The Witches' Time-Key
by
Ceane O'Hanlon-Lincoln

A Sleuth Sisters Mystery
Book one in the bewitching series

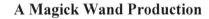

A Magick Wand Production

"Thoughts are magick wands powerful enough to make anything happen– anything we choose!"

Cover Design by Ceane O'Hanlon-Lincoln

To all those who have ever stood on a windy hill in Ireland—
Stood and listened— and heard the ancient whisperings of
The Old Ones;

To fellow time travelers everywhere;

And to my husband Phillip,
Who bought me my ticket …

The Witches' Time-Key

by

Ceane O'Hanlon-Lincoln

A Sleuth Sisters Mystery

~By Ceane O'Hanlon-Lincoln~

In this paranormal-mystery series, Raine and Maggie McDonough and Aisling McDonough-Gwynn, first cousins, are the celebrated Sleuth Sisters from the Pennsylvania town of Haleigh's Hamlet. With their magickal Time-Key, these winning white witches are able to unlock the door that will whisk them through yesteryear, but who knows what skeletons and dangers dangle in the closets their Key will open?

One thing is certain– magick, adventure, and surprise await them at the creak of every opening door– and page-turn.

In the first book of the bewitching **Sleuth Sisters Mystery Series,** *The Witches' Time-Key*, these "mystery magnets" seek answers to the haunting questions connected to their own quest and to a series of murders and legendary lost jewels at Barry Hall, a noble estate in County Clare, Ireland, where a chance encounter with a fellow Pennsylvanian leads them.

More Sleuth Sisters adventures, romance, spice, and surprises abound in:

Fire Burn and Cauldron Bubble, book two of the *Sleuth Sisters Mystery Series*
The Witch's Silent Scream, book three of the bewitching *Sleuth Sisters Mystery Series*

Watch for *Which Witch is Which? Coming soon!*

~~~

Also by Ceane O'Hanlon-Lincoln:

Autumn Song, a harmonious medley of short stories threaded and interwoven by their romantic destiny themes and autumnal settings. Each tale in this compelling anthology evokes its own special ambiance– and sensory impressions.

O'Hanlon-Lincoln never judges her characters, several of whom resurface from tale to tale. These are honest portrayals, with meticulously researched historic backdrops, intrigue, surprise endings– and thought-provoking twists.

For instance, in "A Matter of Time," which side of the door is the main character on when the story concludes?

From the first page of *Autumn Song*, the reader will take an active role in these fascinating tales, discovering all the exciting threads that connect them.

How many will *you* find?

~~~

The award-winning history series:

County Chronicles
County Chronicles Volume II
County Chronicles Volume III
County Chronicles Volume IV
County Chronicles: There's No Place Like Home!

If you haven't read this author's *County Chronicles*, then you haven't discovered how thrilling history can be! With meticulous research and her "state-of-the-heart" storytelling, Ceane O'Hanlon-Lincoln breathes life into historical figures and events with language that flows and captivates the senses.

~~~

The Witches' Time-Key
~ Cast of Characters ~

Baranya "Barry" Bartok– The brilliant and beautiful investigative reporter at WIIP, Pittsburgh TV, whose Gypsy soul warns her of danger– but the magnetic Rob Carroll and Ireland are temptations too strong to resist.

Robert "Rob" Phillip Carroll– The virile owner of a Dublin-based travel agency suddenly finds himself lord of the manor, Barry Hall, a family estate in County Clare. The peril Rob has faced during his worldwide adventure expeditions is *nothing* compared to the danger awaiting him in his native Ireland.

Phillip Barry– The wealthy great-uncle of Rob Carroll and mysteriously departed lord of Barry Hall. Was he the victim of an "accidental suicide"– or a cold-blooded murder?

Katherine Foster– This friend and co-worker at the Pittsburgh TV station warns Barry of more than one jeopardy.

Joe Skinner– Barry's sadistic boss at WIIP, Allegheny County News Center, is fast to crack the whip with his ultimatum– and the worst is yet to come.

William Lawrence– This no-account accountant is a control freak where Barry is concerned. The spawn of wealthy parents, he is used to getting what he wants.

Francis Xavier Dillon– Youthful and spry for his sixty-odd years, "Frank," Barry Hall's manager, has the lilt of County Clare on his tongue and a ready smile on his face– but what is in his heart?

Nora Dillon– The "Mrs. Danvers" of Barry Hall, she has a talent for suddenly appearing and disappearing that Barry finds *unnerving.* Could there be something dark and sinister just beneath her professional veneer?

Máire Nolan– Nora's pretty, eighteen-year-old apprentice dreams of becoming a writer, little guessing what Fate holds in store for her.

The Gardai, Sergeant Dugan and Detective-Inspector Haggerty–
They called Rob's great-uncle Phillip Barry's death an accident, but
haunting questions still linger in the ghostly mists surrounding Barry
Hall. Could a devilishly clever collusion be at work here?

Patrick F. Conroy– The distinguished, silver-haired solicitor
reveals an intriguing– and glittering– bequest attached to Phillip
Barry's will, concluding, "Fulfill your birthright." That legacy is not
the only thing replete with secrets. Solicitor Conroy is concealing a
secret or two of his own.

Margaret Conroy– Rob's cousin and the solicitor's wife, this grey-
haired Amazon would like nothing better than to be mistress of
Barry Hall. The question begging is: Just how *far* is Mrs. Conroy
willing to go to realize her ardent desire?

Dr. Daniel Rafferty– Compassionate and professional, this
physician adamantly believes that the suffering, man or beast, should
be *helped* into a better world.

John McHendrie– Barry Hall's work-shy gardener is quick to offer
extra assistance. Meanwhile, his slighted duties in the Love
Garden's labyrinth puzzle his employers.

Brian Carroll– A storm blows Rob's older brother back into his
life, but neither contentious Carroll will reveal to Barry the dark
secret of their stormy relationship.

Maeve O'Brien– A cast-off ex-girlfriend, this forceful, fiery
redhead persistently pictures herself as Mrs. Robert Phillip Carroll.

Timothy Callahan– The Shannon Blazers' Master of the Hunt has
his *own* reasons for wanting Rob out of the picture.

Sheriff Brennan and the "Forty-Fivers"– Frank's card-playing
cronies are good men to have around– in a "pinch."

Raine and Maggie McDonough– First cousins, these bewitching
Pennsylvania history professors, from the faerie-tale town of

Haleigh's Hamlet, are not divulging any information about their mysterious thesis. Just who *are* these savvy– self-appointed– "Sleuth Sisters" anyway?

Aisling McDonough-Gwynn– She and her husband Ian, former police officers, are partners in their successful Black Cat Detective Agency. The third of the trio of Sleuth Sisters, the blonde with the wand can't make the journey to Ireland with her two cousins, but she "travels" with them nonetheless.

Beau Goodwin– Raine's "Beau" and neighbor is a superior veterinarian, with an extraordinary sixth sense. After all, his patients can't tell him what's wrong.

Hugh Goodwin– Beau's semi-retired veterinary father– whose amazing sixth sense matches his son's– has an avid appetite for mystery novels and an amazing aptitude for solving them that the Sleuth Sisters find absolutely "wizard."

"Trust to Time to set matters straight."
~ Old Irish adage

"Time, some know you as Destiny, a fortune teller. Others call you a great healer. Perhaps you are the conductor in this symphony we call life. Whatever you are, you are *magick*, for, as love– you are *eternal*."

~ Author Ceane O'Hanlon-Lincoln

~ Prologue ~

Raine set a tray with two mugs of spiced cider on the massive, claw-footed table. Dropping into a chair, she plucked a piece of lint from the hooded, black velvet robe she was wearing, then looked up at her cousin through a veil of lashes so black and thick, they appeared to weigh the long, delicate lids above them. "All packed and ready to go?"

"Just about," Maggie answered, adjusting the belt on her green dressing gown, a robe that little concealed her voluptuous figure. "I have a few last-minute things to pack, that's all." She picked up one of the steaming cups, but paused before taking a sip. "I have a stomach-full of butterflies. Don't you?"

The more petite Raine nodded. "Granny used to say that if you've butterflies in your tummy, invite them into your soul– and soar with them toward your dreams. Those butterflies will remind us that we *must* succeed in our quest." After a moment, she added, "And we will … if we keep to the path of the Great Secret."

History professors Raine and Maggie McDonough were sitting in their spacious kitchen at Tara, their Queen Anne Victorian home just outside the quaint village of Haleigh's Hamlet, Pennsylvania, their agenda spread over the antique oak table between them. It was the day before their departure for a long-awaited journey linked to a sabbatical leave from their teaching duties at Haleigh College.

The last rays of the setting October sun, through one of the house's many stained-glass windows, cast jewel-toned light on the handwritten sheets, and the windowsills sparkled with rows of varicolored crystals. Among them were amber for vanquishing negativity, dis-ease and disease; amethyst for healing and inducing pleasant dreams; aquamarine for calming the nerves and lifting the spirits; citrine for cleansing; moonstone for new beginnings and intuition; peridot for release from guilt; rose quartz for unconditional love; tiger's eye for strong protection; sapphire for insight and truth; emerald for bliss, loyalty, and wealth; and ruby for energy, passion, and vigor.

Behind the two women, the tall kitchen-cabinet doors, too, shimmered with stained glass. Above them, from the dark, massive ceiling beams of abiding English oak, dangled bunches of dried herbs and flowers. The old house had all the modern conveniences, but in the kitchen especially, Raine and Maggie preferred the Old Ways.

Surrounded by a black, wrought-iron fence with fleur-de-lys finials, the turreted 1890s home was crowded with antiques, and the cousins' wardrobes replete with vintage clothing and a collection of *very special* jewelry, most of it quite old. The pair had a magickal flair, each for her own brand of fashion, each possessing the gift to *feel* the sensations cached away in every one of their collected treasures, "As if," as they were prone to say, "we are living history."

A long line of McDonough women possessed the gift for sensing, through proximity and touch, the layered stories and energies of those who previously owned vintage articles.

The grand old lady who built this house came from Ireland, bequeathing her female heirs a special Key– and a great deal of magick. Over the long years, the McDonough manse gathered within its stout brick walls a myriad of secrets. Tara, as it became known, was a grand old house, not the most beautiful residence in the world, but unquestionably one of the most unique– as were its mistresses. McDonough women could make magick just by walking into a room. Hallowe'en was their favorite holiday.

And then there were the cats– five at the moment. But, after all, it was a *big* old house, and it literally purred with love.

"Other than the fact that we fly into Dublin and depart from Shannon, everything else is totally devoid of reservations. We'll be free to move about as we please, starting with Trinity for intense research … Newgrange, then the area roundabout the Hill of Tara. From the Dublin side, we drive northwest. Here are the agreed-upon stops." The raven-haired Raine pushed a sheet of paper toward flame-haired Maggie, pointing to each site with a black-lacquered fingernail. "The Aran Islands, then from Galway to Tipperary, next to Waterford, Cork, Kerry, Limerick … we end in Clare; fly home from Shannon."

Slipping on a pair of designer glasses, Maggie perused the sheet with its penciled notes in the columns, took a draft of the cider, then let fall the weighty words, "So … Poulnabrone's the spot?" It was a question, though it hardly needed to be.

Raine gave a slight nod, locking eyes with her cousin before scooping up the itinerary and sliding it into a large brown envelope. "Of course, our agenda is always subject to change, depending–" her pretty face clouded for a moment, before she shook off her doubts, her husky voice taking on a cheerful note– "on what unfolds," she finished resolutely. "And if … *when* we succeed, the sky's the limit!"

"Nooo," Maggie mused, tapping her cup with a fingernail, glossy scarlet to match her sensuous mouth, "not even the sky!"

Raine tilted her tousled black head, and her fair cheeks suddenly took on a rosy tint. "*Not even that,*" she repeated dreamily, looking for the moment like a sassy, playful waif with her short, asymmetric, jet-black hair, the jagged bangs, point-cut, dipping seductively over one eye, a little ebony curl over the opposite cheek. Raine was a sexy, somewhat naughty pixie, who was destined to keep her looks and her youthful appearance. Pixies, after all, are enduring.

Maggie was another of those women who would be forever young, and she was most definitely sexy. Perhaps it was her sense of humor that helped retain her beauty and allure. Maggie laughed often. She gave a short laugh now; but it was not her usual expression of amusement, a laugh that was almost musical. This laugh carried a hint, just a hint, of something dark. "I just hope we don't encounter a point of no return. Sorry," she quickly amended, catching sight of the flicker of fear that sparked in Raine's eyes.

Able even to read each other's thoughts, the pair were more like sisters than cousins. For one thing, they both had identical eyes, arresting to anyone who looked upon them– the "McDonough eyes" the villagers called them– tip-tilted and vivid emerald, the color of Ireland itself, fringed with sooty black lashes, and blazing with unquenchable life.

Both women accentuated their eyes with intense makeup. Both possessed the McDonough skin– rich cream, glowing and flawless– that, together with their hair and matchless green eyes, rendered each dramatically striking. Friends summed them up by saying, "Raine and Maggie have that intangible something that makes them unforgettable."

No one ever forgot a McDonough woman.

In all fairness to the pair, they did not collect hearts as one collects seashells or butterflies, and yet …

At the moment, Raine, who was usually fearless about plunging into tomorrow, was feeling her confidence and optimism beginning to slip. "A point of no return?" she echoed, the fear on her face quite evident now. Instinctively, her hand rushed to the antique talisman suspended on a thick silver chain around her neck. She brushed her ringed fingers across the large emerald embedded in the center of the amulet's silver and black-enameled surface. A myriad of tiny gems of moonstone, garnet, emerald, ruby, sapphire, amethyst, citrine, and various hues of quartz and topaz glittered in the treasured heirloom. For a long moment, Raine seemed to study the piece, as if seeing it for the first time.

"Darlin'…" Maggie purred, stretching in her most feline manner and lifting her heavy, shoulder-length hair from the back of her neck, dark-red flame that in certain luminosity, such as this, rippled blue lights, "relax. I have no doubt we'll succeed." After a pensive moment, she added, "I wonder if *it* will follow us to Ireland?"

A shadow passed over Raine's glittering green eyes, and she nearly shouted, "Don't even voice it! Perhaps we'll get a break while we're away."

Leaning back in her chair, Maggie directed her emerald gaze out the window, to the woods aflame with the fiery colors of autumn. A black cat leaped from the floor into the comfort of her lap, and she began to stroke its glossy, velvet coat. "I'll miss the cats."

"So will I. I'll miss Tara and our sleepy little valley, especially at this time of year when it is the most beautiful." Her voice, with her thoughts, drifted off, "Autumn … when the veil wanes, and the line between this reality and the next becomes *misty*. But," she said when her musing moment passed, "we're fortunate that we have Aisling. And my Beau."

Maggie laughed again, and this time it was her spellbinding laugh that sort of tinkled through the air, pure and perfect, and light of essence. From under her robe, she extracted the talisman she always wore on a silver chain around her neck. Maggie's heirloom piece matched Raine's exactly, except that the large center stone in hers was a blood-red ruby. Tracing a finger over the amulet's bejeweled surface, she said, "There's indeed something to be said for having the mystical power of three. And your veterinary boyfriend right next door."

"Indeed," Raine echoed. "And you'll miss your beaux too." Her lips curved into a little cat smile, "The lot of them! But it will all be worth it." She bent her head to take a drink from her mug, watching her cousin from beneath the thick, inky veil of her lashes. "For a moment there, I thought you were having second thoughts."

"Not second thoughts, but I can't deny pushing a few devious doubts from my mind all day. I keep thinking that–"

Raine cut her off with a brisk wave of her hand. "Nothing but positive thoughts! We *must* keep to the path of the Great Secret. A month to six weeks in Ireland isn't *that* long. If all goes well ... if we pull this off, we'll be able to do all the things we ever dreamed of. And time will be of no importance."

"None at all," Maggie concluded, resettling herself in the antique kitchen chair, the full red lips curving in her mysterious Mona Lisa smile. *Ooooh, the possibilities...*

Glancing down at the airline tickets on the table, Raine mused aloud, "There's no denying we're taking a chance leaving our jobs for a whole year to complete this project. The risks, all of them, *are* great, but it's our chance to–"

"Prove ourselves," Maggie interposed with quiet force. "Granny left us more than just this house and a great trust fund."

"Remember how she liked to quote William Jennings Bryan? 'Destiny is not a matter of chance– but a matter of choice.' I suppose we could say that our history is the foundation of our destiny," Raine dimpled.

Smoothing a fiery lock of hair from her goddess-like features, Maggie smiled, "*Touché!* We've been summoned to unlock a mystical portal– a portal that will unveil a world of ancient mysteries and hidden knowledge. So mote it be."

A sudden sense of power fired Raine's confidence, and now it was her turn to repeat the ancient phrase, "So mote it be." She reached down and picked up a second black cat that, on silent paws, had entered the room and walked to her. Gazing intently into the depths of its mesmerizing pumpkin-colored eyes, she recited, "Once upon a time, there were two ... *pioneering* college professors from an unheard-of little hamlet in the backwoods of Pennsylvania ..."

The cat still in her arms, she wandered to the front porch, where her eyes found the moon that was just making its dramatic appearance over the adjacent mountains.

Who is ever going to believe this?

"The distinction between past, present, and future is only a stubbornly persistent illusion."
~ Albert Einstein

Chapter One

At approximately the same time, Pittsburgh investigative reporter Baranya Bartok stood on that city's Grandview Avenue, gazing at the full hunter's moon with its angry red ring. Her thoughts were disquieting.

Blood on the moon. A halo around the moon is always a sign of disruption. And when it's a double ring, like this one, all tangled and snarled, anything can happen. Trouble. And trouble is like love ... it comes unannounced and takes over before you even have a chance to think. The wind whipped her dark auburn hair wildly about her face. *I'd better get inside. This storm's going to be a doozy!*

The bright October day had rendered a damp, chilly evening. Great drops of rain began to pelt her as a city bus roared by, the words across its side, "Joe said it would," referring to one of the area's most popular weather forecasters. She turned, locked her car, then raced for the front porch of the tall, stately Mount Washington house, where she rented the top-floor apartment.

A passing male neighbor paused to wave and stare after "Barry," who made a striking appearance, with her long, wavy hair and knit, forest-green cape billowing behind her in a whirlwind of autumn leaves.

As a local celebrity and TV newscaster, Baranya, with her dramatic looks, was used to attention, though she was always personable and friendly. Tonight, however, she was preoccupied. She could not shake the keen feeling all day that something was about to happen that would change her life– and blood on the moon was definitely not a good omen.

Arriving breathless at her apartment, Barry fished out her keys, unlocked her door, and turned the old-fashioned switch. Light flooded the cozy room, a room warmed by bright splashes of color, reflecting her Eastern-European heritage and her fascination with the mystical. Still preoccupied, she tossed her purse on a claw-foot stand, slipped out of her cape and hung it on a mahogany coat tree in the corner.

As always upon returning home, she was drawn to the huge living-room window that overlooked the lighted city where Pittsburgh's three rivers meet. "The Point," with its illuminated fountain, glittered as though awash with diamonds. For several quiet moments, she remained standing at the rain-splashed glass, looking at the spectacular view.

Nighttime Pittsburgh from Mount Washington is a faerie-tale place.

Then her gaze and her thoughts, once again, came to rest on the moon with its warning of violence and possible death.

I'm tired. I've been burying myself in work lately. Perhaps I'm overreacting. And I'm lonely ... but I'd rather be alone than with Bill again. When I think of him, 'alone' is not so bad.

The driving force of the hot water over the lush curves of her body soothed her, and she could feel the tension loosening as she showered. But by the time she sat, cozily enveloped in a favorite robe before her bedroom mirror, the day's signs, full of portents, again returned to haunt her– vague, misty imaginings that told her nothing specific.

Blood on the moon.

Picking up her brush, she vigorously stroked her hair until the rich auburn color fairly glowed in the soft light. With upward strokes, she smoothed a cream into her golden skin. Then, momentarily, she studied her reflection. Her high cheekbones, sultry dark eyes– eyes more black than brown– and full lips were a model's dream, but, unlike some women who possess such beauty, Barry was devoid of vanity.

I will do a reading. Whatever it is– I have to know.

Baranya placed the last card on the dark-green, cotton cloth, sipped her cup of foamy, fragrant Chai tea, and studied the layout before her.

The High Priestess. Secrets. Mystery. It seems ... I will be forced to make a choice. And I will have to choose carefully, for once I open one door, the others will be sealed to me.

The Lovers. Indecision. Confusion. Of a sudden, a sole Tarot jumped out at her.

Barry picked it up, looking closely at its face. *The Empress, the Venus symbol of Love everywhere–* on her shield, her dress, behind her on the cushioned throne; around her neck, the seven planets formed a necklace, demonstrating the domain of Love over the entire universe.

Love ... someday. I'm more confused than ever. I'll pick a resolution card.

With her left hand, Barry drew a single Tarot from the remainder of the deck. *The Hermit.*

Several minutes passed, the only sound the loud ticking of the clock on the living-room mantel, as Barry deliberated over the card's colorful depiction.

Presently, the wise counsel of the ancient oracle, with his hooded robe, staff, and his lantern held high, rose up to challenge her: *In the days to come, you will have to listen to your inner self. Fears and doubts will plague you. You will have many questions, but the answers are available– Seek and ye shall find.*

The young woman reached for a warm shawl, wrapping it snugly around her against a sudden chill.

***

Barry exited the mobile news van, "WIIP– ALLEGHENY COUNTY NEWS CENTER– 'PITTSBURGH'S MOST ACCURATE NEWS'," painted on its side, to brave the brisk October wind whipping off the river. Carrying a reporter's notebook, a pen tucked behind her ear, she hurried to the front entrance of the TV studio, pulled open the door, hurried past the reception area and up the flight of stairs. At the top, she paused just long enough to let her fingers fly across the buttons on the security door, using the code to gain access to the production area.

With a cameraman following in her wake, Barry swept briskly through the news scribes busy at their computers, then hurried past the editing base, tarrying briefly at her friend Katherine Foster's desk in the production pit, where she exchanged their familiar "thumbs-up." Taking a deep breath, she rapped lightly on the door of the large, glass-wrapped office to her right, the plaque on it reading: JOSEPH P. SKINNER– EXECUTIVE PRODUCER.

"We got it." Barry silently let out her breath.

Skinner yanked his trademark cigar from his mouth– to his indignation, unlit, since the building went "smoke free." "Don't just stand there! Get the copy ready, and make it snappy! I have another assignment for you at Carnegie Music Hall. It's not your usual snoop job, but I got no one else free to handle it. "

Look at him! Barry thought, glancing up from her desk at her cigar-gnawing boss in his adjacent office. *He can't smoke, so he uses the damn stogie as a pacifier. Too bad it doesn't work!*

Within a half-hour, Barry was once again in the mobile news van. She perused the assignment sheet, reading aloud, "Robert Phillip Carroll presents *Adventures for Everyone.* Expedition travels compiled … best-selling book." Crossing her long shapely legs, Barry sat back, glancing over at Danny, the cameraman, who was skillfully maneuvering the van through the crowded Pittsburgh street. "Probably an arrogant Tarzan type. Should be interesting though."

The young man returned her glance, a sharp note of apathy in his voice. "Yeah, they're always interesting."

"Damn!" Barry came to an abrupt halt, on the front steps of the music hall, to check the damage to her high heel.

"What's wrong?" Danny, toting his camera with attached light apparatus in one hand, a duffel bag in the other, stopped inches behind her, nearly knocking her down.

"I broke my heel!"

"Barry, we're late as it is!" The young man shifted his weight, his expression registering his impatience.

"At least it's still on. C'mon, let's get in there!"

The lecture hall was dark as the two newspersons entered as quietly as they could. A travel film was in progress, and Barry could see that a reading-stand had been set up at the side, where Robert Phillip Carroll stood narrating, the only illumination, other than the projection itself, a small circle of light on the lectern.

Barry stood against the rear wall, allowing her eyes to adjust to the dark.

On the screen, an expedition on camels moved across an exotic desert scene. Within moments a dozen or so horsemen, their voices raised in barbarous shouts, bore galloping down on the caravan. Turbaned, with blue veils masking their faces, the riders carried antiquated muskets, but the horses they rode were the beautiful and spirited Arabians Barry had often admired at the horse shows she occasionally attended.

With a charming Irish accent, his voice deep and resonant, the speaker intoned, "My clients and I had a few unsettling moments when these Tuareg tribesmen … *greeted* us. The Tuareg are the fiercest nomadic tribe in all of North Africa. They wear the veils to keep the sand out of their noses and mouths. After awhile, the dye stains their faces blue. These gentlemen were just curious as to what we were doin' on their turf."

While the cameraman waited in the rear, Barry moved toward the last row of auditorium seats, her loose heel squeaking. The lecturer paused, and she could *feel* his eyes as she settled in for the remainder of the presentation. Across the screen, the Sahara tribesmen galloped off and away from the camel-riding caravan.

"In this business, you learn to take care of unexpected situations to the best of your ability." There was another slight pause, and Barry sensed that the speaker was remembering, reflecting on past perils and thrills. "Expedition travel teaches one as much about himself as it does about foreign cultures ..." –Again she felt his intensity– "... *more* perhaps. For those who crave this type of travel, there's still plenty of adventure to be had."

The film ended, and the assistant scurried to turn up the lights. At that moment, Robert Carroll came from behind the lectern, and Barry took instant notice that he was tall and powerfully built, with broad shoulders and an easy, confident manner.

"Helen Keller once said that 'Life is either a daring adventure– or it is nothing.' On that note, I'll thank you for your attention and for inviting me to Pittsburgh. You've been most accommodatin'," he quipped, glancing out the windows at the misty rain, as the attendant raised the blinds. "This is the first time on my US tour I've come across real Irish weather!"

The audience laughed then applauded, some standing and beginning to leave the lecture hall. Barry stood and, joined by the cameraman, made her way toward the front–to Robert Phillip Carroll.

Aside from the Silver Screen, Barry thought she had never seen a man with such wide shoulders, so heavy with muscles.

Packaging him nicely, he's not Tarzan at all. More like a modern-day Rhett Butler. Hmmm, love the mustache and that little bit of grey in the black hair. And such a virile face ... wickedly handsome. Those expressive brows do more for a girl than a set of large biceps. 'Course he's got those too. And those ... tiger eyes, not quite green, not quite amber– "Hi!" Barry extended her hand, hoping, for the first time in her life, that it was not damp. "Baranya Bartok, WIIP, Allegheny County News Center."

"Rob Carroll." His smile rose to eyes that flicked expertly over her. *Now here's a woman ... nice. Ver-ry nice.*

Barry caught her breath. *Firm handshake. I like that.*

There was a cool recklessness in his face and an innate humor in his eyes as he smiled at her, revealing perfect white teeth beneath the thick, ebony mustache.

"We'll take but a minute of your time"– she returned his smile– "if you'll permit us to cut an interview."

"Why not?"

"Welcome to Pittsburgh, Mr. Carroll. Can you share with our viewers some of your favorite expeditions?" Barry extended the microphone toward Rob, who had set his book up next to him on the lectern. Before them, the cameraman was taping, the camera and attached light apparatus on his shoulder. Behind them, people were still filtering out of the hall.

Rob rubbed his jaw. "Well now, that's difficult to say. I've several, actually: camera safaris in Kenya, hang-gliding in the Alps, wind-surfing in the South Pacific, diving in the Caribbean … I'm also partial to South American treks."

Barry glanced down at her notes. "What was your most *frightening* experience?"

Rob considered for a moment. "I'd say that took place about a year ago, during a jungle expedition on the Amazon. A client accidentally fell overboard," he laughed quietly to himself, remembering, "but we managed to fish him out before the piranhas got him."

Barry smiled with him. "Why have you chosen this life of high adventure?"

This time Rob did not hesitate. "Anything else would bore me. I like the challenge of being in an ever-changing situation where I constantly have to prove myself."

"Talk about *proving* yourself, how does it feel to be on the Best-Seller List?"

Again, the author laughed. "I'd much rather be in the bush than sitting at a computer, writing a book. It's still hard to believe it made the List."

"What's next on your exciting agenda, Mr. Carroll?"

"This is the last stop on my tour. Tomorrow I'll return to my travel agency in Dublin, look in next at my London base, and then," he gestured with a devil-may-care attitude, "who knows? Life is full of suprises!"

Barry nodded to the cameraman, "That's a wrap." Then she turned back to Rob. "Thank you, Mr. Carroll. We'll use this tonight on the 'Eleven-o'Clock.'"

"Rob," the deep voice intoned.

When they shook this time, Rob held her hand for a beat longer. Then, for an even longer moment, their eyes held, and Barry felt an electric current pass swiftly through her body. The spell was broken when the cameraman's voice reached her from what seemed like a great distance, though he was but a few inches away. "We'd better get back with this tape, Barry."

This is, without a doubt, the most ... undeniably **male** *individual I have ever met. Deliciously irresistible.* Her gaze still fixed on Rob, Barry replied to Danny's plea with a wave of hand, "Go on; I'm through for the day. I'll go home from here." *I wonder if there's anything of substance inside Mr. Carroll's great packaging? Could he be as good inside as he is on the outside? And be single?*

Danny took a couple of steps, turned, and with a bemused air began, "But, how–"

Recovered– somewhat– Barry was quick to cut him off. "**Go on**, I have a few things to take care of." *Like figuring out how I can get this terrific hunk to carry me off to that proverbial castle in the sky.*

In a moment, Barry sat down in one of the front-row seats, examining anew the shoe with the broken heel. "You say you like the challenge of proving yourself in a situation. Can you fix this?" *Or a heart that's become a little too fragile?*

A smile leaped to Rob's tiger-like eyes.

He moves with the grace and ease of a tiger too, Barry mused. *And he's looking at me like I'm dinner. Be careful. Be careful.*

Kneeling before her crossed legs, Rob took her slender ankle between his fingers and removed the shoe. *These are th' loveliest pair of legs I've had th' pleasure of... or would like to ... .* "I don't believe anyone's ever worn shoes like this on safari, and I don't think this *can* be fixed. I'll buy you a new pair before we go to dinner."

Barry swallowed, her heart beating faster. *What luck that Skinner had no one else to send on this assignment!*

Rob raised one ebony brow, and a roguish grin played about his features, the elongated dimple in his right cheek becoming more pronounced. *I can't remember ever seeing a more beautiful woman. Quick-witted too, with a sense of humor. And spirit.*

Oooh, those eyebrows. She sat back, studying him. *It's all I can do to keep from reaching out and touching him, running my fingers through that glossy black hair.* For a long moment, she stared at him, then she laughed, "You're a Sagittarian, aren't you?"

"As a matter of fact, I was baptized Catholic."

"Let's see," Barry tilted her head, "you're a leg man and you've a penchant for travel and adventure. Great sense of humor … most definitely Sagittarius."

"Twenty-nine November. Do I pass?" *I hope so,* he admitted to himself.

Seated at a huge window overlooking the city, Barry was more relaxed as she and Rob companionably shared their meal at Cliffside, a restaurant atop Pittsburgh's Mount Washington. Since it was a bit early, only a few of the tables were occupied. The intimate candleglow of the room, the excellent cuisine and wine, the soft music, and the faerieland view of the three rivers and city below made the evening festive and even more special.

"*Barry.* My mother's maiden name was Barry." Rob poured more wine in each of their glasses.

Leaning back in her chair, Barry took a sip of the garnet-red liquid. "That's kind of a coincidence. Do your parents–"

"My parents were killed in a plane crash over four years ago," Rob interposed.

On impulse, Barry reached over and laid a hand on his. "I'm sorry. My parents are gone too. They died when I was quite young. Any brothers or sisters?"

Something, in the candleglow, flickered in the depths of his eyes, then it was gone. "An older brother. We were never close; it's years since I've seen him."

It was as though a shadow had come between them, and several moments passed in silence. "What's your job *really* like?" Barry asked suddenly.

A look flitted across Rob's face, and Barry got the warm feeling that whatever that shadow was, it was now exorcised.

"*Different.* That's the word I could use to describe my job. Different from most other jobs … and different every time, the places, the situations, the clients. Isn't yours like that?"

"That's why I like it. For the first few years, I had a newspaper desk job. I *had* felt challenged in the beginning, but after awhile," she shook her head with the memory, "it got so that I'd start off my day by reading the Help-Wanted section. I remember how imprisoned it made me feel. It was all I could do not to grab my coat and purse and make an escape each and every day."

Rob motioned for the waiter. "I know what you mean. Travel's my life, and I hate my life disrupted by routine. That's why I have managers for my agencies in both Dublin and London. I need to be active, and I love the out-of-doors. I couldn't stand being trapped behind a desk all day."

"Would you care for dessert this evening?" The waiter began clearing away some of the dinner things.

Rob gestured to Barry, "Go on, have a sweet. With a figure like yours, you can afford it."

"Thank you," she answered demurely. *He's sweet. And I adore his Irish brogue.* "I'll skip the dessert, but I'd love coffee."

The waiter nodded and poured the steaming aromatic liquid for Barry, caught Rob's eye, then filled his cup.

"I have a grand idea! After we've finished, let's go dancing. Have you an early day tomorrow?" He sipped his coffee, watching her over the rim of his cup.

He's so natural, so easy to be with. "As a matter of fact, I don't."

***

The River-View Inn, at Station Square, twinkled with lights as Barry and Rob walked toward it from the riverside lot, where Rob had parked his rental car.

A scattering of boats bobbed on the river. At night their radiance reflecting off the water fascinated her, but this night the spell was strengthened by this extraordinary man whose arm she now held. Barry pointed to the large riverboat *Majestic* gliding gracefully into its pier. In the distance a warning bell from a barge, navigating the fog pockets, reached them, as the low cargo boat slowly floated away from the incandescent city.

"Aren't the lights beautiful? I miss the steel mills. When I was a little girl, I used to love to see the endless stretch of mills ablaze in the night sky. Rob, you had to see it– red, orange, white– a spectacular fiery drama. They're history now."

"You love this city, don't you?" Rob paused, placing his hand over hers, where it rested on his arm.

Barry's gaze swept the glittering surroundings. "Yes," she answered. "Don't you miss Ireland, when you're away so much?"

"I do that. It'll always be home. And someday, it's where I'll settle."

Just as they arrived at the elite inn, Barry glanced up at the moon, and a chilling sensation of doom shot through her. Shaking off the feeling, she asked, "But you'll still go off, from time to time, on expedition?"

Rob pulled the door open, holding it for her. "From time to time."

***

"You're a terrific dancer," Barry said as he drew her closer, his cheek resting next to hers.

"If I am, it's due to the inspiration I'm feeling tonight."

Her heart seemed to flutter. *Unlike a lot of men I've met, Rob Carroll, you don't advertise. You're magnetic yet subtle. And something else ... .* She gazed up at his face. He seemed to be studying her expression with one brow slightly raised. *Mysteriously sensual. Yes, that's it.* She laid a hand on his broad chest, snuggling closer and breathing in the intoxicating woodsy scent he wore. *And the way you move ... I wonder ...*

Medieval-style wall sconces and the subtle glow from the table candles softly illuminated the room, and since it was a weeknight, the dance floor was not crowded. From the bandstand, a live orchestra was playing popular tunes from a bygone era.

"This has always been one of my favorite songs," she murmured, as they floated in each other's arms to the evocative slow rhythm. "Of course, Judy Garland's rendition is the best, but this orchestra is really bringing it to life. It's the *perfect* piece of music for tonight."

"You're perfect," he answered.

Something ... perhaps the thing we call Destiny, seems to be weaving us into a sort of magickal spell ... or web. With a sigh, Barry closed her eyes, deciding to enjoy the moment. A delightful fantasy began playing on the movie screen of her mind in which she was stirring Rob to an exciting passion, making him her willing captive. *If only this moment could last– forever.*

As they moved together to the enchanting music, Rob lightly kissed her on the forehead. She raised her eyes to his, and for a dizzying moment, she felt as though she might faint.

Their eyes held, speaking to the heart's hollow, each to the other, of shared dreams– a gossamer wisp of youth, regrets, and hoped-for destinies.

How can I have such an absurd rush of longing for this perfect stranger? Oh, and he does seem so very perfect. Be careful, Barry, be– **Hush!** she silenced that inner voice, running a hand over his shoulder to thread her fingers through the ebony hair at the nape of his neck. "I have three days free this week. Do you *have* to leave tomorrow?"

"My time's my own." *Making love to her would be like laughing in the face of danger. Sweet death in a starburst of bliss. You're a free spirit, Robbie, and free spirits don't tie themselves to anything or anyone. Best watch your step with this lass.* But in a moment, he said, "Perhaps you could show me round this 'big small town,' as you call it. Pittsburgh is more of an *intriguing* place than I would ever have imagined."

Their lips met, and in the midst of that magickal kiss, the music continued, as Time waited and they spun round, lost in each other and the spell that was enveloping them both and whisking them far, far away–

Somewhere over the Rainbow.

"The real secret of power is the consciousness of power."
~ Charles Haanel

Chapter Two

"October is the year's *dramatic* month. It's the jewel in the ring of time!" Barry laughed, as the pair strolled, arm-in-arm, the following day, through the park, all the while her thoughts singing, *Fall is glorious. Fall is breathtaking. Fall in love.* "The vibrant colors, the crisp air, the tangy smells– I love everything about October! Take a deep breath! The air is *spiced* with the scent of fallen leaves and woodsmoke. Just look at that tree over there! It's like a painting."

The Point at Pittsburgh was ablaze with the fiery hues of autumn, and though late in the year, a myriad of blooms still dotted the numerous flowerbeds and the Parisian-style vendor carts along the winding paths that skirted the sun-splashed river.

Rob smiled, reaching up to touch her face. "Aye, a day like this is like a canvas from one of the Impressionists. Renoir perhaps. You never mentioned it, but do you travel much?"

"No," Barry answered, "but I've always wanted to." Through the bright canopy of foliage– russet, red, orange, green and gold– the obliging sun made dancing patterns of light on their faces and shoulders.

"C'mon." Rob pulled her toward one of the nearby vendor carts. "A dozen of th' red ones," he gestured, indicating the velvety garnet buds.

"Yes, sir." Beaming, the elderly man quickly chose, tissue-wrapped, and extended the bouquet to Barry, who, accepting it, returned his warm smile, delighted as a child with a surprise gift.

"Rob, that's so sweet! Thank you." For an intoxicating moment, she breathed in the heady perfume, then standing on tiptoe, she placed a hand on his chest and kissed him firmly. "You darling! How did you know red roses are my favorite?"

"Sure 'n that's an easy one! I knew because, in a word, they are *unrivaled.*" He tilted her chin upward to receive his kiss. "In another word," his lips traveled to her ear, there the whispered caress– "*You …*"

"… Are lovely. And you could get to be a habit altogether," Rob pronounced. "I'm glad you suggested dinner aboard this fine vessel. I must say, I've enjoyed it."

"I thought you would. This *grande dame*'s one of the largest old-fashioned riverboats afloat."

They stood, close together, at the rail of the open-air third deck, as *The Majestic* slowly made her leisurely way past the wonderland of lights that was nighttime Pittsburgh. The pleasant, sensuous sounds of the river lapping against the stern, the purring swish of the boat's great paddle, and the soft dance music reached them. The air was brisk, and after several minutes, Barry wrapped her long, fringed shawl tighter about her.

"Are you cold?" Not waiting for an answer, Rob pulled her into his arms, his large, warm hands sliding under the soft red cashmere of her wrap, sending instant heat to her body. In a moment, his lips came down on hers, and she melted into him, the kiss transporting her again to that mystical land beyond the rainbow.

***

In the misty moonlight, the high-arched ruins of the fifteenth-century friary evoked an eerie atmosphere. The lower Shannon of County Clare, Ireland, was studded with ruins such as this, where in owl-light, mist and fog, especially at this time of year, one could readily imagine ethereal figures abroad in the chill of an October night.

Samhain– Hallowe'en. One can *feel* it in the air, in the darkness, in the whispering winds. 'Tis a time of death– for the ancestors, and the Old Ones, are more accessible now than at any other time. It is a season, too, of divining, an interval to scry the coming year. Dreams become more vivid, as shadows deepen. Omens, signs and portents are omnipresent, and the "Sight" is remarkably sharper. At *Samhain*, the very winds have something to say– for those who can hear them, and who dare to listen.

Standing sentinel in an open field, surrounded by its churchyard graves, the ancient friary at Quin had become the nocturnal meeting place for two sinister figures. Two figures who were, indeed, engrossed in the subject of death. Two, in fact, who were consumed– with *murder*.

"I hate these bloody fags, but it's pretty hard t' get a pipe goin' out 'ere. Got a lucifer?"

The taller shadowy figure struck a match and, shielding the flame from the wind, lit the other's cigarette, their features taking on a ghoulish appearance in the feeble light.

"Won't he taste the stuff in his drink?"

"You won't need much. Couple-a drops'll kill a man of …" he grimaced, pursing his lips, "fifteen stone or there abouts. Just make sar-tain you put it in the right drink!"

"I'm not that bloody stupid! Are you *certain* he'll be there? When did you say he–"

"He'll be there. After the old bastard's wake. I mapped it out perfectly." He pulled a sheet of folded paper from his jacket pocket. "Here! I wrote everything down. See that you study it in advance, then destroy it. That always works best f'r you."

"Right, Mate; 'e's a dead man already. He just doesn't know it yet."

***

Rob's sweeping gaze took in the open-air markets along Pittsburgh's Strip District. "This reminds me of a set for a turn-of-the-century *film*." He pronounced the word in two syllables, in the Irish manner of speaking. "You sar-tainly are an accomplished tour guide. I'm thinkin' I may have to convince you to come to Ireland and work for me." He squeezed her hand, as they sauntered past the various shops and markets, Barry receiving a friendly greeting, here and there, from a variety of ethnic merchants who recognized her.

"You must shop here often? They all seem to know you. I'm jealous."

"I come here at least once a week to shop, but people know me from TV too." She glanced over at him. "Why are you staring at me like that?"

"Sorry. I can't stop looking at you. You're by far th' most beautiful woman I have ever met in all my travels … anywhere."

Barry paused on the walkway. "Oh, Rob, you're very flattering, but *I'm* not beautiful."

"You can't be serious? You have to know how incredible you look."

"My lips are too full. And so is my figure. Did you ever see those models? They're all so slender."

"Spindle-shanked you mean. Your lips are luscious. They … give rise to all kinds of erotic fantasies. As for your body, 'voluptuous' is the word that comes to my mind, among others. You are a goddess, Barry. A *sultry, **sexy** goddess.*"

"I'm thrilled that *you* think so. I never liked my dark coloring either. I always wanted to be blue-eyed, fair and blonde."

"I've never been attracted to blondes."

She bit her lower lip. "Rob … would you answer a question for me, without taking offense?"

"If I can." He edged her toward an antique shop, where the enamoured pair, her hand in his, gazed into a window, and into the past.

"When you're on safari, or ballooning over the chateaux country of France, whatever wherever, do the bored ladies of the *beau monde* expect more than the contracted thrills?"

Rob turned from the antique shop's window display to her, their eyes locking. Swiftly, that quick humor she had come to identify with him rose to his greeny-gold gaze. "No, luv, that's only in the films. However, I did have a very persistent lioness after me one memorable moonlight night near Tsavo. Ver-ry persistent, as I recall. Let's go into this shop, I want to purchase a souvenir."

It was the most beautiful antique, heart-shaped locket, the exquisite black enameling, over the glow of gold, characterizing it with the 1860s. "And don't tell me you can't accept it. I want to buy you something for making these three days the most delightful holiday of my life." When she started to protest, he placed a finger to her lips. "Here now, allow me to put it on for you."

Barry turned and lifted her hair, as Rob placed the gold chain of the rather large heirloom around her neck and fastened the clasp. "I don't know quite what to say. It's beautiful." She fingered the puffed heart, her own brimming with emotion. "I–''

He kissed her, and words were of no importance. "Perhaps, dear lady, you will see fit to place me in a special chamber of *your* heart. And since this is my last night here, 'tis La Mont for dinner. The desk clerk at my hotel informed me it is *the* place to dine with a lady of quality. Then an evening at Heinz Hall. I rang them this morning and discovered there were still good tickets available for *Wicked*. We're all booked in. I saw it in London; it's *extraordinary*, so I know *you* will enjoy it."

Barry reached out and placed a tentative hand along the side of his face. "Let's not say *last*, Rob. It sounds so final. *Good-bye* will be difficult enough." She moved closer to the pier glass in the shop's interior, admiring the antique locket resting against the black cashmere of her sweater and wondering who may have been the witchy lady with Rob the first time he saw *Wicked*.

Behind her, the object of her heart put his hands on her shoulders, his eyes, too, in the glass, admiring. *I could lose myself in this lass. I could ...very easily do that.*

The long, silver limousine hissed through the rain puddles to a stop at the curb before Rob's hotel entrance. "Are you sar-tain?" He softly kissed her mouth, then traced a finger, light as a feather, over her lips, sending a shiver of anticipation through her body.

"Quite."

The uniformed chauffeur opened the door and helped Barry from the vehicle. She had turned heads all evening in a long, amethyst velvet dress and matching cape that fastened at the throat with an ornate silver clasp. A huge, hot-pink muff, that matched the lining of the cape, completed the captivating ensemble.

Rob, also in evening attire, and who had turned a few heads himself, escorted her quickly inside, for the night was unseasonably cold, and the rain was coming down in sheets. Within minutes, they were alone, cozy and warm, in the elevator en route to his top-floor suite.

"Nervous?" His mustache began playing sensory games with her skin, as he slowly pulled off her gloves, lightly kissing each delicately-tapered fingertip.

She let out her breath, but a zillion butterflies still fluttered to escape. His soft little kisses, exquisite little caresses, were slowly driving her crazy. "I don't know *what* to call it; I've never felt like this before. It's–"

"Bewitching," he murmured in her ear.

She ran her slender fingers with their dark-amethyst lacquered nails through his ebony hair, and when their lips met, she was whisked, with the most delicious sensation, away again, on that magick-carpet ride she thrilled to in his presence. "I feel … almost faint," she breathed.

His response was to pull her against him, his back against the elevator wall, his mouth traveling its unhurried sensuous way from her lips to her cheek, her ear, there a whispered word …

A thrill rocketed through her, as the elevator settled, and the doors roared opened.

Barry's glance round the sumptuous suite of rooms came to rest on the bottle of champagne in an ice bucket. She smiled, depositing the muff on a nearby chair. "You were rather sure of yourself."

With a laugh deep in his throat, Rob came up behind her, his arms slipping round her waist to draw her close. "Not at all." He began kissing her neck. "My publisher sent it up three days ago. If we want it, we'll need ice. Shall I see to it?"

"No, Mr. Carroll, I'd rather you see to this," she said playfully, beginning to undo the clasp of her wrap.

"Slow … and easy," he crooned, catching her hand and usurping the unfastening of her velvets. His eyes held her, as he removed the cape, then began his teasing game of skill with her dress.

For several moments, Barry was spellbound by the big-cat sorcery of his gaze. Now her hands, too, busied themselves to undo the buttons of his shirt, sliding it off his wide shoulders.

"Barry," his kiss was deep, lingering, "I don't want this to be one of those one-night things. I must …" his open-mouth kiss consumed her, as he pushed the dress from her shoulders, letting it fall to the floor at her feet, "… see you again." His mouth felt like fire on hers. "Again… and again."

"Please," she moaned. "Pleeease–"

The sudden loud ringing of the telephone quite near to where they stood startled both from their enchantment.

"Bloody hell," Rob growled, moving to the annoyance and picking it up. "**Yes!**"

Barry sank down in the chair a few feet distant, watching him. *Why didn't he just let it ring?*

For some moments, he was silent, listening to what she perceived was a male voice. Though the disembodied voice on the other end of the line was audible, she could not glean any of the conversation; but by the look on Rob's face, whatever the caller was saying was completely unexpected.

"Just a moment," Rob said, sitting down on the couch by the phone, "I'll write that down." Leaning over and opening a drawer, he extracted a pen and a pad of paper. "Go on. Yes, I've got it."

Again, Barry could hear the barely audible voice as Rob continued to listen. "I've hardly been in the room," he responded. "Right. Thanks, Elliot. Aye, I will that." He replaced the receiver, remaining motionless for what seemed to Barry a long, uneasy time.

"What's wrong?" She moved to his side in her plum-colored teddy, laying a hand on his shoulder. "Was it bad news?"

"That was Elliot, the manager of my agency in Dublin. He's been trying to reach me. He rang me up a couple of times here today, but said he didn't want to leave what he had to say in a message."

"What's happened?" She dropped down beside him on the couch, taking his hand between her own.

"My great-uncle Phillip Barry has died." Rob seemed to reflect for a moment before he went on. "He's named me heir to his estate in County Clare, and I must be present at the readin' of the will. Elliot has already made my travel arrangements." He clutched her hand in both of his. "I'm sorry, Barry, but I must leave," he glanced at his watch, "soon. Can you help me?"

"Yes, of course. I'm so sorry about your uncle." She studied his face. "Rob, I told you it would be difficult to hide things from me. There's more, isn't there?"

"Much more, luv. Elliot said that there's something *mysterious.* Some special bequest attached to the will, which is part of the reason I must return to Ireland straightaway. He also said that my uncle … committed suicide."

"Oh, Rob, I am sorry. Was he suffering? A *great*-uncle … how old was he?"

"Aye, he was sick, and old, but he did *not* commit suicide. That is quite *impossible.*"

Less than an hour later, Barry and Rob were in her car as Barry drove him to the airport.

"Why is that so impossible? You said yourself your uncle was quite ill, in pain, and confined to a wheelchair. A man who had once been so active, perhaps–"

"You didn't know him," Rob interposed mildly. "He had a saying he was fond of, the Barry credo actually, 'The Lord hates a coward.' No, there's something wrong. *Something.* And I intend to find out what."

A shiver ran along Barry's spine, the cold chill of doom she had sensed a couple of nights before, returning to haunt her. "Have you spent much time with him, since you're away so much?"

"I haven't seen much of him the last few years," Rob admitted, reflecting. "He was a crotchety old character. I don't think he ever let anything or anyone get the better of him."

"When did you see him last?" Barry asked, glancing over at Rob, who was staring straight ahead, seemingly deep in thought. "You know, he may have changed since you last visited him. Medication can alter—"

"No. I saw Uncle Phillip just prior to my coming here for this book tour, and he hadn't changed a bit. That was not quite two weeks ago."

Barry speeded up, skillfully maneuvering the car into another lane. "Think back. Does anything stand out in your mind about that last visit?" Again, she glanced over to Rob, who looked pensive.

"He was as crotchety as ever … threatened to horse-whip me and cut me out of the will," he laughed.

Barry looked at her passenger, the oncoming lights from other vehicles gilding his tiger eyes– eyes that seemed, in the luminosity, to gleam with the memory.

It had started to rain again, this time more like descending mist than rain, and the night had turned even colder. Barry hurried with Rob across the parking area to the main entrance of Pittsburgh International Airport. He was wearing what Barry called an Indiana Jones hat and, under an open raincoat, an Irish tweed blazer over a black turtleneck sweater and flannel slacks. *He looks like the model for a "Come-to-Ireland" poster,* Barry thought as she watched him out of the corner of her eye.

When they were nearly at the entrance, Rob stopped, put his valise down, and in an instant, his hat was in his hand. "Don't come any farther, Barry, I'm worried about you driving if this turns to freezing rain, and it looks as though it might. I'm sorry our evening was spoiled." He stroked her face with the back of his fingers.

"Rob, I understand. I do. Perhaps you can come visit for the holidays; I have some time off then. Or I could come to Ireland. I'll have a week. It's not much, but …" Her voice trailed off, leaving the sentence and the thought unfinished.

"I'll call you when I get back. We'll talk then." He glanced down at his watch. "I'll miss my flight if I don't go now."

Resolutely, he moved toward her, they embraced, and he kissed her lightly on the mouth. "Good-bye." He picked up his suitcase and started away.

Barry stood, watching him go, the sensation of doom returning so poignantly that it nearly overcame her. But in a moment, he dashed back, took her firmly in his strong embrace and kissed her again– long and deeply.

Without a word then, he turned and walked hurriedly away, through the descending mist and the fog, dipping his head and replacing the fedora. Replete with grace and charm, that single motion, under the glow of a Victorian streetlamp, tore more savagely at her heart than anything else had done.

Unaware of the wet and the cold, Barry stood gazing after him, until he pulled open a door and entered the terminal. "Good-bye," she whispered. *Oh, Rob ... Rob, will I ever see you again?*

When she returned to her car, she was chilled through. She started the car engine and sat for a moment, shivering. *I'll call you when I get back. We'll talk then. What had he meant by that?* Tears stained her cheeks and flooded her heart. *'I'll call you.' Famous last words. The kiss of death.*

The sudden ringing of her cell phone startled her out of her reverie. She reached down and lifted it from her bag. "Hello."

"Hello, Barry. I knew I'd get you on your cell."

"Bill! And you knew that because?" *Oh, why did **he** have to call?*

The voice was calm, low-pitched and– menacing. "I know everything about you. Don't you know that?"

Her shivering was uncontrollable now, as she scanned the dash for the heat control switch. "What do you want?" She flung the words at him.

The caller responded with a low laugh. "What do you think?"

"I told you I never wanted anything more to do with you. What part of 'It's over!' don't you understand, or is there something wrong with your memory?" She turned on the wipers, letting the defroster do its work on the windows.

"There's nothing wrong with my memory. That's what haunts me. Doesn't it you? I have such *pleasurable* memories." He savored the word 'pleasurable' as though it were ice cream.

"I have a memory, of your hitting me and calling me obscene names, and that's the one ... **two** that haunt me. I don't know how I could have been so stupid!"

"It will never happen again."

"Oooooh, you're right about that."

"I told you I was sorry. Can't you find it in your heart to forgive?"

"I did that– *once*. You said it yourself– '*Never again!*'" She disconnected, set the phone down and put the car in reverse, talking aloud to herself as she slowly guided the car out of the airport parking lot. "Why did he have to call and put *his* stamp on tonight? It was almost as if he *knew* ... . Forget it; think about what you're doing. The roads are getting bad."

The fog was thick and swirling. She struggled to see what was looming, virulent, before her, fear rising as bile in her mouth. Two figures, each dressed in what looked like cobwebs, their robes hooded, oversized, so that their faces were veiled in shadow, came out of the eddying mists. They moved as though they had forever, but she *knew* they had a plan– a purpose– and that their plan was *to kill.*

Thick and swirling .. can't see. Someone is hurt. I must try, try to help. She attempted to move, but the mists held her, and her feet felt as though they were mired in cement.

Slowly, surely, the fog began to lift, dissolve, and then, on the ground, she could discern the injured, perhaps dead, man. She could see his form clearly now. *His face ... I must see his face!*

Gingerly, she moved closer, kneeling beside him. *Rob! Blood! So much blood!* Blood on his face, head, and on the ground beside his body.

From a distance, a deep voice was trying to reach her, a lament of warning, and it seemed to be repeating the same word over and yet again. All at once, she heard it, like the tolling of a requiem bell–
Mur-der! Mur-der! Murrr-der!

With a start, she awoke, sitting up in bed, her body drenched with perspiration.

The Strength Tarot is telling me to rely on my intuition. Barry held the card to the bosom of her robe. *I cannot let Fear overcome me. It is the strongest of negatives, its opposite, Love. I must act out of Love, not Fear.*

Barry drew three runes from the blue cotton pouch. On the familiar green cloth, spread on the kitchen table, she laid the trilogy of apple-wood chips face down from right to left, the same direction, as in Hebrew, that they are read.

With a sigh, she turned the first one over. *Journey. Union. Reunion. This rune is inciting me to assume my quest.*

Turning up the center rune, Barry pondered on its symbol. *Disruption. This rune is ... a "skull and crossbones." I am being warned. There is nothing inconsequential here. The more trenchant the confusion, the shattering, the disruption– the more significant the change.*

The last rune, the one on the far left now. The Horse, symbol of movement, new hearth and home. A new life. OK, and I know it's crazy ... but I can't help feeling that, somehow, real horses will figure in this intrigue.

Barry sat back in the kitchen chair, her fingers brushing the apple-wood runes. *This whole reading is shrouded in danger, mystery, and something else, but I cannot fathom what. Something quite strong is at work here. Love. Yes, oh yes. But I must draw one more– a Crisis rune.*

Barry closed her eyes and reached into the pouch, her fingers seeking. The runes felt cool and smooth. She touched each one, waiting for the familiar tingle, that trickle of energy that pricked her fingertips. "Tell me," she commanded, focusing on the issues pressing on her mind and heart. "Please tell me what I need to know in my life *now*. Help me to decide what to do."

The runes were silent.

Then, suddenly, the magick happened, and she drew the final rune, placing it on the cloth before her, symbol-side down. With bated breath and trembling fingers, she turned it over.

It was blank.

Only one of the runes is blank. Blank is closure, blank a new beginning. This rune can foretell a death. Or the death can be metaphoric. This, above all the others, calls for an act of pure and absolute courage.

Barry took up the battered old book that she had received years before from a beloved aunt. She leafed to the desired section, reading aloud, "'The blank rune evokes our greatest fears; however, there is nothing that cannot be deflected, changed. We all have choices. Free will.'"

Her eyes continued to scan the page, as she read on, "'… and no power on earth or beyond is greater than Love. The blank rune should be translated as proof of communion with your infinite– ultimate destination– for, synonymous with this'"– a loud crack of lightning made her jump, followed by a deep roll of thunder– "'is the rune's own name– **Destiny**.'"

Chapter Three

"Robbie!"

In Shannon's arrival terminal, Rob, carrying his suitcase, turned in the direction of the resounding voice to see Frank Dillon hurrying toward him.

Though in his sixties, the black had not faded much from Frank's thick, wavy hair, nor the mischief from his clear blue eyes. With the lilt of County Clare on his tongue and his ready smile, Francis Xavier Dillon was a youthful man, a wiry, jovial sort with the definite gift of what has been called, since Elizabeth the First, "Blarney."

Frank and his wife Nora had been managing Barry Hall for the past thirty years. This last was on both their minds as Rob extended his hand to his late uncle's longtime estate manager.

"Y' have me sympathy, lad."

"Thank you, Frank, and for coming to collect me."

The older man guffawed. "'Tis nothin'. Th' car's just outside," he gestured with a jerk of his head in the intended direction.

The ride from Shannon International Airport to Barry Hall was a mere ten-minute drive in Frank's Ford Focus. As the overseer talked nearly incessantly, Rob, from the passenger's seat, took in the rolling hills dotted with familiar white cottages, the smoke from their chimneys curling from pungent turf fires. Sheep grazed over the forty shades of green, and scattered round about were the various castle ruins of Ireland's turbulent past.

"… Old Phillip could be a divil, ofttimes *hard* t' wur-rk for, but everyone who knew him respected him. 'Tis a pity we couldn't reach you in time for the wake. Nearly th' whole county showed up. Ah! I'm t' remind you about your meetin' with the solicitor."

"When is that?" Rob asked, glancing over at Frank.

"Tomorra night. Just so you know ahead o' time. Gives ya a chance for a bit o' rest."

"I'm thinkin' of stopping by Doc Rafferty's place after I speak with the solicitor."

"Why?" Frank nearly shouted, immediately softening the timbre of his voice. "I mean, why wud ya want to pay a visit t' Rafferty?"

Ready to answer, Rob was paused by the startled expression on Frank's face.

"I didn't mean t' pry, lad. It's … I …" Frank seemed to fumble for words, "Are ya sick?"

"No, nothing of the sort. I want to talk to him about Uncle Phillip." Rob thought he detected a hint of anxiety revisiting Frank's features. *Now what in bloody hell is goin' through his head?* "How's Nora?" he asked, changing the subject.

"Always th' same." Frank seemed again to search for the right thing to say. "A man couldn't ask for a better wife. She'll have a grand Irish breakfast ready, time we arrive back at the manor."

Rob cleared his throat. "Frank, I want you to know that I intend for everything to continue in the same fashion at Barry Hall. I know you and Nora must be concerned, but there's no need."

A look of relief passed over Frank's features. "I don't mind tellin' ya, lad; we were a tad troubled. Nora … *och!* You know how women like to fret."

Rob grinned, "I do. Tell Nora to rest easy. We're all family, are we not?"

Frank's blue eyes under his bushy black brows brightened. "Sure 'n I'd like to think we are! By the bye, there are some repairs that need tendin'… nothin' much. We contract large jobs out, but Barry Hall has always had a full-time gardener. The garden's in rather a state of disarray ,… now wud you be listenin' t' me? I don't mean to burden you with everythin' at once'st." Frank paused in his ramblings, then with a sidelong look at Rob, he added, "They say death comes in threes." As Frank had intended, he had Rob's full attention.

"Who besides Uncle Phillip has died?"

"Tom Mannion, our gardener. You remember Tom, don't you?"

Rob was a bit taken aback. "It's sar-tain I do. What happened?"

"Tom was not a sprightly lad, to be sure. Would've been sixty-eight next month."

"Was it his heart?" Rob asked.

"Apparently so. He was found in his cottage by a neighbor, night before last." Frank shook his head. "Card club won't be th' same without ole Tom. I knew him since we were lads together."

Absorbed in thought, Rob responded automatically with an understanding nod, then turned his attention to the window. Through the lacework of trees, the village of Quin, with its fifteenth-century abbey, stretched before them in drowsy, sunlit tranquility, and beyond, the plain of East Clare was bespeckled with the ancient forts of a bygone age. *I'd like to show Barry this place so near to my heart. But for now, I must settle these matters concerning the estate and my uncle and whatever this ... enigma is surrounding his death.*

Presently, Frank brought Rob out of his reverie. "Robbie, is somethin' else troublin' ya?"

"Sorry. Indeed, Frank, there is something weighin' on me. This business about my uncle's suicide. I know you told me that everything points to an *accidental suicide–* God, isn't that phrase a contradiction in terms?" he mused quietly. In a moment, however, his voice rose sharply. "I tell you something is not right, not right *at all*, and I intend to find out what."

A look of alarm fleetingly crossed Frank's expressive face, and for once he was silent, as he pulled the car into the circular drive in front of the imposing seventeenth-century manor house. "Looks like we've unexpected visitors."

A white police Ford Mondeo was parked in front of the main entrance. As soon as the pair got out of the car, Frank extracted Rob's valise from the boot, while Rob walked immediately up the front steps of the house to greet the uniformed man in blue, who was just exiting the front door. "Rob Carroll," he said, extending his hand.

"Sergeant Dugan," the hefty, ruddy-faced Garda replied, grasping Rob's hand in a firm shake.

Frank, right behind Rob, exclaimed, "Dugan! What bit of business brings you out here?"

"It's about my uncle's death, isn't it? I *knew* it wasn't suicide." Rob lifted the suitcase from a visibly anxious Frank, setting it down at the door, where the three men stood, facing one another.

"Lad, we've closed the case on your uncle. As far as we're concerned, his death was an accident," the middle-aged officer stated flatly.

Rob shook his head. "That's what Frank informed me, but what drew you to *that* conclusion?"

"We pieced together the scenario the night of your uncle's passing, and came to the *logical* conclusion that Mr. Barry got up during the night, probably in pain, and took a second dose of his medicine himself, this after Nora had already administered his bed-time measure. We discovered a residue of the stuff on the bathroom sink and floor. He must've fumbled with it. That second draught was enough for cardiac arrest. We believe, however, *it was accidental*." This last was delivered with what Rob interpreted as a mix of condescension and annoyance.

"Poor old fella," Frank lamented, "in pain every minute of his life, sometimes s' bad, he couldn't sleep nights. Perhaps someday the law'll change, and those who suffer will be allowed to go peacefully."

Rob looked at Dugan, whose intense hazel eyes shifted from Frank's to his.

Suddenly aware of their reaction, Frank exclaimed to Rob, "Sure 'n don't we do it f'r th' sufferin' beasts!" Then he focused his eyes on the sergeant. "You still didn't say what brings you out here today?"

The Garda's reply was swift and totally unexpected. "Th' matter of Tom Mannion's death."

Now Frank and Rob exchanged astonished glances.

"Let's go inside," Dugan indicated with a courteous sweep of his arm. "Everyone's in there."

The three men entered and moved down the foyer, turning left into the public room.

This was a cozy chamber with a large stone hearth, a deep-green divan and settee, and a pair of burgundy Morris chairs. A well-equipped bar with its mirrored wall occupied one end of the room.

Seated in one of the large armchairs was Frank's buxom wife Nora, who, Rob noticed, was obviously upset. Her faded red hair was pinned neatly up in a bun, and her long-sleeved, grey linen dress with Irish-lace collar was impeccable. Seated on the settee was Máire Nolan, Nora's pretty eighteen-year-old apprentice, who was dressed like her mentor, except that Máire's dress was black. She, too, appeared to be agitated, as she brushed an errant strand of strawberry-blonde hair from her face with a shaking hand.

Before a spirited fire in the hearth, stood a tall, authoritative man with impressive shoulders in a trench coat, who was scribbling in a notebook.

"Frank!" Nora sprang from her seat, rushing over to him. "They're sayin' Tom was *murdered*!" Her eyes darted to Rob. "Excuse me, Mr. Carroll."

"Jaysus!" Frank started. "Who would want t' murder Tom?"

Sergeant Dugan raised his arms in a peremptory manner. "Please, everyone, sit down and be calm." He indicated the taller, more slender, agent in the trench coat. "This is Detective-Inspector Dennis Haggerty from the crime squad, down from Dublin." Dugan removed his cap and smoothed his ginger hair.

With worried face, Nora sank into the Morris chair, and Rob and Frank moved forward to shake hands with Haggerty, as Dugan introduced them. "This is Robert Carroll, the new owner of the estate, and Frank Dillon, his resident manager." Rob and Frank both sat, while the two Gardai remained standing.

*I'm not **publicly** the new owner*, Rob thought, looking sharply at the sergeant.

"To get right to th' matter," Dugan began, his eyes meeting Rob's, "the undertaker rang us up when he noticed some splotches on Tom's hands. We ordered a postmortem straightaway. Now it looks as if cause of death is poisonin' by a lethal herbicide absorbed into th' body. The herbicide breaks down the central nervous system. Stops th' heart." The sergeant paused for a brief moment. "We, in turn, rang up the crime squad in Dublin."

Inspector Haggerty stirred a lump of sugar into the cup of tea he had been sipping. "We found a spilled can of th' stuff in your gardener's shed. Whoever spilled it got it on th' work gloves."

"What are ya sayin'?" Frank queried. "That someone staged an accident?"

Haggerty cocked his head with its shock of white hair. "I am. Someone wanted to make it look like your man was a bit careless … that the herbicide was absorbed through th' skin causin–"

Frank met the inspector's gaze without flinching. His bushy black brows drew together, and his eyes shot blue fire. "Don't stand on ceremony. Get to th' point, man! What was th' cause of Tom's death?"

Unruffled, Haggerty took a sip of his tea, the action deliberate, weighty, as though he enjoyed the drama of the moment. "The postmortem revealed a lethal dose of th' same substance in Tom's stomach. Doesn't take much. Two or three drops will kill a man weighin' fourteen, fifteen stone." His steely gaze scrutinized the assembly.

Frank lowered his head, speaking more to himself than to anyone in the tension-filled room, "Mother of God! Whoever th' murderer was … why would he want to poison Tom?"

"You said 'he' as if you know the murderer to be a man," Haggerty noted aloud. "There are far more women poisoners wanderin' about the world than men. Poison is more commonly a woman's weapon, but you said 'he' as if you are sar-tain it is a man."

"Seems to me you're th' one wanderin' about," Frank shot back.

Haggerty shrugged off the remark, continuing, "We're attemptin' to trace Mannion's movements in the last couple of days. That's why we need to question you, Mr. Dillon, your wife, and your maid here." The inspector took up his notebook anew, raising his voice an octave. "Now, we know Mannion liked to stop f'r a pint or two after wur'rk."

"Frank," Dugan asked, "do you recollect anything unusual about that evenin'?"

Frank pondered a long moment, running his fingers through his thick salt-and-pepper hair. "Mr. Barry's funeral was that mornin'. I don't remember anythin' unusual in regard t' Tom, except that he and I raised a few glasses to th' departed afore he left. We were both a bit unsteady on our feet. You know how 'tis, we had many a tale to trade. I don't remember much after that, save Tom tellin' me he was goin' t' stop by Kelley's Pub."

Haggerty, who was writing in his notebook, paused and looked up at Frank. "Can you remember what time he left here?"

Frank thought for a moment. "I can't recall exactly, but I'd say it was … round six, or there abouts."

Haggerty finished the last gulp of his tea, then set the cup on the bar, fixing Frank with his persistent scrutiny. Imperceptibly, the inspector's manner changed. It was hardly noticeable except as a slight hardness in his voice. "Then Mannion had several drinks *here*, b'fore he started off?"

Frank swallowed, tossing an uneasy glance at his wife, whose worried expression visibly deepened. He gave a slight nod, answering, "A few."

Rob, who had been taking this all in, got up and moved to the bar, where he poured himself a stiff drink. "Well now, Sergeant, don't you think you should reopen that ruddy file on my uncle's *accidental* death?"

***

"Go ahead; call me crazy, but I know I'm right." Barry poured herself a cup of coffee at the beverage station in the producers' pit, where her friend Katherine Foster stood, shaking her sleek blonde head and staring at her incredulously.

"Destiny, huh?" Katherine repeated dryly, shifting her weight to lean a slim hip against the wall.

Or rather a matter of need meeting Destiny, Barry thought.

"Do you intend to see him again?"

"I hope to, yes. Oh, Katherine, it was the most wonderful three days. The first night he took me dancing, and all those great old songs were playing. I'm in love. For the first time in my life, I am really, unequivocally, in love!"

"How long has it been since you and Bill broke up?" Katherine took out her compact and began refreshing her lipstick in the small mirror.

"A couple of months." Barry rolled her eyes, casting off the memory in a dismissive wave of her hand.

"Barry," Katherine pursed her freshly rouged mouth, "I can't blame you for being excited. I saw your interview with him, but I hope this is not a rebound thing, and I hope, for your sake," she lifted one perfectly penciled brow, "this guy's nothing like Bill."

"Believe me, Rob is the total opposite of Bill. When I think back on how controlling that weasel was," Barry took a sip of the office coffee, grimaced, but downed a swallow of the bitter brew, "I don't know how I could have been so stupid."

"You weren't stupid that long, sweetie. Rob looks and sounds like your knight in shining armor, but why do I get the feeling there's something wrong with this picture?" Katherine popped a couple of aspirins into her mouth, swallowing them with her coffee.

"Because there is–" Barry caught sight of their boss through his glassed-in office. "Ooooh, Skinner's watching us. I'd better get back to work." She tossed her empty cup into the wastepaper basket. "We'll talk later."

When Barry returned to her desk, her phone was ringing. She reached over and grabbed the receiver, sliding into her chair. "Bartok."

"I just felt like ringin' you up, Bartok," a deep Irish voice intoned.

"Rob! I'm so glad you called. Is everything all right?"

"No, it isn't. I've just been hit with more complications. It's too involved to discuss on an overseas call, but–"

"Rob, listen to me, I had a dream. I am rarely wrong when I get these premonitions. I *feel* there are two people scheming to kill you." Except for a sibilant hissing sound, there was complete silence on the line. "Rob! Are you there?"

"I wish I were there, luv– *with you*."

"You must take this seriously."

"I take *you* seriously," he said softly.

"I dreamed that a murder is in the–"

"Our gardener has just turned up murdered, and because of that, the Gards have agreed to investigate my uncle's death. I knew he had not committed suicide." Again, there was silence. "Barry … Barry?"

"I'm frightened for you," she answered, her voice barely a whisper.

"Don't be. Once the officials get this snarl of events untangled, and I get this place runnin' smoothly–"

"What do you mean?"

"Barry Hall, the estate I've inherited … *likely* inherited. There's a vast amount of property that goes with the old manor. Though it houses only a maximum of six guests at any one time, the place has a reputation in these parts … fox hunts, fancy dress balls, that sort of seasonal thing. Adhering to its traditions, I intend to keep it operating as an inn."

"The estate you inherited is an inn?" Barry repeated almost to herself.

"Yes, but it's closed to guests now, due to the deaths. I'm sorry, Barry, I am going to have to ring off, but I'll call again in a day or so."

"There is danger surrounding you! Please, please be careful," she admonished softly before hanging up, her hand lingering for several moments on the receiver. *How fortunate for someone in the travel business ... a princely and, it seems, **flourishing** inn. Stop it, Barry! This isn't Bill you're talking about!* Oh, Rob, she slowly drew her fingers from the phone, running them through her mane of dark mahogany hair, *please be careful!*

"And I mean *careful*," Katherine cautioned *sotto voce*. "He's in a foul mood today. If I were you, I'd wait to ask him about the rest of your vacation time."

"Oh, Katherine, if I waited till he was in a good mood, I'd be waiting till those clichéd cows come over that fanciful hill and home. I hate to grovel, but I have no choice." She locked eyes with her friend, "I mean ... all he can say is 'no.'"

"That's not *all* he can say," Katherine mouthed to Barry's squared shoulders, as the latter marched off in the direction of Joe Skinner's office, her fingers crossed behind her sweatered back.

"So, you see, Mr. Skinner, if you permit me to take the rest of my vacation now, I'll work through the holidays. I wouldn't ask– and I never have before– but I have some crucial personal business to take care of, and I could really use that week now. I'll work over, when I get back." She let out her breath slowly, struggling to keep her demeanor.

Joe Skinner yanked his unlit cigar from between yellow teeth to bark, "Okay, you got it, but I can't let you have a week. Six days. That's the best I can do. You're the one covering that convention in town." He waved a pudgy hand at her, "*hell-lo* ... the AMA convention?"

Barry nodded. "Thanks, Mr. Skinner." She quickly turned on her heel to exit the office before he could change his mind, his thundering voice following her.

"You make sure you're back in this office bright and early Monday morning– or your problems **will** be crucial!"

***

At the entrance to the narrow, tree-lined way, the wooden sign creaked on its pole and chain in the chill autumnal wind. The placard's words– *The Black Cat Detective Agency*– curved above the sooty, arched figure of a fierce-looking cat– were barely discernible in the fading light of the murky October dusk. In a sudden flash, the headlights from a car entering the lane seemed to enliven the cat's golden eyes, making them momentarily glow in the near-darkness.

Like the footfalls of a spectral night-creature, the tires of Raine's cream-colored 1953 MG TD made crunching sounds on the gravel, as she and Maggie motored up the narrow, twisting drive to the stone house that served as home and business for their cousin, Aisling McDonough-Gwynn, and her husband Ian. Aisling had inherited the charming property (along with the means to start the agency) from her grandmother McDonough, whose husband had used it as a hunting lodge.

Former cops, who had worked together as detectives on the Pittsburgh police force, the Gwynns were master sleuths. Nonetheless, it was not sleuthing that brought Raine and Maggie to the Gwynns' forest home this bleary night– that is, not *conventional* sleuthing.

With her usual bright manner, "Merry," the Gwynns' blonde five-year-old daughter, enthusiastically greeted them at the door, the family's huge black cat, Merlin, spilling over in the little girl's arms. "The 'aunts' are here!" she yelled, shooing the cat to the house's interior and clapping her hands with joy. "The 'aunts' are here!" Then, reaching up, she bestowed hugs and kisses that were energetically returned by Maggie and Raine.

"Meredith Gwynn," a female voice called from the kitchen, "you go up and take your bath and get into your PJs. Seven o'clock rolls around mighty early, and you know how hard it is for you to drag your little tush outta bed in the morning!"

In the candleglow of the secret "room-within" the darkened study, the three McDonough cousins completed their all-important spell, chanting in unison inside the sacred circle, their voices increasing in volume in the locked, soundproof alcove, "Now we say this spell is cast. Make it so this spell doth last. Do what ye will and harm ye none. It is so; let it be done. So mote it be; blessed be!"

The trio raised their arms, the bell-sleeves of their hooded black robes falling to their shoulders, as they concluded their ritual. "Oh, Guardians of the Watchtowers, angels, and spirit guides, by our will, we release you. Thank you for your guidance. Return ye now to your place of power. So mote it be; blessed be!" With their wands, then, they released and dispersed the conjured energies.

Seated on the arm of an overstuffed chair in the Gwynns' rustic study, Aisling looked like the proverbial "tall, cool blonde."

Maggie often said of her "gum-shoe" cousin, "Aisling has the ability to silently project that she is an authority, very professional our gal, yet she has understanding and compassion for others."

Tonight, however, the third of the trio of Sleuth Sisters appeared a tad uneasy, as she listened to her cousins' "travel agenda." When they finished, she stood, her long slender, blue-jean-encased legs carrying her the short distance to the fireplace, where she remained silent before the lively flames for a pondering moment.

Finally, she turned to face Raine and Maggie, who, devoid now of their robes, sported similar, casual attire and were seated side-by-side across the room on the leather divan.

Reaching inside her white, cable-knit sweater, the leggy blonde pulled her gem-encrusted amulet free, lifting the heavy silver chain over her long, ash-blonde hair. She held the antique heirloom out to her cousins, the scatter of smaller jewels on its surface glittering in the firelight, the center stone a large sapphire. "I want you to take this with you. You'll need its energies."

"It's far too risky!" Raine and Maggie both exclaimed nearly simultaneouly, but Aisling waved their protests aside.

"It's far too risky *not* to take it with you." The emerald green of Aisling's intensely made-up McDonough eyes glistened with the emotion she was feeling. "And when it's time, *I'll* be with you as well."

As if on cue, Raine and Maggie removed their talismans from around their necks. Linking arms, the trio held before them the three necklaces, bequeathed to them years before by their grandmother, Aisling Tully McDonough, who had inherited the very special totems from her grandmother.

The amulets fit together perfectly, forming a Triquetra, the ancient Celtic knot symbolizing all trinities– *and infinite power.*

As sisters of the moon, the cousins knew that in ancient times, before it was known as a magickal symbol, *talisman* carried a far older definition. From the Greek *telesma* meaning "complete," a talisman was any object that completed another– *and made it whole.*

From the study's window, the moon's silver glow sparked a blaze of light from the fitted talismanic pieces, as the Sleuth Sisters united their voices to invoke in perfect harmony, "The power of three shall set us free! So mote it be! Blessed be!"

"For every evil under the sun,
There is a remedy, or there is none.
If there be one, seek till you find it;
If there be none, never mind it."
~ Mother Goose

Chapter Four

Barry leaned back against the headrest of the comfortable *Aer Lingus* seat and closed her eyes. She had had to change planes at Kennedy, since Pittsburgh offered no direct flights to Ireland.

*Skinner must really like the work I'm doing to cut me this break. The man simply does **not** cut breaks. It's taken me quite awhile to gain his grudging respect, and I'm risking a lot by taking off now, but I've learned that you have to do what you think is right at the time. And I truly believe this **is** the right thing to do.*

Barry accepted a diet cola from the flight attendant. Pouring some into the plastic glass she lifted from her tray, she took a sip, her thoughts returning to Rob. *But what if he doesn't have the same feelings for me? Wonder if all he was feeling was something physical? I don't really know that ... yet.*

*The fact of the matter is this: Though I just met Rob, if I really believe these feelings I have for him are real, coupled with believing what I do about the danger he's in, then I **must** do this, job or no job. I can always find another position in my field, but I don't think I could ever find another Rob Carroll. I've been burned before, so, as difficult as it would be, I think I'm tough enough to move on, if he doesn't share my sentiments. God knows I've had my heart broken before.*

The point is I've come across plenty of brass and ... "fool's gold"! But to discover pure twenty-four karat, now that's rare, rare indeed! Rob Carroll is a treasure. I'm not just talking about the handsome packaging, though that alone is enough to take my breath. He's a good man, a man of substance. And, if ever I had a sixth sense about anything, I acutely sense that he would never hurt me, or any woman. Not like Bill. Horn-rimmed-bespectacled-three-piece-suit-Mr.-Pseudo-Respectable Bill, who, I found out, not only hit me, but his ex-wife and a couple of ex-girlfriends as well. What a polished act he had! Barry gave a slight shiver. *I don't think I would have been so vulnerable, if he hadn't come along right after Gran died. Anyway, aside from my job and Pittsburgh, which I love, but ... .*

For a moment, her thoughts drifted off to home and Pittsburgh. *What else am I really leaving behind? Since Aunt Lizzie and Gran have both passed on, I have no one. It's so depressing spending holidays alone, seeing husbands and wives, children, families all together, their faces smiling and happy.*

Hearing a giggle, Barry turned her head to watch an enamored couple across the aisle. The man picked up the woman's hand and kissed it, whispering into her ear.

Yes, I'm doing the right thing. If Gran and Auntie were here, they would say that nothing should stand in the way of Love.

*I'm worried, not just about the danger I feel surrounding Rob– that's bad enough– but I'm afraid that he, used to so much freedom, would never **want** to settle down. He may never want to give up the exciting, carefree life he's living.*

So …if it works out, why couldn't I join him in his career? I believe I'd really like that, for a few years anyway. Then, we could have a family. And as for my work, I could still write. In fact, traveling with Rob and assisting him in his profession would be the best thing for my writing. Of course, all of this depends on how Rob really feels about me. The thing is– I won't have much time to find that out, about five days, tops. Is that even possible?

Barry opened her eyes. She turned and noticed for the first time the passenger sitting by the window next to her. The woman was elderly, probably in her eighties, with snow-white hair and a pink and white complexion. It was, however, her eyes that caught Barry's attention. They were the most brilliant blue she had ever seen, and they really did twinkle.

"You look like y' have somethin' weighty on ye'er mind, lassie." The old woman smiled warmly.

A bit taken aback, Barry inclined her head. "I have. I can tell by your voice that you're Irish. I'll tell you something," she leaned companionably toward her seat-mate, "I think an Irish brogue is the most charming accent in the world." She offered her hand. "Barry Bartok."

In spite of her fragile seafoam appearance, the crone grasped the hand in a surprisingly firm shake. "I'm Maura. Maura O'Rourke. I was visitin' my daughter and her family here in New York City, but 'tis good to be goin' home. I've been away nearly six months." She cocked her head, her azure gaze bright. "Will this be ye'er first visit to the Emerald Isle?"

Barry nodded. "Yes, it will."

"Then," she patted the younger woman's hand, "*Go n-eiri an bothar leat, agus go sirbhe Dia duit.* I wish you luck on your journey, and may God assist you in your quest. We've a legend in Ireland that ye've probably heard– the pot of gold at the end of th' rainbow." Mrs. O'Rourke twinkled again, and there was a mien of perception in her bright blue eyes. "I hope ye find what ye'er lookin' for, lass. I've a keen Irish feelin' ye've been searchin' f'r a long time." After a moment, she added, the look in the vivid depths of her eyes deepening, "Be bold in what ye stand for … *and careful what you fall for.*"

Barry got out of the cab, paid the driver and stood in the circular drive, looking at the aristocratic seventeenth-century manor with its understated elegance. In the center of the driveway loop was a flowerbed, graced by large blooms in rich autumn hues. A carpark occupied an area on both sides of the mansion. Diagonally in the background was a picturesque, ivy-covered carriage house and, beyond, a grove of stately oaks, their faded leaves clinging tenaciously to the intricate array of branches, as though they dreaded the bleak arrival of winter.

Seeing no one about, Barry drew in her breath. Then she started up the curved stone steps leading to the manse's massive front door. A huge brass doorknocker in the creation of a lion's head, its mouth open in a silent roar, confronted her. *Vis-à-vis* with the toothy guardian, Barry lifted the polished grip and firmly rapped three times. Presently the heavy oaken door was opened by a uniformed housekeeper, whose demeanor, Barry perceived, was straight out of Du Maurier's *Rebecca*.

"May I help you?"

"My name is Baranya Bartok. I'm a friend of Mr. Carroll's. Is he here?"

Nora's eyes quickly appraised the younger woman before answering in a voice as formally efficient as her appearance, "Mr. Carroll's takin' his breakfast now, and I'm afraid he cannot be disturbed. Perhaps if you'll tell me–"

A familiar voice reached Barry from somewhere inside. "If it's the Gards, Nora, please show them into the dining room."

"As you can see, Mr. Carroll is quite busy at the moment, but if you care to leave a message, I'll see that he gets it."

Barry sighed, but her voice was firm when she spoke. "I have come all the way from America. I've been on a plane all night without a wink of sleep, and I–"

In an instant he was there, a look of surprise and pleasure illuminating his handsome face. "Barry! This is brilliant!" He waved his arm in a welcoming gesture, as he moved swiftly forward toward the door where Barry remained standing. "Come in! Come in!"

Smoothly moving Nora from her battle station in the doorway, Rob enfolded Baranya in his eager embrace. "How did you manage this? Never mind. I'll wager you're tired and hungry. Nora, this is Miss Bartok, a very dear friend of mine, and we must give her the royal treatment. Barry, this is Nora Dillon. She and her husband Frank have managed Barry Hall for years … couldn't do without them. Nora, would you mind preparin' some more of those delicious rashers, eggs … and there's plenty left of your fine soda bread. Ah! 'Tis good you're here," he sang, focusing once again on Barry and giving her yet another bear hug.

"Mrs. Danvers," however, with whom, over Rob's shoulder, Barry came nearly eyeball to eyeball, seemed none too thrilled with the idea of Rob having a visitor, longed-for or otherwise. As a reporter in the field, Barry was used to opposition, even downright hostility, but, in the steely-grey eyes of Nora Dillon, Barry read an outright declaration of war.

"She'll want a wash-up," the housekeeper returned gruffly. "I'll have Máire show her upstairs to a room."

"Mr. Carroll said you are a writer." Máire took the embroidered, garnet wool dress Barry handed her, slipping it onto a crochet-trimmed hanger. The younger woman was immediately in awe of the beautiful American visitor, and the two had taken an instant liking to one another, as, together, they unpacked Barry's things. "Are you, m'am? A writer, I mean?"

"I write news copy for a TV station. Why do you ask?" She handed the maid a knit dress in a rich shade of forest green.

Máire smiled shyly, pausing in her task of unrolling and putting away Barry's packed apparel. "Y' see, m'am, it's like this. I have a secret desire to write. I know it's not possible for university, or anythin' so grand as that, but I've been readin' books on creative … *prose* they call it, and–" The maid stopped, her hand reaching for a turquoise silk blouse, which she draped onto a hanger. "Ah, would y' be listenin' t' me now! 'Tis only a dream."

Barry set aside a crimson wool skirt and matching blazer. "Máire," she began, laying her hands on the girl's thin shoulders and looking into her eyes, "'Reach high, for stars lie hidden in your soul. Dream deep, for every dream precedes your goal.' My aunt and my granny who brought me up used to tell me that all the time, and before she passed on, Granny told me the pair of them would be '… sittin' on the stars in the gem-studded night sky, spilling to me, from gossamer veils, a myriad of shimmering inspirations– like stardust– to enhance my dreams.'" She smiled, asking, "Now, do you want *my* advice?"

The enraptured Máire nodded, "Indaid, I do, m'am!"

"Continue to *read,* everything you can, and learn to be a good listener. Everyone you meet knows something you don't. And, even more important, learn to be *observant*. It's how I was trained, and it has served me well."

Her duty of getting Barry settled in momentarily forgotten, Máire turned a radiant face to Barry, "My *da* tells the loveliest stories. If I could tell a story, on paper, th' way *Da* entertains us nights before the turf fire, I'd be followin' in the grand family tradition of *seanchaí*."

Taking the final item from the single valise she had brought, Barry tilted her head, "You're going to have to translate that last for me, Máire."

A sheepish little grin curved the girl's lips. "Storyteller," she obliged, smoothing the soft, pretty sweater and putting it into a heather-scented bureau drawer. "A *seanchaí* is a storyteller."

"Write those stories down, Máire, and remember– dreams pursued are dreams won," Barry finished kindly, returning the smile and accepting some fluffy towels, before heading for the adjoining bath.

Just as she was about to step into the hot, lavender-scented water Máire had drawn, Rob's voice reached her.

"Are you dai-cent?" He tapped on the partially open door.

"She's in the bath, Mr. Carroll," Máire replied, indicating the closed door behind her.

Rob nodded, raising his voice to be heard. "Barry, now that you've eaten, why don't you try and sleep for a few hours. I have an appointment early this evening in Ennis. I'd like for you to ride with me, if you're not too tired. Máire could wake you in time."

"I'd like that," Barry called out, sinking farther down into the deep claw-foot tub, the sensation of impending danger momentarily banished by the steaming, scented water. She drowsily closed her eyes and imagined herself in a faerie forest replete with wildflowers of every imaginable hue– with a teasing undertone of Rob's woodsy aftershave. *Yes, yes, yes, dreams pursued are dreams won ...*

***

"So, now that I've caught you up on all the happenings, what do you think?" It was raining, and Rob was driving Frank's car with caution on the winding road to Ennis, where his meeting with the solicitor was scheduled to take place.

"Rob, this reiterates what I was trying to tell you yesterday over the phone. I believe strongly there are people plotting to kill you. Why do you think I came all the way to Ireland? You're in danger." She reached over and laid a gentle hand over his on the gearshift. "It feels odd sitting on the driver's side, with someone else driving."

Rob laughed. "Seems, though, we're providin' you with th' same soft weather as Pittsburgh." He squeezed her hand. "Rain is a good memory-jogger, isn't it? We Irish like to say that when there is rain on the roof and a warm meal in the belly, it is time to look over our shoulders and remember." He glanced over at Barry and winked, causing her to instantly blush.

I remember, she mused. *Oh, I do so remember ...*

"About the solicitor," Rob continued, "Patrick Conroy has been the family's solicitor ever since I can remember. He's married to my cousin Margaret. She's the only other near relative I have, though I don't really know her or her husband all that well. Margaret is some twenty years older than I, so I never really spent time with her as a lad. And as an adult, except for the occasional fall hunt or fancy dress ball I attended, I've been away a lot." He paused for a moment, then commented, "I should invite them over for dinner one evening soon. Yes, I'll do that," he mused aloud, navigated a sharp turn, then glancing over at Barry, remarked, "I want Margaret to meet you. And I want you to come in with me to the solicitor's. You've a good head on your shoulders, and what is that you Americans say, 'Two heads are better than one'? "

Barry, too, was pensive. *Only near relative? I thought he told me he has a brother.* Aloud, she said, "I was thinking that perhaps you ought to make an appointment to speak with your uncle's physician as well. You may learn something you could turn over to the police."

"My plan exactly! I can see we're going to make a good team. We don't need an appointment. Dr. Rafferty is a close family friend. We'll stop by his place en route home. It's only about a kilometer from Barry Hall. Uncle Phillip thought highly of him, both as a friend and a doctor. Like so many doctors in rural Ireland, he still makes house calls. When my uncle first learned he had cancer, he took it all in stride, saying, 'I have Faith, Hope and Rafferty, so I've naught to fear.' Aye, Doc Rafferty was devoted to my uncle. In fact, I'd go so far as to say they were almost like brothers. You'll like him." He flashed her a bright smile. "By the bye, have I told you how much it means to me to have you here?"

Barry smiled too. "Five or six times, but you can tell me again, if you like."

Solicitor Patrick F. Conroy sat behind a massive oaken desk in his Ennis office, looking down at the legal documents before him. Silver-haired and bespectacled, he was a tall, trim man who appeared to be in his early sixties.

Barry glanced around the lamp-lit room. Legal volumes lined two of the walls. An electric fire took the edge off the evening chill, and, through the leaded diamonds of the open-draped window, a tree branch, in the gloaming, surrendered its leaves to a persistent autumnal wind and rain.

"… I understand," Rob replied, "but I prefer that Miss Bartok stay."

The solicitor's poker face remained unchanged. "Very well, as you wish." His gaze focused on Rob. "As we discussed on the telephone this afternoon, you are the sole heir. Your great-uncle saw fit to leave a sum of money to the Dillon family for their faithful service. The rest, including the entire estate, he leaves to you." Conroy paused here, giving his next words additional weight. "I must add, there is a provision. Mr. Barry stipulated that the Dillons be retained for as long as they wish. He hoped that the manor house continue as an inn until such time as you may wish to reside there yourself."

Outside, cars and lorries whished over Ennis' wet cobblestone streets, and an occasional horn honked. Rob cleared his throat.

"I've already informed Frank that I want everything to continue in the same manner at Barry Hall. In a few years, I do plan to retire there."

Conroy gave a slight nod. "Your uncle hoped you would," he mumbled, glancing down at the papers on the desk, needlessly restacking them into a neat pile. "Mr. Barry was a good businessman," the solicitor shifted to the next focus. "He was solvent when he left this world. In fact, his securities amount to well over a million euros." Conroy extended a legal-bound document to Rob, concluding, "Those are the figures. Of course, it will be somewhat reduced by taxes, but you will be a wealthy man."

Rob perused the proffered sheet. "I knew my uncle was frugal, but I honestly had no idea … in a way, I feel strange taking this."

Conroy looked startled. "Under the law, it's yours. Of course, you're not obligated–"

A grin played on Rob's expressive face, one black brow lifted, as he stared for a quiet moment at the grim-faced solicitor. "I didn't say I wasn't going to take it."

Uh-oh, Barry thought, watching Conroy. *I don't know if I like this guy or not. He seems like a no-nonsense man right down the line– a typical lawyer with no sense of humor.*

For an uncomfortably long moment, Conroy regarded Rob over his wire-rimmed spectacles. "You are fortunate to have someone as trustworthy as Francis Dillon in your employ," he stated impassively, though the remark bit stingingly like an insult.

Rob's voice lost its note of sport. "I quite agree." He turned slightly in his chair, sending Barry a quick wink when the solicitor glanced down again at the neat stack of papers on the desk before him, his fingers smoothing the edges perfectly even.

After an awkward silence, Conroy removed his glasses. "There's one more item I must discuss with you, Robert."

Rain beat on the diamond-paned window, and the errant branch flailed in the strong wind, making, along with the leaping flames in the fireplace, eerie shadows on the walls and ceiling. Rob leaned forward in his chair, whilst Conroy extracted an old-fashioned trunk key from an envelope on his desk. A feeling of anticipation coursed like an electric charge through Barry, and she subconsciously moved closer to Rob.

For a long, silent moment, the solicitor stared at the key, as though he dreaded relinquishing it. Then he handed it over to Rob. "Here is the key to your great-uncle's trunk, to be found in his private apartment at Barry Hall. Inside, you will find your great-grandfather's diary. Read it carefully. Mr. Barry instructed me to this point only. He wanted you, the legal heir, to study the diary and then," Conroy too leaned forward, gazing steadily at Rob over his glasses, "to *fulfill your birthright*."

* * *

Situated in the scenic village of Quin, Dr. Daniel Rafferty's home and office occupied a neat, two-storied, ivy-covered building with a Georgian entrance, the door bright with kelly green paint and glowing brass. The doctor himself reminded Barry of a beloved uncle, though his speech carried the lilt of Eire.

"I was just about to have a bracing cup of tea. Won't you join me?" he said, picking up a small bell and ringing it.

"Thank you, we will," Rob answered.

"Sit down, please." The kindly physician indicated a divan, and Barry and Rob sat next to one another, the doctor across from them before the fire, in a somewhat worn but comfortable armchair. "I get rather chilled this time of year. Gravitate toward the warmth of the fire." He sent them a warm, avuncular smile. "Must be my age, like old Prince there." He looked to the Irish setter stretched out before the hearth, who opened his eyes upon hearing his name, yawned, then immediately went back to sleep.

Barry went over to the dog and stroked his silky head. "He's a beautiful animal. How old is he?" Kneeling beside him, she continued running her hand over the lustrous surface of his mahogany coat. Prince gazed up at her with grateful eyes.

"Poor old fella is fourteen now. His arthritis gives him a bit o' trouble, but he still enjoys our walks." Rafferty blinked rapidly. "When it's his time, I'll not let him suffer. He'll pass over without fear or pain." The doctor nodded to himself. "Robert, I want to convey my sympathy to you over the loss of your uncle. He was a good man and a dear, dear friend I respected and sorely miss."

Rob leaned forward and laid a hand on Rafferty's thin shoulder. "And I want to take this opportunity to thank you for the excellent care you gave Uncle Phillip. He always felt he was in the best of hands."

Presently a trim, uniformed housekeeper came in carrying the welcome tray of tea. After setting it down on the coffee table, she dropped a half-curtsey and swept briskly from the room. With the tea things stood a pot of jam, glistening like rubies, alongside a plate of scones, still warm from the oven, and a platter of hearty ham and cheese sandwiches.

"Now, what is it I can help you with, Robert?" Dr. Rafferty rose and poured a cup of tea, looked to Barry and asked, "Sugar? Cream or lemon?"

"Just sugar, please," she replied.

He dropped two lumps into her tea and handed her the steaming drink.

"Sugar and cream for me, please, Doctor," Rob volunteered. "I'd like, first of all, to learn anything I can about my uncle's state of mind at the last."

The doctor extended the requested cup to Rob, answering without hesitation, "His state of mind was good. He'd get quarrelsome from time to time, but that, as we both know, was his nature." He poured himself a cup of tea, adding both sugar and cream.

"Dr. Rafferty, tell me the truth as you know it. Do you think my uncle committed suicide?"

Again, the physician did not hesitate with his response. "Not on purpose, definitely not intentionally. The empty bottle of his medication was found in the sink, where he must have dropped it. How much he took, how much went down the sink we'll never know. What's troubling you, lad?"

"I do not believe there was a suicide, intentional *or* otherwise. *Foul play.* And I told the Gards as much."

Rafferty's eyes widened, and something seemed, for a moment, to sputter in their depths, but he remained silent.

"Rob," Barry said, pensive, "wasn't anyone in the manor house with your uncle nights? Wouldn't they have heard noises, when he got up?"

"Nora had taken to sleeping in the room across the hall from Uncle Phillip, rather than in the carriage house, where she and Frank reside. She used a wireless intercom to hear if he called her during the night. As for noises the night he died, she said she heard nothing unusual, no sounds of his stumbling round, or anything falling. Apparently, he had knocked a box of tissues and a plastic tumbler off the nightstand, but they would have made no real noise on the carpet."

Barry leaned forward, fixing her gaze on the doctor. "Could Rob's uncle have been mobile after having taken his regular nightly dose of morphine? I mean, wouldn't that have made him ... I don't know the proper word, but certainly more than drowsy?"

Pursing his lips, the elderly physician inclined his head. "Phillip was an exceptional case. He was, as you well know, Robert, a ver-ry determined man. If he made up his mind about something ... ." Doctor Rafferty seemed to recall a particular incident, for he suddenly gave forth a chortle, shaking his head at the reminiscence. "He never had a stroke. His arthritis never prevented him from getting about, though he needed his cane. The morphine administered a few hours earlier would have diminished enough, permitting him to get to the adjoining bathroom unassisted, if he had a mind to, and that's perceivably what he did. His covers were pulled aside and draped over the floor, and he was lying sprawled across the bed."

Rob patted Barry's hand. "How much of the liquid morphine was in that bottle, do you suppose? When was his prescription last filled?"

The doctor thought for a moment. "Frank picked up the morphine sulphate, his liquid morphine, only a couple of days before."

"Then the bottle would have been ... say three-quarters filled?" Rob queried.

"Oh, yes. Phillip had been asking Nora to increase his nighttime dose, so that he could sleep without pain the night through. We were already giving him the maximum dosage, twenty milligrams ... a teaspoonful every four hours. Let me take the liberty of interjecting that Phillip was fortunate to have such good people looking after him. The Dillons *loved* your uncle. Know this, lad– they did everything in their power to relieve his suffering. Anyroad, Nora told him she *did* increase his dosage, that the latest refill was more potent, though the teaspoonful before bedtime remained the same. A little psychology," the elderly physician smiled. "But she said he *knew*. No one ever put anything over on your uncle."

Rob finished the last of his tea, setting the cup down on the coffee table before him. "*Someone* did," he said with finality, "and I intend to find out *who*."

"The moment you decide that what you *know* is more important than what you have been taught to believe, you will have shifted gears in your quest … "

~ Ralph Waldo Emerson

Chapter Five

"I think I found it!" Raine carefully extended the ancient tome to Maggie, her gloved finger indicating, *sans* touching, the place on the yellowed, brittle page.

Maggie adjusted herself in the straight-backed chair and began her perusal. The cousins were seated at a reading table in the old library building of Dublin's esteemed Trinity College.

While Maggie read, Raine relaxed in her chair and stretched, cat-like. Her shoulders ached from the days of endless research. She tilted back her head, and her gaze took in the superb barrel-vaulted ceiling. "You know, Mags, Trinity houses over two million volumes. And I feel as though we've looked through at least half of them."

"Well, it's paid off. *This*," Maggie's whispered words carried the intensity of her emotions, "is what we've been searching for." Removing her reading glasses and momentarily closing her overworked eyes, she gave a long, protracted sigh of relief. "Without that letter from Professor Burns, I *know* they never would have permitted us access to this rare and truly amazing collection. Thank God 'n Goddess I spent my senior year at Trinity. And what a year it was," she added, placing her hands behind her mane of flame-red hair, leaning back, and smiling slyly with the memory.

Raine flicked a bit of dust from her elbow, then pushed the sleeves of her Aran sweater up her arms. "Hmmm. You must have managed to get *some* work done. In fact, Mags, you seemed to have left quite a good impression on your professors here, especially with Professor Reilly."

Maggie responded with a look sated with mischief and mystery.

"Uh, huh," Raine shook her head. "You little devil! I think you've had more love affairs than the Empress Josephine! It's …" she struggled to think of a suitable phrase, giving up and saying simply "too much."

"Too much of a good thing is … *won-der-ful*, darlin'. Truly, it is."

"Yes, well, back to work," Raine responded. "Let's be careful to copy everything exactly as it appears here. We can't afford to make even one tiny error or omission. And let's hurry. Our allotted time with these books is nearly over." Raine took up her pen and continued writing in her notebook.

Maggie laughed, "Yes, ma'am! Then we're off to Tara."

Rising 500 feet from the surrounding Meath countryside, the Irish Camelot, the Hill of Tara, rose proudly, the ancient seat of *Ard-Rí na hÉireann*, the High Kings of Ireland.

"There's nothing here! It's just a grassy mound." A group of American tourists swarmed over the vivid green terrain, blaringly intruding on Raine and Maggie's carefully planned afternoon.

"Tara, Hill of Kings, is a place for mystic communion, for recollection … and imagery," Raine nearly shouted in disapproval, her green eyes blazing with impatience. "If they're so disappointed, perhaps they won't stay long, and we can get back to work! Nothing here! As the Irish would say, 'What cheek!'"

Maggie slammed her notebook shut. "Why, oh why, do the wrong people travel, and the right people stay at home! What did they *expect* to find? Scarlett and Rhett?"

"Who knows?" Raine watched as the motley crew spilled over the hillside, scattering in all directions. "They make me angry," Raine hissed in a harsh whisper. "If they would stand still and quiet, they could conjure the royal court, there," she pointed, "as it was in the glory days of the High Kings. One hundred and forty-two strong, and long before records of either Greece or Rome. And over there," she indicated, "were the five chariot roads radiating, star like, from Tara, crossing all of Ireland. Imagine it now … during the Great Harvest Feast, the roads would be thronged with princes, peasants, druids, harpers and other musicians, all traveling to Tara. And spread before us was the great banquet hall. I can almost see and hear the guests, well over a thousand of them, eating and drinking, laughing and exchanging fine stories."

"Descartes said, 'Travel is almost like talking with men of other centuries," Maggie stated with a renewed twinkle in her eyes.

For several moments, the enraptured Sleuth Sisters stood soaking in the splendor of Tara, the magick and the energy of the place. "It's easy to see why Tara was chosen as the seat of the royal power. It has such a commanding, all-round view."

"That was, of course, the military reason. But there was another reason the Celts chose this as the seat of their kings. It had formerly been a Stone-Age burial site, the remains of which are … there," Raine pointed to the steep knoll, "and therefore had *sacred* significance. Oh, to travel back to 500 B.C. ..." Raine went into instant reverie.

"Come on," Maggie urged after a few moments, her thick, wavy red hair blowing in the brisk breeze. "Let's walk a bit. I don't think these people will stay long. Likely they'll be bored in jig-time."

Side by side, the magickal duo walked to the *Lia Fail*, the cylindrical Stone of Destiny, where they stood in quiet contemplation.

"Listen!" Raine stretched out a hand and snatched Maggie's arm in a painful grasp. "Do you hear that?"

"Ouch ... what?"

"*Listen.*"

A wind had risen, whispering past their ears, and carried on it were, what seemed to be, the ancient voices of the Old Ones. "Do you hear it now?" Raine stood perfectly still, listening with breath abated.

Maggie turned and her countenance answered for her. "Do you suppose it's coming from the Destiny Stone? Let's move closer."

The pair leaned against the mystical landmark. "Legend says that the *Lia Fail* roared three times when a *true* high king sat upon it at his coronation."

"It's not a roar I hear." Maggie cocked her head, hardly daring to breathe. "It's more like–"

"Machinery ... a transmitter or something running." Raine turned slightly and stood as still as possible, holding her breath. "Hmmm, it's sort of a ... humming sound."

"That's it! Can you still hear," she let fall the last two words softly, hardly daring to speak them, "*the voices*?"

"Faintly. But I still hear that humming."

At the summit, the whisperings in the wind grew noticeably louder. "Raine," Maggie said, opening her oversized purse and drawing out her notebook and a pen, "we must try to take down what those elusive voices are saying."

"Yes," Raine nodded excitedly and hurriedly drew from her own bag her journal and a pen. Both began furiously to write, pausing often to listen intently. "It's so difficult to understand. It must be Old Irish ... *has to be*."

"Write! We've got to try." Maggie labored over her notebook.

After several minutes, they had seized a few words and phrases, but it was difficult to concentrate with the tourists milling around them, talking and taking photographs, some carrying on in an irritating manner.

Suddenly Maggie's face took on a look of dismay, the expression seeming to melt away suddenly to utter disappointment.

"What on earth is wrong with you?" Raine asked, staring at her cousin's odd expression.

"Look!" Maggie flung out her hand, the index finger pointing to the brow of the hill, where a grasshopper-green tractor was chugging along, the farmer's radio tuned to one of Ireland's many Gaelic-speaking stations.

It was the magickal hour when the day's light dwindles into twilight that Raine and Maggie returned to the Hill of Tara. They had decided to sit and work at the entrance of the sacred passage grave, not far from the Destiny Stone. Diligently, for what seemed like hours, though an hour and a half would have been a more correct estimation, they pondered in the stillness, devoid now of tourists, neither speaking, each lost in her own mystical fantasies.

Raine's emerald gaze drifted over the peaceful landscape, misty now in the Irish eventide. "I just *know* I heard Old Irish before that tractor—"

"Hush." Maggie held up a hand for quiet. "*Listen.*" The familiar wind rose, and with it, the voices of the Old Ones. This time, since no one else was about, they came louder and more distinct.

"Focus!" Maggie urged, beginning to write into the notebook she held. "If you don't recognize a word or phrase, jot it down phonetically. We'll succeed this time!"

Raine picked up her pen and notebook that she had laid on the ground at her feet. But no sooner had the pair begun to scribe, when Raine stopped abruptly, her eyes fixed on the gathering darkness before them. "Maggie ..." she pointed with a shaking forefinger.

Without looking up, Maggie replied, "Get that flashlight from my purse, would you?"

"Maggie," she tried again, "*look!*"

Following Raine's pointing finger, Maggie saw that a figure was manifesting, glowing golden in the chill and haze of the Irish night.

"It's ... a woman," Raine stammered, reflexively shrinking backward.

The shimmering, ethereal figure floated in the misty moonlight like the echo of an evocative song, while smaller, individual lights– a court of lesser entities from the luminous realm of faerie– seemed to follow. Presently, the faerie court fell into place behind and on both sides of the dominant figure.

"Fear not, Sisters, I am Dana," the golden-haired faerie announced in the old tongue, "Goddess of the *Tuatha De Danann*. We who, when the world was yet young, held dominion on this isle until the sons of Mil, whom ye call Gaels, came, usurping our reign," Dana raised her eyes and arms skyward, "but not our powers. Nay! Ne'er our powers."

The glowing figure looked directly at the Sisters and smiled benevolently. "Humankind has forgotten our race, but ye, I know wherefore, have not." She smiled again, a strange smile, yet now, it generated no fear. "List' ye, and I shall bestow unto thee the sacred Time-Key. This ye, steadfast, have sought and earned–
The Key to safe passage."

***

"I think we need to return to Trinity to consult an expert." Maggie pushed the notebook away, resting her eyes by turning her gaze out the window, of their room at Fitzpatrick Castle, to the green pastoral scene beyond.

"But," Raine countered with a frown, "if we seek too much help, we'll lose sole possession. Perhaps we should just go back to their library and give it a further go in there? We could hardly travel with all our own hefty tomes! I know I'm not a master at this, but I do believe we've got the Dana segment right." She turned a page of her journal, slid her reading glasses on, and began scanning the section to which she had just referred.

Maggie moved across the room and flopped down on the bed. "While you were recording that, I was attempting, without complete success, to translate those other legends we unearthed. The ambiance of our work arenas has most assuredly helped in freeing our thoughts, but I think we *do* need to go back to Trinity to seek out expert assistance."

From the nightstand, she picked up a jar of cream and began, pensive, to massage it into her flawless milk-and-apricot skin. "You've made a valid point, though, regarding our need to protect our work. We cannot allow anyone to–" Maggie bolted abruptly to her feet, an eagerness brightening her face as she struck her forehead with the palm of her hand, "We've been cramming our heads so full of information, it's shoved out our common sense! Here's what we're going to do."

***

Rob switched on a small stained-glass lamp as he and Baranya entered the late Phillip Barry's private apartment. The scents of oil soap and camphor permeated the air. Since his arrival at Barry Hall a couple of days before, Rob had been occupying his great-uncle's suite of rooms. This was, however, the first time Barry was seeing this section of the house, and her eyes swept the old-fashioned bedchamber with its massive, intricately carved rosewood furniture.

Everything was clean and tidy, and the polished wood glowed the color of a fine wine. Pristine, white Irish-lace curtains framed a large window overlooking the labyrinthine gardens below. On opposite walls from one another were two fine oil portraits. While Rob switched on more lamps, Barry moved to read the brass nameplates– *Phillip Barry* and *Robert de Barry.*

"Robert was Uncle Phillip's father and my great-grandfather," Rob volunteered.

A yawning greystone fireplace took up an entire wall, above which were the De Barry family crest and an impressive collection of medieval weapons. Bagpipes occupied a space on the fourth wall, where gilt-edged, leather-bound tomes overflowed a vast bookcase. Lastly, Barry's gaze came to rest on the massive canopied bed, elaborately carved antique rosewood, matching the preponderance of the suite of furniture.

At the foot of the bed was an old trunk. When she turned to look at Rob, Barry saw that his attention, too, was focused on the heavy, brass-bound trunk.

"No time like the present," he said, retrieving the key from his pocket and dangling it for an electrifying moment before her. Then he extended his hand to her like a strong, warm invitation into his life.

Together, they knelt before the unopened trunk, and Rob inserted the key, which turned easily, releasing the lock. Then he raised the heavy domed lid, disclosing several faded family photographs taped to the inner cover. Inside, on the very top, was a thick, cream-colored envelope with Rob's name, *Robert Phillip Carroll,* written boldly in Edwardian script across the fine parchment.

"Let's go over there, luv." Rob indicated a settee next to one of the stained-glass lamps. "The light will be better."

Carefully, Barry adjusted the lamp so that the light shone directly on the letter in Rob's hand. When she sat down beside him, he unfolded the thick missive, penned in the same curly script as the envelope, and began, slowly, to read aloud.

"'*My dear nephew, as you read this, I will have gone to my heavenly reward. I always knew you had a love of adventure. This is why I have no doubt you will unravel the enigma of Barry Hall. Your great-grandfather, Robert de Barry, in the year 1890, was betrothed to marry a young Spanish woman whom he had met at Newmarket-on-Fergus, this county. The young maiden, Carlotta Maria Montoya Velazquez de La Coruna, Galicia, resided there with her family whose business in Kinsale was, like my father's, importing-exporting. My father was deeply in love with this dark-eyed beauty, who, by all accounts, was willful and verily bewitching.'*"

Laying aside the epistle, Rob paused to lean over and kiss Barry, taking her face gently between his hands. "We'd better … concentrate on the letter. There's a danger we'll forget why we came in here," he murmured between kisses.

"Yes," she whispered, delicious shivers rippling through her, "a very great danger. You … you do such strange things to me, Mr. Carroll."

"Do I now?" His voice was raspy. "Should I stop then?"

His hands skimmed over her, igniting a fire that she was helping to enflame by moving against him. "Ooooh," she purred, "that is so nice."

He continued to stroke her. "You make me forget myself … ah … m'Lady … forget even why we came in here."

"We said there was … that danger. Yes," she murmured, "*that* is even nicer."

"This," he whispered, continuing his magick. "Or this?"

As dizzying rapture enveloped them, spinning them upward in their progressive flight to the stars, a sudden, loud noise caused them to stop and quickly turn to look– at the empty doorway.

"Probably the radiator," Rob whispered in her ear. "You know how these old houses are … full of knocks and," he kissed her soft mouth, "things that go bump in the night."

"Like Nora," Barry sighed and, picking up the letter, handed it back to Rob.

His eyes held hers. "Oh, we most definitely are in danger," he murmured.

Captivated, she ran a finger lightly over his thick mustache. *I wonder if you know just how great a danger? It's as though I'm under your spell.*

"*Verily bewitching*," he repeated, gazing into the ebony depths of Barry's almond-shaped eyes.

"Read," she commanded, sighing again. "I really do want to know what happened."

"Yes, m' Lady. '*So infatuated was my father,*'" Rob read on from his great-uncle's bequest, "'*that he commissioned the gardens with their love theme to be added to the estate. They were to be a wedding gift for the bride.*'"

Barry rose and moved to the window, where she looked down on the lamp-and-moon-lit labyrinth below. She could almost envision Robert de Barry, the way he looked in the painting– age forty perhaps– overseeing a myriad of workers who labored feverishly to complete the maze of gardens– a green cathedral created by the Goddess herself– the Cupid in flight, and the fountain with its marble likeness of Venus. From the window, she could see the luminated Goddess of Love, where she occupied a niche in the fore brick wall, the water jetting from a large open seashell, its rainbow mist enchanting.

"'*In addition,*'" Rob continued, "'*he commissioned a famous London jeweler to make up a parure, a set– which my father designed himself– consisting of a ring, a magnificent ten-carat emerald surrounded by the very finest diamonds, and earbobs, the tops of which were five-carat square emeralds surrounded by diamonds, suspending rare emerald drops, inspired by the fountain. However, the pièce de résistance was the necklace-- a rivière of fourteen exceedingly large and fine emeralds, each surrounded by old, European-cut diamonds, separated by pearls, dream-born, too, from the fountain, and suspending a peerless, even larger, single drop-shaped emerald, the clasp itself a flawless ten-carat diamond.*

"'The parure is unique and, needless to add, worth a king's ransom. Understand, Nephew, that my father chose emeralds, for, as a student of mythology, he knew this was the stone dedicated to the goddess Venus. As with the Egyptians and the Romans, emeralds fascinated him for the legend of their mystical powers– if one gazes long into the cool green depths of a fine emerald, he will be drawn into those depths– and into a telling dream.'"

Barry moved from the window back to the settee, again sitting next to Rob. "She must have been some lady," she remarked. "I wonder if there's a photo inside the trunk."

Rob looked up from his uncle's bequest. "We'll look when I finish the letter. There's not much more." He located his place and read, *"'On the eve of the wedding, the precious set was delivered to Barry Hall. The London jeweler had sent the ring to be engraved, as my father had instructed, with the young lady's initials and the words "To Destiny" on the inner surface of the band. Alas, when my father examined the ring, he was furious– the engraver had erred. The initials were wrong! Superstitious, he took this to be an ill omen. And it was, for that very night, his adored Carlotta would betray his love. Before the stroke of midnight, she eloped with a dashing Spanish marqués, leaving her betrothed heartbroken and wrought with despair.'"*

Since meeting Rob, Barry's natural clairvoyance and clairaudience skills had kicked into overdrive. Her eyes closed and she saw, across the movie screen of her mind, the raised arms of the marqués lifting the sultry, capricious Carlotta, wearing a long hooded cape, onto a spirited black stallion. Then the tall, darkly handsome man sprang into the saddle behind her, and they were off at the gallop down the deserted, moonlit strand, dissolving into the mists, the terrible beauty of the ocean crashing mightily against the rocks in the foreground.

"Barry. Barry, are you all right?"

She opened her eyes. "Yes, of course. I was imaging the scenario. You must admit, this is all quite exciting. A *marqués* ... is that Spanish for marquis?"

"Right."

"Read on."

Rob raised an ebony brow. "The plot thickens," he grinned. Again finding the desired spot, he continued aloud, *"'The following morning, your great-grandfather was left standing at the altar. The family never learned the details of what happened that fateful morning. My father would never speak of his lost love. Five years later, he married your great-grandmother.'"* Rob indicated with a wave of his hand, "Barry, there's a wedding photograph … over there on the bureau."

Barry crossed the room and picked up the ornately framed photo, bringing it over to Rob in the light. "He looks to be in his mid-forties, his bride perhaps ten years younger."

Rob held the old Victorian frame as together they studied the image. "Neither looks happy, do you think?"

"No one seemed to smile in those old photographs, Rob."

"Let's read on and get to the mystery." Locating his place, Rob continued his recitation. *"'The emerald jewelry was never again seen. To the end of his life, my father did not divulge what he did with his intended wedding gift for Carlotta. I never saw the jewels, of course. They had disappeared before I was born. However, I did come across the original designs, in my father's private papers, after his death. I include these for you. My brother James and I searched every inch of Barry Hall, but we never uncovered so much as a single clue to the whereabouts of the missing treasure. Our own investigations revealed no trace of it ever appearing on the world market. The only record my father kept was his diary, which I leave to you, hoping you will recover this legacy. If you fail, it may be lost forever– or worse still, at some point in future, be found by a stranger.*

"'You have inherited the adventurous spirit of the first De Barrys to come to the shores of the Emerald Isle in 1169. With my death, the Barry name disappears from Ireland, but I trust you will carry on the great Barry heritage and tradition, including the fancy dress ball, held each October, the fall hunts, and the grand festivities at Yuletide. Nothing should extinguish the bright light of tradition here at Barry Hall– not even my death.'" Rob paused here for a moment. *"'Affectionately, your great-uncle, Phillip Robert (de) Barry.'"*

Barry placed a hand on his. "He seemed like someone I would have liked. His talk of heritage and tradition reminds me of *my* grandfather."

Rob nodded, and Barry sensed he did not trust his voice for a moment. "I can well-imagine his father ragin' at that courier from the jeweler. If his temper was anything like my uncle's, there must've been bloody hell to pay." He pulled out the faded original designs of the emerald jewelry, the ring, the earbobs, and the fabulous necklace. "Can you imagine what this is worth today?"

"A king's ransom, as the letter states."

Rob refolded the thick sheets, then slipped them back into the envelope, laying it aside. "Let's search the old trunk."

"Your uncle must have liked poetry … especially the Irish poets." Barry laid several volumes on the floor beside them, her attention captured by the cover art of a small book atop the pile. She opened it and began scanning the yellowed pages. "Speaking of enigmas, listen to these ethereal lines from W.B. Yeats' 'The Tower.' Your great-uncle, or someone, marked this passage: *I pace upon the battlements and stare/ On the foundations of a house, or where/ Tree, like a sooty finger, starts from the earth/ And send imagination forth/ Under the day's declining beam, and call/ Images and memories/ From ruin or from ancient trees/ For I would ask a question of them all.*"

She looked up, her brow furrowed. "I wonder…" she tapped her fingers on the pile of books, "if this holds for us a hidden clue?"

Rob shrugged, taking the book from her and scanning the passage she had just recited.

Barry held up a couple of other tomes. "Here're those books on Egyptian and Roman mythology he spoke of. Be careful, they're so old, they're falling apart."

"This must be the diary." Rob unwrapped something cached in an old oilcloth. "It is." He passed his hand over the embossed initials *R. de B.* on the leather cover. Despite the oilcloth wrap, the old journal was cracked and withered with age. "Before we begin reading this, let's see what else is in here. What's this wrapped in a sheepskin?" He worked at the tie, then–

They answered in chorus, "More bagpipes!"

Next, Barry lifted out a carved wooden box, opened it and handed it to Rob. "Looks like your uncle, or someone, was a war hero."

"Uncle Phillip," Rob replied. "A Celtic warrior in the grandest tradition. Hello … what's this?" Something shiny at the bottom of the trunk had caught his immediate interest. His fingers sought, found, and raised for them both to consider a tiny, very ornate key. "Now, what do you suppose *this* will unlock?" After a moment, he added with a chortle, "'For I would ask a question of them all.'"

"Here's a box of old coins, Rob."

The sudden sound of squeaking floorboards nearby startled the pair. They quickly turned to see Nora standing in the shadowy doorway, her face as somber and effective as her erect, grey-uniformed figure.

"Excuse me, Mr. Carroll," she began, her voice carrying on it the efficiency of thirty years of service, "but Frank asked me to inquire if you'd like to come down to the public room for a drink before dinner."

Rob stood, stretching. "Thank you, Nora. Tell him we'll be down directly."

Nora gave a silent nod, her penetrating grey gaze lingering for a beat on Barry. Then she was gone.

Barry rose and whispered into Rob's ear, "She's like a phantom. I hardly ever *hear* her. It's as if she floats rather than walks. She gives me the creeps."

Distracted, Rob studied the little key in the palm of his hand. In a moment, he tossed it into the air, snatched it, and set it on the bureau, next to the trunk key, after which he pulled Barry into his muscular embrace and kissed her soundly. *I have never experienced any woman like this one. She's at once sexy **and** innocent.* "Why don't we go down to have that drink and a good dinner, then," his voice lowered, as he murmured against her lips, "perhaps we might find some time to be alone later."

A thrill blazed through Barry's body. *Oh, yes,* she thought, *yes,* returning his kiss in full measure.

A lively fire burned in the hearth, its reflection in the bar mirror bright and cheery. Frank had already poured a shot of Jameson into two thick Waterford tumblers.

After handing the drinks to Barry and Rob, he pulled himself his usual stout, hoisted his glass, his eyes fixed on those of his new employer. "May you be in heaven a half-hour b'fore the Divil knows ye'er dead."

Barry's glass slipped from her fingers and fell with a thud to the heirloom, clan-crested carpet at her feet.

Chapter Six

Frank finished sopping the spilled whiskey from the carpet. "No harm done, these Waterford tumblers are as enduring as Ireland herself." He deftly poured another two fingers of the twelve-year-old Jameson Redbreast into a clean glass, handing it to Barry, who was eyeing Rob's drink askance. *I can't let Rob drink that!*

"I don't know what's come over me," she lied, with a wave of her hand, nearly succeeding in knocking Rob's drink from his grip. "I'm as nervous as a cat. Let me have *your* drink, Rob; I feel a bit shaky."

When he handed her his tumbler, the glass immediately slid from her fingers, falling to the hearthrug at her feet.

"Oh!" she exclaimed, her hand rising to her mouth. "I can't believe I did that! Please forgive me. I'm not usually this clumsy."

Again Frank rushed forward with a cloth from the bar. But this time, Barry took it from him. "No, no, let me. I'm so embarrassed. I don't know what's wrong with me."

Rob removed the bar rag from her shaking hand, took her by the arm and led her to the settee. "Here now, sit down. You're suffering from jet lag and these strange happenings, all so close together."

"You'll feel better after a shot of this," Frank added, pouring fresh drinks from the bottle. "*Uisce beatha*, water of life, we call our whiskey." He handed a drink to each of them. "Now," he smiled his bright smile, "let me try a toast anew." He raised his glass of foam-topped stout. "May th' wind be always at ye'er backs, and may th' sun shine warm upon ye'er faces!"

"*Sláinte!*" Rob returned, touching his glass to Barry's, then Frank's. "To your health."

"*Sláinte,*" Barry repeated softly.

All three drank then, as three pairs of eyes measured one another over the rims of the thick, lead-crystal glasses.

"Frank," Rob began after a brief silence, "my family has relied on you for years, so I know I can confide in you now. I learned this evenin' of the special bequest attached to Uncle Phillip's will. I'd like to enlist your help to sort this out, if I may."

Frank tilted his head. "Whatever 'tis, I'll do what I can." Catching sight of something in his peripheral vision, Frank turned. "Ah! Just the thing, th' ver-ry thing!"

"A little somethin' to go with your drinks." Nora entered, holding a tray of hors d'oeuvres. Soundlessly, she glided across the room, depositing the silver tray on the bar. "I'll be puttin' dinner on th' table shortly."

"Thank you, Nora," Rob said, taking the tray and offering the savories to Barry and Frank, before sampling a canapé himself. "Superb salmon. It's your cookin' that makes Barry Hall so special," he said, sending the grey-uniformed housekeeper a jocular grin.

Nora surrendered a half-smile. "Sure 'tis simple fare, but there's plenty of it." She crossed the room, pausing in the doorway. "I'll ring when dinner is served."

The Jameson was sending a warm, cozy feeling through her body, and Barry sat back in the settee, beginning to relax. In the large mirror above the bar, she caught sight of Nora lingering in the foyer, just outside the half-open door. *She's pretending to be tidying up out there, but she's eavesdropping again!* Barry's gaze, at that moment, locked with the older woman's, and the grim-faced housekeeper sent her a withering black look before disappearing from view.

Seated in one of the public room's comfortable chairs, Rob was thoughtfully nursing his drink, while at the bar, Frank was munching a canapé. "Frank," Rob said after several seconds had passed, "about that bequest … tomorrow is soon enough to begin."

Frank ceased chewing, and his voice carried a hint of the disappointment stamped on his face. "Sure, lad, sure."

"What do you make of this business about Tom?" Rob asked, reaching for another salmon appetizer. "Is there any way he could have swallowed th' stuff accidentally?"

Frank shook his head. "That makes no sense." He took a sip of his stout then added, "Nor does murder f'r that matter. No one stood t' gain by his death. He was a widower, no children. And he didn't own much." His expression and his tone softened. "Not much at all, at all. Except f'r a good heart and th' gift of laughter. God rest him."

"God rest him," Rob repeated.

For a moment no one spoke, then Barry said, "You mentioned that there were a lot of people here the day of the funeral. There may have been a good number in the pub too. I wonder if perhaps Tom Mannion didn't get a drink meant for someone else."

Frank considered a moment. "I suppose anythin's possible," he shrugged. "I'm thinkin'… if he had th' poison on his hands, he could have eaten somethin' at the pub, and–"

"*That*," Rob surmised, "may have been the accident."

***

"Aisling, we've news. Big news!" Raine blurted excitedly into her Blackberry. I don't want to discuss the matter in detail over the phone, but suffice it to say that we're close, mighty close." She tossed a bright smile to Maggie, who returned the gesture from the passenger seat of their rental car, parked on a busy Dublin street, the lights from an on-coming vehicle illuminating the "Sisters'" blissful faces.

From their smart phone, Aisling's voice rose in excitement. "Already! You can't be serious!"

"Oh, we're serious all right! Look, we're exhausted and famished. We haven't had a bite since cockcrow, and it's past eight in the evening here. We'll keep you informed, so don't turn off your phone."

Aisling's voice crackled over the overseas line. "You're breaking up!"

Raine ran her fingers through her gamine hair, brushing the long, jagged bangs out of her left eye. "Yes, we're both fine. Uh, huh, we're taking turns wearing your amulet, depending on what each of us is doing." More sputtered dialogue reached her. "Say again."

Aisling repeated her last words.

"And we could say the same to you. Don't worry about us. We're *always* careful." Raine gave a short laugh, replying, "We're not planning on it. Talk to you later."

When she disconnected, Maggie asked, "What aren't we planning? What did she say right before you rang off?"

"She said, and I quote, 'Don't get mixed up in any murders over there. It isn't good for you.'"

***

The grandfather clock in the foyer was striking the eleventh hour, when Rob exited the kitchen with a snack tray and started back up the stairs at Barry Hall. Noticing a light under his beloved's door, he rapped softly. "Are you awake?"

In a moment, the bedroom door opened to reveal Barry. She was wearing a long apricot silk wrapper, and her long hair was slightly disheveled. "I'm awake, come in. I couldn't keep my eyes open downstairs, but when I got into bed, I just couldn't fall asleep."

"I couldn't sleep either." Rob entered and closed the door. "I was reading the old diary, and I got hungry. But I'll share. *Bionn an rath i mbun na ronna* ... there is luck in sharing." He sent her a wink, setting the tray on the nightstand. "Bread and jam. We're mad for jam in Ireland. And the hot milk is laced with *uisce beatha*. It will help you sleep."

"What is it?" Barry asked, picking up the tankard and sniffing.

"Have you forgotten your first Irish word? *Ish-kuh* **ba-ha**," he pronounced, "Irish whiskey."

"Oh, Rob, I'm so worried. This whole matter about the jewels makes me even more fearful."

"What do you mean?"

"I *mean* that I know now why I dreamed someone, or more than one; in fact, it looks like more and more," she rambled, then stopped, and tried again. "What I'm trying to say is that I truly believe there's more than one person plotting to kill you– for the jewels, the estate ... isn't it obvious?"

He rubbed the side of his face with the back of his hand. "I intend to pursue the matter, beginning with the diary. I've been reading ever since I went to bed, but nothing seems to conjure a clue."

"Do you have it with you?" Barry sat on the bed, where she plumped the pillows before resting her back against them and the headboard.

"Right here." Rob pulled the journal from the oversized pocket of his cashmere robe.

"Let's read it together." Barry patted the bed beside her, and he settled cozily next to her, carefully opening his great-grandfather's old diary.

Gingerly, he leafed through the yellowed pages, finding the place he had marked. "Listen to this," he said, beginning to read. "'*She is one of those women born to love and to be loved. She is alive, passionate– full of fire and zest. It is truly intoxicating to be in her presence. She is Ecstasy, her lust for life contagious. I need her;*

*without her, my life has no balance, for I am so conventional, I bore even myself. Carlotta loves with every fiber of herself– with her soul as well as her body. Her kiss ... oh, how I love her! I am under her spell. To love Carlotta– or rather, to **adore** her– this is my only desire in life.'"*

"I'd say he was smitten." Barry bit into a slice of bread spread thick with black currant preserves. "Hmm, this is good. Bite?" She held the snack to Rob's lips.

He took a bite, then leafed forward a couple of pages. "Wait till you hear this bit." He read on. *"'I cover her portrait with kisses. If I should go on loving her, and I were the only one who loved– this, of all roles, is the one I cannot play. She has taken possession of my very soul, enslaving my senses. I only hope she has not fallen in love with me through a caprice. I could not bear it! I stifle this sentiment which is beneath my dignity. She is so beautiful, my dark-eyed Venus, so graceful, so sweet of face– yet, there is something– something just below that adorable surface. I cannot say! I feel old tonight– a hundred years old. God help me, I put **nothing** before her.'"*

Barry gave a sigh, taking a sip of the hot milk and whiskey. "Oh, Rob, I think this is the most romantic tale I have ever heard."

"You've not heard the ending. Listen to this. *'I am wretched! I warned you, did I not? I sensed it even at the moment my heart was about to be involved. My cruel Venus! Ah, but all this foolishness is demeaning to me, a De Barry! I have never really believed in happiness. Is life worth making such a fuss? She never loved me. And now, I cannot wish her happiness– if inconstancy can ever bring happiness. I am avoiding the word "perfidy," for, as I have disclosed, true love never existed in her heart. She inspired in me a delirium that was degrading. Never again will I allow myself to place such nonsense over all other nature. As far as I am concerned, she is dead, along with all those senses she awakened in me. All is buried– never to be uncovered. Gone– with her memory– forever.'"*

Rob looked up, adding, "That was entered on the date of the intended wedding. Look," he said, extending the leather-bound diary toward Barry. "The last entry is a passage in Gaelic."

"What does it say?" Barry asked, setting the drink on the tray.

"I have no clue," Rob answered. "I intend to ask Frank's help on this tomorrow."

"I thought you knew Gaelic."

"We learn it in school, of course, but I am not proficient enough to translate this."

"I wish we could find a portrait of Carlotta. I wonder–"

"You know something?" he interposed, leaning over her and enfolding her in his powerful arms. "She reminds me of you." He kissed her deeply, then began nuzzling her neck, his mustache sending thrill after thrill to every part of her.

That melting, all-consuming sensation swept like hot, molten lava through her body; abruptly then she pushed him away. "Oh, thank you very much."

A look of perplexity passed over Rob's face.

"I remind you of Carlotta! She sounds rather mean-spirited and capricious, don't you think?"

He kissed her again. "But exciting … ver-ry, ver-ry exciting."

Barry laughed softly and moved to settle more comfortably in his pleasurable embrace, when something caught her attention. She hastily put her finger to her lips and pointed across the room. "Shouldn't she be in the carriage house?" she whispered in Rob's ear.

Rob turned, and they both stared at the elongated shadow under the closed door. As quietly as he could, Rob eased himself from the bed, stole over to the door and, with a single motion, flung it open.

No one was there.

In robe and slippers, with lighted "torch" in hand, Rob crept down the stairs of the dark, still manor. Suddenly he stopped, thinking he had heard a sound below him. Warily now, he moved down to the first landing, a floorboard protesting under his weight. Not wanting to turn on lights and warn the intruder, he continued moving as silently as he could, the narrow beam of light guiding his slow progress.

At the bottom of the stairs, he turned into the dining room, searching with the flashlight the shadowy, moon-washed chamber. Something creaked behind him, and he whirled, but one by one, the bizarre black shapes looming in the corners and recesses of the spacious room vanished, exorcised by his beam of light.

Satisfied that no one was there, he exited the way he had come in and, crossing the foyer, entered the public room, opposite. Here, too, he deliberately moved his ray of light over the ghostly shadows cast by the moon through the window behind him.

Nothing.

He stood for a time, listening intently, but the only sound the ancient house surrendered was the loud ticking of the large grandfather clock in the entrance hall.

The small pool of light still guiding his steps, Rob moved stealthily down the hall, past the kitchen, to the rear of the house. As he entered the mudroom, he could hear the soft murmuring of the wind. A quick scan with the flashlight revealed a partially open window. He closed it, then unlocked the back door and stepped outside into the chill air.

Glancing around, Rob was momentarily struck by a sudden discovery of nighttime beauty– the intricate branches of the majestic oak, reminiscent of black Spanish lace across the pearly moon.

Hearing a noise to his right, he spun round. Shining his light before him, he moved cautiously to the rear left side of the house. Someone had knocked over a garbage can. Stooping, he righted the can and replaced the cover.

A small grey tabby wove its way around Rob's bare ankle.

"Púca, you little devil! Shouldn't you be down at the stable on mouse patrol? This is th' time o' year when the little varmints are lookin' for a warm place for the winter!"

"Meow" came the negative reply.

He reached down to extend his fingers toward the cat in a gesture of friendship, and the tabby rewarded him with a loud purring. It was then Rob caught the moving shadow of what looked like a man at the entrance to the Love Gardens. *Could be a man or the shadow from one of those branches.* Without hesitation, however, he entered the maze of gardens, the labyrinthine paths lighted by flickering torch lamps.

Gingerly, he made his way through the inky, moving specters along the twisted pathways, a snapping twig or a rustle of leaves causing him to direct his flashlight sporadically about him. *Someone's out here, toying with me.* Panning the darkness with the beam of light, he thought he caught a glimpse of the shadow-man up ahead. *If it is someone, he seems to be heading for the fountain and the Venus.*

Arriving at the rear of the gardens, Rob paused, quite still, listening to the sounds of the night mingled with the cascading water from the fountain. The wind had picked up, and from somewhere in the distance, a night bird called out. Several moments passed with the peaceful burble of the water the only other sound that reached him.

Suddenly, the tranquility was shattered when a huge cement urn crashed violently from the wall, missing him by mere inches, a shrill feline scream accompanying it, the shards scattering and hitting his feet. Jumping hurriedly to the side, Rob turned and sprinted from the serpentine gardens, in hot pursuit of the elusive shadow-man.

At the exterior of the rear garden wall, he carefully moved the shaft of light from his torch along the ground.

A man's footprints were clearly visible in the soft, damp earth.

"Those footprints could have been made earlier, but I don't think so. I learned a trick or two from a Masai friend in Kenya." Rob sat on the bed next to Barry. "Be that as it may, the cat would not have been strong enough to push that heavy urn over, not even the wind could have toppled it, as strong as it's blowin' out there tonight. Whoever our intruder was, those prints tell me he's a brawny bastard."

"Oh, Rob, you could have been killed!" Barry threw her arms around him, kissing him in a frenzy of emotion.

"Well now, it was worth it to have you do that And I give you leave to do it any time, luv." He smiled, drawing her closer and running his hand along the fine contours of her face. "Let's not trouble ourselves with these confounded matters any more tonight. I'll speak to Frank about the prowler in the morning. I want him t–"

"No!" Barry interposed. "As far as I'm concerned, he's a suspect. Promise me you won't say anything until we glean some information of our own. Unless, of course, you want to discuss it with the police."

Rob looked thoughtful as he paced a moment in silence. "Perhaps you're right. I don't think I'll talk to the Gards either. They haven't seemed too interested in anything I've had to say thus far, anyroad. Sure 'n we've had all the interruptions we're goin' t' have for one night." He reached for her, pulling her against him. "Earlier, I thought Nora would never finish her tidyin' up. Now," he crooned, nibbling her ear, "where were we?"

Barry sighed softly, and he could feel her abandoning herself to him as he gently laid her down on the wide bed. She reached out to him, and she seemed to tremble as he bent to kiss her, murmuring words, in his enchanting way of speaking, along her ear. His hands too were magickal as they caressed her, exploring her body in its silk apricot nightdress.

Soon, the thin layer of silk and wisps of foamy lace were too restricting, and he peeled them from her golden skin. For several heated moments, he looked at her, then he quickly stripped the robe and shorts from his own body.

How powerful he is ... like a legendary Celtic warrior of old, she marveled.

But he was all tenderness and warmth, and as they lay together in the silver moonglow throughout the night, they *both* realized that they were, indeed, destined to come together– their bodies and souls merging into a cascade of falling stars and ascending fiery comets.

"The most beautiful thing we can experience is the mysterious."
~ Albert Einstein

Chapter Seven

Raine and Maggie entered the crowded Dublin pub and headed for a quiet table in the rear.

As soon as they sat down, Maggie pulled out the notes and translations they had just obtained from the head of the language department at Trinity. Lowering the hood and shucking her grey, rain-soaked coat from her shoulders, the striking redhead glanced down at the notebook. "I think it's going to come out the way we surmised, and I can't wait till we get back to the room to get started."

Raine leaned forward, an excited expression lighting her face. "Professor Burns' letter from our good ole Haleigh College is certainly serving us well. Do you think your prof friend at Trinity was suspicious in any way?"

Maggie raised a dismissing hand, shaking her head. "I don't think so. We took the words and phrases completely out of order, and we tossed so many extras into the mix, for good measure, that I really don't see how he could draw any undesirable conclusions."

"You're right, of course. And the way you kept flattering him, flirting with him, I don't think he was even aware of anything else." Raine grinned. "He still fancies you."

Maggie rolled her vivid green eyes. "He's very good-looking, but very married nowadays." Opening the logbook, she quickly scanned the hand-written sheets, stopping at the page where the morning's notes were located. She was just about to speak, when the waitress came to their table. Hastily, her hand still in the book, she closed it, and they ordered drinks and a light meal.

While the Sleuth Sisters ate, they filled in the missing words, with the translations from the Trinity language professor, that were necessary to their odyssey. "Backward," Raine supplied. "That one means 'backward' in Old Irish."

"And that really guttural-sounding phrase … look! It *is* what we thought!" Instantly Maggie lowered her voice, glancing round at the other patrons. No one seemed to notice the two Americans at a corner table in the hindmost area of the lively pub. She extended the book for Raine to see the passage she was referring to.

"The spirals at Newgrange!" Raine could hardly contain her mounting excitement.

"Yes, and read on, now that we have all the words filled in. There is a *double* meaning connected to those spirals. It's not only what I thought, but read ... do you see what I mean?"

"I do!" She patted her cousin on the back. "I am always impressed with your instinctive wisdom for ancient symbols and symbolism, Mags! Not only will we be able to succeed in our quest, but we can literally turn back the–" She stopped abruptly, glanced quickly around the noisy room, then let the translation sink in for her consciousness to absorb. "It all hinges on that one word. The power is in the word, and the word–" she caught herself again, her anxious gaze scanning the room. Still no one was paying any mind to them. "I opt for scrapping our itinerary and making straight for Clare," Raine said, setting her reading glasses back on her head, and reaching for a savory vinegar-seasoned chip.

"No, it will serve us better to wait. At *Samhain*, the veil between the worlds will be gossamer thin. There will be the Oneness that," Maggie lowered her voice even more, leaning forward as far as she could toward her raven-haired cousin, "the Oneness that will cinch it. So there is no reason not to take in at least some of the other sites we have on our agenda."

"I agree," Raine yielded, her husky voice even throatier with the emotion she was feeling, "and from those additional sites, we may gather *more* energy. I have a feeling we'll need it, even with Aisling's contributions. *At least our first time.* In my excitement over the translation, I stupidly forgot about *Samhain*, the time of death and rebirth. But, most importantly, it's a time for the Old Ones. How could I have lost sight of their significance in this, *their* contributions, when from the start, I could hear their words in genetic memory, *feel* their ... *urging* in my very bones and in my blood?"

"When we pay homage to the ancestors at *Samhain*, they, in turn, will honor us, in that night ahead, when we cross to take our place with those who have gone before into the greatest mystery of all." Tears had started in Maggie's magnificent eyes, then suddenly she began to laugh, and Raine shot her a questioning look. "It'll be a trifle awkward when, for our doctoral, we document our sources before the exalted thesis committee." She slipped on her reading spectacles, jocularly viewing her cousin over the gold designer frames. "'It was like this, honorable– *distinguished*– fellow colleagues of letters, we were awaiting the Great Stag. We got a

John Deere. We heard voices, and a faerie appeared.' I pray the board doesn't dismiss us as irrefutably … *crazy!*"

"We'll be in good company," Raine shrugged. "Let's see … Joan of Arc, Napoleon, General Patton, Abraham Lincoln, Edgar Allan Poe, to name but a few. Harry Truman talked about the ghost in the Lincoln Bedroom of the White House, and–"

"OK, let's get back to work."

Raine felt the weight of Maggie's stare. "What? I was just trying to make the point that *they* heard voices … experienced the paranormal, and they weren't *crazy*," she snapped, her Irish temper flaring.

"Not all of them anyway."

Raine stuck her tongue out at her cousin. "Don't be such a cat!"

Maggie laughed. "Here, read the last line." Again she attempted to hand the book to Raine, who, like a willful child, ignored it, continuing, with pouting lips, on her soapbox.

"Not only have several famous people in history seen and heard supernatural phenomena, but every time there is unusual sunspot activity– as there was back in the fifties– actual sound waves from the past are picked up by television and radio stations worldwide."

A charming blush suffused her fair skin. "Just think, Mags," she whispered excitedly, "'the Great Secret, to quote Emerson, 'is the answer to all that has been, all that is, and all that will ever be.' And now," Raine seemed to take on a magickal glow, "*we* are in possession of the Secret. We hold the *Key* … the missing link between modern science and ancient mysticism!"

The petite brunette took a sip from her mug of foamy black stout. "Einstein himself said that matter and energy are interchangeable, and that nothing is ever lost or destroyed. And he said that one day, science and what we accept on faith will come together to simply be called," she brought her forefingers to meet for emphasis, "'*Truth*,'" she finished with a flourish of hand and a clicking of tongue.

Maggie munched a forkful of clams, washed it down with a pull of stout and opened her mouth to speak, when again Raine interposed.

"A good portion of what we uncovered today boils down to mind over matter." This Sister too munched happily on a fried clam, "an amalgamation of the simple truths taught by all the great avatars." Her cheeks took on more pink. "And aren't we constantly discovering that all truths are simple!"

Dreamy, Raine rested her little pointed chin on her ring-adorned hands, the fingernails, as always, lacquered a glossy ebony. *My God! Blown out, this can literally transform the physical world. We are, each of us, the masters of our own world– of the universe! The real secret of power is the consciousness of power!* After a poignant moment, she voiced aloud, "Legends that endure for centuries do so for a reason. Now, what did you want to show me? Levitation, these clams are good!"

Though Raine's passion matched her own, Maggie smiled, always intrigued by her cousin's fervor for every project they undertook. "You've been preachin' to the choir, darlin'; no need to convince *me*, and let's keep our voices down. In the wrong hands, this … *secret* could cause havoc." She handed her cousin the book, which Raine, this time, accepted, slipping her reading glasses over her pert nose. In a moment she looked up, a startled expression on her animated face.

"Does that surprise you?" Maggie asked, popping a vinegar-seasoned chip into her mouth. "According to ancient Irish legend, that could make the quest more successful. Now," she leaned back in her chair, a finger to her chin, "where do we find a … *worthy* recipient?"

Raine sipped her Guinness, thoughtful and uncommonly quiet.

"Know what?" Maggie lifted her brows in query. "I don't think we'll need to do much searching for a worthy recipient, as you put it."

"You're right," Raine concluded as she signaled for more of the establishment's delicious fried clams. "It *has* followed us, and it will present itself in a timely fashion– as always."

***

Bright morning sunlight flooded the high-ceilinged dining room as Barry and Rob, seated close together at the lace-clothed table, finished the huge Irish breakfast Nora had prepared.

Leafing through the old diary, Rob sipped his strong breakfast tea. "Barry, we can't delay this thing. Before we know it, you'll have to return to the States, and we both want to take every advantage of your time here now. We need to find someone to translate this passage straightaway, I–" he paused abruptly. "Frank, is that you?"

The manager's booming voice reached them from the kitchen area. "Aye! Be right there!"

Barry sent Rob a cautioning look. "Perhaps," she whispered, moving even closer to him, "you should get someone else–" Her gaze moved to the doorway, and she quickly sang out, "Good morning, Frank."

"Mornin', lass, Rob," he nodded. "Did you sleep well?"

Rob patted Barry's hand, which rested on her lap under the table. "That's another thing about Barry Hall. I always sleep long and deep."

Frank's smile was mischievous, and his voice, to a blushing Barry, sounded rather cryptic when he spoke. "Ah, yes … that's th' ver-ry thing f'r you, th' ver-ry thing."

"Frank," Rob said, "won't you join us for a cup of tea? I'd like to have that talk now, if you've the time."

"What's that they say, 'Time and Tide wait for no man'?" Frank helped himself from the long buffet, then took a seat next to Rob at table. "I'm at ye'er sar-vice."

Frank set his cup down, settling back in the ornate dining-room chair. "Like you and everyone else round about, I knew about the legendary emerald jewelry, but I never believed it to be hidden here on the estate. If y' ask me, ye'er great-grandfather sold th' jewels after he was jilted. Why would he have kept them? That, t' me, would have been daft."

Pouring himself more tea, Rob stirred in a lump of sugar before responding. "We don't know what he did. However, I quite agree that he was– I don't want to use the word 'daft'– let's just say he was not in a rational state after Carlotta."

Frank stood and moved to the fireplace, taking out a pipe. "Mind?"

Barry and Rob answered in near harmony, "Go ahead."

Frank patted his shirt pocket, mumbling to himself, "Where's me lucifers?" He lit the pipe, then tossed the match into the sputtering fire. "From all accounts, lad, ye'er great-grandfather was much too frugal a man not to have liquidated somethin' of such value." He got the pipe going nicely, and the mellow aroma of black cherry permeated the air. "Especially when it had such painful memories attached to it."

Assimilating what the men were saying, Barry helped herself to more of the steaming tea, stirring in both cream and sugar, as she had come to prefer since coming to Ireland. "I agree with Rob," she said, when the men had stopped talking, "the man was crazy about Carlotta. Hurting the way he was, he could have done just about anything."

"Besides which," Rob added, "both Uncle Phillip and Grandfather believed he *did* keep the jewels. I've been thinking that it was almost as if he kept them as a costly reminder of his great folly, a lesson he wanted over and yet again to remind himself of. That's why I think he cached them somewhere he would have noted day after day in his routine. I know the manor has been searched several times in the past, but I have a feeling he would not have hidden them in the house. If they still exist here on the estate, I opt for the grounds. In his diary, Great-grandfather states, '*All is buried.*'"

Frank puffed his pipe thoughtfully. "Whilst I've been a member of the Barry household– and that's some thirty years– the buildings and the grounds– and remember, lad, just how vast of an area we're talkin' about here– have been painstakingly searched, and more 'n once, as ye've said."

During this last exchange, Barry had been sitting back, listening; now she sat forward, an idea coming to her. She was just about to speak, when she caught herself, thinking better of it for the moment. *I'll wait till Rob and I are alone.*

Rob picked up the leather-bound journal, turning to the page he had marked. "Frank, there's a passage in Gaelic that appears at the end of the diary, after the last entry. I'm not proficient enough to translate it. Can *you* give it a go?"

Frank set his pipe in a large ashtray on the mantel. "'Tis sar-tain I can, lad. I speak and read the old tongue." He took the diary from Rob, looked down at the marked passage, and an expression of surprise fleetingly touched his features. A moment later, he handed the book back to Rob. "But not enough to do us … *you* any good, I'm afraid."

The way he hesitated … . Has he really no clue what it says, or did he, in fact, decipher the passage? Barry frowned.

Suddenly, Frank snapped his fingers. "Sure 'n I can help you! I have a friend, a schoolmaster. He teaches th' *Gaeilge*– **he** could translate th' passage!"

"How convenient," Barry murmured *sotto voce.*

Slightly startled, Rob looked to her, one black brow raised in the sexy way she had come to love. "Grand!" he replied to his manager, his eyes still on Barry.

"I'll ring me friend." Frank again took up his pipe, seemingly considering the matter at hand.

"When do you think we can see him?" Rob closed the diary, slipping it into the pocket of his tweed blazer.

Frank paused, puffing thoughtfully on his pipe. "He's busy most *days* ... perhaps tomorra evenin.'"

"Don't hang about. Arrange it as soon as possible," Rob requested, "the sooner, the better."

Frank was hesitant again, Barry pondered. *He's usually so quick to respond. I wonder ...*

***

"It couldn't be much farther." Raine pulled the car off the narrow, rural road to have yet another look at the map her cousin held.

"Five miles ... let's see, that's about eight kilometers west of Tuam," Maggie dragged a scarlet-glazed fingernail across their route. "I believe we've covered nearly that. Let's drive a bit more, down R 333. That should take us right to it."

Raine guided the car back on the road, and they continued toward their destination. Within a few minutes, they saw it– a prominent wooded hill, the summit studded with prehistoric remains scattered, like hidden jewels, among the hawthorns, bracken, heather and gorse.

"Knockmaa," Maggie pronounced as the rapt pair walked from the car to the hilltop. "Some say Queen Maeve is buried here."

"The important thing," Raine recounted, "is that this mound is sacred to the Old Ones, for it was granted by Dagda, king of the *Tuatha De Danann* and the first to ever master the harp, to Finbarr, king of the faeries."

Once they reached the summit, they stood looking out at the impressive vista– a broad checkerboard of green farmland crossed by murmuring brooks and a shining ribbon of lazy river. Below, black and white cows swayed heavily at milking time across a country road, their bells sounding in the enchanted stillness.

"Do you feel it?" Raine spoke quietly. A slow smile curved her lips, and her emerald eyes seemed to look beyond, to a past clearer to her vision than the present. "Magick yet engulfs this place. It's quite strong ... drifting around us in currents and making my senses tingle! Do you feel it, Mags?"

Maggie lowered the hood of her grey raincoat, freeing her fiery mane of dark-red hair, then she inclined her head and, closing her eyes, raised her arms skyward. "Yes, oh yes ... I can feel the power of the *Sidhe*. The *Tuatha De Danann* were highly skilled in the arts of Druidry. Great Goddess! They could call the wind by whistling for it! Imagine it, Raine, accomplished necromancers that they were, they knew no limits of time, and it is said they were capable of changing shapes at will." She lowered her arms and opened her eyes. "If you could shape-change right now, what would it be?"

Raine's expression turned instantly playful. "Normally I would say a black Bombay cat like my Panthèrra, or Black Jade and Black Jack O'Lantern, but here and now, I would change into one of those ravens up there, and soar on an air current over this special place, brimming with its secret lore and its mysteries, and I'd absorb all the magick that I could." She looked to Maggie. "Why is it, do you think, that most people do not believe in what they cannot see or hear?"

After a brief reflective moment, Maggie replied, "That's an easy one– *fear*. Of being scoffed at. And fear of the unknown, the unexplained."

Raine gave a quick nod of agreement. "C'mon, let's walk around Cashel's ruins."

The stone fortress was so old, no one had ever determined its exact age. The walls, three feet thick, were of successive heights. And the Irish moss covering the stone seemed to lend even more antiquity to the place.

"Legend says that the *De Danann*– and oh, they were a beautiful people, the people of Dana– possessed an invincible weapon of Light," Raine mused, "but they chose not to use it against the invading Gaels, who, with honor, offered fair combat for possession of this 'Emerald Isle.' Opinions differ on what happened to the *De Danann*, who then disappeared from Ireland while the Gaels stayed. Some say they went underground, others that they returned to the planet from whence they had come, a few remaining to intermarry with the Gaels."

"Look," Maggie pointed, "there!"

Raine turned and, after moving to the spot where Maggie stood, stared down at the delicate little stone steps built into the walls of the ruins, steps too small for any human to have used, steps that coiled seductively round enchanting Irish legend, steps that led straight to the height of the imagination of anyone, over the long centuries, who viewed them.

"Humankind may not recall the *Tuatha De Danann*, but," Raine breathed, *"they are here now.* I can *feel* them, and you and I know they guard, still, the timelessness, the magick, the shape-changing in the land of ever-youth and feasting, gemmed with wondrous glittering castles, but now relegated forever– *to faerie.*"

***

A struggling sun was shining faintly through a gap in the cloudy sky; and over the shimmering verdant patchwork of green and woods about the stately manor, a steady, soft rain was falling as Frank pulled his Ford into the circular drive. Rob and Barry exited the car with the estate manager and hurried up the front steps into the house, escaping the drizzle.

"Nippy day like this, you should be sittin' cozy by th' fire with your lady," Frank said when they entered the foyer. "Afore y' go upstairs, wud y' be wantin' a wee nip to take th' chill off?" As he doffed his tweed cap and shook it, droplets of water sprayed the air.

"Why not?" Rob removed his hat, tossing it to a peg on the wall. He ran his fingers through his windswept hair, then escorted Barry through the doorway to the public room.

As expected, a cheery fire was burning in the hearth. Frank went immediately behind the bar, where he mixed short Jameson and sodas. Rob and Barry sank appreciatively onto the settee, relaxing before the warmth of the fire.

"You shouldn't be too disappointed, lad." Frank handed him a tumbler. "If th' Gaelic passage were meaningful, don't you think ye'er grandfather and ye'er uncle would've made use of it?" He offered a tumbler to Barry.

"You're right, of course," Rob answered, "but I thought we'd be able to find some small clue they had overlooked. I can't help being disappointed that all it turned out to be was an overly sentimental ode. A soppy love poem!"

Now it was Barry's turn to look disappointed. "Overly sentimental! Soppy! Not at all! Personally, I think the poem's alive with … stimulating thought and genuine feeling."

Rob shrugged absently, ruminatively taking a sip of his whiskey.

Frank, too, appeared lost in thought. A brief silence hung over the room, broken by a loud crack of lightning and the rolling sound of thunder. "Robbie," he said finally, laying a weathered hand on the younger man's shoulder, "they've an expression in prizefightin'. 'Anyone can take a hit. The trick is in th' gettin' up again.' Ah," he snapped his fingers, "afore I forget, I hired a new gardener this mornin'. Name's John McHendrie. Says he has experience. Th' poor man practically begged me f'r work, bendin' me ear with his life story, how he's been down on his luck of late. We'll see how he does. That garden needs tendin'."

"Very good," Rob nodded. He laughed then. "You know how they say that God invented liquor so the Irish wouldn't rule the world? I sometimes think he invented obstinacy so that we could be the best at something."

Barry turned a vexed expression on him. "I thought the English were known for stubbornness. 'Johnny Bull' and all that."

"The Brits don't have a monopoly on bullheadedness. I intend to sort out every last mystery surroundin' this place, find the lost jewels and … fulfill my birthright! Tossing back the remainder of his drink, Rob stood, and set his empty tumbler on the bar. "I'm going upstairs. Frank, thank you for everything. You've been most obligin'."

"Th' Divil you say!" Frank's outstretched arm took in the cozy hearth-lit room. "Barry Hall is me home."

Pausing near Barry, Rob bent to kiss her cheek. "I'll see you at dinner, luv. Remember, the Conroys are joining us this evening. You may wish to nap a half-hour or so whilst you can. With all the goings on round here, you haven't gotten much rest."

Hiding her miffed feelings, Barry attempted a smile. "See you at dinner."

Still in a distracted state, Rob exited into the foyer and started up the stairs. A loud knocking sounded at the front door. He turned and came back down, mumbling, "Can't be the Conroys; it's too early."

There was another loud crack of lightning, followed by a long peal of thunder, as he pulled opened the heavy front door. The storm swept in– wind and rain, along with several dead leaves from the verandah. Before him stood a tall, burly, raven-haired man with fervid blue eyes, wearing seaman's attire and holding a duffel bag.

"Brian!"

"A change of feeling is a change of destiny."
~ Neville Goddard

Chapter Eight

"I've been out to sea all these years, and I thought that it was time I reconnected with my family ... *whilst I have family left.*" His duffel bag on the floor, Brian stood in the foyer of Barry Hall, nervously twisting his seaman's cap in his large hands.

"If I had seen th' Divil himself when I opened that door,'t would've been less of a shock!" Rob looked down at the extended hand, hesitated, then held his brother's eyes for what seemed a very long time, finally gripping the proffered peace offering.

"I rang you up at your London agency. They put me through to Dublin, and your man Elliot told me you were here, and why." Brian looked down at his feet, seemingly searching for the right words. "Look, Rob, I want to put you at ease about this business of the inheritance. I quite understand. I was never close to Uncle Phillip. As I said, I've been away all these years, and now that I'm approaching middle age, I ... well, it seemed like a good time to–" He moved quickly forward and embraced his brother, giving him a hearty slap on the back. "It's good to see you, Rob."

Before Rob had time to react, Barry entered the foyer, taking his arm. "Are you going to introduce me? I couldn't help overhearing your conversation from the public room." *Rob and Brian look alike. I wonder if they **are** alike?*

Slipping his arm around her waist, Rob drew her a little nearer. "Brian, this is Baranya Bartok, a very dear friend. Barry, this is my long-lost brother, Brian."

"Pleased to meet you, I'm sure," she said, extending her hand.

"Don't be so sure," Brian responded with a wicked grin. "You don't know me yet," he winked.

Barry laughed.

"Ah, there it 'tis! That forthright Yankee laugh. You *are* American, are you not?"

Barry nodded, "Yes, I am."

"Tell me, Barry, what is it that makes you Yanks so strangely naive and innocent?"

Barry cocked her head, answering, "I don't think we are. Are you so cynical?" she asked amiably.

Brian chuckled, "Let's just say I have a sneering disbelief in certain things," his eyes shifted to Rob's, "as well as in certain individuals."

Now what, do you suppose, he meant by that? Barry mused.

Rob was quick to observe that while Barry and Brian shook hands, his brother's gaze had traveled over her. "You look like you just jumped ship. Are you staying?" Rob's voice conveyed more than a little of the annoyance he was feeling. "Should I have Nora set an extra place at table? Or are your maritime obligations such that you'll be returning to your vessel?"

Somewhat taken aback by Rob's uncharacteristic lack of hospitality, Barry looked quickly at his profile. His jaw was set in a tight, hard line. *I wonder what the problem is between them? Yet another enigma of Barry Hall.* She looked to Brian, who smiled down at her in a way that made her smile back. *Both brothers have the same coal-black hair and strapping frame. Rob's more muscular, Brian more beefy. And, except for the color, both have the same intense eyes.*

At the moment, Brian's fervent gaze was fixed with unconcealed delight on Barry. "It would indeed be a *pleasure* to join you for dinner. Did I hear you say, 'Nora'?" Brian pronounced jestingly, shifting his eyes to Rob. "Is she still runnin' th' show here?"

At that instant, the somber housekeeper appeared in the foyer. "Good-evenin', Mr. Carroll."

Brian rushed over and gave Nora a bear hug. "Nora old gur-rl! Y' haven't changed a bit. Has she, Rob?"

"I could say th' same f'r you, sir." Nora straightened the snowy-white bib of her starched apron.

Perhaps it's my imagination, Barry thought, studying the older woman from a few feet distant, *but she seemed to send Brian a look. The question begging is– was it her usual one of disapproval, or was it a cautioning signal?*

"Leave your bag; I'll have Frank see to it. I've sent him on an errand, but he'll be back directly. Dinner will be in about an hour." Nora vanished into the kitchen.

"Splendid!" Brian's eyes swept his surroundings. "All th' saints! I haven't been down at the Hall f'r years! Nothin's much changed I see." He chortled, "Except that it's a helluva lot quieter since the ole divil has taken his leave. Now, I could really use a drink," he announced, rubbing his hands together and heading for the warmth of the public room.

***

Frank was at his customary position behind the bar, when Barry entered the room to join the men. She had bathed and dressed for dinner in a striking garnet knit dress that accentuated her curves to perfection. Her long dark hair was swept becomingly to one side with an antique comb studded with faux jewels the same claret color as her dress.

"Lovely!" Brian, who was nearest the door, turned and, in a polished, courtly manner, picked up her hand and kissed it, his look lingering on the deep décolleté of her dress. "Hmm, Jasmine. How appropriate for such a goddess as yourself."

Rob's eyes flickered for a moment, but only a hint of danger carried on his voice. He came immediately forward and lightly kissed Barry's cheek. "He's right, you know," he delivered softly. "You *are* a goddess." After escorting Barry to the settee before the hearth, where he took a seat beside her, he turned to his brother. "As I recall, you never did answer my question, Brian. I trust your visit here will be brief."

With a grin shimmering in the deep blue depths of his eyes and at the corners of his mouth, Brian shifted his attention from Barry to Rob, "I was hoping you would offer me a little hospitality. At least until I find my own place. I've just retired from the sea." He lifted one black brow, and his eyes again flicked to the décolleté of Baranya's dress. "I'm a ship … seeking a harbor."

"Here we go," Frank intervened, extending a glass to a bewildered but curious Barry. "One sparkling water with a twist."

This is a twist all right. There're some weird twists of fate at work here, she thought.

Rob turned toward the bar to collect Barry's drink, mumbling through clenched teeth, "Bloody hell." He handed her the frosted glass with its wedge of lemon perched on the rim.

For the second time that evening, Barry gazed in surprise at the man she thought she was beginning to know.

Brian, on the other hand, seemed to be enjoying himself immensely, and the mischievous grin still danced about his features. "What was that, Brother?"

Three firm knocks sounded at the front door. "That would be the Conroys," Frank declared, wiping his hands on the bar towel, and then moving with purpose toward the foyer.

***

Barry dissolved in laughter, "Oh, Brian, where I come from, we would say you really know how to spin a yarn!"

"When ye've met as many people as I have, and been as many places, that's not such a task." He gestured toward Rob, "Or for you. Congratulations on your book."

Rob responded with a frosty nod.

"Yes," Margaret endorsed, "congratulations are in order for your book, Robert. I must say it was the perfect fireside reader. A *ver-ry* good read."

Margaret Conroy sat across from Rob and Barry, next to her husband Patrick, in Barry Hall's companionable public room. The solicitor's middle-aged wife was tall and mannish, with broad shoulders and thick ankles. She looked at the world through no-nonsense, wire-rimmed spectacles, and her short-bobbed, grey hair– not a salt-and-pepper grey, nor an iron-grey, but an odd slate shade, the even grey of a Maltese cat– did nothing to flatter her somewhat horsey face, a face she made up with only the lightest touch of unflattering color. This evening Margaret sported a two-piece tweed suit and sturdy shoes, and Barry guessed correctly that tweeds or riding togs were her habitual attire. Focusing her shrewd myopic eyes on Barry, she asked, "What do *you* think of this Gypsy lifestyle of Robert's, my dear?"

Barry cleared her throat, recrossing her shapely long legs. "Since I am of Romany extraction, and as you've alluded, I think it's wonderfully exciting that Rob has gotten to see and experience so much of the world."

At mention of the word "Romany," Margaret gave a slight start. "Rom … a Gypsy! How … *colorful.* What exactly do you *do* in America?"

Barry's face flushed, but her voice was cool and level. "I am a television investigative news reporter."

Margaret's features took on a look of distaste, her expression suggesting that she had just caught wind of a bad smell. "I see." She shifted her weight in the chair, as though to gear herself up for what she was about to deliver. "Not to cast aspersions on your country, my dear, but I have always held the opinion that in America especially, those of your chosen profession seem to go way beyond the pale. It's as though they have a license for being meddlesome and intrusive. Instigators and downright spies, I daresay, the lot of them! American telly ... hump!" Margaret mumbled, in conclusion, under her breath.

Talk about meddlesome and intrusive! What is her problem? It's as if she– stand your ground, Barry! "Some of what you say is true, Mrs. Conroy, but we do believe in freedom of the press and the people's right to know in America. A lot depends on the individual media source or the journalist. Personally, I have always practiced what I consider honorable journalism. Freedom of the press is simply a part of the great paradox of freedom."

"Like America, Ireland ranks first-rate in the world for press freedom." Rob squeezed her hand and held it. "It's but one of the many common denominators we share."

Not to be put off, Margaret's steady gaze lingered on Barry. "By the bye, you do ride, don't you? *That* is a part of the great paradox of being Irish. Horses are the most important aspect of our lives here in the country. Riding is in our blood."

Barry stifled the response on the tip of her tongue. "I had a couple of riding lessons as a child, but I wouldn't say that I–" she looked to Rob, who intercepted for her.

"Since it's been awhile, I will be instructing her all over again." He gave her hand another encouraging squeeze, which she warmly returned.

"I look forward to the fall hunts here at Barry Hall. They really get my blood up!" Margaret continued with an ungainly flourish of the hand that nearly swept her husband's drink from his grip. "We'll just have to invite her to ride to th' hounds with us, won't we, Robert?"

I wonder if anyone's ever been tempted to throw a saddle over her fat rump? Ride to the hounds, huh? That's fence-jumping and– Ooooh, no! Definitely not for me, Barry decided.

"Pity," Margaret continued, looking down her long nose at Barry, "you won't be proficient enough to ride with us this season. Tell me, Cousin, what do you think about this business of old Tom Mannion's death? Personally, I think it's a lot of rubbish. Happenstance! Of course it was an accident!"

"For now, I think I'll leave that to the Gards," Rob answered in a tone that firmly closed the door on the subject.

Barry was studying Margaret intensely. *Did a look pass between Margaret and Frank? I saw something pass between them ...*

Margaret uttered a sharp exclamation of annoyance, quickly maneuvering an assertive foot back into the conversational door. "I hope you've found yourself a new gardener. In the interim, I could always come over here and whip those gardens back into shape. You know, of course, I've won first prize ten years runnin' in our local flower exhibitions. Why, my Savoys grew so large, I had to move the neighbor's fence! Cultivatin' roses is both an art and a science. Now, listen carefully. There are five major mistakes people make with roses, and, as I've said, I am just the one to–"

"Frank," Rob interposed, "has just hired a new gardener. I have no doubt he will be capable in his duties. But I appreciate the offer, Margaret."

"Tradition is what makes Barry Hall the place it is," Conroy declared. "I think that is what my wife was attempting to convey. Weren't you, dear?"

*Now I **know** a look just passed between Margaret and her husband.* Barry moved, on impulse, a bit closer to Rob.

Margaret snorted a mirthless little laugh, and with her cocktail napkin, she fiercely brushed a morsel of salmon from the corner of her near-lipless mouth. "**Attempting**! I'm layin' th' cards right out on the table here, Patrick. Tradition is *everything* at the Hall!"

"Oh, I don't think you need concern yourselves about heritage, tradition 'n all that sort of ballyhoo. My brother is like our parents in that respect; the past is everything. As for me, I prefer living in the present," Brian avowed with his usual devil-may-care aplomb. "Live for th' here and now. That has always been my motto!" He immediately returned his attention to a tray of appetizers on the bar, food he seemed to be devouring like there was no tomorrow.

"Perhaps you have the right idea," Conroy replied, visibly eager to shift the focus of discussion. "I can't remember who said it, but I read once that the past is history, the future a mystery, the present our gift to ourselves. And that's the reason it's called 'the present.'"

*I wonder if **his present** with tallyho Margaret is such a gift,* Barry mused. *I can't imagine any man, even the stuffy ole solicitor there, wanting to take her to bed. I must stop. This is sheer meanness! Try and be nice, Barry.* She took a sip of her sparkling water, and smiled, with as much warmth as she could muster, over the rim of her frosted glass at her horsey nemesis on the opposite side of the room.

"Are you going to keep up the traditions of Barry Hall or not, Robert?" the insufferable woman blurted abruptly, ignoring Barry's gesture of friendship.

"That is my intention, yes." Rob sipped his drink, seemingly unruffled by Margaret's assault. "Fancy dress balls and all."

"I am heartened to hear that. I just don't know *how* you intend to do it from points all over the globe." Margaret sent her cousin a look full of challenge. "I quite expected to receive a notice in the post, announcing the cancellation of the ball this year, what with Phillip's death and all." She popped a canapé into her mouth, and immediately reached, toward a tray on the coffee table in front of her, for another.

Rob cleared his throat. "It was Uncle Phillip's explicit directive that the ball be held in spite of his death."

"In spite," Margaret spat in a low aside to her husband, head down, dabbing furiously at her mouth with her napkin. "Yes," she voiced louder, raising her head, "that sounds like old Phillip."

"To a 'T'." Brian accepted a curried egg from the tray the uniformed Máire was now offering to the assembled guests, sending her a wink.

The little maid's cheeks flamed a deep scarlet. She deposited the tray on the bar and hastily exited the room.

"These remind me of the curry dishes I enjoyed in the Indies." Brian snapped up another spicy egg.

"I'd wager," Frank began, picking up the fireplace poker, "that between you and Rob, there wouldn't be many places in the world you haven't seen." He stirred the fire in the hearth, and the flames leaped and snapped.

"You'd likely win that bet. I've put in at every major port you could name." He looked out the window at the storm, seemingly in reverie. "And some out-of-the-way places I'd bet even Rob never heard of." Brian stared at the sprightly manager a moment, suddenly giving forth a loud chuckle. "Remember, Frank, when Rob and I were lads, how you used to say we were so ver-ry different, one from the other? Actually, I think we turned out rather alike."

Rob seemed for an instant to choke on his drink. He started to say something but held his tongue.

"We both have the wanderlust and a need of high adventure. Excitement," Brian ran on, apparently oblivious to his brother's annoyance. "We simply channeled it in different directions. You know, Barry, when th' pair of us were wee lads, I, being the older by a couple of years, was, *f'r a short time,* bigger, and I was, simply put– a *bully.* We fought quite a lot," he laughed. "However, there's nothin' like a life of discipline t' take that out of ya!" Brian tossed back his Jameson, and a sad expression settled on his features. "Rob, I know you probably still hold it against me that I did not come home for the funeral when our parents passed on, but … everyone has to deal with loss in his own way. Quite frankly, I couldn't deal with it. You know well that *Da* and I were not on th' best of terms when I left home. That made it even more difficult for me."

Rob mumbled something under his breath that Barry did not catch. He slid his arm along the back of the settee, behind her, and his tiger eyes held his brother's equally intense look. "Didn't I hear, a few years back, that you had married?"

Brian grinned, "If you did, you heard wrong. In all my travels, worldwide, I never found the right woman for me." His look shifted, settling over Baranya. "Never even came close."

A trifle uncomfortable, Barry stared down at her hands. *He's bold. Boldly charming, however. As for Rob, I've never seen him this rattled. The tension between him and Brian is as sharp as a dagger's edge. Surely he's not jealous of his brother, though I'd bet my life they were always fearsome rivals.*

Máire reentered the public room, glancing nervously at Brian, who sent her another wink from his position at the bar. In a timid voice, the maid announced, "Dinner is served." She dropped a little curtsey, then scurried into the hall.

"Grand!" Brian rose, his dancing eyes by chance meeting Barry's. He flashed her a rakish smile. "I'm as hungry as a wolf."

Frank, carrying a tray of glasses, headed, with his usual quick gait, for the kitchen. Brian moved toward the foyer, gallantly ushering the Conroys, Rob and Barry ahead of him.

Just as they were about to cross into the candle-lit dining room, Rob swiveled round, and, eye to eye with his brother, muttered, "I'll thank you to curb your shaggin' depravity in this house."

"… Never forget the last time we put in to Bridgetown in Barbados. We went into a favorite pub and had just settled in for a quiet evenin' of drink and chat, when who should come into th' place but crew from th' Brit merchant fleet. At first 'twas nothin';

we kept to ourselves. But after a pint or three, the b–" Brian coughed, catching himself in the midst of his full-swing narrative, "*Brits* started castin' aspersions upon us, the sons of Belial gettin' bolder and louder by th' minute. Finally, Liam started singin' a rousin' rendition of 'Follow Me up to Carlow,' and when he belted out th' line, 'And would ye let a Saxon cock crow out upon an Irish rock? Fly up and teach 'em manners!' he did just that. Poor little Aidan was so scared of th' thing turnin' into a real Donneybrook, that he ducked behind me, shakin' in his number-six shoes. 'Keep your back to th' wall,' I told him. 'I'll keep the blighters away from ya!'"

Frank, the Conroys, and Barry laughed, and Brian relaxed in the dining-room chair, pleased with himself and the impression he was making on his audience. All except, that is, for Rob, who rolled his eyes and tried, as best he could during the entire dinner, to ignore his prodigal brother.

"Brian, I think *you* should write a book! You've got more stories than any *seanchaí* of old," Margaret exclaimed, her last forkful of Nora's fluffy twice-baked potatoes en route to her mouth.

"Not me, I don't think I could sit still long enough." The ex-sailor helped himself to another generous slice of lamb, sluicing it with mint sauce.

"You could always hire a ghost writer," Conroy added. "You and Rob could even think about working on the next one together."

"Ho! Imagine that! Rob and I shut up together for th' time it would take to write a book! I think not, Patrick, though if I only bothered to try, I could be just as brilliant as that brother of mine," he laughed.

"Laziness is a heavy burden," Rob muttered aside to Barry, who responded by nudging him to silence, under the table, with her foot.

"I don't want to overstay my welcome here," Brian was saying. "I've plans of my own to get under way."

"You seem to be a man of many talents. What do you think you'll do, now that you've terminated your sea career?" Margaret gave her mouth a final pat with her linen napkin and sat back in the chair, her large hands folded in her ample lap.

"Of that, I'm not entirely sar-tain … yet. I've a couple of business prospects, to which I'm givin' careful consideration. I don't intend to stagnate. I'm like Rob in that; always in motion, I am." Though the others had all finished, he helped himself to yet another potato, dressing it copiously with butter and chives.

"I wish you well in whatever endeavor you choose, Brian, and if there's ever anything with which I can assist you, please feel that you can call upon me." Conroy, by force of habit, took out his pipe, then, thinking better of it, returned it to the pocket of his tweed jacket.

"I will … I will that," Brian replied, polishing off the last of the food on his plate.

Now it looked as though Brian and Patrick Conroy exchanged looks, Barry observed. *Perhaps I'm being overly– Noo, I've been a reporter long enough to note that something passed between them, and that wasn't the only mysterious look exchanged this night.*

Máire came in and, with eyes downcast, dutifully repeated, "Nora says you may retire to the public room for coffee and brandy now, if you like." She started for the kitchen, when Brian caught her eye, sending her a grin loaded with enough sexual innuendo to sink the last ship he was on. She rushed out, her face burning.

Everyone filed back across the foyer, the tall Conroys leading, next Rob, with his arm around Barry's waist, Frank following, then Brian, who lingered, his eyes scanning the floor near his chair. "Be there in a minute, I seemed to have misplaced my lighter again." He moved the chair and spotted the lighter lying on the rug. Stooping, he retrieved it, looking up to see Máire standing inches away.

She hurriedly stepped back from the table, where she had come to fetch the bowl of fruit. "Excuse me, Mr. Carroll."

"Excuse you? For what?" His voice was like a caress. Standing, he moved, in a slow hypnotic gait, toward her. "Such a big bowl for such a wee lass. Here now," he murmured, reaching out to take it from her, "let me help you."

"No! I mean, Nora told *me* to take it into th' public room. Please, sir." She inched to the side, trying, like a trapped and frightened hare, to make her escape, but Brian blocked her way, an arm on either side of her, the wall to her back.

"I only want to help." His face was quite close, his lips dangerously near to hers, his lowered gaze lingering on her partially open mouth. For a devilishly long moment, it looked as though he might kiss her, but he did not. Instead, he gallantly ushered her ahead of him with a dramatic and courtly sweep of his arm.

Máire made a speedy retreat with Brian's low laughter following her, just as Rob peered into the dining room, a scowl darkening his features.

"What?" Brian asked in a poor attempt at innocence, another low laugh escaping him.

* * *

"Well, we know we can trust Frank," Margaret stated with conviction. In their car, en route home from Barry Hall, the Conroys were discussing the evening's events.

"Tradition *is* everything where Barry Hall is concerned! When I think that if he marries her, a *tinker* would become the Hall's mistress, I want to scream. Can you imagine it? A foreigner *and* a tinker! And the way she dresses! You *know* she must have a past. I just wonder what it is? How can Robert even consider someone like that?"

"Your point?" Patrick asked. "You seem to think this is all some sort of soap opera!"

"My point– and it's as sharp as ever it was– is *tradition*! Patrick, did you even hear a word I said?"

Conroy glanced over at his wife. "How could I not? Margaret, ever since we first married, all these long years, you've always expected me to play my role to the hilt. You've not, however, held up your end. If you intend for this grand scheme of yours to succeed, you had better do as I've advised you. Did you take care of the matter we discussed yesterday evening?"

Margaret sat up straighter and drew in a long breath. "I did not! And I don't see how you could even ask such a horrid thing of me. I just can't bring myself to do it! It is *not* necessary; I tell you!"

Conroy tossed his wife a look boiling over with exasperation and anger. "It *is* necessary!" he answered through clenched teeth. "How would the Lady of the Manor like visiting her husband in prison?"

"Oh! I don't know *why* Phillip didn't leave Barry Hall to us! He should have, all things considered. We are the ones who value … *appreciate* the place! And we're the ones who have the knowledge and experience to perpetuate the centuries of custom, decorum and conventions associated with the Hall. Not to mention old Phillip's heavy pockets of a million-plus euros with which to do it! Rob won't even *be* there half the time. How can that *snip* of a girl hope

to carry on the traditions there? I shall never get over it– never!
Everything will go straight to hell. Straight to hell, Patrick." She
shot him a quick searching look. "Do you hear me?"

Again, Conroy glanced for a fleeting moment, from the road,
toward his wife. "No, Margaret, that is *not* going to happen."

The garden was misty, and the early-morning sun felt good on his
upturned face as Rob entered the Love Gardens and ambled, in a
reflective mood, through the maze of pathways. Presently he
happened upon a rotund, middle-aged man in work clothes, busily
trimming the yew hedges.

"Top o' th' mornin' to ya, sir!" The gardener touched a finger to
the tweed cap he sported.

"And th' rest of th' day to you," Rob returned with a burst of
laughter that released, for the moment, his worrying thoughts. He
extended his hand. "Rob Carroll. And you must be John
McHendrie."

The new employee smiled, his expression cherubic, shaking
hands in as lively a manner as Rob had ever encountered. "Right ye
aire! McHendrie's me name; gardenin' me fame."

Rob nodded. "Glad to have you with us. Carry on then."

A finger to his cap in acknowledgment, and McHendrie went
back to his trimming.

Rob walked on, through the labyrinth of pathways. Soon his
aimless wandering led him to the fountain with its charming statue
of Venus in her niche in the wall, an artesian spring supplying a
constant flow of water from the large open seashell at her feet.

Mother Nature and a sequence of gardeners, of a century past,
had provided a delightful profusion of cascading ivy that covered the
brick wall on both sides of the marble statue. But Father Time, in a
covenant with Destiny, had lent character to the love goddess' lush
curves. Facing her weathered form, Rob flopped down on an old
stone bench.

It was peaceful in the gardens, the only sounds being the snip-
snip of McHendrie's clippers in the distance accompanied by
occasional birdsong. His thoughts were scattered as he breathed in
the crisp morning air, pungent with the woodsy October smells of
boxwood and decaying leaves.

Goddess, what secrets do you hold? Still in a distracted state, Rob
stretched his long legs out before him, staring at the entrancing

Venus. It wasn't long before he turned his head, certain he sensed someone watching him. He could see no one about, but in a moment the sound of McHendrie's jovial voice reached him. "Top o' th' mornin', lassie!"

Barry came into sight on the yew-lined path. Pleased to see her, Rob patted the stone bench beside him. When she sat down, he picked up her hand and, with both of his, pressed it to his lips.

She smiled. *Well now, perhaps Brian's a good influence.* A silence hung between them, each occupied yet with private thoughts. She breathed deeply, filling her lungs with Ireland's sweet morning air. "You don't like your brother much, do you?" Barry waited, but the silence, except for the occasional bird, prevailed. "Why?"

It was several moments before Rob answered. "I have my reasons." He turned toward Barry. "*You* seem to like him well enough. In fact, you never took your eyes off him the whole evening."

Now it was her turn to be silent. After an awkward moment, she opened her mouth to speak then stopped. Something had stirred in the bushes, and the pair looked toward the noise, but nothing was there. She turned to Rob and pushed a finger into his chest. "Uh-huh, and I'll tell you what I observed. Maybe it's just the reporter in me, but for one who claims he's been out to sea all those years, his skin is not weathered the way a sailor's would be. Now, your face– and it's such a nice face–" she touched his cheek, "proclaims to the world your life of quest and adventure … my gallant knight-errant."

Rob gave a snort reminiscent of Margaret. "Perhaps most of Brian's sailing was by moonlight."

Barry sent him a quizzical look. He grinned, taking her face in his hands, tilting her mouth upward, his gaze lingering on her parted lips, glossy with a tint of russet. "A little moonlight would be nice right now." He drew her closer, and his mouth came softly down on hers. "I'm glad you're here. Why so quiet? What are you thinkin'?"

"I'm thinkin', Mr. Carroll," she tweaked his mustache, "that you look ever so handsome in that Irish tweed cap."

He smiled, removing the cap and playfully setting it on her head. "I'm sorry if I seemed distracted last night."

Barry flicked the bill of Rob's cap, lifting it a tad from her forehead. She studied him an instant before responding, "You were noticeably quiet at dinner."

"It's all these mystifyin' … overlapping events. First there's my uncle's unsolved death. Didn't it seem to you the Gards, at first, anyroad, were rather cavalier about the matter?"

Barry thought a moment. "What could *they* have to hide?" She slapped the cap back over his tousled black hair.

Rob lowered his voice. "What or who? I've been thinking that there could be a collusion at work here. Perhaps even with the Conroys … I don't know. A man hasn't got a corner on virtue just because his shoes are shined." He adjusted his cap to its customary position on his head.

"Hmmm, a collusion … maybe even more than one," she finished virtually to herself. *It's entirely possible. And maybe there's no connection whatsoever between the complicities.* Realizing that Rob had just uttered again the word "collusion," she asked, "You mean for the treasure?"

"What else? It's legendary in these parts."

"Now that you mention it, the Garda could well be involved in the whole mess … with the Conroys," she glanced quickly around, "or with Frank and Nora," she said quietly. "You did say you noted anger when you pressed that Dublin detective to reinvestigate your uncle's alleged suicide." For several moments, Barry seemed to consider this new thought. "Of course," she rambled, twisting a strand of her dark auburn hair, "what you perceived as anger could just as well have been irritation that you believe the Garda didn't do a thorough job in their initial investigation. Speaking of the Conroys, they didn't seem to care for me much. *She* didn't, anyway."

"A pox on them! They've always been a stuffy pair. Don't let Margaret fluster you. It doesn't matter what either of them thinks, for, as I told you, blood aside, I hardly know them." Rob paused, glancing again behind him. "I can't help feeling … prying eyes."

Barry turned, her gaze skimming the area. To their left, the yew hedge stirred, but neither saw evidence of anyone about, and the sound of the gardener's clippers was still audible from a distance. Unexpectedly, a few feet away, a mouse scurried out of the maze of hedges, a small grey tabby pursuing it.

"Our little Púca isn't the only shape-shifter around here. Next," Rob continued with his former discussion, "comes Tom Mannion's strange, unexplained death, and, to cap th' lot, look what last night's storm blew in."

"Rob, I don't know how I can return to Pittsburgh Sunday night in the midst of all this. I do know we'd best be watchful– deaths seem to come in threes."

"That's exactly what Frank said." He laid a cautioning hand on her arm, his voice low. *"Listen."*

In close succession came a snap of shrubbery, frightened bird cries, and a mad flapping of wings, as a gathering of sparrows took sudden flight from a nearby hedge. Barry and Rob sat motionless for several seconds, but the only other sound was a brisk breeze that carried on its October breath the sharp, bitter smell of decay.

Rob held the back door open as Barry entered the manor house. Lost in thought, the pair made virtually no noise coming through the mudroom and down the carpeted hall. *I can't shake the feeling that someone was watching us,* Rob brooded.

*Someone **was** spying on us out there. Who? I can't dwell on that now,* Barry thought. *I'd better figure out what I'm going to say if and when I telephone Skinner. It would take a miracle to have this web of intrigue unsnarled by Sunday night. Web ... cobwebs! Yes, of course! That's why the killers wore cobwebs in my dream! That and the mental cobwebs Rob and I are trying to clear away.*

The pensive couple moved down the hall, freezing when they heard the sound of anxious whispering coming from the kitchen. "... Out of here!" Nora decreed. "'Tis the only way!"

"Ye'er plan's a good one," Frank responded. "We'll–"

"Whist! I thought I heard somethin' out there."

"They wouldn't be comin' in th' back door."

"*Och!* D'ya want them t' hear ye, man?"

Frank peered into the hall and, seeing Barry and Rob, came forward, a sheepish expression on his face. "Ah! Back from ye'er toddle so soon?"

"That maze of gardens is nothing compared to the puzzles I'm facin'." Rob tossed his tweed cap on the wall peg. "I'll sort this all out, or die tryin'."

Frank's blue eyes brightened. "Now, that's just what Nora and I were chattin' about, lad. You won't solve any puzzle, if ya wur-rk at it steady. I've taken th' liberty of makin' a dinner reservation at Bunratty Castle for th' medieval banquet tomorrow evenin' for th' lot of us. Before ya know it, Barry will have to return home, and she has not seen anythin' at all of Eire yet. Early tomorra mornin', let's take your lady all about, to places you haven't visited since you were a wee lad, what say you? It'll clear your mind and help ya t' think."

Rob and Barry exchanged glances, and laying a hand on Frank's shoulder, Rob answered, "I think it's a grand idea! Before I forget, the rental place is sending a car round. I wish now we hadn't sold Uncle Phillip's old Austin, after he wasn't permitted to drive any longer. Fact is I want Barry to get used to drivin' here."

She turned wide surprised eyes to Rob.

"What?" he responded to her astonishment, not giving her a chance to speak. "If you can navigate rush-hour traffic in Pittsburgh, you can easily drive here, luv."

From her position in the hall next to Rob, Barry could see in the kitchen, through a crack in the partially open door, Nora's white-cuffed sleeve.

"By th' bye," Frank said, suddenly remembering, "I asked Brian to join us, but he said he had business every day this week in Ennis, something about layin' plans for th' next chapter of his life, but he agreed to accompany us to the castle. Ah! And he said to tell you that he won't be long under your feet, for he niver could stand t' be idle."

Frank glanced out the window and noticed the gardener leaning on his rake. "There's McHendrie usin' his rake as a bleedin' prop again. I'm off to give him a list of things he's to knock off whilst we're out tomorra. I hired him as all-round handyman as well as gardener. If he doesn't get those saddles and leathers oiled, they'll rot with th' damp." Frank charged out the door then, making a beeline for McHendrie.

As soon as the manager left, Barry seized Rob's hand, pulling him up the stairs, down the hallway, and into her room. She shut the door before speaking in a whisper. "Did you see!"

"What?"

"That woman would make a great international spy."

Rob lifted a brow questioningly.

Barry spoke in a low, rapid whisper. "She was lurking behind the kitchen door, listening to every word you and Frank said. I don't know about you, but, personally, I don't trust either of them."

***

"Oh, Rob, I don't know if I can do this. It feels so strange. Especially trying to shift gears with my left hand." Barry sat behind the wheel of the rental car, as the two of them started out of the manor house carpark and down the tree-lined lane to the main road.

"Of course you can do it. If you're nervous because you think I'll shout at you or scoff at your mistakes, I assure you I have no intentions of doing either."

I swear Rob and I can read each other's minds. "Oh, I'll make mistakes. I just hope they're not too grievous. I figure, though, if I'm only doing about twenty-five miles per hour, I'm not going to hurt us. Or anyone else."

"Mistakes are how you learn, luv. You're doing fine. I trust you with my life. See," he said, leaning back in the seat and stretching his legs out in front of him, "I'm relaxed and content with you behind the wheel."

Barry let out her breath, and a little smile curved her full mouth. "Robert Phillip Carroll, you are a treasure. Do you know that?"

He considered her fine profile a moment. "Am I?"

"Yes. You have a way of treating me ... graciously, that makes me feel regal, like a great lady."

Rob leaned over and kissed her cheek. "You are not only a great lady, you are *my* lady. It's very easy to have faith and confidence in you, not to mention other, more intense feelings. You will be drivin' as if you learned here, in no time at all, at all. Of that, I am quite sartain."

"I'll try, Rob." They were coming to a crossroads.

"Stay on this route. It'll take us past Knappogue Castle; you've not seen it as yet."

Barry nodded, keeping her gaze fixed on the rural road stretching through the undulating, green countryside ahead of her. "I feel more relaxed already."

"Sure 'n it takes a bit of gettin' used to, like anything else." He gazed out the window for a few moments, silent. "As for the string of mysteries at Barry Hall, well, we've a sayin' here in Ireland, 'Trust to Time to set matters straight.' I'm of the opinion that old saying holds a riot of truth. Here comes a lorry, stay to the left ... well done!"

Eight kilometers later, they came to the castle.

"Would you like to stop and have a look-round?" Rob asked.

"I'm just starting to get the hang of this. Let's keep driving for now." With only a minimum of difficulty, Barry shifted gears and rolled to a full stop at yet another crossroads. "Which way now?"

"Take R 462 south. We'll drive down to Sixmilebridge. It's a pretty little village I think you'll enjoy seeing. Have-a care to stay to the left now, for this road is quite narrow and somewhat windin'. 'Tis th' proper speed you're doin', hold her there, for we may have t' yield, now and again, to a herd of sheep. Ver-ry nice, ver-ry nice."

Barry smiled to the soothing timbre of Rob's voice as she eased the car onto the rural road south. *Bill would have yelled at me at least fifty times by now, picking on every little thing he could. He'd have laughed and said my learning to drive here was hopeless too. Anything to make me feel inferior, so that he could better **control** me. Control was his thing. I know now that was the only way he could feel like a man.*

"What a difference," Barry whispered, she thought, to herself.

"Sorry?" Rob asked.

"Just thinking aloud. How am I doing?"

"You are perfection," he answered.

An old lady, dressed entirely in black, a worn shawl over her shoulders, was walking along the road, coming toward them. She struggled under the weight of two heavy baskets laden with purchases from the nearby village. "Pull over, luv." After the car came to a stop, Rob jumped out and went to the woman and spoke to her. Within a few moments, he was putting the baskets into the boot of the car and helping the matronly wayfarer into the backseat.

"This is Mrs. O'Laughlin, Barry. I told her we'd be happy to take her to her home. Turn round, and steady on, down this road. 'Tis but four or five kilometers back the way we've come."

"Now I know who y' aire! The new owner of the manor! Ah, ye'r th' talk of the county, you aire." The old woman smiled, pleased that she had recognized her rescuer.

Rob turned halfway in the seat to face Mrs. O'Laughlin. "I am, am I?"

"Aye. I'm a nosy old biddy; 'tis th' blather round the pubs. You and your gardener ... once removed. Poor ole Tom. Some folks aire sayin' 'tis queer that he died– not havin' been sick a day in his life– so sudden like. And right after your uncle passed. I'll be rememberin' him. Not an easy man t' forget, that one! Accordin' t' some, a ver-ry snappish man … shockin' rude sometimes, yer uncle. There were some round here who resented that rudeness, and there were those who did not, because he was s' rich. Oh, there's lots of waggin' tongues, but not much sense bein' made from all of it. There *is* a piece of it, though, I should pass on t' *you*. D'ye remember a lad, 'bout your age, name o' Tim Callahan? The other evenin' in th' Shillelagh, your name came up, with Callahan *roarin'* that th' last thing we needed round here was an absentee landlord."

Rob raised a brow, a tad taken aback.

"Aye, that's what he called ya." Mrs. O'Laughlin nearly shouted. "Black words, those! I didn't hear the entire conversation, mind– and some would say 'twas only th' liquor talkin'– but *I'd* wager he's holdin' a *mean* grudge against **you**, boy-o."

Barry's troubled eyes met with those of the woman in the rearview mirror.

Mrs. O'Laughlin, however, quickly looked to Rob, who again raised a quizzical brow. "Tim Callahan … I vaguely recall the name, but I can't put a face to it."

"He's the manager over t' the O'Brien place. An' I hear he's t' be the new Master of the Hunt for the Shannon Blazers." The elderly woman adjusted her shawl. "Pull over Lass; I'm gettin' out here."

Rob shrugged. "I've hardly met the man. I wouldn't know what he'd have against me."

Barry brought the car to a rolling stop at a narrow lane leading to a tidy, whitewashed cottage nestled, just a few feet distant, among a bounty of rose bushes, a few late blooms showing faded red, pink, and yellow. Rob lightly exited the vehicle and opened the door for their loquacious passenger.

"I'll be thankin' ye for th' ride, lad. Sure 'tis an angel ye aire to help an old woman like me." Rob moved to the boot of the car and lifted out her baskets. She took the parcels from him. Her lively pea-green eyes, peering over her spectacles, fastened on his, and in a low tone murmured for his ears only, "Ya can't keep any secrets round here, laddie. Somethin' 'bout a feisty redhead perhaps?" She gave a little chuckle, turned and started up the short path to her cottage.

Rob stood for a reflective moment, looking after Mrs. O'Laughlin. "And I know just the redhead," he muttered to himself.

When they were again alone, Barry reached over and placed her hand over Rob's. "Yet another thing to guard against. Rob, this is getting *really* unsettling!"

"Ho, now! Don't go gettin' yourself unduly frightened over something like that. Pub blather is common in these parts. Trust me on this. It means next to nothing. Now let's get back to your drivin'. I must say you have nearly mastered th' skill of it!"

She threw her arms around Rob and kissed him, her mind taking a reeling detour to a slippery Pittsburgh road nearly a year earlier:

It was getting dark; Bill was driving, Barry in the passenger seat, as they headed to her apartment from a nearby restaurant, where they had just had dinner. Frozen sleet and rain made the familiar road a nightmare as vehicles fishtailed and skidded over the glazed surface of what was commonly referred to as "black ice." Suddenly a paperboy stepped out to cross at the curb, as Bill ran the red light just as it changed. Though they did not hit the boy, he fell. Barry had screamed, but the controlling William Lawrence refused to go back. By the time they arrived at her place, Bill was so thoroughly angered by her crying– he had called her crude names and shouted at her at the top of his voice the entire rest of the way home– that, upon entering the privacy of the apartment, he struck her hard across the face with the back of his hand.

She kissed Rob again, snuggling into the masculine curve of his shoulder. *Please let me be seeing what is **really** there this time. I am such a dreamer, such a hopeless, incurable, as they say, romantic, that I only ever see what I want– **hope**– is there. Please let me be right this time. **This time** I have got to be right!*

"What was that for?" He began kissing her neck before she could reply.

"For being a good Samaritan." Tears stood in her dark eyes.

"If my mother were alive and in need, I would hope someone would stop and help her. Or you, for that matter. I would hope that–"

I'm right what I'm thinking, because ... "You are a treasure," Barry repeated, kissing him again. "An absolute treasure." To herself, she added, *and worth every risk I am taking!*

***

"You keep focused on that *windfall*, and never mind the risks. That's *my* department."

The rambling ruins of the ancient friary were witness again to the shadow-men as they stood among the gravestones, scattered helter-skelter across the dark, lonely churchyard. Near to where the two men stood, plotting their next foul deed, an owl in a hawthorn tree hooted thrice.

"Listen … did you hear that? Restless spirits roam these hills, 'n that wasn't a good omen. Reminds me … let's see now; how does it go?" He snapped his fingers. "'Alone and warming his five wits, the white owl in the belfry sits.'"

"Are you turnin' daft on me?" The taller of the two dark figures hissed, waving, with violent gesture of hand and arm, his partner in crime to silence. "I'm startin' to wonder just what's sittin' in *your* belfry!"

Choosing to ignore the affront, the shorter entity glanced nervously around. The moon had risen, and the place was bathed in a ghostly, pale light. "Perhaps that's *just* what I am … *daft!* Murder's a bit of a sticky wicket, what! I don't know how you ever talked me into this. You said–"

"Bugger what I said! You listen to me, you *eejit.* You're in this muck now just as deeply as I am. *One body each.*"

The stubbier figure groaned. "Don't remind me."

"I'll be remindin' you t' keep your wits about you! Never mind the friggin' owls! As for tomorrow night, I've already formed a plan. Even worked out a back-up scheme, depending on how it plays. And *you,"* the taller shade pointed a long finger at his accomplice, "you just continue to play out your role."

"What do you think I'm about?" The shorter shadow pulled himself up to his fullest height. "Larry Olivier could do no better!"

"Right, I'll see to it you get an award. Just don't get carried away. Everything's going smoothly for us."

"Thus far."

"Always the pessimist."

"Not always. I've never stepped out of character."

The taller shadow poked the squat silhouette in the chest with that long, warning finger, emphasizing each of his words. "That would be bleedin' deadly. Bleedin' deadly," he repeated, his voice taking on an even more sinister timbre.

As if on cue, the owl hooted three times over, and the bare hawthorn branches, as the moon shifted from behind the clouds, took on a portentous, skeletal appearance.

Chapter Nine

"B'hold the ancient Cliffs of Moher! They rise nearly seven hundred feet above th' roarin' sea. 'Tis a grand sight!" Frank exclaimed proudly with the familiar sweeping gesture of his arm. "Look at all those birds … gulls, puffins, ravens, thousands of them. They build th'r nests in th' limestone cliff walls." At that, several boisterous gulls swept gracefully past on an accommodating current of sea air. "Ah, gives new meanin' to the phrase 'free as a bird,' doesn't it? *Free as a bird,"* he repeated dreamily to himself, as he gazed out over the magnificent vista.

Barry, Rob and Frank stood on the footpath atop the moss-covered Atlantic edge, like the Fates at the rim of the world, overlooking the foaming breakers. The sheer, rough-hewn cliffs stretched, like a dark, jagged finger, over nine kilometers out into the endless ocean.

"Th' Cliffs are like we Irish. Forces can hammer us f'r centuries, but nothing can destroy us!" Frank's denim-blue eyes flashed, and his salt-and-pepper hair blew fiercely back from his face, his usually booming voice greatly diminished by the might of surf and wind.

With her hand in Rob's, Barry gasped at the natural drama surrounding her: the tempestuous fury of the foaming, grey-green breakers crashing with violent force against the majestic cliffs, the spray ofttimes as high as modern skyscrapers; the wild shrieks of the soaring, swooping sea birds; the shimmering brilliance of lush green moss leading to O'Brien's Tower in the misty distance.

And the green! Green was everywhere, in every conceivable shade, not only in the trees and grass but in the very air– a verdant glow filled with magick. "Rob, it's as though someone carpeted this whole island with glittering emeralds."

"In a way, Someone did," he returned.

The wind lashed her long dark hair about her face, its salty breath stinging her skin and her eyes. From a pocket of her trench coat, she took out a tissue and dabbed at a tear.

"You all right, luv?" Rob nearly shouted, though he stood close, giving her hand a squeeze.

"I'm not sure if it's the wind or the *power* of this place. It's–" she raised her arms, spinning round and shouting with the sheer delight of doing so, "wild and wonderful and … terrible, and so incredibly beautiful!" She breathed in the tangy sea smells, grasping Rob's wide shoulders, dizzy and a little drunk on the magickal nectar of the Old Ones, on whom Frank had expounded on the way up the winding cliff road. The wind whipped; the waves crashed, and whitecaps and sea foam emerged all around them.

Rob laughed with her, wrapping his arms tightly about her and kissing her firmly on the mouth. "Steady on, now! The cliff edge is no place to stand when a thunderous sea batters it. On a day like this, th' fury of th' wind n' sea can whip pebbles the size of golf balls up from the strand, hundreds of feet below us. A heavy rain, like we had last night, can loosen parts of the cliff edge and send us plummeting into the Atlantic. It's happened." He pointed. "See those warning signs?"

"Aye!" Frank shouted. "*Signs.* 'Tis a *banshee* wind today, so it is. Listen to th' sound 'n fury of her!" He cocked his head, and his vivid blue eyes took on a wild look. "D'ya hear her? There's nothin' like th' cry of the banshee. It chills ye'er bones!"

A gust shrieked eerily past Barry's ear, carrying on it the unearthly notes of the flutes and tinwhistles from the Irish musicians she had remarked along the steep cliff road. "What's a *banshee*?" she asked with a sudden shiver, grasping Rob's arm.

Ignoring the question, Rob gestured north, toward a dark gothic structure in the distance. "The tower! Let's walk up to it!"

The trio started up the path leading along the jagged cliff top toward the highest point.

"Th' *banshee*," Frank explained, "is the white faerie woman who keens in the wind, portending a death, a death hovering–" he stopped suddenly on the path, looking up at the rapidly darkening sky and pointing, "like those ravens there– yet another omen– what we call Death's shadow."

Barry stood between Frank and Rob at the cliff edge. Behind them in the distance, at the approximate midpoint of Moher's jagged finger, was the gothic outline of O'Brien's Tower, its stone walls dark and forbidding against the backdrop of infinite sky and sea.

"This was good today, Frank." Rob's amber gaze took in the resplendence of their surroundings. "I had nearly forgotten how it is here ... so–"

"Mystical," Barry finished. "There is something *mystical* about this place ... about Ireland. I can't explain it. There were places we visited today that sent forth a strong feeling of another world. Of a very old world, long past. Even the wind seems to whisper of ancient secrets."

"Aye," Frank intoned, the wild look leaping once again to his eyes, as he reached inside the inner pocket of his jacket. "And there are some things destined to remain just that– *secrets.* Secrets forever."

***

"What if we can never go home again?" Raine stared out the side window of the rental car, at the passing, late-afternoon scenery. "Never to see our loved ones again, our cats, the horses … our home." She groaned. "I've not been sleeping. And I should *know* better!"

Maggie glanced over at her cousin from her position behind the wheel. "That is *not* going to happen. Let's just make sure we don't get separated from one another."

"What!" Raine turned her fervent gaze on Maggie. "Do you think *that* could happen?"

"I hope not."

"Maggie, we've got to stop this!" Raine nearly shouted. "Do you hear what we're doing? We're just liable to end up imprisoning ourselves with our own negativity. The bars we're building around us, we're creating with fear, and we both know that's *the* greatest negative– and the most destructive."

Maggie did not respond. Her eyes were fixed on the road, but her fine profile told Raine she was in total agreement.

"Ok, let's get back on track. We both know the Great Secret responds to thoughts, no matter what they are, so we've got to stay focused on the positive. We've worked hard. We've done all our homework– years of intense, meticulous research! All we have to do now is keep our minds fixed on our goal, on the end result. This is the quintessence of 'mind over matter.' And we're experts at that old game! We've nothing, absolutely nothing, to fear! In fact, it's just as FDR once said– 'The only thing we have to fear is Fear itself!'"

"That's what I love about you, Raine. You're a great cheerleader." Maggie flashed her cousin a warm smile. "I'm *positive* … we can do this!" She drove for a few moments in silence, then asked abruptly, "Where *are* we anyway?"

Raine lifted the map from the console, studying it in the fading light. "Pull over. I can't really tell."

In a moment, Maggie guided the car off the road and switched off the ignition. Heads together, the two women perused the map of County Clare. "Didn't that guidebook say that the medieval banquets are nightly at Bunratty Castle?"

Raine reached down and picked up a paperback travel book, opening it to an earmarked page. "Yep, nightly." She tilted the open guide toward Maggie, who read the information on the illustrated leaf.

"I'm getting hungry, aren't you? I vote we go to Bunratty and take in the festivities. It'll be fun, and it will help take our minds off our impending mission, not to mention boost our dwindling spirits and put us back on a positive track." She glanced at the antique gold watch pinned to the lapel of the deep-purple blazer she was wearing, then ducked her head a bit so she could see the threatening sky. "Wind's rising, and it's getting dark. I hope we're not in for a storm. We'll have time to check into a hotel first. What say you, the Old Ground?"

"A noble establishment. You've got my vote on both counts," Raine answered, settling back into the seat.

"Right!" Maggie started the car and eased back onto the road, while her cousin opened her purse, extracted compact and lipstick and executed a quick makeup repair.

With her fingers, Raine fluffed her short, black hair. Then she lowered her window and breathed deeply. "Oh, ye-ah, I can smell it. I love storms!" After they had gone a mile or so, her hand sought the ancient talisman around her neck. Tranquility filled her. "The lady said, 'Safe passage,'" she stated; "everything will work out the way it's supposed to. It's drawing nigh to *Samhain*. The veil between the worlds grows thinner each night. I can *feel* it in the air. In the night. You know, Mags, out of the blue, I have an overwhelming feeling this banquet will prove more interesting than we might think." Raine smiled, and her glittering green eyes danced. "The guidebook says there'll be bagpipes, and you know how they always buck me right up! Tell me again what you heard the lady say as she faded. I like to hear it on your voice."

"With the magick inside each of you, go thee, now, and unlock the great Secret of Time. Go– and meet thy destiny!"

In the public room at Barry Hall, Nora Dillon, dressed in mufti, paced before the window, stopping every once in awhile to look out onto the circular drive in front of the house, or at the niggling ticking clock on the mantel above the fireplace. This evening, the only fire burning at the manor was the one inside the housekeeper as she continued her vigil at the window.

Dressed in flannel slacks, turtleneck sweater, and a navy-blue blazer, Brian sat in one of the room's Morris chairs, nursing a drink. "It's after seven. I'm beginning to think you're right. Something's gone amiss."

Outside, the sound of a car engine sent Nora flying into the foyer. The opened door revealed Frank, his face anxious, coming up the curved stone steps.

"Well?" Nora's face was a thundercloud, as her fists found her ample hips.

Scowling, Frank maneuvered Nora back into the foyer. "Hush, woman." Through the opened door, Nora saw Barry and Rob coming up the front steps, Rob wiping his hands with a greasy rag. "Sorry we're late." He sent her a little-boy grin. "Did Frank tell you? We had a flat."

Nora shot her husband a look of vexation. Hands clenched at her sides, her voice held in check, Nora replied, her eyes sweeping the trio in the hall, "Tea's been and gone. You've but an hour to have a wash-up, dress, and get to th' castle."

Rob saluted. "Yes, m'am." He took Barry by the arm, and the pair hurried up the stairs to their rooms. At her door, Barry whispered, "Rob, did you notice? She seemed almost surprised to see us. And did you see how Frank was desperately trying to keep her from saying something?"

Rob shrugged, thoughtful. "I did. However, let's not rush to judgment. I hope that photo Frank took at the top of the cliffs turns out. It should be *dramatic*, to use your word. We'd better hurry. Whoever's dressed first, rap on the other's door."

He started away, dashed back and caught her just before she stepped inside her room. Taking her face between his hands, he entangled his fingers in her wind-tousled hair, kissing her, then he quickly entered his own room, closing the door after him.

For a long, radiant moment, Barry stood leaning against the door jam, in the wake of that kiss, which had been at once tender and sensual.

She had no sooner started to undress, when a knock sounded at the door. "Rob! I have to get ready!"

"It's Máire, m'am. Mrs. Dillon sent me up to assist you."

"Oh, good!" Barry opened the door, holding before her the sweater she had just removed. "Come in, Máire. What do people wear to these castle affairs anyway?"

Her shower, makeup and hair done, Barry emerged from the bathroom, wearing lacy black undergarments. She saw that Máire had laid out a long knit dress in a forest green trimmed in black frogging. Barry quickly pulled on a pair of sheer taupe pantyhose and slipped into the garment Máire held for her, which buttoned completely down the front, the tiny buttons covered with the same wool fabric as the dress itself. Next, she slid her feet into a pair of black suede pumps, then donned a matching forest green headband for her mane of dark auburn hair. "Máire, could you bring me that little jewel case? There," she pointed, "on the nightstand."

The maid handed her the scarlet silk case. Barry selected a heavy gold bangle, sliding it on her arm, and a pair of plain gold hoops for her ears. While she was putting in the earrings, a rap came at the door.

"Is it safe to come in?" Rob called from the hall.

"Yes, I'm ready. You're looking dapper this evening, Mr. Carroll!" she exclaimed to Rob when the door opened. Turning to Máire, she asked, "Please get that long black shawl out for me. That's the one, thank you."

Dressed in grey flannel slacks, Aran-knit sweater, and a tweed jacket that Barry noted complimented his golden topaz eyes, Rob entered, and the little maid bobbed a curtsey. "Doesn't she look lovely, sir?"

Coming forward and kissing her cheek, Rob whispered in Barry's ear, "You are a vision." He inhaled her perfume, reminiscent of the scent of jasmine. "Máire," he began hoarsely, "go and tell them we'll be down in a minute."

As soon as the maid left the room, Rob pulled a small, black velvet box from the pocket of his sport coat. "This was my mother's," he said, raising the lid. "I want you to have it."

"Oh, Rob … your mother's? What is it?"

"Let's open it and see." He extended the box toward her, removing a dainty gold harp encrusted with tiny, sparkling diamonds. "The symbol of Ireland," he said softly.

"It's beautiful!" Her eyes shimmered with tears. "Oh, Rob, I'll treasure it forever." *How I love this good man. I never ever want to be without him.*

"Let me pin it on for you." He started to do so, but, fearful he would jab her with the pin, he began undoing the top buttons of her dress, so that he could more easily secure the brooch to the bodice. The intimacy of this, in combination with the way she looked, the scent of her, her full breasts nearly spilling from the scraps of black lace that was her bra, proved too much for him, and he began kissing her, his mouth traveling down her neck. She whispered his name, her shaking breath warm and sweet.

Their breathing was such that neither noticed Nora in the doorway, until the housekeeper coughed. Startled, they both turned, still in their embrace, to see, like a dash of icy water, her severe, reproachful expression.

Before disappearing from view, she chided, "Frank has the motor runnin'."

Rob whispered into Barry's ear, "So did I." However, when a blushing Barry broke away to button her dress and repair her lipstick, he muttered, looking out the door, "Blast th' woman!"

To Rob, Barry whispered, feigning a brogue, "Sure 'n didn't y' have me purrin' too, Mr. Carroll."

Ensconced in the backseat of Frank's Ford, between Rob and Brian, Barry, with such dignity as she could rally, was still feeling the flush of embarrassment. In the front next to Frank, a peeved Nora sat with her mouth pursed in disapproval, as the car rolled out of the circular drive. To the right of the lane, a smiling McHendrie was leaning on his rake. He raised his hand in farewell, and Frank paused the car, winding down the window. "Don't forget about those saddles."

"No, 'tis at th' top of me list."

Frank nodded, wound up the window, and the Ford started off again. Barry turned to see McHendrie check his watch before leaning again on his rake, as he stood, looking pleasantly after them.

"'Tis a good thing th' castle is but a couple o' minutes away," Nora fretted, "or we'd never make th' before-dinner festivities. The music is the evenin's best offerin'."

"I'm anxious to get there myself," Brian responded with a wicked little grin to Barry, "as you may have guessed, I've been in dry-dock too long."

Chapter Ten

The echoing skirl of bagpipes greeted the arriving guests. As the group walked toward Bunratty from the carpark, Barry stopped on the path to gaze at the Gothic castle, colossal grey against the night-blue sky, its narrow slit windows glowing golden, a huge Irish tricolor waving proudly from its highest tower. Round about, the tree-sprinkled grounds, too, were romantically lighted. Pipers and castle personnel in colorful courtly attire were positioned on either side of the entrance, as well as at the drawbridge.

"There's nothing modern," Barry mused aloud, "a glimpse, and I am whisked back to that medieval world of knights and fair ladies. How old is this castle? Oh my, it even has a moat!"

"Bunratty's fifteenth-century. Wait till you see inside. It's completely restored to its ancient grandeur, furnishings and all." Rob took her hand in his, his eyes doing magickal things to her. "Tonight you *shall* be whisked back in time, my love."

"Know something? I've always loved bagpipes. But I thought pipers *blew* into them," Barry remarked.

"They do in the war pipes, the Great Highlands. These are the Irish pipes, *pib uilleann*, literally 'elbow pipes.' The pipers use the elbow to pump in the air, then force it out. See," he indicated the pipers at the bridge.

Her gaze swept the scene, soaking in as much of the fanciful ambiance as she could. "This is all so romantic. In Pittsburgh, if something is two hundred years old, it's *old*. But here, we're talking centuries and centuries."

On the path ahead of them, Nora, Frank and Brian waited. "Centuries and centuries," the housekeeper repeated. "That's how long it's takin' us t' get in there."

"Come on, you love birds." Brian took Barry's other arm, and the group proceeded to the entry of the drawbridge.

"Oh, no!" Nora stopped abruptly, nearly causing Barry, just behind her, to trip.

"What in th' name of all th' saints is th' matter?" Frank all but shouted.

For the umpteenth time that night, the housekeeper appeared rattled. "I f'rgot m' purse. Ye'll have to go back f'r it. We won't be able to get in. The tickets are in that purse!"

Reaching into the inner pocket of his sports coat, Frank produced the tickets with a theatrical flourish. "No, m' lady, I took them out of your purse before we left … and a good thing too!"

"Y' still have t' go back f'r my purse!"

"Why, pray tell?" Frank flicked the held-up vouchers with a thumb, "I have the tickets."

Nora's voice took on a sugar Barry, for one, had never before heard. "Now Frank, be a darlin'. My medicine, my eyeglasses, y' know I need them. Th' purse is in th' carriage house, on the stand by th' door."

"What th' divil d'ya need ye'er glasses f'r? An' you kin take ye'er ruddy medicine win we return!"

In a flash, Nora's face and demeanor changed. "Off with you!" she shushed.

Frank cringed, embarrassed before the others.

Barry turned away, whispering to Rob behind her hand, "Now that's the Nora we all know and love."

"Bloody hell," Frank muttered, handing the tickets to Rob. "Go on inside, lads, with th' ladies and enjoy th' festivities. I'll be back in jig-time." Frank hurried off in the direction of the carpark, while the rest of the party continued across the drawbridge to the joyful skirl of the pipes

At the castle entrance, the host, dressed in fifteenth-century hose and doublets, greeted them with a sweeping bow, "M' lords. M' ladies." In the gallant fashion of that bygone era, he offered each a piece of bread, dipped in salt. "For safe stay and journeys."

Before partaking, Barry murmured to Rob, "*We* should ask for the whole loaf."

At that moment, a striking colleen with flowing chestnut hair, dressed in a puffed-sleeved, emerald velvet gown, came forth to usher them into the Great Hall. Now it was Brian's turn to whisper an aside to Barry, "Journeys end in lovers meeting."

Spellbound, Barry stood inside the great castle, looking about. Flaming wall sconces illuminated the vast reception hall, where gowned serving wenches moved amid the merry guests, pouring goblets of mead. Medieval tapestries and weaponry, suits of armor, authentic furnishings, and three magnificent Irish wolfhounds set the enchanting scene– and mood– releasing a myriad of faerie-tale fantasies across the fertile field of her writer's imagination.

To hold the autumnal cold at bay, fires roared in enormous twin hearths at opposite ends of the Great Hall, and in the background, two harpers, in scarlet and sapphire velvets, sat caressing their instruments so that the gilded harps "sang with the wind," providing period music.

"Rob, this is wonderful. I was afraid it would be … oh, I don't know, carnival or commercial. It's anything but."

He kissed her cheek. "I told you it would be a magick-carpet ride into the past."

"Don't you like your mead?" Rob queried, noting that Barry had hardly touched her drink.

She wrinkled her nose. "Bit too sweet for me. What's in it?"

"Honey," Rob replied. "You don't have to drink it. I'll get you a mineral water."

"Oh no, don't bother." Barry glanced around. "Nora, where did Brian go? He's been so quiet tonight."

"Be right back." Rob started off in the direction of the arched doorway through which they had just passed.

"Here he comes." Nora indicated Brian, who was walking toward them.

"Sorry," he began. "Seems that gorgeous damsel is married. More's th' pity. Hul-lo!" He sent a wink across the way to a bouncy little blonde, who received it with promise.

When the saucy minx returned Brian's wink, Nora pursed her mouth, muttering under her breath, "Hussy."

About to comment, Barry felt a tap on her shoulder. Turning around, she faced two women, both pleasing to look at, both dressed attractively and holding golden goblets of mead.

"Excuse me," the taller, flame-haired lady smiled, "but … aren't you … I'm sorry, I can't, for the life of me, remember your name; please forgive me. I know it begins with a 'B.'"

"Baranya Bartok!" the other woman, petite and raven-haired, supplied with a snap of her bejeweled fingers.

"We're going to be terribly embarrassed if you aren't," the redhead remarked, but–"

"I am." Barry offered her hand. "You sound like Americans, but is it possible you're from Pittsburgh too?"

"Maggie McDonough," the taller woman with the fiery locks said, grasping Barry's hand in a firm shake, "and this is my cousin,

Raine McDonough. We're from Haleigh's Hamlet. It's less than an hour southeast of Pittsburgh. We've seen you so often on TV, on the news, that we simply *had* to come over and speak to you."

"I'm glad you did," Barry smiled, lighting up. "I know the Hamlet! A cluster of old Victorian, castle-like homes, lots of stained glass, gingerbread, and old money. A historic little college town, the Hamlet and the college both named for, if I remember correctly, a coal mogul's wife, whose family endowed both the college and the theatre. It was one of the first stories I did when I started working at the station. It really *is* a small world, isn't it? I especially remember your community theatre. Right out of a faerie-tale ... *gorgeous* sylvan-lake setting, but I can't recall the name. *Shady* something, or is it–"

"Whispering Shades," Maggie supplied.

"'The little theatre in the woods,'" Raine added, quoting from the theatre's flyer.

"I loved it there when I did my research. "Don't the locals say the theatre's haunted?"

"Oh, we most definitely have a resident ghost!" Maggie laughed. "And she's a very protective ole gal!"

Catching sight, with her peripheral vision, of a curious Nora, she quickly amended, "Forgive me. This is Nora Dillon, and Brian Carroll."

Tearing his gaze away from the very receptive– Barry had noticed– blonde guest with whom he had been making eye contact, Brian bestowed on the two Americans his most winning smile, his eyes devouring them. "Delighted."

"I'm beginning to wonder what's happened to Rob," Barry said, scanning the hall. "And Frank's not back yet either. I hope he hasn't had car trouble again."

Nora mumbled something inaudible, casting Barry one of her withering looks.

Barry released her breath slowly, ignoring the housekeeper's veiled dig. "I can't help thinking that something is wrong." She peered round her two fellow Pennsylvanians, talking more to herself than anyone. "It's like everything else of late– *an enigma, a mystery.*"

Maggie and Raine immediately exchanged poignant glances. "Seems it's found us," Raine said, nudging her cousin.

"Wherever we go," Maggie replied under her breath.

"And right on cue," Raine confirmed *sotto voce*, a smile curving her crimson lips.

Nearly together, Nora and Barry, turning toward them, asked, respectively: "What did you say?" "Sorry?"

"Well," Raine began, "we're kind of famous where we're from, in our own little *environ*."

"You see," Maggie continued, "we seem to be magnets for mysteries. In fact, the folks in our hometown have nicknamed us the 'Sleuth Sisters.'"

"And," Raine added, "the soubriquet has proven rather ... *à propos*."

Brian, who had just sent the blonde object of his attentions another enamored signal, shot a surprised look at the "Sisters." "You're detectives?"

Raine gave a short laugh, the dimple in her left cheek deepening. "Oh no, college professors." She made an airy little gesture, with her ringed fingers, to herself, "American history and Celtic legend and lore," then to Maggie, "archaeology and history."

Brian's practiced eye studied the attractive pair– the sassy, green-eyed Raine with her intense eye makeup; short, raven hair, the long, jagged bangs dipping alluringly over one eye, the cut reflective of her gamine personality; and the voluptuous, sexy Maggie with eyes the same vivid hue and tip-tilted shape, and hair as fiery as her essence. "I never had teachers like you when I was in school. If I had, I'd probably be a lifelong scholar. More like film stars, I'd say." His amorous gaze took in the women surrounding him. "I feel as though I'm in a lovely flower garden, the blooms so colorful, so contrasted– and each a work of art."

"A *hungry bee* in a flower garden," Maggie whispered to Raine. "Reminds me acutely of my ex."

"Now, you," he said, gesturing to Raine, then picking up her hand and kissing it, "are downright enchanting. Utterly mysterious. His eyes swept over her, taking in the black, stand-up collar of the Gothic-style dress she was wearing, the long sleeves coming to points over the tops of her slim, ringed fingers tipped with glossy black nails. "The way you dress ... *witchy*. Uh-huh, a real witchy-woman here. It suits you ... and causes men to wonder about you." He seemed to study her for a long moment. "I'd wager you can turn that personality of yours on and off at will. You can retire into yourself when you want to be aloof, and then, suddenly, a turn of the head, a graceful movement of the hands, the smile, the dimple– and the spell is cast. Ah-huh! There! You see! And you," he shifted his focus to Maggie, kissing her hand while his gaze skimmed the deep décolleté of the vintage, forties-film-noir, black cocktail dress she was wearing with its sheer bodice and sleeves, "are as alluring a woman as ever I've encountered– a sorceress who can bewitch a man with a look." The blue of his eyes seemed to deepen to cobalt, "Yes, ver-ry much so– *'tis Gilda you are*! I'm totally seduced by the sorcery of you both. Indaid, I am. Your eyes ... as I said– *spellbinding!*"

Maggie turned to Raine, rolling her bright emerald peepers, the gesture causing the latter to stifle a snigger.

"Barry, *our Barry*," Brian continued, oblivious to the Sleuth Sisters' scorn, "is sultry, seductive. We don't need to dwell on that, or my brother will have my head. And Nora ... ah, Nora is like a fine wine. She continues to improve with age."

The housekeeper relinquished a half-smile.

"Nora, darlin', you should smile more often. Haven't I always told you that? Bliss becomes you." Brian sipped his drink, and his attention reverted back to the Sleuth Sisters. "I don't mean to pry, but shouldn't you be in the classroom this time of year?"

"Usually we are," Maggie responded, "but we're working on a doctorate. It's collaboration, and as long as it coincides with the subject matter of the thesis, one is permitted, even encouraged, to travel."

Temporarily distracted from her concern for the absent men, Barry asked, "A doctoral. That's impressive. What's the subject?"

One pair of McDonough green eyes darted to the other. "What a leading question!" Maggie laughed, charmingly sidestepping the question.

"We're not at liberty to say," Raine said after a somewhat uneasy moment, her feline eyes taking in the effect of Brian's polished act on the receptive blonde tourist. "You see, we intend to have it published."

Trained to a career of investigative interviewing, Barry pressed, "Can't you tell us generically, at least, what it's about? You've piqued *my* curiosity."

Again the Sisters looked to one another. "Let's just say it revolves around our history-related travels," Raine offered. You know how obsessed we Irish are with history. We're forever dredging up the glories that stretch back over memory and myth."

"To what specifically," Barry pushed.

The Sisters remained silent.

"Another mystery," Barry laughed. "Just one more clue?"

"Now you have *me* curious too," Nora chimed in. "What *is* it about?"

But the expressions of finality on both their faces left no doubt that Raine and Maggie had closed the door on the subject.

"The mystery is where we're going to stay tonight." Maggie gave Raine a subtle jostle as Brian sent the blonde yet another suggestive look.

"Yes, and I don't fancy sleeping in the rental car." Raine watched the blonde, whose eager gaze had darted to a handsome, russet-haired man, who had begun speaking, with Irish brogue, to a group of newly arrived visitors. Remarking this, Brian moved toward his objective whose shrill voice had elevated in a piercing laugh.

"Have you no hotel?" Barry questioned. She, too, couldn't help noticing the ex-sailor's antics. It looked as though he was just about to reel in his catch.

"We thought we would, but things didn't work out," Maggie answered. "We never thought the Old Ground would be filled this time of year. Convention of some sort." She took a sip of her mead. "Wouldn't you know! And we did so want one of the old noble hotels."

"Perhaps," Barry began, purposefully ignoring Nora's disapproving face, "I can help you with that."

***

The night was especially dark, as clouds scudded across the eerily-ringed moon. Máire Nolan made the Sign of the Cross, stopping on the path through the tangle of trees to Barry Hall. Fragments of things, since childhood, she had heard in whispers about the ghosts of *Samhain* echoed now in her fanciful mind, causing her to further hasten her steps. Never had the woods seemed so eerie, never the familiar footpath to the neighbor's estate so long and twisting.

Remote, dark, and ever-mysterious, the woods lay in watchful silence, the grim quiet broken by the occasional raucous cry of a bird or the groan of a tall, half-fallen tree. Shadows came to life in the thin shaft of her electric torch, and everywhere she imagined eyes– animal, human, or of the netherworld she knew not which– staring at her from the darkness of the surrounding trees. The bare autumnal branches seemed to reach out for her with claw-like hands; and the forest floor of dead leaves, softened by the recent rains, clutched at her feet, preventing her from swift progress.

Try as she did, she could not banish the keen sense that unseen eyes were watching her, and once she even thought she heard an unearthly voice whispered on the wind.

Crossing herself again, she glanced behind her, whispering, as she did, an ardent prayer of protection. A rustling in the brush sent her hand flying to her mouth, and she quickened her steps.

"If I had not forgotten the watch *Da* worked so hard to give me for m' birthday, there's no way I'd be out after dark this close to *Samhain*. No way **at all, at all!**"

Yellow eyes glowed at her, and a sudden, loud flapping of wings caused her heart to skip a beat. The owl hooted, as its sharp talons clung to a low branch, and Máire stopped dead, petrified.

"Sure 'n the veil between the worlds is lifted this night," she breathed.

Then, an unexpected rushing in the underbrush sent her heart and her feet racing. Grasping her ankle-length skirt, she ran in terror, slipping on the wet leaves and nearly falling, face forward, when her foot caught in an exposed tree root. Breathing hard, she continued to run, her silky strawberry-blonde hair blowing about her flushed face.

With her Celtic clairvoyance, the stumbling girl looked, yet again, back over her shoulder, certain she would see grotesque entities on her heels.

I've got to catch me breath. She paused, focusing the narrow beam of light from her torch on the path ahead. A sudden, unearthly sound on the wind froze her blood.

A púca ... **or the banshee!** *God 'n Mary help me! Steady on; 'tis not far now.*

Willing herself to continue walking, she struggled to control her fear by trying to recall where she had last seen the watch.

"I know where I left it! It's in th' old gentleman's bedchamber. I laid it on the dresser when I went t' clean th' bath," she whispered to herself, delighted that she would not have to search the shadowy, empty house for the treasured item.

Ten minutes later, using her key, a shaking Máire let herself into the dark, still manor. Her training as a servant and her natural light step rendered her entrance nearly soundless.

The small circle of light from the flashlight guided her quiet steps to the top floor and the heavy door of old Phillip's suite of rooms. With those thoughts on her mind, she turned the knob and entered the chamber, stopping suddenly.

"Oh, Mr. Carroll, excuse me. I didn't think anyone would be here. Did y' happen to find me watch? I–"

Máire's words caught in her throat, and her face registered fear as the man, partially in shadow, moved menacingly toward her.

"Oh! Nooo … ye'er not–"

A large gloved hand clamped over her mouth. "Well now, lassie, it must've been th' Divil himself who brought you here this night."

***

"Wait a minute! The 'Sleuth Sisters'! Now I remember you!" Barry exclaimed, as she, Nora, and the Sisters were escorted by a brightly robed colleen to one of the long banquet tables in preparation for the first *remouve*. They took their seats, beneath flaming wall sconces. "Yes, the station did a piece on you a couple of years ago. Didn't you aid the police in solving that missing-child puzzle … in White Oak? It had authorities baffled for months."

"That was us," Raine answered. "A most dreadful case."

"You *are* rather famous in our neck of Penn's Woods! Very talented, both of you."

"Something always seems to lead us to the right source when we're in need of answers," Maggie replied modestly.

Again Barry's glance swept the Great Hall. "I'm worried. It doesn't bode well that Rob's been gone all this time, and Frank should have been back at least twenty minutes ago. God only knows where Brian is. Uh-huh, and I notice that little blonde has vanished too."

"Her talons were far-reaching tonight," Maggie remarked, laughing when she noted the expressions on the others' faces. "Raine and I encountered her earlier this week, at Galway. She's a busy little beaver, that one."

The rich odors of roasted meats and savories permeated the hall, and Barry found herself surrounded by the dancing notes of the jigs and reels, her heart pounding with the primal rhythm of the *bodhrán*.

"If they don't get back pretty soon, they'll miss a delicious dinner," Maggie commented, her gaze sweeping over the tempting medieval fare a trio of the costumed wenches were serving the neighboring table.

"Look, no forks, only knives and these little, wooden paddle things," Raine pointed out. "Not to worry, we are to tie on these bibs." She snatched up a green one, fastening it around her neck.

"It'll be rough going, but scads of fun," Maggie laughed. "I've done this before, a few years ago, when I lived in Ireland."

"You lived in Ireland?" Barry asked.

"For several years," Maggie answered. My ex-husband is Irish. We met my senior year in college, which I spent at Trinity. We were married after my graduation."

"I think I know what's keeping Frank," Nora blurted, somewhat disconcerted. "I'm afraid I may not have left the purse on the hall table, as I told him. It may be in our bedroom. I hope he has sense enough to look there." Nora's expression suddenly changed to one of relief. "Speak of th' Divil, and he appears."

In his usual rushing manner, his face flushed scarlet, Frank entered the banquet hall, toting a black leather purse under his arm. He wound his way through the tables toward his group with a mien of unease. The banquet was in full tilt when he sank with exhaustion into the chair next to Nora. "I finally found it," he sighed, exchanging pointed looks with his wife, their faces suddenly taking on sinister masks under the flickering wall sconces.

"Barry, can you forgive me?" Setting a bottle of sparkling water on the table next to her plate, Rob slid into the chair next to her. Leaning over, he kissed her cheek. "You'll never believe this, but I thought I had seen a ghost, and since it's *Samhain*, Hallowe'en to you, I thought I'd better check it out."

Barry sent him a strange look, and he laughed.

"A white hunter I used to know in Kenya." A faraway look passed over Rob's features. "Thought he was dead. I mean I had *heard* that he was. Anyroad, I had to converse with him, luv. He saved my life once." He laughed again. "Always told me I lived a charmed life. I am sorry, Barry, I never meant to stay away that long." He glanced about, his eyes scanning the merry, supping guests. "Where's Brian?"

"Speak th' Divil's name, and he appears," Nora repeated, her grey eyes fixed on the entrance.

Everyone turned to see Brian strutting toward them and looking, for all the world, like the proverbial cat that ate the canary. "Sorry," he said, gracefully slipping into the remaining empty place. "I seemed to have gotten … *waylaid.*"

The others exchanged glances. A few moments later, tousled and her lipstick smeared, the blonde reentered the hall, taking a place, directly behind Maggie and Raine, at table. Leaning over to speak to the female friend seated beside her, the obnoxious woman remarked somewhat theatrically in what was, for her, low tones, "My third– and best– Irishman. Juicy details anon." When her eyes found Brian, the blonde smiled, and he cast her a look sated with secret meaning, blowing her a kiss.

"Looks like she's been 'rode hard and put away wet,'" Maggie quipped under her breath to Raine, who stifled a giggle.

Several minutes later, a group of costumed castle staff burst into song, and Raine abruptly stood, whispering into her cousin's ear. Maggie rose too, and the pair quickly exited the banquet hall. "Nancy Drew comin' through," Raine muttered as they pushed through a press of people.

The cubicles were all occupied when Raine and Maggie entered the "Ladies'." As the pair waited near the door, a familiar shrill voice reached them from one of the stalls. "I couldn't, at first, decide which one I wanted, but you know how partial I am to–"

"Good-night nurse!" a second voice interposed sharply, reaching the Sleuth Sisters from the adjacent cubicle. "What did you have to go and …"

***

"… Kill the bird for?" The shorter of the two shadow-men gasped, his voice taking on a hysterical pitch.

"You've answered it yourself– I had no choice in th' matter. She walked in on me. I couldn't let her talk, now could I?"

"All this killin'! I didn't bargain for it."

"Bit late for that, isn't it?"

"I didn't; I tell you!" In the moon's glow, the shorter figure searched frantically for a smoke. Locating the pack, he extracted a cigarette, and with shaking hands, placed it between his cracked lips.

The taller shadow-figure flicked on and held a lighter, his face a mask of evil in the wavering light, as he bent to shield the flame from the soughing wind. "It's not as if we *planned* t' kill her, now is it?"

In the stillness of the ancient ruins, they could hear the softly rippling stream that separated the friary from St. Finghin's church. "I don't know ... all this killin' ... it's making me barkin' mad! How are we going to make this one look like an accident?! Tell me that!"

The taller shadow shrugged. "No way to do that." His demonic laugh reverberated in the midnight churchyard, the medieval ghosts of Quin witness to his callousness. "I made it look like a rape."

"A rape! This isn't London, Mate!"

"No, for sar-tain it isn't."

The shorter figure, in the eerie moon-and-fog-drenched yard, sent his accomplice a frenzied look, and there was indeed a madness that peered from his eyes, as he exclaimed again, "A rape! Bloody hell! There's most likely never been a rape round here!"

"There has now, or so they will think. The Gards won't conclude anything more than that. They haven't sorted anything out yet; have they? No, and they won't. Stupid sods that they are. And, round about, the pub talk is grist for our mill."

With a bloodcurdling whine, the shorter shadow seemed to sink to a black stump.

"Steady on! I did a first-rate job hidin' th' body. 'Twill be awhile b'fore anyone finds it. That'll work to our advantage. Clues fade with time."

"All this killin'... I'm losing my mind, I tell you!"

"You're playin' your role to perfection. Steady on, I say, and there'll be a bonus in it f'r you."

"I hope we're done with murder now. We've got to end all this killin'!"

In response, a cold, keening wind blew the fog about the pair in wraithlike streams– slithering it round them like something of pure evil.

"No," the more sinister of the two replied, "no, there's one more– *one more yet.*"

Chapter Eleven

The wind had fallen, but from off the sea, a chill permeated the night air. Flickering torch lamps and faerie-lit trees, together with the hunter moon cast golden splashes of light over the shadowy Love Gardens. Through the maze of yew-lined pathways, Barry and Rob strolled, hand-in-hand, as they discussed the mysteries besetting them.

"I still say the strongest clue is the word 'buried.' Barry looked up at Rob's brooding profile. "It's my guess the jewels are *not* in the house."

Rob nodded. "I'm convinced they're buried too ... *somewhere* on this estate. Mind, that includes the gardens, the woods, paddock– where do we begin?"

"A couple of days ago, at breakfast, when you were discussing the diary with Frank, I happened to think of metal detectors. So much has been going on, I haven't had a chance to mention it to you. But I suppose they have been tried."

"Likely, but, over the years, there have been improvements on such equipment. I've already ordered the best there is. Frank will be picking it up early Monday." Rob paused. "What about your job?"

Barry rested a hand on his chest, her eyes fixed on his. "That depends on how you answer my next question. Do you want me to stay?"

His response was to pull her into his embrace and kiss her. "Very much."

Her breath came rather quickly as she replied, "Okay. I'll phone Skinner."

"Are you sure about this, luv? I don't want to be the cause of any lost opportunities."

"There are no lost opportunities," Barry replied, patting his cheek. "Don't you know that?"

"It's settled then!" Rob caught her hand and pressed it to his mouth. "This will mean you'll be here for th' fancy dress ball. Fantastic! But first things first. Tomorrow's Sunday," his face took on a deliciously wicked expression, "I'm sar-tain we'll find something to keep us occupied." He kissed her again. "But come Monday morning, we begin our treasure hunt in earnest. We'll start here, in th' gardens. I don't know why exactly, but I think this is where he buried those elusive jewels, and most likely within the inner, heart-shaped labyrinth. Now," he gave a low laugh, "that narrows it down to about three acres of digging."

"Rob, I hope you're okay about the two Americans. I should have asked you in private if they could stay. You really had no choice but to oblige, the way I put it to you, right in front of them. It's just that, even though I never met them until tonight, we are practically neighbors." She sensed rather than saw his smile.

"Happy to help."

The pair walked on, Barry's face, in the flicker from the torch lamps, mirroring her troubled thoughts.

After a few moments, Rob paused. "Now what's on your mind?"

"*Murder*. And it's not just reporter's instinct. There were no accidents here. Someone wanted those two people dead. We have got to use caution. As impetuous as we both are, we'll need to watch over each other."

"I like the sound of that." He put his arms around her, drawing her close. "You know," he said, kissing her between phrases, "all the puzzles ... all the new people and places ... the banquet ... all this morbid talk about murder. You've had a ver-ry trying time of it. I'd better get you to bed."

A thrill ran through her. "Yes," she answered in a whisper.

He kissed her again, and desire swept all other thoughts from their minds.

Arms around each other, they started back toward the manor, when suddenly Barry stopped, her gaze focused on an upper-floor window of the carriage house across the way. "Look." She squeezed Rob's arm. "It's *her*." The white lace curtain settled, behind which the shadow of a woman was discernible. "Do you really trust them?"

"I do that."

"But in my dream, there were two people–"

"Not those two. Come on." He took her hand, and they exited the gardens.

"Don't let Nora bother you. She is a bit of a meddler, but th' lady has a heart of gold."

"That," Barry concluded, "is what I'm afraid of."

On the huge antique bed, in the warm glow from the fireplace, Barry wrapped her arms around the man with whom she had fallen deeply in love. His kisses were eager, passionate, and as intoxicating as hot, spiced wine. She ran a delicate fingertip across his lower lip, tracing its outline with a butterfly touch. "Have you loved many women, Rob Carroll? No," she amended instantly, "don't tell me. I don't want to know."

He kissed the tip of her finger as it paused on his lips. "I love you," he said, his gaze moving slowly and deliberately over her. "I love everything about you– your beautiful midnight eyes, so full of secrets and promise; your enticing mouth, made for words of love and melting kisses; your hair, so dark, yet so full of lights; your goddess-like body," he teasingly ran his hand over her silky skin, from her neck to the gentle mound of her belly, "and your ardent Gypsy soul."

Her lips parted, and she was blushing again. "As I love everything about you– your thick, ebony mustache, the green-gold of your tiger eyes, your smile. I love the way you smile … as though you are in possession of an amusing secret." She pulled him close, her voice low and silky, "Love me. Love me now."

In an instant her lips were under his, her words melted away by the fire of his kisses. At this moment, there was only the crackling fire, their breathing, and the tiny, pleading noises in her throat. He covered her with kisses, her hands moving restlessly across his back and neck, stroking his hair, caressing, the tips of her fingers conveying her urgency. It seemed the very air in the ancient bedchamber was charged with pulsing heat and energy.

"I love you … I love you so," she whispered again. She had never felt such abandonment. *If we could not have been together tonight, I would surely have died.*

Presently, Barry leaned over and touched his chest with her lips. Their skins, in the fireglow, seemed brushed with gold, and when she spoke, her voice seemed to come from deep within her essence–

"I will be here with you … for as long as you want me."

His kiss wakened her, and she stretched luxuriously, as content as a hearth cat. "Hmmm," she hummed, "how nice to see you when I open my eyes. Let's not get up yet. It's so pleasant just lying here … together." She smiled, and her look was one of open sensuality. *The power of a woman*, and, not to be distracted by her own musings, she stretched again, arching her back, all the while watching him through lowered lashes.

He leaned in with the exquisite slow grace of the tiger that resided in his soul, leveraging his muscular body over hers for a long, anticipating moment– a moment that seemed suspended in time– and though he had not even touched her, he drew her energy to him with his sheer power. This time, their love-making was slower, more leisurely, and somehow more intimate, touching, in each, the inner core– that secret, special place that only true love can ever hope to reach.

"Rob, if ever you tire of me, please tell me; don't keep me hanging on. I know how easily bored you can get … how in need of excitement. I don't think I could stand it if–"

"Are you serious?" He drew back, gazing down at her. "I will never tire of you." His kiss was long and full, and oh, so sweet. "What does that tell you?"

"I want to be everything to you– *everything*."

"Come on now!" Rob delivered an affectionate smack to her bottom, before getting out of bed and heading for the bath. "It's a grand day, and we've lots to do!"

Barry rolled over, put her hands behind her head and replayed their magickal night and morning across her mind and heart. A smile curved her lips, and she basked in the warmth of the memories. From the adjoining bath, she could hear water running as Rob prepared to shave.

"Let's begin with a horseback ride. By that time, Nora will have a hearty meal ready," he called. "Actually, the staff is off today, but Nora has agreed to make us breakfast."

"No!" Barry sat straight up in bed. "No horses! I told you horses would somehow figure into this intrigue."

His face lathered in shaving cream, Rob appeared in the doorway, a towel wrapped around his waist. "Darlin', what are y' goin' to do? Consult th' damn cards every mornin' t' see if it's safe to get out of bed?"

Out of the recesses of her mind, his voice and manner conjured the Barry-Carroll credo– *The Lord hates a coward.* With a sigh, she swung her feet to the floor, stood and moved to the open closet door, pulling on his robe. "If you can find me a pair of boots, I'll do it."

It was after breakfast when Barry, Rob, Raine and Maggie ambled down the path that led to the stable. All four wore breeches,

Aran fisherman sweaters, and high black boots. Except for the sweaters, the riding togs were the property of Barry Hall. Rob hurried on ahead to tack up the horses. The picturesque stone stable was about a quarter-mile from the manor, a scenic tramp through a copse of young beech trees.

"I don't know whether to call my boss after lunch, or if I should wait until late tonight. Perhaps later would be better," Barry reasoned, "my plan being to reach him at home, around seven or eight in the evening, Pennsylvania time. If he's ever in a good mood, it may be after he's had a good Sunday dinner. What do you think I should do?"

"From what you've said about the man," Maggie began, "forget trying to figure a time to make what you have to say more acceptable to him. I'd say you'd be better off giving him *more* time to get someone else to cover that convention for you."

"I agree," Raine said. "Call him right after lunch."

Maggie smiled. "Again, we want to thank you and Rob for providing us with such nice quarters, and for inviting us along this morning. Do you ride much?"

Barry made a wry face. "I had a couple of lessons as a child, and I've gone a time or two at the park, but I'm no *equestrienne*."

"I hope we're not intruding on your private time with Rob," Raine remarked.

"Don't be silly. We *want* you to join us." *You don't know how much. I figure Rob won't be too daredevil with you two along.*

"We appreciate it. As much as we like to travel, we do miss our horses when we're away," Raine replied.

Maggie nodded. "And the cats."

"You have your own horses?" Barry ventured. "I suppose you ride pretty well then," she added, biting her lower lip.

Raine dimpled. "Honey, we could ride before we could walk. My, what a charming stable!"

Barry forged a smile, but it came off as just that.

Maggie laughed. "Raine's my first cousin, though, since childhood, we've been more like sisters, and I can tell you, she's been known to stretch the truth. We didn't start riding till we were about four or five."

An almost audible sigh had started to escape, but caught in Barry's throat, coming out as "Sh--" She abruptly stopped herself, groping for a similar-sounding word. "S-sure is fine weather for a ride, isn't it, ladies?"

"… So you see why we are so worried about Máire." Barry rode between Raine and Maggie, Rob a little farther ahead, as the four guided their horses across a shallow, rock-strewn stream. "I don't know why I'm telling *you* all this, but I trust you. It's just a feeling, but I've learned to trust my instincts … well, most of the time," Barry finished.

"And I've got a strong feeling all these things are connected," Raine concluded.

"All, perhaps, except this last. Because of all the previous goings-on, this concern for Máire may be premature, and maybe not." Maggie tossed Raine a look. *Witches recognize their own*, she thought. Aloud, she said, "Raine and I are like you, Barry. Clairvoyant. Some call it 'second sight,' but these gifts manifest themselves a bit differently in each of us, depending on the circumstances."

"My feeling is that we'll have news of Máire, good or bad, before too long … today or tomorrow." Raine patted her horse, a dapple grey with a black mane and tail.

"My family referred to it as the 'Sight' too. I just *know* things sometimes," Barry revealed. "I suppose you could call me a psychic child. I had the usual invisible playmates, but I also had vivid dreams that warned of death, accidents, and such."

"That is something Maggie and I, and our other McDonough cousin, Aisling, could do from a very early age," Raine added. "We would sit and listen to our grandmother teach us the meaning of colors and dreams. She taught us the use of crystals, gemstones, and herbs, and the importance of spending time in nature."

"Grandmother was a wise woman," Maggie added, reining her horse in a bit to keep alongside Raine and Barry. "She would read the future and fascinate us with her wisdom and her gentle spirit. She was this great lady who showed us by example that nature must be an integral part of everyday life, that the further we moved away from it, the more unsettled we'd become." Suddenly remembering something, Maggie gave one of her delightful laughs. "One of the things she always taught us was to be careful what we wished for. How right she was!"

Raine nodded approvingly. "Our granny taught us so much. For example, when people talk to me, they say a great deal more than their lips deliver. I dream sometimes too, and later, that event will unfold just like the dream. Some might find that strange."

"I've never found it strange," Barry replied. "As I said, I share that gift. The Sight has never failed to add to my sense of destiny."

Making eye contact, the Sleuth Sisters nodded in unison.

"We have something else in common as well," Barry continued. "Your wonderful grandmother sorely reminds me of my own wise granny." Barry was beginning to relax in the saddle, and she could not help thinking how much she liked these two fellow Americans. *I feel such a strong bond with these two ladies, as though I've known them all my life.*

"Raine, Aisling, and I come from a long line of wise women on both sides of our families," Maggie began. "In many aspects of our lives, we prefer the Old Ways. Women like us emit energies that attract all sorts of dreams and visions, not to mention spiritual healing. We can bend the forces of fate for our own destinies, as well as the fates of others ... though one must be careful about that. Mysterious and paranormal occurrences constantly surround us."

Maggie sent Barry a warm smile. "We all have a tendency to fear what we don't understand. You mustn't be afraid of this gift, dear. I sense that you are sometimes ... to the point that you have, on occasion, denied the gift, refusing to allow it to work for you." Again the striking redhead reined her horse in. "Your innate powers can help you gain mastery over your life. They'll help you to follow a true path– a *lighted* path with clarity."

Maggie locked eyes with her cousin. "Raine and I suspected from the first time we conversed with you that you were a kindred spirit." She smiled her Mona Lisa smile, and her eyes twinkled, "a 'Sister,' shall we say?" Stroking her horse's sleek neck, she exclaimed, "How good it is to be riding again!"

"You didn't mention your mothers. I never really knew mine. She died when I was a baby. Were you close to yours?" Barry inquired, curious.

Maggie and Raine seemed to answer in chorus, "Not as close as we were to Granny McDonough."

"Since our fathers retired this year, our parents have been traveling. To some of the most remote areas of the world," Raine added. "They're consummate explorers, and we're happy they're enjoying themselves. They check in with us periodically."

"What did your fathers do?" Barry asked.

"They're archeologists. As brothers, they grew up with similar interests, majored in the same field, got their doctorates at Harvard, and worked most of their adult lives together on various archaeological investigations, ending their careers at the Smithsonian," Maggie answered. "They were constantly afield on one dig or another. Once in awhile Raine and I accompanied them, but, for the most part, we were with Granny McDonough in the big, rambling Victorian house she left us."

"So you weren't lonely then?" Barry asked.

"Mercy, no!" Raine exclaimed. "Our family made a fortune in coal, so we enjoyed a privileged childhood, bursting with travel, a spectrum of experiences, and lots and lots of fun. I remember one excursion especially. It was in Nepal the summer Maggie and I were nine. We were riding atop an elephant with our fathers when the beast sensed danger. A large tiger was in the tall grass. Now, mind, tigers don't attack elephants … usually. But, apparently, this elephant didn't know that, and she started backing up– right into a tree. Pow!" Raine gave a swift wave of her bejeweled hand, the rings catching a beam of sunlight and flashing emerald fire. "The jolt unseated Maggie and me, and we tumbled to the ground where we heard the tiger growl. He was close, but we didn't know exactly where he was until suddenly we saw him. I think Maggie and I both saw him simultaneously, as we locked eyes with him in the tall grass. Meanwhile, our fathers had jumped off the agitated elephant, and, guns at the ready, took aim, all the while shouting at the tiger, along with the guide, who had begun banging on a drum. With all the force we could muster, Maggie and I yelled, '**Don't shoot!**' To the tiger, we whispered, 'Go on now; **scat!**' Needless to say, that's exactly what he did. It all happened so fast."

"Weren't you scared to death!" Barry exclaimed.

Raine shook her head. "No, we weren't. In that suspended moment, we felt our spirits merge. I shall never forget looking into those great golden eyes and feeling as one with that magnificent big cat. It was surreal, like nothing before or since– *an epiphany.* We had discovered we could communicate with animals."

Maggie tossed Raine an affectionate glance. *"You're* the one blessed with *that* very special gift."

The riders had come to a meadow. "Let's pick up the pace a bit," Rob called good-naturedly to the women. He urged his horse into a trot, the three other horses following.

Maggie looked over at Barry, who was still conjuring images of Raine's tiger tale, though the eyes she was seeing, in her mind's eye, were Rob's.

"Post, honey. Like this," Maggie instructed.

Barry got into sync with the rhythm of her chestnut mare, and the jolting vanished. "I had nearly forgotten. It's like a rocking chair. Almost." *Or will be when we shift into the next gear, which I know Rob'll want to do any minute now.* "I wish I had a saddle horn. This little English affair is no bigger than a postage stamp."

"What you need is a Spanish saddle," Raine suggested. "It's a happy compromise. You're so tense. Relax. It'll make it easier to keep your balance."

Rob turned his mount and trotted alongside Barry, the Sisters moving up ahead. "Looks like you're doin' fine. Want to try a canter?"

I knew it. "I don't know, Rob. I'll have nothing to grab onto, if I need to. I was just saying how I miss a saddle horn."

"Bah! Grip with your legs. You always have brakes– just rein her in. Firelight is well-trained. Come on, let's give it a go!" He nudged the big black into a canter, the other horses reacting at once.

The canter quickly escalated into a full gallop, and for a few seconds Barry felt the exhilaration, the freedom, and the oneness with her horse, as they raced across the long, wide meadow. Then her mare stumbled slightly, and Barry, grasping wildly for the absent saddle horn, lost her balance, falling to the ground with a thud.

Rob immediately reined in, wheeled his hunter and dismounted in what appeared to be nearly the same fluid motion. He ran to her side. "Are you all right!" His face clearly showed his concern as he bent over her, extending his hand.

"Yes." *He must think me hopelessly uncoordinated.* Barry got slowly to her feet.

"Are you sure, darlin'?"

"It's only my pride, nothing more, that feels slightly wounded." She rubbed her posterior. *And my backside.*

"Here, let's get you brushed off." Rob began dusting the dirt from her breeches, and Barry winced. He kissed her forehead, smoothing back her tousled hair. "I'm sorry, luv. I didn't intend for you to damage yourself."

"Don't worry; it won't slow me down any." Barry looked up at him and smiled.

"Glad to hear it." His mustache tickled her face. *She looks magnificent even after a tumble. And there's courage there besides.*

Raine and Maggie came cantering back to where she and Rob stood, their horses nearby. "Are you okay?" Raine shouted.

"Yes, I'm fine, really," Barry answered, a blush suffusing her face.

"Best thing is to get right back on," Maggie said firmly.

"She's right," Rob concurred. "Come on. I'll give you a leg up." He led her over to the grazing red mare, where he put his hands together, forming a makeshift step for her to mount easily. "By the bye, you fell like a pro, nice and loose. Always go with it, and sort of roll. Never put your hands out to break the fall. You did just right, a *perfect* fall."

"Thanks," Barry smiled ruefully. "I'm happy to hear that."

He patted her thigh. "Poor darlin'. Tell you what, I've got to get back to both my Dublin and London agencies by phone after our ride this morning. I can't let my businesses go to hell. So you'll have an hour or so to rest, or whatever you wish to do, before we tackle our next adventure today. Perhaps, since we've a big day tomorrow, a nice long drive, or something soothing. There, there, the worst is over now."

Is it? Barry started at his words. *Suddenly, I don't think so.*

***

"There now, aren't you pretty?" Barry brushed Firelight with gentle strokes, admiring the way the mare's hide was beginning to gleam like her appellation in the shaft of bright sunlight streaming through the stable. "I think you're beginning to like me," Barry added, rubbing the blaze on the handsome forehead. In response, the mare gave her groomer a shove with her head, the large doe-like eyes half-closed in ecstasy. "Well, I think it's nice that you and I can have this intimate chat. The ladies have taken off for some historic site nearby, the old Abbey I believe, Frank is out and about on some errand or other, and Rob is busy on the phone for awhile.

So it's just you and me, baby. Can we talk?" Barry giggled at the way the mare was looking at her, as if she understood every word.

"I'd like that" came the unexpected reply.

Barry whirled to see Brian striding toward her. He was dressed in corduroy trousers, an Aran sweater and Irish tweed cap. "Oh, you gave me a start! Were you eavesdropping on our private conversation?" she asked mildly.

"I confess I was." He smiled, leaning against the wall near her. "You made such a pretty picture, that I really could not help myself."

Barry continued to brush Firelight, but an uncomfortable sensation was beginning at the pit of her stomach. "Do you like animals?"

"I never gave them much thought." His penetrating gaze never wavered as he languished against the stable wall. "People interest me much more. You, for instance. Tell me about yourself."

"My life would seem rather bland to someone like you, who has seen just about every country in the world." Barry swallowed, then placed the brush back on the shelf where she had found it. She returned to the mare and began undoing the snap that secured the horse to the cross ties.

"Let me help you." Brian quickly moved to her side and, taking the lead rope in hand, led the mare to the stall, where her name appeared on the door plaque. He removed the lead rope and was about to close the door, when Barry spoke.

"Let's take off the halter as well. I heard Frank say he never leaves them on."

"You got it." Brian started to unhook the halter, when the mare threw her head up, catching him on the jaw, and causing him to bite his lower lip. "You red-hide bitch!"

He raised his hand and was just about to bring the halter, with its metal fastenings, down hard across Firelight's face, when Barry hurriedly stepped inside the stall, grabbing his arm and stopping him in the nick of time. **"Don't!"** The mare was nervously stamping about, making frightened noises, her large brown eyes showing white. "Don't hurt her!" She fiercely yanked the halter from his grip.

Brian laughed, pushing the mare back from them and guiding Barry out of the stall. His arm had snaked around her, and now she could feel the pressure of a firm hand on her lower back. He closed and secured the stall door before taking hold of Barry's arm. "Sorry if I alarmed you, but you have to show an animal that size who's boss." His hand remained on her arm, and his hot blue eyes bored into her, making her ever more disquieted.

Barry looked down at the offending hand, then back into those mesmerizing eyes. "I don't happen to agree. I've always been of the mind that gentleness and patience go farther than force or maltreatment."

Brian yanked her toward him. "Perhaps you're right. I could use a little of that myself." His lips were on hers in an instant, his arms pressing her against him in an iron hold, his hands moving with precision over her.

It all happened so fast that Barry, though she struggled, was taken completely off guard. Jerking free of him, she slapped him hard across the face. "How dare you! Who do you think you are to maul me like that?" Her face burned scarlet, and her bosom heaved with the fury and outrage she felt from the assault on her person.

"Afraid Rob will find out?" His hand shot out, and he took another firm hold of her, pulling her into the open door of an empty stall just inches from where they stood.

"Let go of me!" Barry gave him a sound kick to the shins, pulling away in a vain effort to break his grasp.

He clamped a huge hand over her mouth. "He'll never find out, unless *you* tell him. And I don't think you want to be the cause of a fight to the death between us, do you? That's assuming he believes you. But nothing will ever erase the pictures he'll have of us in his mind." He laughed a low, wicked laugh as he pushed her down into the straw, pinning her beneath him with his heavy body. With one hand he fumbled with her sweater, revealing her lacy bra.

Barry bit down on the hand that covered her mouth. "Get off!" She nearly succeeded in shoving him aside, so surprised was he by the pain her teeth had rendered.

His hands quickly seized her around the neck, pushing her back down in the straw, as she gasped for breath. "You little hypocrite! I saw th' way you were lookin' at me the other night, like you wondered what it would be like."

His mouth moved over her, and with his teeth, he opened the front-hook bra. "Quit fighting me! Do you want us to be discovered? Think about that now." He removed his hand from her mouth, and Barry screamed as loudly as she could, but again his hand came down, cutting off her voice. She kicked and struggled to free herself, but he was a powerhouse.

Suddenly a loud noise reached them, and Brian stopped, raising himself and listening. It was just Firelight kicking the walls of her stall, but it was all Barry needed. With superhuman effort, she jammed her knee in his crotch, pushing him off her and scrambling out of the stall.

Brian yelled, his hand over his injured anatomy, as he writhed in pain. She yanked her sweater down over her loosened bra, and started to run, when she saw him starting out of the enclosure toward her. In desperation, she grabbed for the bridle she had removed from Firelight and, swinging it with all her might, hit him in the eye with the iron bit, making him cry out in pain anew.

"Now I suppose you'll be tellin' Rob, you little tease!"

"No." Barry stared at him in mingled horror and satisfaction as blood dripped from the cut over his eye. An angry red welt was already rising, a white streak down its center. "But you get your own place, just as fast as you can *get!*"

He reached up and felt his eye, his fingers coming away bloody. "You cut me." His face took on a staggered expression.

At the door of the stable, where she had backed away, the bridle still clutched in her hand, Barry paused, her voice low and dangerous, her face reminding him of a hunt-cat, the eyes narrowed, "You keep away from me. If you're fool enough to try that again, I'll aim lower."

Barry ran the whole way back to the manor, and by the time she reached the end of the bridle path, she was panting. Before coming out of the trees and rounding the corner of the house, she rehooked her bra and brushed any remaining straw from her sweater and riding breeches. The realization of what had transpired in the stable had begun to settle over her, making her legs feel somewhat weak. In addition, she felt suddenly chilled, and she wondered briefly if she could be in shock. Running her fingers hurriedly through her hair, she stepped inside the foyer, with the intention of going straight to her room.

Nora was on the telephone, which was located just beneath the stairs. The housekeeper turned, raised a hand to signal for Barry to wait, and spoke briskly into the receiver, "She just came in. Hold please."

Nodding her thanks and thinking it was probably Skinner calling, Barry accepted the receiver. Taking a breath and hoping her voice sounded normal, she said, "Hello." She watched as Nora busied herself with a bowl of fresh-cut autumn blooms from the garden. She stood but a yard or so away, and Barry knew she was listening avidly.

"Barry?" a familiar masculine voice queried. "What in heaven's name are you doing in Ireland?"

Bill! Exactly what I need right now, she thought bitterly. "How did you get this number?"

"Your office gave it to me. Now will you tell me what you're doing in Ireland? *They* didn't even know."

"That's entirely my business," she answered flatly.

"Is that any way to talk to me? After all, I'm the one making the first move to patch things up between us. You don't still hate me, do you?"

Barry gave a short laugh, shaking her head at the audacity of the man. "I don't hate you, Bill. For that, I would have had to feel something intense to begin with."

"I can see you're in one of your moods. When are you coming home?"

"That, too, is my business. What I can't seem to make you understand is that it is over. You find someone else to torment, because it's not going to be me."

He started to say something else, when Barry cut him off. "No, *you* listen! And I'm only going to say this one more time, for *if* you'd be foolish enough to bother me again, for any reason, I'll get a court order. So, listen carefully to my final words: *It is over.* Don't ever call me again." She started to replace the receiver, pausing at his next words.

"All right, let's stop the game playing! I just wanted to see if you were going to tell me yourself. I *know* why you're in Ireland. I saw you with him here in Pittsburgh– the Point, the Strip, Cliffside, shall I go on? And I checked–"

Barry could feel her anger rising, but she struggled to keep a rein on her churning emotions. "There's a law against stalking. Do you know that? It's *over*! I'm telling you, if you don't leave me alone, I'll get a court order. It's as simple as that."

"No, it's not." The sibilant voice was chillingly calm. "No one writes me off like that. Just remember, Barry, I know where you are. I always know where you are … *both of you.*"

"William Lawrence, you really are a bastard." She slammed down the receiver. For a moment she stood, shaking, frozen to the spot by the phone. *Get hold of yourself, Barry, there's an ocean between you and that SOB.* She took a deep breath and started down the hall to the foot of the steps, where she stopped in her tracks. Rob was poised on the stairs, and by the look on his face, she was sure he had heard at least a portion of her conversation. Nora, now with a feather duster in hand, moved a few feet distant, flicking the duster over the public room furniture, where the door was wide open.

"Barry," Rob called softly, extending his hand. "Come here." He started down the stairs, meeting her halfway, intending to put a comforting arm around her, when she rushed into his arms, sobbing.

"Do you want to tell me about it?" He kissed her wet cheek.

"He was … so awful," she wept, clutching him as though she were drowning, and causing his strong arms to tighten around her. "I don't know how I ever … Oh, Rob, hold me. Please hold me! So awful … so awful." *Please God, protect this good man, please don't ever let anything happen to him … please!*

"There, there, go ahead and cry. I will never let anyone hurt you. Don't you know that? Hmmm?" He stroked her hair, and his lips brushed her ear. "Were you serious about him? Did you love him?"

"I thought, at first, that I felt something for him; I don't know if I'd call it 'love,' but he showed me rather quickly that he had a cruel streak. He was so controlling, so abusive. It was a short-lived relationship, and when I broke up with him, I never thought he'd bother me again." She paused, finishing with intensity, "I never wanted to hear from him– *ever again.*"

"Steady on now. I guarantee he'll stop bothering you. I know his type. He's a windbag, a braggart, an abuser of women, all signs of a coward." Something flickered in his eyes, and she tried to grasp where and when she had seen that determined light in their amber depths before, but it was just out of reach, floating in memory like a dandelion puff on a forgotten summer's breeze. He lifted her chin and kissed her. "Believe me?"

"Oh, Rob, I don't know *how* you can say that he'll never bother me again. He was *watching* us, everywhere we went in Pittsburgh, and he said–"

A growl escaped from the big cat that dwelt in Rob's soul. "Th' Divil roast him! It doesn't *matter* what the tosser said." And a look of such ferocity sprang into his eyes, that Barry was struck speechless.

He took her face in his hands, and the force of his steady gaze held her, his love enveloping her like a protective shield. "If he ever harasses you again, he'll live to regret it," he finished, and though his voice was soft and low, his tiger eyes held a danger not to be denied.

Chapter Twelve

"Rob, I'm scared!" Barry exclaimed, as the pair exited the back door of the manor.

Carrying the metal detector Frank had picked up for him earlier, Rob tried not to let the back door slam, as he and Barry emerged from the mudroom, on their way to the gardener's shed for shovels and whatever else they might need for a vigorous session of treasure hunting. "We don't know for sar-tain that anything is wrong. Let's go over what we *do* know, and then, perhaps, whilst we work, we'll think of a logical explanation. 'Tis sure that when Máire's family rang up Nora last night," he lowered his voice, glancing quickly about, "our favorite snoop got chapter and verse."

They followed the narrow path leading around the outside of the Love Gardens to the tool shed, which was hidden from view by trees and shrubbery.

"Well," Barry began, "no one has seen Máire since she left here after work Saturday, the night we went to the castle. Her father told Nora that she had left her watch here and that she decided to walk back to get it. Máire told her parents she was going to her sister Brigid's place, as she sometimes does for the weekend, to help out with the kids. She hadn't planned on going, because it was so close to *Samhain*, but since she had to go back out anyway for the watch, she told the parents, as she was leaving, that she might as well go on to Brigid's; it wasn't much farther. The sister didn't expect her, because she knew Máire's fear of the dark, especially at this time of year."

"It's a wonder Máire wasn't missed at Mass," Rob speculated.

"The parents and Brigid attend the same church," Barry explained, "but different masses, so Máire wasn't missed until rather late last night. That's when her parents telephoned Nora. They had already called Brigid."

"Sounds to me like our little Máire has a boyfriend," Rob concluded. They were nearly at the shed.

Barry paused on the path to throw Rob a sudden quizzical glance. "You don't really believe that's the reason for her disappearance. I hardly know Máire, and I know she wouldn't *scheme* anything. It's not her nature. Something is terribly wrong here."

He kissed her forehead. "Now don't jump to conclusions. I'd wager by the time we go back up to the house for lunch–" He suddenly remembered something, pointing toward the manor, "Nora reminded me not to be late for lunch. And she said that since she has no help today, we would all be eating in the kitchen."

Just as they were about to enter the shed, the Sleuth Sisters, wearing tunic-length pullover sweaters, long skirts, socks and lace-up paddock boots, came down the path toward them from the gardens, walking briskly.

Raine sported a becoming bottle-green corduroy hat that sort of rolled back from her radiant face. "Hi!" she called with a brisk wave. "Thought we'd take a nice long hike before lunch. The weather here is so invigorating."

"Your best bet would be the bridle paths," Rob indicated with extended arm.

"Thanks. See you at lunch then," Maggie called cheerfully, her flame-red hair, adorned with a purple scarf tied becomingly to the side, wisped about her face in the crisp morning breeze.

When Barry and Rob entered the gardener's shed, McHendrie appeared to be snooping through the contents of a cabinet located in a dim corner of the storage area. He wheeled and faced his employer, his look one of surprise.

"What's your job for today?" Rob queried.

"I was just about t' get to the day's tasks, Mr. Carroll, sir, but I can't seem to find me prunin' shears." He started rummaging through a jumble of tools on the potting bench.

Rob moved across the area and lifted the sought-after item down from a wall hook. "Aren't these pruning shears?"

"Saints 'n angels! I was lookin' right at 'em! Isn't that ofttimes th' way of it?" He took off his cap, and scratched his greying head. "But I could have *sworn* I hung them over here," he indicated an empty wall-hook close to where he stood. "I *know* I did! Must've been th' faeries who moved them!" he chuckled, slapping the cap back on his head and accepting the shears from Rob. "Thank ye kindly," he beamed.

"Will you be needin' these two shovels? We'll be doin' a bit of diggin' today." Rob handed one to Barry.

"Help ye'erselves. I'll be on th' hop with me own chores." And though his words rang of ambition, the gardener's feet remained planted where he stood.

Armed now with the equipment they needed, Barry and Rob started out of the shed.

"Mr. Carroll," McHendrie called after them, "I don't mean to overstep me bounds, but bein' a newcomer to this part of Ireland, I've been hearin' a lot of blather in th' local pubs about the legend of Barry Hall, and I want you to know that I wish y' luck in findin' the lost treasure. If you need any help, I'd be obligin'."

Rob nodded, "Get on with your work. If we need help, we'll call you."

"I'll be here! Good-day t' y' then!" A finger to his cap, and the gardener exited with the shears and a wheelbarrow, mumbling audibly, "Someone moved those pruners. Likely th' same one who moved me rat poison yesterd'y! How kin I git me wor-rk done if I can't find me tools!" A moment later, he began whistling a lively rendition of *Skibbereen*.

Carrying their tools, Barry and Rob headed for the Love Gardens. At the top of the heart-shaped yews, near the Venus, they set the shovels and metal detector down. "Let's start here," Rob said, handing Barry a pair of work gloves, then drawing a pair over his own hands. "I haven't pressed you for details on how it went with your boss when you rang him yesterday. I was waiting for you to tell me, but now I see I must ask. He gave you th' hammer 'n tongs, right?"

For a moment Barry was silent, then she let out her breath, saying, "Not at all. After I told him I needed more time, he was calm and quite succinct. 'Take all the time you need,' he said. 'You're fired.' Then he hung up."

"Of all the cheek!" Rob moved toward her, taking her in his arms. "I'm sorry, darlin'. This is my fault."

"Now you look here, Rob Carroll. Coming to Ireland and remaining here were totally *my* decisions. And I have no regrets, so the subject is closed. Except for the fact that someone was listening, on an extension, to the conversation. I distinctly heard a click after Skinner banged down the phone. I don't think I need to ponder at length on who it might have been."

"Now, Barry, you don't know that. It could well have been your boss's wife, or someone else at his house. You rang him at home, didn't you?"

Barry shook her head. "That click was on *this* side of the Atlantic, and I think we both know who was eavesdropping … *again*."

After about an hour and a half of enthusiastic digging, Rob leaned on his shovel, looking over at Barry, who was wiping dirt from the last item they uncovered, a silver chain, from which dangled a little heart-shaped locket. "Are you thirsty?"

"I am," she answered, glancing up from her task. "Must be the bacon … rashers we had for breakfast." She pried the locket open, staring down at the faded sepia-tone photographs inside. "Look, Rob, it's quite similar to the one you gave *me!*" Her hand strayed to the hollow of her throat to touch his gift. She had taken to wearing it nearly every day since he had presented it to her in Pittsburgh.

Rob moved to her side and, glancing down at the opened, unearthed locket in her hand, looked into the faces of a couple, judging by her Gibson-girl coiffure and his handle-bar mustache, of more than a century past. "Do you think he loved her as much as I love you?" he murmured into her hair.

"I think … no. No one is capable of the kind of love we have. It isn't possible."

He kissed her softly, pulling her into the circle of his arms. "I do love you, Barry. And I'm glad you're feeling better."

She laid her head on his muscular chest and, for a wonderful fleeting moment, was at peace with the world at large.

"I'm going up to the house to get us somethin' to drink. Take a well-deserved rest. I'll be back in a tick."

Barry sat down on the stone bench, stretching her legs. *Oh, God, please don't let anything spoil our love. Don't let anything happen to Rob. I love him so.* She suddenly felt tired and utterly drained by all the events, emotions, and the tensions of the past several days. She put her face in her hands and began sobbing with deep, soul-searing grief. Once the tears flooded forth, she let them come, feeling a release from the stress she was under.

"Barry, what's wrong?" a quiet female voice asked at her side.

She stopped crying, removed her hands and looked up into the concerned faces of Maggie and Raine. "I'm all right. It's … a combination of things these last few days … all the stress and worry, and I suppose, I'm just plain tired." She hurriedly pulled a tissue from a pocket of her jeans and wiped her streaming eyes.

The Sleuth Sisters sat down beside her, Barry sliding over to make room. "I take it, it didn't go well with your boss, huh, kid?" Maggie asked.

Barry shook her head. "But that was no shock."

"If I'm not being too personal, you and Rob didn't have a quarrel, did you?" Raine had removed her hat, and her short, black hair was adorned with a long, bright red scarf, tied, like Maggie's, jauntily to one side. "Maggie and I found a bridle on the path, as if someone had left the stable in a flurry, forgetting they even had it and losing it along the way."

Barry dropped her eyes and toyed with the tissue she was holding. "I did that, but I didn't have a quarrel with Rob. Can you tell me why I seem to attract jerks– Rob excluded? Is there something wrong with me?"

A look flew from Raine to Maggie.

"Barry," Raine began, "I used to do that very thing. It wasn't because there was anything terribly wrong with me. It was quite simple really– I was a giver, and I was attracting all the takers. Until I could recognize a pattern, I couldn't break it. Finally, I realized that I no longer wanted a relationship that was twenty-five–seventy-five, or worse, with me always on the lesser end. I wanted a fifty-fifty partnership. I'm no longer drawn to," she flicked her fingers to symbolize quote marks, "the 'bad boys.' Grant you, there are times Beau and I are twenty-five– seventy-five. Sometimes he gives more; sometimes I do, depending on who's in need, but we have a good balance. Beau wants to marry me– he's always been there for me, since we were children really. God knows I love him– and sometimes I think he's spoiled me for other men– but I want to keep things as they are for awhile. I like being a free spirit."

"I had an unsuccessful marriage," Maggie stated. As I told you, we met my senior year at college, here at Trinity. Rory McLaughlin is handsome and wealthy. I had everything my little heart desired, except his fidelity. But I have no regrets. Rory and I get along fabulously now that we're divorced. Other than that damn roving eye of his, he's a great guy, flat out likable, though certainly not husband material. I find Liberty a far better husband than he was.

My point is," Maggie continued, brushing aside a stray lock of her fiery hair, "don't think you're the only woman in the world who has played the fool to some horse's ass of a man. We nearly all have." She laughed her effervescent laugh, and it was like a jet of champagne bubbles bursting into the ethers. "Some of us are becoming the men we wanted to marry. Not in a literal sense, of course."

"Women are capable of more extremes than men," Raine remarked. "They can be more cruel, or ever so much more nurturing than a man, so there are those men out there who–"

Barry started crying again.

Maggie shook her head at Raine to convey silence, when the raven-haired Sister began again to speak. "What's happened, honey?" she asked softly, laying her arm across the sobbing girl's shaking shoulders.

In halting words, Barry related what had happened in the stable between herself and Brian, concluding with the perfectly timed overseas call from Bill and why she did not tell Rob about his brother. "He and Brian hate each other. I think they must have been, since childhood, *fierce* rivals. And *I* do not want to be the cause of more trouble between them. They're both hotheads. *Please, please*, do not tell *anyone* about this, for I fear for Rob enough as it is. I think he would really–" she stopped herself. "I just don't want Rob to get into serious trouble over me. I handled it."

Raine's vivid green eyes seemed to glitter for a moment. "Yes indeed, I'm most happy to say you did. Brian boy should be sent to the Vienna Boys' Choir as a permanent soprano." To herself she thought, *My cats are black not my magick, but what an entertaining notion that is!*

Maggie lifted her head in a silent "Touché!"

Barry smiled. "You know, I was telling Rob that I noticed Brian does not have the weathered skin of someone who has spent years on a ship. But those stories of his *do* ring of authenticity. In my line of work, I was trained to be observant. Then I thought if he had been an *officer* … I mean he *is* educated and could well have been an officer, he would have worn a regulation cap, which would account for his *un*weathered complexion."

"I'm not so sure about that," Raine countered. "I have an uncle who just retired from the Merchant Marines. He has a problem with skin cancer, and he was a captain and always had to wear a regulation cap. He said he was never without it on deck, but the sun's reflection off the water did its damage anyway."

Barry shrugged. "Right now, I'm more worried about my problem with Bill. When he said he always knows where Rob and I are, a jolt of fear shot through me. It did, literally."

Raine's jet brows drew together in quick anger. "Don't let him continue to torture you! You're doing exactly what he *wants* you to do! Think! If the twit saw you with Rob … well, anyone can tell at a glance that Rob's nobody to fool with. What's this Bill do?"

"He's the Chief Finance Officer of a large Pittsburgh-based corporation owned by his father. I met him at a party, and he subsequently did my taxes. The thing with Bill is that his family has money, and he's always gotten his own way, everything he always wanted." After a moment, Barry asked, doubt carrying on her voice, "Do you *really* think his harassment is all talk?"

"Bullying is the first sign of a coward," Maggie answered, echoing Rob.

"Succinct and correct in one," Raine chimed.

"Forget about Bill altogether," Maggie said with force. "He's history, a history *lesson*, I hope."

"I hope you're right, but you don't know him. I'm so filled with guilt! I mean I so regret that I ever–"

Maggie cut her off at the pass with something that sounded like a cross between a snort and a chortle. "Regret … guilt, that's wasted energy, honey! You can't build on it. It's only good for wallowing in. Anyway, don't you know that mistakes are the price tag for living a full life?"

Raine gave a rueful laugh. "Show me a woman who doesn't feel guilt, and I'll show you a man," she pronounced in her husky way of speaking.

"I'm also afraid for Máire." Barry dabbed at her eyes with the tissue. "I have a feeling that Brian … she could be lying dead somewhere!"

Raine's tip-tilted eyes narrowed. "That hatred you mentioned that Brian harbors for Rob was undoubtedly the reason he attacked *you*."

"I agree," Maggie said. "Jealousy is a powerful motive." She thought for a moment. "If he *has* put his big mitts on Máire, it's more likely that he seduced her, and now she's ashamed to face her family. She could have run away. I promise you, we will get to the bottom of this. Let's hush now," Maggie cautioned of a sudden. "I see Rob headed this way. We were going to ask him if we could ride again this week, but we'll save it for later." She squeezed Barry's hand, "We didn't mean to lecture." Then flicking Barry's chin upward, she whispered with a warm smile, "Chin up now."

Barry waved after them as the Sisters started briskly off on another of the hiking trails.

As soon as they were out of ear-shot, Maggie remarked to Raine, "There's more than meets the eye at work here. It's elusive and moves in shadows."

"Hey!" Barry yelled to Rob, who was taking a short break from their digging. "I found something!" He immediately started digging in the spot she indicated, hitting metal after only a few minutes.

"This could be it," he said, using his gloved hands to clear away the last bit of dirt. Gingerly, he reached into the hole, extracting a pocket watch. After glancing at it, he passed it to Barry, who cleaned it off with a rag. "Ach, blast it! What does that come to?"

She examined their latest find. "I think this is real gold." Picking up the can they were using to deposit their loot, Barry related, "In addition, we've got some coins; a little gold cross; the locket; some horseshoe nails, and a couple of horseshoes. Oh, and this little gold and ... ruby perhaps ... hair ornament."

"The jewelry was probably lost over the past hundred years by guests stopping here at the manor. The pieces look old, antique, or at least vintage." He flopped down on the stone bench. "I don't know about you, but I'm thirsty again. And mighty peckish."

She shot him a startled look.

Noticing, a smile sprang to his eyes and spread, slowly, to curve the full lip beneath his ebony mustache. "It means, lass, that I need food. I stand before you a hungry man."

"You stand before me a filthy man," she joked.

He glanced down at his soiled clothes, then at his watch. "We've been working for over three hours. Let's walk back to th' house. Then, after lunch, we'll have a gallop; it'll do us good."

Barry sighed. "I don't know why you want to take time for riding, when we should be concentrating on the treasure. We just went this morning." *And I thought I did pretty well too, all things considered. I'd like to leave it at that. Somehow I feel as though I'm tempting the hand of Fate.*

He stood, sliding his arm around her waist, as they started in the direction of the house. "We'll take up our shovels anew immediately after our ride. I want to get you beyond this phobia you've developed over horses."

"It's not a phobia, it's ... never mind." She sighed again. "Rob, we have to rethink this thing. I feel we're right to search within the heart maze of the Love Gardens, but my mind keeps drifting back to a fragment of that poem. What did it say? 'Love points the way,' or something like that? My money is on either the statue of Venus or the Cupid. Either is Love personified." Barry was museful several moments, then said more to herself than to Rob, "Maybe … the treasure isn't even buried." She paused on the path. "Maybe it's–"

His butterfly kiss halted her words. "I'm too hungry to think any more now. Come on," he pulled her by the hand, glancing again at his watch, "you know how Nora is about mealtimes."

When Barry and Rob entered the mudroom, they again encountered McHendrie, who had just finished washing his hands. "I heard your contraption go off several times. Any luck?"

"None whatsoever." Rob accepted the soap from Barry, then lathered his hands.

Through the doorway, Barry was watching Nora whose ears had perked up with McHendrie's query. The gardener tilted his head, stating in his gentle manner, "Could be th' glitterin' legend about this place is nothin' more 'n fantasy, Mr. Carroll, fantasy puffed up by years 'n years of clack and chatter."

"What's th' word on Máire?" Rob asked as he and Barry took their places at the long kitchen table, next to Raine and Maggie. McHendrie and Frank sat down too, across from the Sleuth Sisters.

"No word," Nora answered, setting a plate of fresh soda bread in the center of the table. "I rang her home this mornin' to inquire after her, but there was nothing. She's gone missing. Needless to say, her family is mad with worryin'."

After everyone was seated, Nora sat down at table with the others.

"Pretty lass like that," McHendrie began, "likely off with a young man somewhere."

"That's the first thing we thought of," Maggie said, "but Mrs. Dillon says she never heard Máire speak of a boyfriend."

"Máire was a good girl," Nora declared softly.

"You said 'was'," Barry remarked. "Why?"

Nora started. "Did I? No reason." The housekeeper shot Baranya one of her blackest looks.

Rob and Barry glanced at one another, as did the Sisters. An uncomfortable silence ensued, while the group partook of the savory lamb stew Nora had prepared.

"Where's Brian?" Rob inquired, spreading butter on a thick, crusty slice of soda bread.

Frank looked up from his stew. "In Ennis, like every day. He leaves early, comes back late. He told me this mornin' he thought he'd be movin' into his own place before th' week was out."

Barry glanced over at Rob and saw that he appeared pensive. It looked as though he was about to say something, but stopped himself. She noted too that the Sleuth Sisters had sent an unspoken message to one another. For several moments, she tried to concentrate on her food, as the assembly ate in what felt like a weighty silence. Finally, she lifted her eyes to the Sisters. "Did you enjoy your walk?"

"Oh, yes!" Raine answered, glad that the awkward hush was broken. "We especially enjoyed the gardens. You're doing a nice job, Mr. McHendrie."

The gardener beamed. "'Tis a foine lady y' aire t' point that out, and I thank ye."

"Mr. McHendrie," Maggie inquired, "if you don't mind my asking, where in Ireland are you from? Your speech differs from the folks here in Clare."

McHendrie cleared his throat. "I'm from the Dublin area, missus."

"Maggie knows Dublin fairly well," Raine remarked. "Where exactly? She might be familiar with it."

McHendrie finished chewing. "I was born 'n raised on Dublin town's North Side. In a typical workin'-class neighborhood." He smiled his cherubic smile. "No colorful stories t' tell."

Maggie returned the smile, her green eyes teasing. "Everyone has stories to tell, Mr. McHendrie. How fortunate you were to have come of age in that area, surrounded by so many of Ireland's significant historic sites."

"We must sound like a couple of lecturing schoolmarms, but travel and history are always so fascinating to us," Raine added.

"Did you reside anywhere near Trinity College?" Maggie asked the gardener.

"Ah, 'twould've been a long traipse for naught," he laughed. "I've niver been one f'r book work. Niver sought a fanciful career. I'm what y' might call a humble handyman … and gardener." He took a forkful of food, then gave a casual shrug. "Me interests always pulled me out-of-doors … inta nature," he gestured with a dramatic sweep of hand toward the window, "where th' winds

refresh, and cares drop off like autumn leaves. Nature 'n sports–
those're me pleasures."

Maggie nodded her understanding, "I quite agree with your
summation of nature, Mr. McHendrie. Nature is the great restorer."
She shifted her interest to Nora. "Mrs. Dillon, you must give Raine
and me the recipe for your soda bread. It's by far the best we've
ever tasted."

Nora acknowledged the compliment with a somber, "I will that."

The gardener polished off the last of his stew. "A foine dinner,
Mrs. Dillon. Thank ye," he pushed himself away from the table and
stood, "but 'tis time I get back to me wur-rk. Ladies," he nodded,
"Mr. Carroll, Mr. Dillon, if you'll excuse me." McHendrie moved to
the door, retrieving his cap from a wall peg that held sundry
household articles.

"Raine," Barry began, "I notice you wear that little magick wand
brooch every day. It's darling. If you don't mind my asking, does it
have special significance for you?"

"I had this made several years ago," Raine answered, touching
the diamond brooch with its wee gold streamers. "It's my
fundamental philosophy of life. I like to remind my students, and
myself even more, that thoughts are magick wands, powerful enough
to make anything happen– anything we choose." She dabbed at the
corners of her mouth and laid her linen napkin on the table.

Barry's expression was full of remembering. "My grandmother
and my great-aunt, who brought me up, advocated that same thing.
Aunt Lizzie liked to say that the real magick is believing in yourself.
If you can do that, you can make anything happen."

"A wise woman," Maggie concurred, sending Raine a look that,
evident by her expression, the latter instantly understood.

"There were some who called us 'witches'," Barry replied a little
sadly. "Not everyone is as enlightened, as understanding, as you and
Raine about the metaphysical, the supernatural world," she paused,
searching for the right words, "or as accepting of those of us these
types think of as … 'different'."

"People fear what they don't understand," Maggie reminded her,
calling to her own mind a phrase of her Granny McDonough's, *Of
course … there are witches … and then there are witches.*

"Well," Raine chimed in with the McDonough gleam in her
emerald eyes to Maggie, "in the origin of many languages, the
concept of 'witch' is derived from the words for 'wise woman.'

*W*oman *I*n *T*otal *C*ontrol of *H*erself ... *witch.* A word both arcane and enigmatic."

"Maggie," Rob asked with humor in his own eyes, "what do you see in your crystal ball for Barry and me."

Barry threw Rob a look of surprise.

Maggie met his eyes, and her own gently twinkled as she laughed her captivating laugh. "Crystal balls are for amateurs ... though I've been known to use mine on occasion." Cocking her head, she looked for a meditative moment at the enamored couple. "I see a *glittering* future. That's what I see."

Rob winked at Barry, who blushed and lowered her eyes, making a pretense of neatly folding her napkin and setting it on the table beside her emptied plate.

"May your lives be filled with blessings bright and beautiful," Raine added.

Frank hastily downed the second helping of his stew along with the last fragments of his soda bread. "Excuse me, I have some errands to knock off in Quin," he announced, sweeping his napkin across his mouth. "Nora, afore I forget, I have a meetin' tonight after supper." Nora sent Frank one of her withering looks, but he broke the spell, got up from the table and quickly crossed the room, where he plucked his car key from a wall peg. "Will you be wantin' me to tack up a couple of horses for you, Rob?"

"Thank you, Frank, but I can do that. You go on," Rob replied.

"Frank," Nora called in a commanding voice. "I want a word with you before you leave." She stood and followed him out to the mudroom. Speaking in low tones, she began, "Frank, how much longer are these nighttime meetin's going to continue? Are you makin' any progress?"

"'Twill all be worth th' tussle in the end, woman, now hush!" With that, he hurried out the back door and headed for the carpark on the carriage-house side of the manor.

Wearing a bothered expression, Nora returned to the kitchen, nearly colliding with Raine, who had gotten up to refill her teacup and was lingering in the doorway. "Excuse me," the housekeeper remarked, before sitting back down at table and picking up her own cup of tea, seemingly deep in thought.

"Ready?" Rob laid a hand on Barry's arm.

"I know your one-track mind. Let's go 'n saddle up."

Once Barry and Rob had gone, Maggie and Raine, alone in the kitchen with Nora, rose too, looking swiftly to one another, after which Maggie spoke. "Mrs. Dillon, we'd like to help you tidy the kitchen, if you'll let us. And I must comment once again on your cooking. The meal was delicious."

"Yes, it was. Thank you." Without leave from the housekeeper, Raine began clearing the lunch things. "After we're finished, we're off on another long walk. This is such lovely country around here, and it helps us think. 'Power walking' we call it."

"It's not fitting that guests should pitch in with the tidyin'-up, but under the circumstances, I would welcome the help," Nora said, getting up and moving toward the sink, where Raine had started piling the dishes.

As soon as Nora's back was turned, the Sisters again made eye contact. For that brief moment, a wordless communication passed between them. Raine slipped Maggie a napkin, and the latter quickly scooped up one of the lunchtime teacups, quickly depositing the cache into her oversized Moroccan leather purse.

"Where first? To the Garda?" Raine asked Maggie as soon as they were away from the manor. The resourceful pair stood in the carpark on the side of the Hall facing the bridle paths.

Maggie's green eyes narrowed. "I think not. Let's save the Garda for last. That way, we can tell them everything at once." She opened the car door and, reaching into the glovebox, pulled out the road map, studying the legend for a few seconds. "Great! The Garda station is on our way home from Ennis. I think … yes, let's visit that other bureau first, then we can take care of all our business in town– with one wide cast of our net."

Raine grinned, moving to the passenger side of the rental car, her fingers gripping the handle. "A little fishing expedition, huh?"

"Uh-huh. For red herring."

The stern uniformed official behind the counter returned the sheet with the Sleuth Sisters' penciled requests to the waiting pair, who stood facing him on the opposite side of the partition. His expression and the tone of his voice told the tale. "I'm sorry," he said, "but we are not permitted to give out that sort of information. It's considered confidential."

Maggie accepted the paper, a slight frown creasing her brow. "We understand. Thank you anyway." She started to turn away, but thought to try again, "Perhaps you could–"

However Raine cut her off, taking her arm and leading her out the door. When they were back on the street, Raine snatched her Blackberry from her shoulder bag. "Mags, any further discussion in there would be about as useful as a teaspoon of salt tossed into the ocean. I'm going to place an overseas call to Beau and Hugh." She checked her watch. "It's about nine in the morning back home. Let's go over there and sit on that bench."

The disappointed duo sallied across the street for the small park-like area Raine had indicated. "Won't Beau be busy now in the clinic?" Maggie asked.

"If he's not too swamped, he'll talk to me," Raine answered. I want to pass the situation by him and Hugh. The reason those two are such good veterinarians is because of their sharp sixth sense. After all," Raine grinned, "their patients can't tell them what's wrong, now can they?"

"A valid point." Maggie pulled a grey, leopard-print scarf from the pocket of the vintage 1950s, misty-grey swing coat she was wearing, put it on, and tied it under her chin. "If you reach Beau, ask him if he or his father wormed Tara's Pride and Isis, and if Hugh has been exercising them. I really don't know what we'd do without those two dear men! The bridle paths they hacked out for us through Witches' Wood, connecting Tara to their place, are such a blessing."

"Oh, Hugh enjoys exercising the horses. It gives him a chance to take Nero and Wolfe out in the open fields. German Shepherds need to run, and Hugh needs to keep busy. I never thought he'd retire, though he considers himself only semi-retired."

They had arrived at the little park.

Raine quickly dialed the country code followed by the number she had committed to heart since she was a youngster, placing the call. "It's ringing," she said, as she and Maggie sat down on the bench, away from prying eyes and ears. "Hello, Jean? It's Raine. Yep, calling from Ireland. I'd like to speak with the doc, please. Either doc, if it's a busy morning there. Thanks."

A few seconds later, Beau picked up the phone in his office. In its beautiful wooded setting, the Goodwin Veterinary Clinic was attached to the long, ranch-style home Hugh shared with his only offspring. Though he had a couple of patients in the waiting room, the morning, thus far, presented Beau with no emergencies. "It's good to hear your muscle-bound voice, Stormy! I miss you. When're you coming home?"

Raine dimpled. "I can't say for sure, but we think it will be within the time span we discussed. How are our 'fur people'?"

Beau accepted the morning mail and a note from his assistant, answering both Jean and Raine in one go, "Fine."

The secretary exited, and Beau continued to Raine, "Are you OK; is everything all right? How's Ireland?"

"I'm fine. We both are. Runnin' on fast-forward as usual." Then after a beat, "Ireland's a magickal place … but how're things there?"

"I wormed the horses, and Dad's been exercising them. Your fur people are eating and doing all the things that cats and horses should do, except that they miss you. But not as much as I do. Oh, and before I forget, I got your MG tuned up. She really purrs now, almost as good as Panthèrra, Black Jack and Black Jade, but not quite as good as Madame Woo. Tell Maggie that Tiger the Tabby has taken a real fancy to me. She'd best be careful; I might just kidnap that little furball."

"Better not! Maggie is quite partial to her latest foundling, and she'd be liable to turn you into a nice, white r-r-r-rabbit when we get back."

"Hmmm, rabbits live rather racy lives," Beau quipped in his teasing manner. "I might not mind that."

"Well, if you think your life lacks 'racy,' Big Boy," Raine snapped, "I–"

"Sheath your claws, Cruella! On second thought, I don't think I could handle any more 'racy.' You're a sex storm with attitude," he laughed.

Raine instantly sweetened. "I'll reiterate that when I get back," she said in her throaty voice.

"Best magick in the world," he answered. And for a moment there was silence on the line.

"We both appreciate everything, Beau, and thank Hugh for us too. Listen, I've got to talk fast to get this all in. I'm positive this won't surprise you, but Mags and I have landed smack dab in the middle of a puzzling mystery."

"Sooo, my little hellcat's been sleuthing again, eh?"

"It's a long story, but I'm going to try, if you've about ten minutes, to condense it for you. Then I want you and Wizard Hugh to mull a couple of things over tonight after supper, over hot toddies. Can you do that?"

"Never would I forsake a damsel in distress. Let's hear it." Beau pointed to his watch, then held up ten fingers to his entering assistant, sat back in his office chair and listened, as Raine launched into the mysteries at Barry Hall.

When she finished, he said, "You two be careful. I'm not comfortable with the idea of your staying in a place where murder seems to be a regular occurrence."

"We're always careful," Raine assured him. "Relate the tale to Hugh tonight, then call me back, and we'll brainstorm. Maggie and I are about to do some sleuthing now, so we'll talk later. Love you!"

Then, before Beau could say anything more, she disconnected, and the Sisters headed for their rental car, with Maggie dialing home to update Aisling and pass the Barry Hall whodunits by their witchy blonde cousin and her husband Ian Gwynn, co-owners of the Black Cat Detective Agency.

In fifteen minutes, they rolled into Ennis. "Let's park here, in front of the cathedral, and walk around. It's our only chance to find what we're looking for." Maggie pulled the car neatly into a space before the cathedral with its tall, spiky belfry.

Raine glanced around. "I feel like we're in a medieval setting, except for the modern vehicles and the clothes people are wearing." She pointed down the narrow street. "Good thing we'll be walking. All these streets seem to be one-way." Again, she looked about her. "Let's take Aisling's advice and simply go up one street and down the next, peering into whatever windows we can, keeping our eyes and ears open for anything and everything."

After more than an hour had passed, the Sleuth Sisters had not seen nor heard anything of Brian. They were just about to give up for the day, when Raine spied him through the window of a hole-in-the-wall pub, sipping a jar of stout and conversing in an animated manner with two other men. "Wish we could hear what he's saying," she whispered to Maggie, standing next to her on the sidewalk.

"So do I, but we'll blow our cover if we go in. And we might just blow it standing here." Maggie quickly took in their surroundings.

"Let's sit over there on that low stone wall. We'll wait till he comes out and tail him."

The Sisters did not have to wait long, for within ten minutes Brian came out of the pub and began striding jauntily up the street.

"C'mon." Raine lowered the guidebook she held before their faces, and the two women started off, following him at a safe distance.

Maggie raised her coat collar. She had covered her fiery hair with the matching grey scarf. Likewise, Raine settled the hood of her black sweater-coat over her hair. Both wore outsized dark glasses. They quickened their pace when Brian sharply turned a corner. For a brief moment, the investigative pair thought they had lost their long-legged suspect. "There he goes!" Raine pointed. "Looks as though he's headed for the square where we parked. Perhaps–"

"He's going into the cathedral!" Maggie exclaimed, somewhat taken aback. "Maybe he's going to confession," she added with a smirk.

"Don't hold your breath," Raine returned. "C'mon. This time, we're going in. It should be dark enough in there to hide our faces. Hurry!"

Upon entering the shadowy church, the Sisters walked quickly through the vestibule, stopping at the last row of pews to allow their eyes time to acclimate to the dark interior. "There he is," Maggie whispered, nudging Raine in the side with her elbow.

Brian was standing at the front, near the altar, in a side aisle, talking in soft tones to a frail-looking, black-frocked priest.

Presently, he took out his wallet and, extracting some bills, offered them to the elderly clergyman. Raine and Maggie observed him shake hands and pleasantly bid the priest good-day before starting down the side aisle for the front entrance, near where they stood watching over the tops of the opened church-bulletins they had snatched up inside the door.

With a tilt of her head, Raine motioned Maggie in the opposite direction, all the while keeping an eye on Brian, who was about to exit the cathedral. "I'm going to follow him. You see what you can find out here." She started away, but Maggie made a quick grab for her spirited cousin, catching her by the tail of her sweater-coat.

"Meet me back here within a half-hour, and *be careful*. I know how daring you can be. Remember what Aisling and Ian both told us."

Raine gave a quick nod and rushed off, her fingers already locating the outsized dark glasses in the pocket of her black cashmere wrap.

Meanwhile, Maggie walked briskly up the aisle toward the snowy-haired priest, who, just having completed a silent prayer before the altar, was slowly rising from his genuflection. "Good afternoon, Father."

He smiled, inclining his head, as if seeking to recognize the speaker. "Good afternoon, my child."

"I couldn't help noticing that gentleman who was making a contribution to the church here. Is there a special charity or fund to which I might donate as well? I'm just passing through– a tourist– but I'd like to donate something. I was moved by his apparent generosity."

The kindly priest looked in the direction of the door, where Brian had exited. "Ah yes, he is a godsend, indaid. This was his third visit, and all three times, he has given most generously for whatever charities I deem the most in need. A ver-ry carin' man, our Mr. Carroll."

Or a very clever one, Maggie thought cynically.

Raine followed Brian as he headed west, walking rapidly past the O'Connell monument. The area was laced with bustling markets and Old-World lanes. After several turns, he came to a rather shabby edifice where he took the steps two at a time and entered the building. Raine climbed the steps and gingerly pulled open the heavy door. Brian was nowhere to be seen. She glanced around her in the gloomy vestibule, its faded maroon carpet worn and frayed. Several mailboxes lined the wall. *Obviously the place is an apartment building. Perhaps he's found a flat of his own.*

From the dark recesses above, the sound of someone knocking reached her. Without hesitation, she ascended the flight of stairs as quickly and as soundlessly as she could, arriving at the end of a long hallway. Peering down the dimly-lit corridor, she saw Brian, a third of the way along the row of numbered apartments, poised to rap again. While Raine pretended to search her purse for keys, the door was suddenly flung open to reveal a woman of indeterminate age with short-cropped, bleached-blonde hair, the color of corn silk, wearing a revealing midnight-blue negligee.

The blonde blocked the doorway to the flat, her words and tone carrying anger. "Well, it's about time! Chatting up the locals in the pubs again, I'll wager! Don't ya know a workin' gurl's got a schedule t' keep? Waitin' f'r you, I missed a chance to go out for a lovely afternoon ride!"

Feigning unlocking the door before which she stood, Raine watched over the tops of her glasses as Brian pushed the blonde back into the flat's dark interior. "That's a bit of a knock, but cheer up, I'll give y' th' ride of your life."

"Huh! All you do is sleep all day."

"Lucky you, I'm stayin' nights now too," he rhymed.

"Says you!"

The door slammed shut.

Still sporting her dark glasses, grey coat and scarf, Maggie was leaning against the rental car, perusing a road map, when Raine came hurrying back, her long, black wrap flung over her arm. "He's not shacked up with Máire; that's for sure. Whoever she is, she looks and sounds like a pro. What now?" Raine glanced quickly behind her. Except for a young boy with his dog, the street was empty.

Maggie looked thoughtful. "The Garda station, then back to Barry Hall. My professor from Trinity will be ringing late this afternoon or early evening with that research we wanted, and I thought we'd go over our notes before he calls, in case we'd have any questions for him."

Raine nodded her agreement. "We'd do well to stay in and work on our thesis tonight. But I've been thinking that soon another vigilant tramp through Barry Hall's woods might also be in order."

Maggie removed her sunglasses and set them down on the counter. "We'd like very much to speak to Inspector Haggerty, please, if he's available."

"He is. Please have a seat," Sergeant Dugan replied, indicating a wooden bench along the wall. "I'll tell him you're here."

Within a few seconds, Haggerty beckoned from the doorway of the inner Garda office, "Come in, ladies."

"I trust, after my phone call, that you've taken the time to, as we say in the States, check us out," Maggie began.

"I did, and I must say, I was duly impressed," the inspector replied.

Raine nodded, then handed the inspector the sheet they had made up. "When we went to their office," she indicated a name and address at the top of the paper, "they refused to give us any information. *You*, we're confident, will have better luck."

"Rest assured we're in no way trying to tell you how to conduct this investigation, but we happened to think, and we figured we could save you a couple of steps," Maggie added with her most charming smile.

Running his fingers through his thick, white hair, Haggerty studied the penciled sheet of questions and notes for a few moments, subsequently raising his steely blue eyes to meet the vivid green gaze of the Sleuth Sisters. "You may be on to something here."

Raine nodded. "We'll bid you good-day then and let you get back to your work."

The Sisters turned to go, when Maggie suddenly stopped, spun round, and with raised hand, motioned Haggerty to wait. Opening her large purse, she pulled out a package, handing it to the detective. "I nearly forgot! We need to tell you one more thing before we leave, and this could prove even more significant."

When the Sisters were exiting the Garda station, they paused at the door, glancing back to discover Sergeant Dugan watching them with an intense expression.

In the Love Gardens of the old manor, the entire area surrounding Venus and the fountain showed evidence of the zealous search Rob and Barry had been waging to find the legendary De Barry treasure. Holes and piles of dirt were everywhere, and a variety of tools lay scattered about. "I want to commend you on your riding lesson today, Barry. You've greatly improved. This system of ours is proving to be a rather good one. Each day, we'll work in earnest toward finding the jewels. And each day, we'll take a break for your riding lesson. There's nothin' like a pleasant canter or a good, all-out gallop to release muscle tension. I swear by it. Come next fall's hunt, we'll have you ridin' to the hounds with th' best of them! And," he said, a flicker in his eye, "you can give Margaret a run for her money. Wait till th' Shannon Blazers see *you*! You'll be *deadly* in your riding togs! Wicked deadly!"

Barry managed a weak smile. *I don't know if I like the sound of that.* Resting on her shovel to gaze at Rob, she mused, *I know one thing though. If I live to be a hundred, I know when I look at him, with his sexy grin and that self-assurance that wraps around him like a cloak, he will always take my breath.* "Thanks to you, I do feel I'm gaining confidence," she said aloud. "Perhaps, too, it's the Gypsy blood. We're supposed to be good with horses." She straightened, turning her head in the direction of the manor. "Speaking of horses, I think I heard the sound of galloping hooves."

"Bad news rides a fast horse," Rob muttered after a few moments had passed, and the boom of Margaret's stentorian voice reached them as she swept through the paths, firing off a whirlwind of orders to a cowed McHendrie.

"Why haven't you pleached that cloister of hornbeams? They're losin' their shapes! Old Phillip is likely spinnin' round in his grave!" A brief silence followed. "And you've not pruned the roses yet either!" Another short silence, and Margaret's voice reached them again. "Yes, I see you've started on them! Well, keep to it, man! We don't want those rose bushes rockin' about in the winter winds! I *must* speak to Robert about all this!" There was another lull, followed by Margaret's thunderous concluding remarks, "Yes, yes, carry on! You seem to be doing a decent job of the yew hedges at least."

*She acts as if McHendrie's **her** gardener!* Barry thought, shaking her head and turning her attention to Rob, who returned her look with a telling one of his own.

"Now there's a tongue that can clip a hedge!" he joked.

Margaret soon appeared on the footway leading to the Venus. Today, she was sporting expensive riding togs complete with silk ascot and diamond stickpin, and as she came barreling down on them, her riding crop in hand, Barry resisted the urge to bolt for cover, feeling as if in the path of an out-of-control tank.

"Yer man told me you were back here." Margaret glanced about, her horsy face suddenly burning scarlet. "What, in th' name of Saint Patrick and all the saints, are you doing, man?" She lunged toward Rob, piercing and slashing the air between them with her crop, accentuating the sting of her words. "Don't tell me you're after believin' that *daft* faerie tale about the lost treasure! All you're doin' is tearin' up the turf here!" Her eyes took in the surrounding area in one dizzying sweep, as her face took on even more of its ugly purple-red hue. "You're makin' a fine mess, a fine mess is all!" A final flourish with the crop, and she fixed Rob with her angry stare.

*Look at her! She's literally fencing with Rob! Careful, Margaret old girl, his are not the eyes **I'd** want to see over a dueling pistol at twenty paces– or at sword-point either!*

Paused in his digging, Rob leaned for a restraining moment on his shovel, staring back at his Amazon cousin, his tiger gaze flaming with held-in anger. But when he spoke, his voice was level. "Margaret, is there an express purpose to your visit today? As you can readily see, we are busy about our work here."

As Barry silently applauded, Margaret seemed to shake herself, and the myopic eyes behind her spectacles showed white. "I came over here to be asked to tea." She glanced at her watch. "It's well after four, but I can see I'm goin' t' have to invite myself." In afterthought, she begrudgingly added, with a slight nod to Barry, "Afternoon, Miss Bartok."

Rob suppressed an urge to laugh. "Let's go up to the house. Barry and I can use a break now, anyroad."

I swear the woman is part horse. Barry smiled suddenly at her private joke. *She is– a big, bad **nightmare**!*

On the way up to the manor, Margaret talked incessantly about the Love Gardens, drilling Rob that she was the only person alive truly capable of restoring them to their former splendor.

"I can see that your new gardener is in dire need of a guidin' hand, Robert. And I am just th' one to train him properly. Frank knows next to nothing about gardening. As for the great mess you've made …" she gave one of her loud snorts, "there's barely time enough to smooth those paths before the ball! I can't for the life of me–"

"I fully intend to restore the gardens to their 'former splendor,' Margaret, as you succinctly phrased it, *after* I conclude my search," Rob stated, cutting her off. "And as for the 'great mess,' I hardly think we'll be trippin' th' light fantastic, this time of year, through the gardens. We've the nice, warm Great Hall for that."

Margaret snorted louder, glaring at Barry, then Rob, who, with a theatrical flourish of his arm, gallantly held the front door open for the ladies to enter. Correctly, Barry intercepted the feeling that he was suddenly enjoying himself.

"Go on into the public room, my dear cousin, and make yourself comfortable," Rob indicated with yet another exaggerated gesture. "I'll tell Nora you're here. Now, if you'll excuse us, we'll have a wash-up before tea."

Once Rob and Barry disappeared from sight, Margaret's bespectacled eyes took in the surroundings. She ran a stubby finger across the fireplace shelf, checking for dust. *If my plan comes to fruition– and I intend to do everything in my power to see that it does– those gardens and this house will look every bit th' way they did in their glory days. Let's see. First of all, I'd change those godforsaken—*

"Oh! Hello, Mrs. Dillon." Margaret turned to see Nora wheeling in a teacart, laden with the four o'clock beverage, scones, and finger sandwiches. "I didn't hear you come in. Lovely. No, no," she held up a mannish hand, "no need to serve me. I'll wait for Robert. Won't you stay and chat awhile?"

Margaret glanced around the room, her pale-blue eyes behind the spectacles coming to rest on the sun-faded draperies. "I have a vintage photograph of this room, taken several decades ago by my father. The damask pattern with the De Barry family crest can be easily replicated by my decorator, Brendan Daly, of the distinguished Dublin firm, Divine Ireland. I've used them for years." She bent her tall, thickset form to run a critical hand over the cushion beside her. "And we could have these done to match. I'll speak to Robert." She lowered her voice to a confidential level. "Tell me, Mrs. Dillon. What do you think of that foreigner he has taken up with? A saucy bit of fluff, don't you think?"

Nora stiffened. "I think quite a lot of things, Mrs. Conroy, but it is not my place to discuss Mr. Carroll's personal life with you or anyone else." Nora locked the wheels of the cart in place near the hearth, where the fire was the only thing warming the room.

"True." A rebuffed Margaret answered, her pursed mouth disapproving, "but surely you don't feel she is a suitable match for the owner of Barry Hall! Really! Couldn't he choose someone from his own rank of life? This girl is … well, she's–" Her eyes darted to Rob and Barry, who were just coming through the doorway. "My, that was fast and furious! I was just tellin' Mrs. Dillon here what I would do with this room. It's become rather shabby, hasn't it?" She made a short sound of reproof. "Pity."

Nora scowled and, leaning toward the hearth, fiercely jabbed the fire with the poker. The flames crackled and spat sparks. She straightened, returned the rod to its rightful place, and exited the room in her usual gliding manner, her tightened lips seeming to sputter an inaudible spark of their own.

"Now, isn't this cozy?" Margaret settled her ample posterior into the most comfortable chair before the warmth of the hearth, a false smile forcing her thin lips upward. "Do let's sit over here. The fire is so inviting." She smiled again, this time more convincingly. "I love this time of year, don't you? You can *smell* October. It has … an indescribable scent all its own. Apples, cinnamon, *barm brack*, fragrant with citrus and spice, hot from th' oven … the crisp, nutty tang of the fallen leaves."

Beneath that hidebound exterior beats the free-spirited heart of an Irish poet! Barry remarked to herself. *If she weren't so overpoweringly bossy, I could almost like the old gal … almost.*

"You know," Margaret continued, "I shall enjoy the fancy dress ball even more this season, as well as the hunt, whenever I think we may have seen our last, what with old Phillip gone. I thought you wouldn't care about our country pleasures." A low laugh escaped Margaret's throat. "Remember– Oh," she stopped abruptly, "you didn't attend last season, did you, Robert? Away on one of your safaris, I suppose. I don't think you made it the year before either, did you?"

"I did." Rob rolled his eyes to Barry, as the couple seated themselves on the divan across from Margaret, who had taken the liberty of pouring the tea. "Cream and sugar?" she asked, looking at Barry, her gaze flicking over the long wool skirt and sweater she was wearing. "That cranberry shade suits you, my dear. It brightens your somewhat sallow complexion, lending it color."

"Just sugar," Barry answered, accepting the cup and struggling to ignore Margaret's thinly veiled insults.

"Barry's coloring is *hardly* sallow, Margaret. It's what I call 'sultry and exotic.' Perhaps 'dramatic' says it too," Rob affirmed, sending Barry one of his winks and reaching over to squeeze her hand.

"Thank you, Rob." Barry smiled her gratitude, returning the hand squeeze.

He stroked the soft flesh of her inner wrist with his thumb, sending a shiver through her.

"Cream and sugar," Rob responded to Margaret's filling his cup. "Thank you." He sipped the fragrant Darjeeling that was the teatime tradition at Barry Hall.

Margaret filled her own cup, liberally added both cream and sugar, then sat back and crossed her booted legs. "Now that I reflect on it, you *did* come home for the ball year before last. You took Maeve O'Brien, as I recall. A beautiful girl that one, and from such an old, respected Irish family, said to be descended from Brian Boru himself. Such lovely fair skin she has, and that red-gold hair! You both seemed so ver-ry much in love." Margaret took a bite of one of the cucumber sandwiches Nora had prepared, then sipped her tea, shaking her head in ambrosial reverie. "Well, I suppose those things happen." She made a quick trilogy of sounds evocative of her esquestrian pursuits. "More's the pity."

At first mention of Maeve, Barry's mouth had gone dry, and she looked to Rob, who was stroking his mustache– a habit she was beginning to associate with disquiet. *First chance I get I've got to ask about this ... Maeve creature!*

"Speaking of the season, this is one *Samhain* during which I, for one, won't be venturing out after dark." Margaret gave a melodramatic shudder that reminded Barry of Firelight, after her saddle is removed. "All these strange, dreadful things goin' on round here."

"I thought you said it was all rubbish," Rob reminded her, helping himself to a cheese and pickle sandwich.

The telephone sounded in the foyer.

"At first I did, but now I am *not so sure*. The Gards would do well to investigate that band of tinkers who have taken up residence down by the Shannon. Them and their gaudy caravans. Untamed savages, I say. Never know what they'll do. They're capable of anything. Why the government puts up with them is beyond me!"

"Miss Bartok," Nora announced, "there's an overseas call for you. The speaker said it was from your office. I told them to hold."

"Thank you, Nora." Barry sent Rob a "what-do-you-know-about-that" look. She stood. "Excuse me, please."

The Sleuth Sisters had just exited their room when they heard Nora on the phone directly below them. At the top of the stairs, the intuitive pair waited, listening intently.

"Hello," Barry spoke into the receiver.

"Hello, Barry" slithered the chillingly quiet voice into her ear. For an unusually long moment, only the sound of harsh breathing reached her.

"Bill! I might have known," she said wearily. With a sigh of exasperation, she started to hang up, when he spoke quickly and loudly, preventing her from doing so.

"You hang up on me, and I come over there and make a scene! Is that what you want? I know you have a guest over there. You see, I'm right down the road."

Her face blanched, and a cold chill shot the length of her spine. "Right down the road?" she repeated, the phone again to her ear. "You can't be!"

"Oh, but I am. At the Castle Arms. It's only a quarter mile from where you are right now, perhaps even *closer*." He pronounced the word 'closer' in such a way that it sounded risqué.

Above, on the landing, the Sisters, pressed flat against the wall and out of sight, strained to decipher the disembodied male voice on the line. "Trouble," Raine whispered into Maggie's ear, causing the latter to silently mouth, "I knew it."

Barry felt frozen to the spot where she stood, her mind spinning her collected fears dizzyingly around in her head. *"Please ... "*

"Oh, that's nice. Now, here's the deal. You come over here and talk to me one last time. You owe me closure, at least. I want to know *why* you left me. It could not have been just for that one–"

"**Two**," Barry retorted, her anger returning and banishing her fears.

"Whatever! I was good to you. Spoiled you even. We have the talk, then I leave, and you'll never hear from me again. I'll accept that it's over. If you don't, I'm coming over there right now, and I swear to you, I will tell them everything you and I ever did together. Would you like that? What will your mick and his guest think of you then? Hmm?"

"Please don't do this."

"I'm in number five. You have ten minutes." The line went dead.

At the top of the stairs, the Sisters exchanged looks. Below them, Barry closed her eyes, took a couple of deep breaths, then made her shaky way to the public room.

"Rob, may I speak to you?" she said in the doorway, struggling to control her voice.

"Excuse me," he nodded to Margaret, who had seized the opportunity to expound on her gardening and decorating talents. Happy to flee, he stood and came into the foyer, where Barry took both his hands between her own.

"Skinner wants me to go over to Shannon, to the airport, and interview Peyton MacCurdy, the famed political leader from the North. He says if I get the interview and fax it to him immediately, he'll give me a good recommendation, and it won't be like I'm fired. Please make my apologies to your cousin. I'll be back within an hour." She kissed him hastily and started for the door.

"What's MacCurdy doin' down here?" he muttered to himself. Hold on! The keys!" he called after the retreating Barry.

She turned, he handed her the keys to the rental car, and she rushed out. Rob started back into the public room, as the Sisters came sprinting down the stairs.

"Rob!" Maggie pulled him into the privacy of the hall. "The call was from that Bill character. Go after her; she's in great danger!"

Rob's face instantly revealed his emotion, a savage light sparking in his amber eyes, as he gently grasped Maggie's shoulders. "Where did she go? Did you hear?"

"No, but I heard her say something like 'right down the road,'" Maggie repeated.

"Thanks," he delivered a firm pat to the Sister's shoulder. "**Nora**!" he roared, darting into the kitchen.

Raine had flown to the hall telephone, where she was frantically dialing.

"What is it?" the housekeeper asked, wiping her hands on her apron as she hurried forth to meet him.

"I need the keys to Frank's car. It's an emergency. Get them!"

Nora rushed back into the kitchen, Rob at her heels. Within seconds, she handed the extra set of keys to her anxious employer, who dashed out the front door, forgetting in his haste to close it.

Margaret had wandered out into the foyer, a half-eaten sandwich in her hand. "How rude! First *she* leaves without saying good-bye, then he, without a by-your-leave, charges out after her. Apparently, he doesn't trust the woman at all! What kind of a marriage would they have? Tell me that!" She turned her sharp, bespectacled eyes on Nora, who was standing in the open doorway, a concerned look on her face, as she watched a frenzied Rob back rapidly out of the carpark and speed away, tires screeching.

"Perhaps a better marriage than you think," the housekeeper answered, her studied gaze on the smoke of Rob's departure.

Arriving at the Castle Arms, a small touristy motel between Barry Hall and Bunratty Castle, Barry paused before number five. She was just about to knock when the door was thrown open, and Bill seized her arm, yanking her roughly into the room. "Get in here, you bitch!" He slammed the door shut. "Now, we're gonna have that long-awaited talk, you and I!" He slapped her hard across the face with the back of his hand, sending her reeling against the wall. "How *dare* you speak to me the way you have! Who do you think you are anyway? Huh? Who?" He came forward and grabbed her again, this time slapping her across the opposite cheek, his signet ring catching her just outside her eye.

Her lip was cut and bleeding. "Please, stop. Why can't you leave me alone? Please, for God's sake, just leave me alone!" She eased away from him, with the intent of making for the door.

"You're not getting away from me without something to remember me by! Come here!" He caught her by the shoulders and threw her down on the bed. In one dreadful moment, he was straddling her, his hands on her throat. "I should just kill you. Do you know that? I think I'll choke the breath right out of you, like this." His hands tightened, and his normally ferret-like features contorted into a mask of scorching rage. "You think you can talk to me like you have! Chuck me aside? **Is that what you think! Do you!!**"

Barry struggled to free herself, her hands clawing at the unyielding grip on her throat. As her air was closing off, her mind freed a remarkably calm thought. *This is how I am going to die. Strange, I never thought **I** was the one in danger.*

Suddenly the door banged loudly open, and Rob burst into the room with the power and ferocity of a killer tiger. He flung himself on Barry's attacker and proceeded to beat him with a vengeance, delivering a savage uppercut to the jaw, followed by several rapid, solid blows to the accountant's soft mid-section, then finishing him with a hard right. This last knocked Lawrence's head backward, causing him to slam against the wall with a bone-jarring thud, slide down and strike his head on the bedside stand. Within seconds, the loathsome man was sprawled on the floor, eyes closed, mouth and nose bloodied.

Barry flew into Rob's arms, and he pressed her tightly to him, stroking her hair and kissing her. "There, there now. I'm here. Let's have a look." That savage spark flamed again in his eyes, but he was ever so gentle as he examined her face, which was red from the force of Lawrence's hand, a welt already rising where his heavy ring had caught her above the eye. There were angry red marks on her neck as well.

Rob grasped her shoulders, his powerful gaze holding hers. "You will never do anything like this again. Give me your word of honor that you will never rush off like that without me when there's a chance of danger. Promise me. Promise!"

She ventured a smile. "I promise."

"Why did you do that?" His large hands gripped her shoulders.

"I didn't want to get you into any trouble."

He pulled her close, murmuring softly into her hair, "Going it alone was not the answer, lass."

Behind them, William Lawrence had come to and was reaching for the nightstand. In the shaft of late afternoon sunlight coming through the high window in the room, something seemed suddenly to drip from his hand, glistening like water. His fingers securely around the steak knife from the tray next to the bed, he eased himself up and murderously lunged for Rob's back, a petrified Barry catching the sunlit-downward-flash of the knife in her peripheral vision, just as the Gardai swept into the room, knocking Rob out of the way and collaring the stunned Lawrence. They held him down, while they deftly cuffed his hands behind his back.

"What the hell do you think you're doing!" Lawrence spit out a couple of loose teeth. "You can't do this to me! I'm an American citizen! Take these off right now!"

"Get up!" Garda Dugan jerked him roughly to his feet.

"You don't understand," Bill bellowed. "This ... *barbarian* burst into my room and attacked me! He's jealous because the woman he thought was his was about to go to bed with *me*! I'm lucky he didn't *kill* me! Look at the difference in our sizes!" He reached a shaking hand to his face. "I think the sonovabitch broke my nose!"

Dugan smirked. "We know you threatened this lady into coming here, and by the looks of her face, you carried out those threats. If we hadn't arrived when we did ... you were just about to stab Mr. Carroll in the back with that knife."

The second Garda was carefully placing the steak knife into a plastic bag.

"You micks are going to be sorry! I don't think you know *who* you're dealing with, but you're sure as hell going to find out! Now, release me at once! I'm the victim here! The victim, I tell you!"

Dugan gave Lawrence a shove toward the open door, his grip on him firm. "Tell ye'er story walkin'."

"You can't do this to me!"

"We can. Move along now!" Sergeant Dugan kept his prisoner moving toward the entrance.

"You can**not**, I tell you! I'm from–"

"We don't care if you're from Mars. Here, assault and attempted murder are serious crimes." He paused before Rob. "You owe your life to those two American professors, Mr. Carroll. One of them phoned us from the manor."

Rob nodded. "Thanks, Dugan."

Barry could hear Bill raging outside as the Gardai were putting him into their vehicle, bombarding them with his newly embellished version of the incident. "Rob, I'm afraid he'll be out in an hour. He can change personalities in the blink of an eye. And when he's a mind to, he can smooth talk his way in or out of anything."

Rob gave a low laugh, putting his arm around her and kissing her forehead. "I wouldn't fret over that, luv. No one recognizes blarney more than the Irish."

From her bed at Barry Hall, Raine reached for her ringing Blackberry on the nightstand.

"Sorry to call so late," a familiar deep voice greeted her.

Hugh Goodwin, in pajamas and flannel robe, sat smoking his pipe in his favorite easy chair before the energetic flames of his fireplace, his two German shepherds lying, heads on paws, at his slippered feet.

"Even though Beau rang earlier, I had a strong feeling you were going to call."

"You'd do well to keep trusting those feelings. Beau related to me the situation there"– A sudden loud barking interrupted his words, and he paused to scold the dogs, "Nero! Wolfe! Quiet!" The barking instantly stopped. "Good dogs." He returned his attention then to Raine. "Sorry about that. They must've heard something outside. As I was starting to say," he glanced down at the ever-present mystery novel lying open on the end table beside him, "It has just occurred to me that …"

"Thoughts are magick wands
powerful enough to make anything happen–
anything we choose!"
~ Ceane O'Hanlon-Lincoln

Chapter Thirteen

Barry awakened to birdsong. Stretching luxuriously in the antique bed, she glanced at the clock on the nightstand. To her surprise, it was after noon. In the darkened room, she put her hands behind her head, deciding to enjoy the rare freedom of being lazy. It was years since she had stayed in bed this long. Years– since she was a child, sick in bed with the flu or a childhood disease– that anyone had waited on her the way Rob had done these last three days. *Oh, Gran, Auntie, I wish you could meet him. I know you would love him too. He couldn't be more caring, more gentle. Surely ... he must love me.* The thought made her smile like a sleepy kitten with a bellyful of cream.

The door opened, and Rob entered, carrying a tray that Nora had prepared for her brunch. "Thought you might be awake and hungry."

Barry's stomach made a hollow sound as the aroma of the food drifted toward her. She sat up, while Rob set the tray down on her lap over the covers.

"You look much better. I want you to stay in bed again today. Nora and I will see to it that your meals are brought up to you." He kissed her cheek, and when she snuggled against him, she smelled of sleep and softness.

"Rob, that is not necessary."

"Nonsense," he interposed. "You slept nearly all day yesterday and the day before. That meant you were *exhausted*. You rest at least another day. Now eat. You need nourishment as well." He handed her a buttered slice of toast from the sterling toast rack on the silver tray.

She accepted the food and began eating, while he sat on the bed drinking a steaming cup of strong Irish breakfast tea he had brought for himself.

I don't want him to think I can't handle danger without having to be pampered days on end afterward. How will I ever expect to share his life of high adventure? Danger is a part of his life. It's what he's all about!

"Rob, I'm not a hothouse plant that you have to pamper. You're right, I must have needed that extra rest, but I feel fine now. I really want to get up today and get some fresh air and exercise."

"One more day in bed will be good for you. After you've finished eating, I'll take your tray, and you try and get some more sleep. Even if you just read in bed, at least you're resting. I brought you some ladies' magazines I thought might interest you." He indicated the colorful periodicals on the nightstand. "I put them there this morning when I looked in on you."

"That was thoughtful. You've been so caring, waiting on me hand and foot. I love you, Rob," she reached out to him. "I love you more and more."

He kissed her hand. "And I you." With a frown he looked at her tray. "Nora's going to be ruffled if you don't finish every morsel. You don't wish to incur *her* wrath so soon after what you've been through, do you?"

She picked up her fork. "I'll eat it all, then I insist on getting up today. I feel great." His expression made her add, "*Really* I do." After taking a sip of tea, she asked, "Any word yet on Máire?"

He shook his head.

"Oh, Rob, I definitely fear the worst now."

"The Gards are doing everything they can … or so they're saying. I wonder about them sometimes." He stirred his tea. "There's still the theory that she ran away, that she is ashamed to face her family for some reason– and that, I suppose, is the most likely explanation. Anyroad, we're in touch daily with the Garda as well as her kin. But no more about that until after you've eaten." He raised his cup to his lips, studying her face over the rim. "You're healing well. That mark's almost faded– it won't leave a scar. You'll be back to perfect for the ball."

Sending Rob a smile, Barry started to eat the eggs and rashers Nora had prepared. *I really am okay. I'm better than okay! In fact, I'm a stronger person than I thought I was! What do you know about that? I am! What was the Eleanor Roosevelt quote I used in that feature on the First Ladies? "Women are like tea bags. We don't know how strong we are until we're in hot water."* She smiled, abruptly coming out of her reverie. "Rob, when *is* the ball?"

He inclined his head. "Day after tomorrow."

"I *must* get up today! I have to find a costume … and my goodness, there's ever so much to do!"

He gently pushed her back against the pillows. "No need to fret. There's absolutely *nothing* for you to do; everything's catered. And

I took the liberty of seeing to our costumes– a knight and his lady fair."

"That sounds romantic."

"Trust me, it will be." He sent her one of his most engaging grins. "Workers will arrive tomorrow morning to begin the decorating, and the caterers will follow. Nora's pressin' your costume as we speak. So rest and recuperate. That's *your* job." He laughed. "I've even convinced *Nora* to wear a costume this year. She gave me a jig and reel about being excused from fancy dress, since she needs to wear an apron, but I won. She's going as a Nightingale."

"A singing phantom!" Barry giggled. "That should be interesting."

"You misunderstand. A Nightingale was a World-War-I nurse. The uniform is complete with a long apron." He tweaked her nose. "And I've instructed our resident 'nurse' to look in on you occasionally this afternoon. I thought I'd go for a quick gallop, then I want to resume the search for the jewels. I've got to ring my offices today as well." He glanced at his watch. "I should do that first. But I'll sit with you whilst you finish eating."

Barry polished off the last of the rashers, then throwing back the covers, leaped out of bed. "Whatever's on your agenda today, Mr. Carroll, count me in! I'm alive and raring to go!"

Rob jumped the big black hunter effortlessly over the fence. Barry, who was doing well up until the stone barrier, pulled the chestnut mare in sharply. Rob wheeled his mount. "Go round, luv!" he called.

"Wait for me!" Dismounting, Barry started leading her mare. Within seconds, she stopped, muttering to herself, "I wonder if he's testing me." She remounted, cantered back for a running start at the fence, then, facing the stone barrier, she paused. *The damn thing's only about three feet high, and today, I feel as if I could jump the moon!*

Patting her mount, she said aloud, "C'mon, Firelight, let's show him what we've got." *The real magick is believing in yourself!*

"Y-AHHHHHH!" She dug her heels into Firelight's sides, and they shot forward. The little mare sailed over the fence with inches to spare. "**Y-y-yes!**" Nearly unseated, but quickly regaining her balance, Barry cantered over to Rob, who was watching her with a visible mixture of amusement and admiration.

"I like your style! It wouldn't win any blue ribbons– yet– but I do, as we say here, bend th' neck to it." Laughing in his teasing way, he leaned over in the saddle to kiss her. "C'mon, I'll race you to those trees!" He galloped off, looking over his shoulder at her, his handsome face roguish.

"No fair! I should get the head start!" A feeling of exhilarating freedom evoked a loud whoop, as she raced across the rolling green landscape that was County Clare.

While the horses grazed nearby, Barry and Rob sat under a willow tree, their backs against the trunk.

"I know; I know, but I still don't trust her! The way she moves around like a phantom, appearing, disappearing– I never hear her enter or exit a room. It's eerie!" Barry began chewing on a blade of grass.

"There's a reason for that. A good servant is trained to be unobtrusive."

Barry tilted her head, considering what he had just said. "I wouldn't know about that. Gran, Auntie, and I never had servants. But, Rob, she– Does a good servant eavesdrop?" she shot at him.

"She's really startin' to like you." He noticed her expression, then continued, "Barry, let me remind you that, discountin' that this is the twenty-first century, this is still *Ireland*. You know she disapproves vehemently of our being together under the same roof. Nora is a typical Irish mother, Victorian prudish and, yes, *bossy*."

"'Bossy' doesn't get it! She's downright tyrannical!"

Rob laughed. "You really don't like her, do you?"

Barry wrinkled her nose at him. "Well, I have to admit she's not as bad as Margaret, the *quintessential* tyrant. Who is Maeve O'Brien anyway?" She launched the question quickly while she had the nerve.

Rob smoothed his mustache with a finger, obviously reflective– and uneasy. "A girl I kept company with for awhile."

Barry tilted her head. "How long is *awhile*?"

"Two years, off and on."

"So you were serious about her?"

"Barry, don't go gettin' your knickers in a twist over–"

"And your family loved her."

"Margaret probably liked her for the reason that Maeve is an excellent equestrienne. As I'm sar-tain you've noted by now, Margaret not only looks like a horse– she thinks like one."

"So what went wrong between you and 'Little-Miss-Hunt-Club'?"

A laugh rumbled deep in his throat. "She wanted a commitment from me. And I couldn't oblige."

*Now, does that mean he couldn't make a commitment to **her**, or at all?* "Rob, will *she* be at the ball?"

"Maeve?"

She raised an annoyed brow. "No, the Queen."

Rob grinned. "I know *she* won't be in attendance."

She gave him a playful slap across the shoulder. "Quit mocking me!"

"I'm not mocking you. I'm tryin' to cheer you."

"Just answer me. Will *she* be at the ball?"

"I suppose she will. Her family has attended in the past."

Barry chewed her lower lip. *I wonder what Maeve will come as? I can just imagine!* Rob, what does my costume look like? I hope it'll fit!"

"I've instructed Nora to hang it in your room once she's pressed it. You can try it on, and if it needs a bit of nip'n tuck, Nora will oblige. Just ask her."

"What if it doesn't fit?" Barry's face conveyed concern.

"Oh, I think it will. I chose the color and the size most carefully." His expression was rakish. "I know my lady intimately enough to choose the proper size and color of her gown, wouldn't you agree? But you'll need to peruse the attic for accessories. We keep all the fancy-dress nonsense up there. You've time enough. As for the others, their costumes will be surprises. I've given your American friends leave to search the attic for their attire. God knows what Brian will sport."

"Rob, are you ever going to tell me why you and your brother so profoundly dislike one another? How did it all start?"

Rob removed his tweed cap, ran his fingers through his ebony hair, then replaced the cap. "I'm not about to ruin today, or any day, by discussing Brian."

Don't press him. Rob Carroll is no man to press. After a few seconds Barry asked, "What's the news on 'Viper Bill'? Have you heard anything?"

"No, but you needn't trouble yourself over him ever again. He'll most likely be sent back to the States with a one-way ticket."

"Rob, I told you his family has a lot of money."

"They have no power here."

"I hope you're right. And Máire? Poor innocent kid. What *has* become of her?"

He shook his head.

"I'm really worried."

"So am I." *Much more than you know.* For an instant, his expression bespoke disquiet.

I suddenly have the feeling that Rob is harboring something ... something. I just can't press him right now.

"We'd better get back to our treasure hunt, and perhaps there'll be some news. Tell you what, let's work a couple of hours, depending on how you feel, clean up, then drive into Ennis. I want to meet with Conroy again. My business there shouldn't take more than a few minutes. Afterward, we can dine alone tonight. And later," he pulled her to him, "when we return home to the manor, I want you back in *my* bed now that you're feeling better. That is, if you're agreeable."

"I'm agreeable," she purred.

His words and the memory of their last love-making, together with the things his hands and lips were doing to her now, quickly aroused her to fever pitch, her vixen coming out to play.

When he drew back, Barry opened her eyes, sultry warm with desire, her voice a pleading whisper, "Don't stop."

"Tonight," he said hoarsely. "We'd better go, or I'll be takin' you here." He stood, offering her his hand.

Barry grasped the hand, meeting his tiger gaze directly, as he pulled her to her feet, a frown creasing her brow. "And I'd be lettin' you, Mr. Carroll."

Rob laughed. "Sure 'tis a wanton I've chosen for a love." He turned toward the horses, but she interrupted him with a kiss. "We really must return to th' confounded digging."

"I'll be *longing* for you the rest of the day." She kissed him again.

"My express intention." Noticing the frown lingering still on her flushed face, he laughed softly, slipping his powerful arms about her and kissing her hair, his hands skimming her lush body. "And in the meantime, every touch ... every glance between us will rekindle our memory of this afternoon and of what awaits us in my bed this night, where, my wicked playmate, you will so get what you deserve… what you desire."

He moved to the horses, picked up the reins and led the animals to where she stood. Ruminative, he adjusted the saddle on Barry's mare. "What continues to mystify me is the incongruity of my great-grandfather. How he could put a love interest before everything else is beyond me. Maybe it was temporary insanity."

In the act of brushing off her clothing, Barry froze. "What did you say?"

Totally oblivious to her reaction, Rob handed her Firelight's reins. "I mean he acted like one possessed. We must consider his irrational state of mind when we begin our search anew."

Barry mounted, ignoring his proffer of a leg up. "You know what? I really don't feel like digging today, or going out this evening. In fact, I'd really like to go back to the house, try on my costume, and then look for those accessories, as you so kindly suggested. Besides, I'd like to ready myself for the ball– my hair, my nails." She had managed to keep her voice level, but her smoldering eyes told the tale.

"But–"

"And then," she cut him off, "I'd like to take your other suggestion of rest and complete relaxation, so I'll not see you till morning. I'll tell Nora I'd like my dinner in my room, alone, if you don't mind."

Holding the reins of the hunter, Rob stood, a confused look manifesting itself on his features. "I don't mind, but I thought–"

"Perhaps you *didn't* think." She turned the mare's head, muttering to herself, "Sometimes I could just slap him upside the head, as we say where I come from."

"Wait! I just thought–"

But she was off at a canter, as Rob stood, perplexed, calling after her, "Ask your American friends to help you with your costume, if Nora's busy!" But she was too distant by then to hear, as Firelight broke into a full gallop to return to the stable.

Presently, he stroked the tall, black hunter's velvet muzzle. "Now, MacCool, what do you suppose she's on about?" The muscular stallion tossed his head, whinnying in response. "Have you th' powers of a sorcerer like your namesake?" Rob joked, "Can y' tell me, huh?"

When he entered the stable a short time later, Rob found Frank busy mucking out a stall. "Shouldn't that be one of McHendrie's duties?"

Frank paused, leaning on his pitchfork. "'Tis. And that's why I'm doin' it again. The man's always tellin' me how much he wants to stay on here, how he'll do this, that. Be nice if he'd just do what he's told." Frank attacked the job with fresh vigor. "Ah, good help is hard t' find. I miss Tom, I do."

Rob led his horse to the cross ties, where he began the task of removing the saddle and bridle. "Perhaps we should interview for the job."

"Let's give it a bit more time. We'll see how he works out," Frank interposed. "Did y' have a good ride, lad?"

"It started out good," he answered, lifting the black Stübben saddle from MacCool's damp back. "You know somethin', Frank? I'd rather be on the Serengeti surrounded by lions or facing a charging water buffalo. I'd know then what to do, or not do. Aren't women confusing?" Rob hung up the bridle, and took up a currycomb.

Frank shot him a playful look. "I think that was the first question Adam put to the Lord."

Rob started grooming the big black in earnest, and Frank went back to his chore.

After a brief time had passed, Frank asked, "What does your heart tell you to do? In some things, 'tis best to ask the heart and not th' head."

"My heart tells me to marry her." Rob resumed brushing, stroking the sleek, ink-black hide until it shone.

Frank pushed the wheelbarrow to the stable door, then moved to where Rob was grooming the hunter. "Then God's nightgown, man, what are you afraid of?"

"Losing the freedom to live the way I do."

The older man rubbed his jaw. "From what I've observed about the lass, ye'ed be sharin' rather than losin'."

Rob seemed to contemplate this, exchanging the brush for a hoof pick. "Maybe I'm too selfish to share my life."

"Do you love her?" Frank asked abruptly.

"So much I can't even concentrate on findin' the treasure." Rob picked up a rear hoof and, leaning against the horse's side, began cleaning out the debris.

"By th' saints! Th' De Barrys are obsessed with somethin' that doesn't even exist!" He put a firm hand on Rob's shoulder. "Lad, if ye've found love, ye've found a treasure. Don't let Fear keep you from what y' want out of life." Frank's denim-blue eyes were intense. "*You* should know that better than anyone."

Rob set the horse's foot down. "Frank, I was feelin' dazed and dejected, but you've given me a good dose of th' best medicine there is."

"I have?" Frank's bristly black brows lifted. "And what's that?"

"The truth." Rob delivered a sound slap to Frank's back, nearly knocking him forward. "I should try and find her and–"

"Whoa there, Robbie, boy-o!" Frank caught him by the arm. "Let her cool down. Best thing f'r that little filly right now. I saw that spark of the Divil in her eyes when she rode in."

Rob nodded, a grin developing round his mouth and eyes. "She was in a dither, and I haven't any notion why." He picked up another of MacCool's hooves and, using the pick, began cleaning it.

"Let her be; she'll tell you when she's ready. They always do. That's one thing about women– they can't keep silent too long."

"You're spot-on about that! Nor do they forget. Women and elephants are alike in that respect."

"And you're spot-on with that one." Frank turned and started for the wheelbarrow.

Rob was reflective. "Frank," he began after a moment of deliberation, "I've been meanin' to talk to you. I think someone has been going through my things."

The manager spun around, an expression passing over his countenance, but so brief was it, Rob had no time to extract any meaning from it.

"Perhaps I'm imaginin' it."

"'Tis sar-tain y' are." Frank snapped his fingers. "Afore I forget, I'd like to invite you to join th' lads 'n me for an evenin' of 'Forty-Five.' 'Tis a club of good cheer– O'Shaughnessy, th' purveyor of spirits; Brennan, th' sheriff; and Garrity, a neighbor. This week it's my turn to host. We'll meet round seven, the evenin' after the ball. Join us; it'll do y' good."

Now it was Rob who laid a friendly hand on Frank's shoulder. "Thanks, but I'm hoping that once the ball is over, our Barry will be over her … spell. I just realized that she and I need some time alone to have a serious talk."

Frank nodded his understanding. "If y' change ye'er mind, we'll be at my place in the carriage house."

Rob untied the hunter and led him into his stall. Then he started out of the stable.

"Are you goin' up to th' house?" Frank queried.

"Aye."

"I'll walk with you."

As they started on the path, Frank said, "By th' bye, Brian asked me to put in a good word for him. And it seems t' *me*, a couple of good words might be, 'Forgive 'n forget.' I hope you two, in due time, can heal old wounds." Noticing the scowl on Rob's face, Frank exclaimed, "Now don't be jerkin' your chin at me! He was wild. But weren't we all, in our stud days?"

"I'd *like* t' say a couple good words to Brian– 'Good-bye and good riddance,'" Rob growled. "Why are *you* so hell-bent on seeing the … *prodigal* and I shake hands?"

Frank shook his head, and his gaze dropped to Rob's hands. "First off," he answered, pushing a finger into the younger man's chest, "it's bloomin' impossible to shake hands with a clenched fist."

When Rob and Frank arrived back at the manor, Sergeant Dugan and Detective-Inspector Haggerty were just coming down the front steps, heads bent as they talked in hushed tones.

"Perhaps they've news," Rob said, as he and Frank walked up the drive to meet the two somber-faced men, Dugan in blue Garda uniform, and Haggerty in mufti, part of which included his signature trench coat.

"Mornin'," Frank called out. "Anythin' to report?"

"Indeed, we have a bit of news," Haggerty replied. "Another of your employees has met with foul play."

Frank looked to Rob, then at the inspector. "Máire. Is she–"

"Dead," Haggerty finished. "Her nude body was found early this morning, in a stand of trees," he indicated, "between here and her home."

"Mother of Mercies!" Frank gasped.

"Funny thing about that," Haggerty continued, "nude body, strangulation, bruises, contusions … everything pointin' to a rape. Only thing, the post-mortem says she's *Virgo Intacta.* We've two thoughts: Either her attacker was frightened off," the inspector paused, "or someone staged a rape scene to throw us off the real motive."

Frank nervously rubbed the back of his neck. "First the old gentleman, then Tom, now Máire. Jay-sus! How am I ever goin' t' get anyone to work here?"

Haggerty was studying Rob with suspicious eyes. "New owner takes over, and you seem t' have a sudden labor shortage. Ver-ry mysterious, these two murders."

Color flamed into Rob's face. "Two murders! You mean **three**! And *you* let this whole mess happen! I told you from the outset that my uncle's death was a murder! And you did nothing but play your stupid bloody games!"

Frank laid a hand on Rob's shoulder. "Easy, lad."

Now it was Dugan's turn to speak. "Murder isn't a game, and we haven't exactly been sittin' on our arses!"

Rob made a sound of utter annoyance. "See that you don't!"

"It looks to us," Haggerty stated, still looking steadily at Rob, "like th' maid was killed somewhere else and her body concealed in those trees, buried under dirt, fallen branches and a rickle of leaves. The girl's family's been sayin' she was on her way over here. She had her own key?"

Still in deep thought, Frank answered somewhat absently, "Aye. What's come to Barry Hall? A bane of evil?"

"My men are searching the estate for clues," the inspector stated. "I have pressin' business to tend to now, but I'll be back. I'll be wantin' to speak to everyone, including the two Americans. No one seems to know their whereabouts at the moment."

Rob nodded. "I know you strongly suggested we take no guests, but–"

"Perhaps it was a good thing you did." Haggerty tilted his head, sending Rob a pointed look. "This isn't th' first time they've aided th' Garda here. They're the ones who found the body. When is that fancy dress ball scheduled for?"

"Day after tomorrow."

The inspector looked hard at Rob. "We can't legally prevent you from having the thing. But it'll be a fecking nightmare for us."

"I really don't see how we can cancel it. Invitations have been posted for weeks, and we have everything in motion."

"No, you can't cancel now. But you can bloody well count on a few more guests."

Rob raised a brow, locking eyes with Haggerty.

"We *will* be in attendance."

Raine and Maggie lifted the trapdoor and stealthily let themselves into the ghostly dark attic of Barry Hall. The faint odor of sulfur drifted on the chill air, and numerous cobwebs festooned the shadowy surroundings.

"Good thing we thought to bring a flashlight," Raine remarked. "Oh, these pesky cobwebs! I don't see a light switch." She tapped the heel of her flashlight, coaxing it to burn brighter.

"Careful where you step," Maggie cautioned. "There may be loose boards. Ouch!" she cried out, rubbing her shin, "I just found one."

"I seem to be in a daze," Raine replied. "I can't get the thoughts of that poor girl out of my mind. Thank the God-Goddess we found her. At least now her family has closure. Last night on the phone, when Hugh planted the seed in my head of how and where we might search, I just knew we'd find her. He had just finished another of the mysteries he devours, in which the killer did practically the same thing."

"Before we quit this place, we'll untangle every snarl in the baffling mysteries that ensnare Barry Hall," Maggie chanted in spell-casting rhyme. *Or die trying*, she added to herself.

"So mote it be!" Raine answered.

"So mote it be!" echoed Maggie.

The Sleuth Sisters glanced around, their meager light revealing an area crowded with boxes of all shapes and sizes, an ornately framed pier glass leaning against a wall, and opposite, some dusty shelving that contained old books. Hanging from the rafters were some antiquated uniforms partially covered by a faded green cloth. Dusty barrels stood to one side, that, upon inspection, disclosed a variety of colorful decorations.

"Doubtless for holidays and the fancy dress balls this place is famous for. Rob told us everything was up here," Raine said. After several minutes of carefully moving about, she noticed an alcove beneath one of the diamond-paned windows, and nestled into it was a huge, battered old trunk. "Maggie," she said in an excited whisper, "we may have hit pay dirt."

Sidestepping barrels and boxes, Maggie moved as quickly as she could to her cousin's side. "We've hit plenty of dirt, at any rate," she quipped, touching the domed lid and hastily wiping her fingers on her corduroys. "Let's hope it's not locked. I don't want to have to disturb either Nora or Rob."

Together, they unsnapped the thick latches, then lifted the heavy top, a cloud of dust rising with it. Raine held the flashlight, while Maggie rummaged through the layers of tissue-wrapped, lavender-scented items. "Oooh, look ... frocks, shawls ... purses ... and shoes– all from the last century! The real McCoys too, I'd say. Maggie, are you thinking what I'm thinking?"

Maggie's beautiful emerald eyes sparkled, and a foxy smile curved her full, red lips. "First chance we get! But, right now, let's concentrate on what we need for this ball."

"Right! Look at these!" Raine lifted a gown and headdress from the open trunk. They look like ... yes, medieval things. Replicas, but gosh ... I wish I could see better."

"I thought I spied some battery-operated lanterns. I wonder ... here thcy are!" Maggie switched on one of the lamps. "Great, they work." Moving gingerly about, she set each of the lights on barrels located on all four sides of the attic. The garret room instantly took on a charm so steeped with atmosphere that Maggie put her hand to her throat, her mouth forming a perfect "Ooooooh! There're three more trunks. Over there!"

"Mags! Herc's a closet!" Raine shouted, her voice seeming to vibrate under the rafters. Opening it, the Sisters discovered, under a protective covering of linen sheets, that the wardrobe was filled with dozens of gowns in every imaginable color. "They're all on padded hangers," she said, removing one of the lacy frocks.

"I think we'll find something appropriate," Maggie breathed, a hand to her bosom.

Unable to contain her excitement, Raine set the lighted flashlight she was holding on some boxes and began searching through the recessed wardrobe. "I feel much like the cinder sweep after her faerie godmother changed her sackcloth to stardust." One by one, they took out the gowns– masterpieces of watered silks, lacy satins, and rich velvets.

Facing the antique pier glass in the corner, the Sisters held each of the ethereal creations before themselves, turning this way and that to get the full effect.

Presently, Raine drew out a lush, forest-green velvet gown accentuated with a long girdle of burnished gold fringe, which the ladies of the medieval era referred to as an "enchantment." "Oh! The darling thing!" The petite Raine held the daring, V-necked, figure-hugging gown before her, the dramatic sleeves cascading to elongated points. Next, she held out the long, sweeping train. "I think it will fit me. I believe even the length will be good. Hmmm," she posed, admiring herself, "'Scarlett O'Hara' trades Tara for Camelot!"

"Here's the perfect frock for me!" Maggie exclaimed. Her cheeks glowing, she held before her a medieval gown in a shimmering shade of garnet red, a deep-purple filigree accenting a scoop-necked panne velvet bodice and flowing silk skirt. "After green, red is my favorite color. Since you're wearing green, I'm for this one. I don't know why people say redheads shouldn't wear red. It all depends on the shade of red, for goodness sake!"

"Your hair is an intense flame, not 'carrots.' That's why you can wear several shades of red." Raine pushed her long, jagged bangs out of her left eye, then turned to her cousin. "The night of the ball, we'll use the curling gizmo you brought with you on your hair," Raine suggested. "Let's leave your hair long and loose. But we'll braid some on each side, like this," she lifted a section of Maggie's hair on each side of her head, "at the temples, then take the braids to the back of the head, like this," she pulled the hair sections together, "and secure them with a pretty ribbon– that trunk over there has lots of ribbons– to harmonize with your gown. If you've some ornament– I know! Granny's jeweled comb you have with you. We'll secure that in the back of your head, where the braids meet. Luckily, I found that black chignon hairpiece cached away in a compartment of my suitcase. It will be the solution for my short hair. I haven't worn it since *Sound of Music*. Remember how I nearly Viennese-waltzed right off the stage and into the orchestra pit?" she laughed.

"That wasn't as bad as breaking an ankle, as I did in *Macbeth*. 'Double, double toil and trouble!'" Maggie echoed in a reprise of the tri-role she had shared with Raine and Aisling. "That was *years* ago. You and I were still in college, but I never got over it! Funny how

'The Scottish Play' almost always brings about some mishap or other. We should've cast a circle of protection at *each* rehearsal."

"And we would have, if we could have done it in secret each time. Someone always seemed to show up early. We did the best we could without giving ourselves away. Our Hamlet gossip is one thing, but spellcasting openly is something else. However, if we do *Macbeth* again, spellcast we shall. Ah, shoes!" Raine bent over a trunk, searching for a pair she liked. "Gosh, these all look so small. I have small feet, but these are … almost child-size and *way* too narrow, all of them." She held out a medieval-style pair with fetching, jewel-encrusted buckles.

"I'll wager none of those will fit. People were so much smaller years ago, and most of these look vintage," Maggie said, tugging without success on the bejeweled satin slippers Raine had handed her. "I give up on the footwear. Remember, we'll have some dancing– and sleuthing– to do. We'll have to choose a pair of our own that will pass. The skirts are long; only the toes will show. We will each need something in the way of a headdress too; I should think."

"Here're some more things we might be able to use." Raine dug through yet another old trunk. "Look! I *love* this headgear!" She raised a tall, pointed blue hat from which a long silk scarf, in a lighter, mystical shade of blue, cascaded. "Gorgeous, but the wrong color for my gown. Green is my color. Oh, here's something." She placed on her head a gold coronet, set with emerald and diamond-like stones, a fleur-de-lys at its center, her black hair escaping in soft little wisps about her witchy-woman face.

"I found something too!" Maggie lifted out a delicate round cap sparkling with gold sequins. "If only those slippers fit! The buckles are a perfect match."

Raine lifted the slippers Maggie liked. "You're in luck, m'lady, the buckles are detachable. You can clip them to your own shoes. Good Goddess! Here's a faux-emerald pair of loose clips perfect for my shoes!" Glancing around, she sighed. "I wish I lived– and loved– during the medieval era, when women were women and men were knights on–"

"Wow!"

The Sisters whirled to see Barry emerging from the top step into the attic room to join them. She dusted a couple of cobwebs from her jeans and cable-knit sweater. "I came up to find some accessories for my costume. Look at all this stuff!"

"What will you be wearing?" Raine queried.

"It's going to be a surprise," Barry answered coyly. "Surprises are fun. I almost feel like a child again. All I'll tell you is that Rob picked it out, and he was right. It's absolutely perfect for me!" She frowned and quickly looked down, fearful she might start to cry, as the memory of a melting kiss before a warm fire tugged at her heart.

"Then why so glum? Oh, dear!" Maggie quickly caught herself, a hand to her mouth. "I'm so sorry. It's Máire. Raine and I feel bad, of course, but we had not met her. You had. Forgive me."

Barry nodded. "Máire, yes, and the fact that I lashed out at Rob earlier today. I shouldn't have; he's been so good to me. I rushed to judgment, and now I'm feeling pretty glum, as you put it. In fact, I'm a ball of tangled emotions."

Raine and Maggie moved forward, each giving Barry a well-needed hug. "Máire's killer will be found. Don't you worry about that," Raine stated with conviction. "When I get a feeling, I'm seldom wrong."

"As for Rob, best to let matters play to Father Time. If Rob's the one for you, Time will tell. C'mon now, let's find you some choice accessories to go with your guise. What do you need?" Maggie asked. "I hope you have shoes. The ones up here are all so small."

"Slippers came with my costume. I could use a hair ornament of some kind. And I was thinking about an elegant belt. It might be a nice finishing touch." Barry glanced about. "Where shall I begin?"

"Here," Raine pointed to the trunk containing the headdress items. The trio started searching the contents until Barry lifted out a gold and silver circlet of metallic leaves, flowers and herbs, the leaves studded with dewdrop glittering "diamonds."

"This is the one!" Barry placed it on her head, regarding herself in the clouded cheval glass.

"With your hair coifed the way I suggested for Maggie, you will be a vision," Raine promised. "I could do it, if you like."

"Thanks, but I really want to surprise everyone," Barry declined. "Now, let's look for a belt. Something *exquisite* that will harmonize with this garland."

"In medieval times, they referred to a belt as a girdle. I seem to remember a glittering one in that trunk over there," Maggie indicated.

Barry crossed the area to the chest Maggie had pointed out, finding the belt almost immediately. Silver and gold and studded with rhinestones, it was wide, coming to a point at the center and tapering to the back, where it fastened. "This is exactly what I hoped to find! Thank you, ladies." Suddenly her face fell. "I just wish Máire … why did she have to die?"

"I don't think anyone can answer that question," Maggie said softly, putting a comforting arm around Barry's shoulders. "Why don't you visualize Máire stepping into the Light and greeting loved ones who have gone before."

"Yes, I will do that," Barry said in a near whisper. "I think I'll take these things back to my room, then rest the remainder of the day. I'm feeling somewhat drained again. I have to look my best for the ball. Maeve O'Brien will be there. She and Rob were quite an item for awhile."

Maggie waved a glittering magick wand, beset with colorful ribbon streamers, she had uncovered in one of the trunks. "Be gone with her!" she cast in the bright tradition of her 'Good Witch Glinda' role. "She has no power here!"

No power here. Barry's mind staggered back to the situation where she had last heard that phrase, the memory causing tears to well in her eyes. "I'm sorry, what were you saying? she asked Raine, who had just mentioned Rob's name.

"I really thought Rob would cancel the ball, but he said his uncle specifically requested that tradition not be interrupted for any reason. I think, though, this ball will bring something significant to the light," Raine declared with a pert nod of her head. "Maggie and I have worked on several cases with the police back home. It doesn't always happen, but sometimes the killer is known to return to the scene of the crime."

***

"Did you have an appointment today, Mr. Carroll?"

Brushing past the receptionist's desk, Rob marched into Solicitor Conroy's Ennis office.

Patrick Conroy removed his spectacles and stared for some moments at the younger man who confronted him across the high gloss of his legal-size desk.

"I know you told me on the phone that you don't have the cheque yet, but I want to talk to you about that! What is your explanation?"

"That seemed rather a large sum, and furthermore, these things necessitate time. Why, may I inquire, are you in such feverish haste for the money?"

Rob made a sound of annoyance. "For restoration and repairs to Barry Hall. I intend, if you must know, to make it a showplace. My great-uncle, as you are well aware, was ill for quite some time, and there are several– costly– matters of maintenance and repairs that have been put off. And, too, I have a few very special ideas of restoration that will be expensive, but salutary to the estate."

The silver-haired practitioner looked uncomfortable as he fumbled, for what seemed to Rob an unnecessarily long time, with the usual sheaf of papers before him. Clearing his throat, he began, carefully choosing his words, "First, there are several matters that I must tidy away for you, and–"

"I recall your telling me that my uncle was 'solvent when he left this world.' Your words exactly!"

"As I have stated too, these things take time."

"Yes," Rob made a gesture of impatience. "You *did* say that. How *much* time? I want to get under way with my plans."

"At this point, I really could not say precisely." He extracted from his waistcoat a large, gold pocket watch, glancing at the hour, his voice taking on a harried tone, "I don't like to rush you, but I have a pressing day today. Perhaps you could come back next week. There's the matter of the taxes, and–"

"That's *your* job! And I suggest you do it!" Rob exploded, losing all patience with the magniloquence of the man. He stood, his hands braced on the desk, as he leaned toward the dour Conroy. "Come here! I don't intend to wait donkey's years to start those repairs and renovations. I'll ring you Thursday next. See that you bloody well have the cheque for me by then!"

"But, Mrs. Conroy, he's with a client!" came the secretary's agitated voice from the outer office.

Rob turned and stormed out the door, colliding with a militant Margaret who reminded him of a lion-of-the-field about to confront a longtime adversary. "Evening, Margaret," he growled without slowing his pace.

"R-r-robert!" she growled, bursting past him through the door to confront her husband, whose face bespoke grave anxiety.

Beyond Rob and Margaret, Conroy could see his secretary throwing her hands in the air in a gesture of exasperation. "I don't know what I'm even here for!"

Slamming her fists down on his desk, Margaret was the second person that day to heatedly challenge her husband. "How **dare** you! How dare you arrange the sale of my horses, my *children,* without my permission!"

"Will you keep your voice down! Do you want everyone to know our affairs? Close the damn door!"

Margaret flung the door closed with a bang, nearly slamming it shut on the hand of Mrs. Byrne, who had anticipated Conroy's desire for privacy. Glancing out the window, she said, "He's gettin' into his car; I can see him. Now, where are my horses?"

"I warned you that if you did not take care of matters, I most assuredly would. How many horses do you need? I've left you three! You saw Robert's face when he raged out of here. I can't put him off much longer. He's demanding the entire sum! This is no trivial matter, Margaret." He removed his glasses and set them down on his desk with a long sigh, rubbing his temples before he again addressed his infuriated wife. "Do you realize what you've done to me, woman? You've forced me to make a choice between humiliating debt and the risk of ending a long and what *was* an honorable law career in prison. I don't fancy spending my retirement years behind bars!"

Margaret fumed in atypical silence.

"I never understood this wild, uncontrollable spending of yours. It's a sickness, I tell you! You've vowed time and again to restrain yourself, and you never have."

"That was because I was so sure th' old bastard would leave us *something*, even if he chose to leave Barry Hall to th' damn Gypsies! After all the extra work you did f'r th' ungrateful man! And him my own cousin! I don't know why you feel so guilty about that money. As far as I'm concerned, it's rightfully ours."

Her hands flat on the desk, Margaret leaned forward till her face was but inches from her husband's. "You're always sayin' I force you into something. Now, you are forcing *me* to do something *desperate*. And desperate times call for desperate measures– once more!"

The loud pounding sounded again at the front door of Barry Hall. After several moments, both the aproned Nora, coming from the kitchen, and Barry, exiting her room and coming down the stairs, met nearly simultaneously in the foyer. But it was the housekeeper who finally answered the urgent rapping, while Barry turned to go back upstairs.

The open door revealed a statuesque woman, dressed in skin-tight, tan riding breeches, a dark-green shirt with a gold stock pin at the yoke, and elegant, handmade, brown leather riding boots. She was holding a crop in one hand, a hunt cap tucked under the opposite arm. A cloud of red-gold hair framed her flushed face, and her violet eyes shot fire. "What took you so long to answer this door?"

Before Nora had a chance to respond, Barry, wearing Rob's amber-hued robe, her hair tousled from pulling her sweater over her head just moments before, came to the housekeeper's defense. "Nora's had to do everything herself lately. She's got her hands full with the up-coming ball."

"Who might *you* be?" the redhead demanded, one brow raised in scrutiny.

"I might ask you the same question," Barry lied, struggling to keep a rein on her emotions. *Maeve O'Brien, you have met your match!*

"I came to see Rob. Where is he?" Maeve flashed a glance up the stairs past a braced Barry, who stood on the first step, unmoving.

A moment later, Maeve's eyes locked onto the monogram stitched on the cashmere robe Barry had snugly wrapped around her lush curves. Even more color suffused the haughty redhead's face. "Obviously, you are the American I've been hearing about."

Obviously. Barry started to respond, her own color deepening, when Nora intervened, her voice resolute and professional.

"Mr. Carroll had to attend to some pressing business matters today. If he has to go into Dublin– as he thought he might– he'll not be back this evenin' at all. There's no point in your waiting." With that, she flung her grey-uniformed arm, with purposeful vehemence, toward the entrance, her expression leaving no doubt that the discussion had ended.

Eyes blazing, Maeve spun on her boot heel and, without a parting word, fumed past Nora out the door to her tethered horse, a tall red hunter that pawed the ground impationately for its rider's return.

With a guttural "Humph!" Nora slammed the door shut, then dusted her hands in her familiar gesture. When she caught Barry's eye, a flash of understanding passed between them– no magick, just the murky mystique of womanhood, each giving the other a harmonious nod.

En route upstairs, a revitalized Barry thought, a smile lifting the corners of her mouth, *Perhaps Rob is right. Nora just might be warming to me! I guess I've made an enemy of you, though, O'Brien– but enemies can be sooo stimulating!*

"Vengeance is in my heart, death in my hand,
blood and revenge are hammering in my head."
~ William Shakespeare, *Titus Andronicus*

Chapter Fourteen

Barry stood back to study her reflection in the large bureau mirror. From downstairs came the sounds of a few early guests arriving. She reached up and adjusted the glass, which tilted obligingly, so that she could view herself from head to toe.

Her gown was a wondrous confection– gossamer, ethereal ivory, dazzling with silver and gold threads and studded with hundreds of "diamonds." *It looks as though it's been spun by faeries.*

She turned, viewing herself from the side. Taking up the sparkling belt, Barry fastened it around her slim waist. Then she picked up the silver and gold circlet, its leaves studded with the same diamond-like stones. Her naturally wavy hair cascaded over her shoulders, the rich auburn color glowing under the overhead light. As per Raine's suggestion, she had braided a section of hair on each side of her face, securing the braids in the back with a rhinestone clip. The glittering metallic wreath fit the crown of her head perfectly, making her look like an enchantress invoked from the pages of forgotten Arthurian legend.

Carefully now, she put the finishing touches to her makeup. A soft russet, blended well, set off her high cheekbones to perfection. The same glossy hue made her full mouth even more inviting. Over her dark, arched brows and naturally thick lashes, Barry lightly brushed a smoky kohl. Taking a bit of the stuff on a fingertip, she deftly smoothed it over her eyelids, smudging it at the corners of each eye. *That did the trick.* She had never taken so much care with her *toilette* as she was doing this night.

I must look as good as I can. Rob will see Maeve and me in the same room tonight, and I must outshine her! She leaned toward the mirror, blending the cheek stain a bit more, adding a light dusting of translucent, shimmering powder on her face and the twin globes of her bosom.

Earlier that day, she had, to her delight, found a hair and body glitter, one in gold, the other silver, that she lightly sprayed over her dark hair, a faint sprinkling of it coming to rest on her eyelids, cheekbones and cleavage. The effect was magickal, and again she smiled at her handiwork.

More liberally than her routine habit, she dabbed her wrists, behind her ears, and the deep valley between her breasts with the heady jasmine perfume that was her scent. Then she slid her feet into the ivory satin slippers adorned with the sparkling buckles that harmonized so well with her belt and headdress.

Suddenly she remembered the diamond harp brooch that Rob had presented to her with such love. *The symbol of Ireland.* She rushed to get it from its resting place in her jewel case.

A tap sounded at the door. "Miss Bartok, may I assist you in any way?" The voice belonged to Nora and came as somewhat of a surprise to Barry, both in its unusually kind timbre and in its offer of help.

"Come in, please."

The housekeeper, wearing her Nightingale garb, entered, closing the door, her eyes taking in the other's costume, her expression remaining bland.

Barry extended the harp to Nora, "Would you mind fastening this for me?"

Nora took the pin and, with gentle fingers, secured it to the bodice of Barry's gown.

It struck Baranya that symbolically she was asking to be accepted into this very Irish woman's world with this one small act.

For an instant, the two women locked eyes, and Nora gave the brooch an approving pat.

I sense that Rob was telling me the truth. She really is starting to warm to me.

"If I may suggest, Miss, a little less severity to your hairstyle. Perhaps a few loose tendrils round the face, pulled free from the braids, would soften the look becomingly. May I?"

Barry nodded and, picking up a slender rat-tail brush from the dresser, handed it to the housekeeper. Then she stood still, allowing Nora to work on her hair.

"There now. What do you think?" The older woman's face still did not convey the least trickle of emotion.

Barry turned toward the mirror. Her cheeks were flushed slightly, and her dark eyes sparkled. For a moment, she stood, staring at her reflection. So great was the transformation from her usual self, that she drew in her breath with surprise and unabashed joy.

This Barry was strikingly beautiful– seductive and verily bewitching. In the glass, she ventured a smile of thanks to Nora.

"Lovely, Miss," the housekeeper returned with a half-smile. "Mr. Carroll will be pleased with your attire, of that I am sar-tain."

As if on cue a second tapping came at the door. "Barry, are you ready? Several of the guests have arrived. And I'm eager to show you off."

Barry flashed Nora a nervous look. "I'll be ready in a minute, Rob. Please go back to your guests. I'll meet you downstairs."

Nora adjusted the younger woman's gown in the back, then without another word, she exited the room on silent feet.

Checking her attire a final time in the full-length mirror on the back of the door, Barry adjusted, on the middle finger of each hand, the fillets that held the points of the long, cascading sleeves in place.

She took a deep breath; she had done her best. Her heart sped. *It was time.*

At the landing of the grand staircase Barry paused, looking down on the flower-decked foyer. Music issued forth from the Great Hall below. The shimmering opalescent glow of a myriad of candlelit wall sconces and crystal chandeliers flickered throughout the richly furnished rooms, and the night wind softly rustled the draperies, carrying inside the woodsy perfume from the fallen leaves and the sleeping autumn flowers of the gardens beyond. Fires blazed in the hearths. A few of the guests stopped what they were doing and looked up at her, their faces mirroring their curiosity– and open admiration. Barry smiled down at them, her smile hinting at mystery and allure.

Brian, grinning up at her, and looking, even more than usual, like a lusty pirate, started for the stairs. But it was Rob, her handsome knight-errant, who greeted her, thinking, as he did, *She always looks stunning. But tonight– tonight she's enchanting.*

He was sporting, over a black turtleneck sweater, a long, pewter grey, loose-knit tunic, reminiscent of chain mail, the large, gold lamé fleur-de-lys on the front catching a glimmer of light from a wall sconce as he moved toward her, past a grumbling Brian.

"Knock me over; why don't you!" the older of the Carroll brothers muttered under his breath.

Oblivious, Rob's attention was focused on Barry, as her eyes were fastened on him. *How handsome he looks ... how sexy in those breeches and boots. To see him tonight is to understand the meaning of the phrase "lord of the manor."*

Taking both her hands in his and kissing her cheek, he whispered, his lips brushing her ear, "You are the most beautiful woman in all of Ireland."

"This is an absolutely perfect night!" Holding her swishing skirts in one hand, Barry spun round in a dizzying waltz in Rob's tender embrace, the rhinestones of her gown and the gold fleur-de-lys on his tunic flashing diamond fire under the candlelit crystal chandeliers and flickering wall sconces. "And so many guests!"

"I'm pleased that so many came. They've come as if there might never be anything like this again. Look at them. They all seem to be totally enjoying themselves too." He nuzzled her neck. "Have I ever told you that you must have faerie blood coursing through your veins?"

"No," she laughed, "you haven't." Then after a moment, she asked, a playful smile curving her lips, "Have I?"

"I believe you do, for I am wholly enchanted ... totally under your spell." His voice lowered, and his eyes took on a dreamy appearance. "I have been, you know, from the moment I met you, in Pittsburgh. Never have I fallen so instantly and deeply in love."

"It happened to me too. I was spellbound from the first moment I saw you."

When the Conroys entered the festive Great Hall, the ball was at full pelt. Garbed as the Duke and Duchess of Windsor, the couple, dressed to the nines, paused just inside the double doors.

The bewigged Margaret, who was toting a stuffed pug, shoved the mock canine under her husband's arm, raising her own to signal a serving waiter, "Over here, my good man!" She snatched a glass of champagne from the gaping attendant's tray. After taking a long pull of the bubbly wine, she squinted, allowing her sharp gaze to survey the area. "I hate these insufferable contact lenses. Miss my spectacles! Well, well, I see Robert has had the help dress in servants' uniforms from the last century, Patrick. A rather nice touch," she added, with a pat to the ridiculous brunette wig. "I'll have to remember that. Look, there are those two American professors I told you about. Kitted themselves out for the occasion, haven't they? I encountered them this morning walkin' up the road, past the friary. There's something about those two ... much too inquisitive for one thing."

"Hmm," Raine purred, sampling a salmon canapé, "these are scrumptious! Nora may be suspect, but her cooking skills sure aren't."

"We'd be wise to watch our food intake. We're liable to come apart at the seams," Maggie cautioned, smoothing the snug waist of her garnet and purple gown.

"I know what you mean." Raine's bejeweled hands skimmed over the sides of her forest-green frock. "This gown fits like a second skin." Her emerald eyes scanned the room, coming to rest on the "Duke and Duchess of Windsor." "I see the Conroys have arrived. She'd really like to get her greedy hands on this place. As far as I'm concerned, she and her husband are *prime* suspects," Raine whispered between bites.

"I totally agree," Maggie replied, ignoring her own counsel and reaching for a canapé. "She's not only big enough to hunt bear with a stick, she's toting a lot of masculine energy, that one. Aggressive, belligerent energy."

"Look at those two characters over there," Raine gestured with a discreet tilt of her head, "the six-foot rabbit and the stubbier gingerbread man. I've been watching them, and they act as if they don't belong here."

"I've noticed. I was just about to call your attention to them. Let's keep watch on those two for sure." Maggie sipped the glass of champagne she held, fixing her tip-tilted cat eyes, over the rim of her goblet, on the strange pair.

"And over there," Raine indicated with a roll of her own feline eyes, "I think we ought to keep track of him as well, the one in the long, black, tent-like robe with the laughing-face mask. He's been watching Barry from the moment she entered the Great Hall."

"It worries me that *Brian* seems overly interested in Barry again. He's done nothing but ogle her all night. Let's keep him under surveillance too. In fact, it's time we got to work." Maggie set her empty glass on the tray of a passing waiter, raising a graceful hand in refusal of a refill. "One of us should start by going over, asking Brian to dance and seeing if we can glean anything useful from the horny brute."

In the blink of an eye, Raine's face morphed from kitten to attack dog. "And I'm the one to do it!"

Maggie's slim, white hand darted out and caught her petite confrere by the beguiling bustle of her green velvet gown. "No, darlin', you're not. You have too much emotional baggage related to that stable incident. I'll go."

"Well … you *are* better at keeping your feelings in check," Raine conceded, readjusting the gold coronet on her head. "I'll take one of the others."

Maggie advanced on Brian, while Raine spun around, bumping smack into the tall figure in the long, tent-like black robe wearing the theatrical face of Comedy, a few hors d'oeuvres dropping to the floor from the plate he held. "Oh! I'm terribly sorry. Let me help you." Turning slightly to do so, she heard him grumble something unintelligible, as he bent and retrieved the spilled food himself. She saw then that he was wearing a double-faced mask, and an icy frisson ran the length of her spine as Tragedy stared ominously up at her.

Raine stood motionless for a meditative moment, the chill she experienced ebbing slowly away. She had learned a long time ago neither to suppress nor deny her gut feelings, and she was not about to start now. Without hesitation, she tapped him on the shoulder. "I'd be happy to get you more hors d'oeuvres," she offered politely.

Comedy faced her again, and for a long moment he said nothing. "You're one of the American professors who're stopping here." His words bore a British inflection.

Raine felt another shiver rush through her, but she smiled, her voice level. "Sir, I feel you have the advantage."

In character with his guise, Comedy laughed a short, hollow laugh. "Ah, but that's how I like it." Then gathering his robe to one side, he quickly whisked a somewhat surprised Raine onto the dance floor.

With a sweeping emerald gaze, Maggie took in Brian's pirate ensemble. "Impressive costume, any pirate in particular?"

His grin was knavish, his gold earring gleaming, as the couple whirled under a flickering wall sconce. "Just my alter ego."

"You don't say? Now that is interesting." She smiled up at him, the smile her most bewitching. "Of all your ports of call, which is your favorite?"

"The West Indies, generally speaking. I liked the climate and the casual way of life in the islands. It quite suited me."

"Raine spent several summers in Martinique and developed an affinity for the place, because of the association with the Empress

Josephine, one of her favorite historic figures. Ever been out to La Pagerie?"

A frown creased his brow.

"The ruined plantation where Napoleon's Josephine was born? It's what the island is famous for."

"Boru's bollocks! I have no interest in history." He yanked her closer. "I live for the here and now." Boldly, his lips trailed lightly across her cheek, and he whispered into her ear, "Dancing with you is like standing too close to a fire. I'm burnin' with desire for you. Can't you tell?"

Long practice had made Maggie adroit at dealing with that one. She dropped her head back, and her full red lips parted in a beguiling laugh as she pulled away from his too-tight embrace. "How you do run on! But you know, Mr. Carroll, hot fires burn out so very quickly."

The music stopped, and Brian guided Maggie over to the bar. "What's your pleasure?" he asked, his voice thick with sexual suggestion.

Maggie smiled her mysterious smile. "Why, Mr. Carroll, you and I don't know each other well enough– *yet*– to share our deepest secrets, now do we? For now, I'll have a Perrier with a twist, thank you, and you can tell me a few of *your* secrets." *Never underestimate the power of cleavage*, she reminded herself. "I'm told I'm a really good listener," she said aloud.

"Have something stronger; it'll do you good," he grinned.

Maggie laughed again, the sound reminiscent of wind chimes. "One reason I rarely drink is that I want to *know* when I'm having a good time."

"Oh, must you keep me guessing?" Raine asked, her tone as sweet as she could make it.

Comedy nodded.

"I detect a British inflection, but I don't think you've spent your entire life there. It's my guess you have lived elsewhere– America perhaps?"

"In the Colonies, yes. A hundred years ago you would certainly have been burned as a witch," Comedy jeered as he expertly guided her around the floor to an evocative rendition of *Greensleeves*.

Not a very polite thing to mention to a witch. Especially not to this witch. She giggled inwardly. *I wonder what he'd say if he knew?* With the ease of custom, Raine dropped her eyelids in a fluttery fashion and displayed her prettiest smile, causing the dimple in her cheek to deepen. "You're not going to keep me guessing till midnight when everyone unmasks, are you? You're such a magnetic fellow that I'm curious as to your association with Rob or his family."

Again he laughed his unpleasant laugh. "What an excellent dancer you are, my dear. Shall we dance out onto the verandah, where, away from this crowd, we can make our own ... *very special* music?"

Now it was Raine's turn to gibe. "Dancing, sir, has always been my favorite frolic. And such good training too. It's the first way a girl learns to guess what a man is going to do before he does it."

"Oh, Rob, I'm having such a wonderful time!" Barry snuggled closer in his arms, as they whirled to the music of a popular Irish waltz.

"I am the envy of every man in this hall." He kissed her cheek. "You know you're a fantastic dancer."

"I never mentioned it, but for years, I studied Flamenco. That's probably why–" Barry stiffened in his arms.

"What is it?" he asked.

"She's here."

Rob raised a brow, looking down into Barry's suddenly cheerless face.

"By the door," Barry indicated with a roll of her dark, almond-shaped eyes.

Rob turned his head to see Maeve standing just inside the room, her long, thick hair a fiery mass about her creamy face and shoulders.

Dressed as an Irish heroine in royal purple, her low-cut, diaphanous gown clung to the voluptuous curves of her figure. A heavy gold torque encircled her slender, white neck. Gold, upper-arm bracelets, in the form of snakes, and an ancient bronze sword, suspended from a gold-tone belt, completed her riveting attire.

At her leisure and with flowing grace– like molten honey– Maeve sashayed into the Great Hall, the flickering lights, above and behind her, seeming to set her ablaze. Whispers took instant flight among the crowd. And like bears to that honey, men were drawn to the enchantress' side, a bold archer taking her hand and pressing it with fervor to his lips. Not far behind were a colorfully attired jester, a blue-faced Celtic warrior, a brassy harper, and an even bolder medieval monk, who stepped swiftly out of character with devilish gusto.

Heedless of the bevy of suitors around her, Maeve bent forward slightly to lift a glass of champagne from an attending waiter's tray, her full breasts straining to spill from the bodice of her daring gown.

In a moment, her heavily made-up eyes, the color of wood violets in deep shade, fastened on Rob. The glossy lips curved upward; the violet eyes narrowed slightly, and discarding the press of her admirers like brushed-away crumbs after an enjoyed sweet, she moved with sinuous purpose across the bedazzled room.

The music was still playing when she tapped Rob on the shoulder and cut in, dancing away with him before Barry had a chance to react– the redhead's lingering, musky perfume taunting.

At the bar, Nora handed Frank a tray of clean glasses. "You'd best keep these fires well stoked, Francis. That Maeve looks as if she's left th' top half of her costume t'home ... along with everything underneath. *Sheer* ..." she muttered under her breath, "strumpet, that one!"

Sporting the colorful silks of a jockey, Frank began filling the glasses with champagne. "Didn't notice," he lied, his merry blue eyes, in the room's large mirror, riveted to that shimmering purple.

"Raine," Maggie said in a low tone, "if Barry hadn't confided in us about what happened at the stable, I'd put Brian aside as a suspect. The man can be downright engaging. Though," her expression turned somber, "there are moments when he reminds me of a voracious animal."

Raine made a wry face. "Yeah, a predator on a ceaseless hunt. As for that double-faced character ... there he is, over *there* now. I'm ashamed to say I got nowhere with him, and no one seems to know who he is. I kept getting the feeling that he was doing his wicked best to scare me off."

"Maeve is holding Rob in conversation over in that corner," Maggie indicated, "and Barry hasn't taken her smoldering eyes off the pair of them."

"In his defense, Rob looks as though he's *trying* to escape," Raine remarked with a chortle. "I wish him luck."

A glass of champagne in hand, Barry stood, staring at Rob and Maeve across the way. *Tonight especially, I wanted him to see only me.* "I'll give her one more minute, then—"

"Am I interrupting anything?" a deep voice intoned.

Barry glanced up to see Brian, his amused expression firing her anger. "**You!**"

"Sheath your claws. I come bearing a flag of truce." His voice was soft and disturbingly soothing. He moved a bit closer, so that they were nearly touching. "I want to thank you for not saying anything to Rob about the other day. And I want to assure you that nothing like that will ever happen again." He ventured a charming smile. "Fact is, I was besotted with you. And with drink. I always did drink too much on shore leave. Fact is, too, I'm ashamed of myself." His intense blue eyes clouded for a moment. "I've been away from civilization for so long, I've forgotten how to conduct myself properly." He ducked his head. "And … I've a demon or two to exorcise, linked to Rob mostly, but I heartily apologize, and I wish you and my brother all the best."

Barry's ebony gaze held his. Not only had his cheeky apology failed to charm her, he had annoyed her the more.

Brian lowered his eyes, looking down for a moment at his booted feet. "If you and Rob make a go of it, we'll be family." He raised his eyes to again meet hers. "Let's put the past where it belongs and seal it with a dance? What say you?" He extended his hand. "Won't you please forgive me?"

Barry glanced over at Rob and Maeve. He was smiling at her, and she was laughing, her head thrown back, her bosom heaving. *He seems to be enjoying her!* Maeve laid a possessive hand on Rob's tunic. Barry grudgingly took Brian's hand with its olive-branch petition, and they danced off, he holding her a bit too tight.

"Brian, who is that man standing in the doorway?" *He looks like Trouble personified.* Barry took in the tall, muscular man with the wheat-colored hair, wearing tight riding breeches, a dark green turtleneck sweater, and mud-flecked riding boots. His handsome face was bronzed, and his eyes seemed to search the crowded room for someone in particular.

"I don't know th' man," Brian returned in a slightly annoyed tone.

As she continued to watch him, the newcomer strode into the Great Hall toward Rob and Maeve, who were sequestered in a corner, across from the entrance. Without a word, the man took a firm hold of Maeve's bare arm. He started to pull her away, his face suddenly a match with her flaming hair.

"What do you think you're doing!" Maeve shouted. "Unhand me!"

Rob moved toward the blond man. "Now just a minute! I can't have you annoying my guests!"

Barry's hand flew to her mouth, and she drew in her breath sharply. The music came to an abrupt halt, and an immediate hush fell upon the costumed assembly, as they held their collective breath.

"I'd never hurt Maeve. You're th' durty bastid who did!" The muscles in his square jaw quivered, as his eyes softened. "I care for her more than anything– or anyone– in th' world." He looked to Maeve, his tone tender. "I always have." Shifting gears, he turned back to Rob. "I've been broodin' on her over at th' Shillelagh for th' past two hours," he stuck out his cleft chin, "and I'm not about t' let you have her, what! So you can hurt her again!"

Barry, like everyone else in the room, was amazed that the fiery Maeve stood listening, open-mouthed but silent. Now, she spoke, and her eyes and her words were surprisingly soft. "Tim, I had no idea. You never ... why did you never tell me?"

Callahan shifted his sea green eyes to Maeve, his words yet heated by his ardor, "I'm tellin' you now!"

A visible look of relief showed on Rob's face. He grinned and moved to Callahan, his hand extended, "And it's a lifetime of happiness I wish you both!"

Tim slid a possessive arm around Maeve's waist, the silence in the Great Hall now broken by random whisperings, as he grasped the proffered hand, and the two strapping men, their keen gazes locked, shook.

Some of the guests burst into applause, but Rob held his hands up for silence. "What's happened to th' music?" He gestured to the orchestra, "Play *Our Wedding Day,* lads!"

The costumed musicians, dressed in medieval hose and doublets, with nodded smiles began the haunting waltz, Maeve and Tim leading. When Rob caught Barry's eye, he started toward her, a broad smile lighting his own face.

"Rob," Frank intercepted, rushing forth, "can you lend me a hand with the champagne? We need t' bring more up from the cellar."

"Sure." Rob fell into step with Frank, and the two headed for the door.

"We may as well continue *our* dance," Brian grinned. Without waiting for her response, he guided her back onto the floor. "This seems to be the night for sortin' things out and settin' them right. I hope *you and I* can–"

His words were instantly halted by the double-faced character in the tent-like robe, who, tapping him firmly on the shoulder, cut in and waltzed Barry briskly off, freeing her from a disgruntled Brian.

"I noticed your costume a little while ago," Barry began, relieved to be rid of Brian. "It's very clever."

Comedy nodded.

"Have I met you?" she queried lightly.

Again Comedy nodded, the laughing face seeming to mock her.

Barry pursed her lips. "And you don't want to tell me who you are. Ooookay. Will you tell me if I guess?"

Comedy shook his head, maneuvering her toward the open door leading to the gardens.

A few feet distant, the Sleuth Sisters were watching the dancers. "Raine," Maggie whispered, "Double-Face is dancing with Barry. Where did Rob go?"

Raine looked fleetingly about. "I don't know. I thought I saw him a moment ago with Frank. Look at Brian. His eyes are glued to Barry again. And I don't like that irascible look on that mug of his."

"Maeve and her new man seem quite taken with each other," Maggie noticed, as the enamoured couple danced past, as if floating on a cloud of ecstasy. "We can't write off Callahan's animosity toward Rob."

"That's top of our list. Or Maeve either. I just happened to think that she–" Raine's eyes narrowed to glittering green slits. "Big Rabbit and Gingerbread Man look to be casing the place. That could mean–"

"Are you thinking what I'm thinking?" Maggie asked, her eyes smiling.

"Probably. But let's be certain." Raine gestured with a movement of her head. "You take the tall bunny, and I'll take the shorter honey."

"Wait!" Maggie uttered in an anxious whisper. "Barry and Double-Face have disappeared!"

Raine glanced quickly around. "Brian's gone too. Let's look in the other rooms. This soirée is spread out all over the place. We must find them!"

Barry struggled, trying in vain to scream, but the double-faced man had pulled her roughly against him, clamping a firm hand over her mouth. Hidden from view of the house, in the shadowy gardens, she continued to resist, but she was caught in his determined hold, as he pulled her deeper into the serpentine paths.

Far from the manor, under a flickering torch lamp, her heart nearly stopped when he pulled a wicked serrated knife from inside his voluminous robe, his eyes boring into her like powerful, black lasers. In a chillingly quiet voice, he spoke for the first time. "Barry, at last we are alone. I told you we would have a final rendezvous, didn't I? Do you know what I was thinking on the plane back over here?"

Barry kicked him hard, but her struggles were useless against him. It was as though he had acquired a superhuman strength.

"I recalled a time in college when I was forced to take a course in Shakespeare. How I resented it! I remember thinking, 'What do I need this crap for?' But now I see that it happened for a reason– a projected purpose." He began drawing the knife along the contours of her face, laughing when he heard the quick intake of her breath.

Oh, God, Please help me!

"The play was *Titus* somethin'-r-other. An opus oozing with blood and revenge. The best part is when the woman's tongue is cut out," he made a horrifying, slicing motion with his knife, "and her hands hacked off ," a weird light kindled in the demonic eyes, "so that she can never speak or write the name of her attacker. How clever and extremely useful to me now–"

"Nora! Find Rob and Frank. Hurry! Something's terribly wrong! Barry has disappeared from the ball! We're going to search outside in the gardens!" Lifting her heavy velvet gown, Raine hastened across the room, grabbing a brass fireplace poker en route for the door.

Close on her heels, Maggie's hand, with its crimson nails and glittering rings, darted out and snatched the antique sword from Maeve's belt, as she and Tim waltzed by.

"Hey!" Maeve shouted, her eyes as piercing as the ceremonial weapon swiped from her costume.

"Cool your jets, Red; I'll bring it back," Maggie called over her shoulder.

When the explosive Maeve lunged at the Sister to retrieve the sword, the thought sped through the latter's own fiery essence, *It's against the Wiccan Rede, but there're exceptions to every rule.* With a quick mumbled chant and a wave of the sword over a stunned Maeve, Maggie dashed out the door after the swiftly moving Raine.

Turning back to her partner, a very randy Maeve murmured into a receptive Callahan's ear, "Timmy, darlin', all of a sudden, I have a wild, insatiable desire for you."

Lawrence was thoroughly enjoying himself now. "No one," he rasped, his Comedy face derisive, "will be able to pin this on me. I've seen to an airtight alibi at home. The fake passport was a cinch, with a little help from my friends, as the saying goes." With an evil gleam in his eyes, he painfully forced her mouth open. "It was your big mouth that got me into all this trouble over here." He brutally brought the jagged knife into position, but when he reached inside, Barry's teeth came down hard on his hand, tearing the fleshy part between thumb and index finger.

Tasting blood, she tried to run, but tripped on the hem of her long gown. In an instant the deranged man had her again, but this time she screamed as loudly as she could, before he threw her to the ground, holding her there, a knee on either side of her. Summoning all her strength, she opened her mouth to yell for help, but the iron hand around her neck cut off her wind.

"You *won't* get away from me this time! And when I'm through, no man will want–"

From the surrounding shadows, Brian flung himself upon the robed figure, knocking him off Barry, who hurriedly scrambled to the side, gasping for air. With a guttural growl, an enraged Bill Lawrence got to his feet, widening his stance and wielding the serrated knife.

"Ho!" Brian laughed, a gleam in his eyes and his manner calm. "That's the wrong thing to pull on this ole pirate!"

Savagely, Lawrence lunged forward, a wild and desperate shriek escaping him, but the stronger, streetwise ex-sailor grasped the other's arm and, twisting it, stabbed Lawrence with his own weapon.

Barry's tormentor fell to the ground, the knife plunging into his heart, the face of Tragedy staring, at a bizarre angle, upward.

With a cry of horror, Barry covered her eyes with her hands. She was trembling all over, when Brian turned and started toward her.

At that moment, Rob came racing up the path. Immediately taking in the situation, he gently drew Barry into his comforting embrace, and she buried her face in the front of his tunic. "There, there ... 'tis over, darlin', all over now." Turning to his brother, Rob said softly, "I'm obliged, Brian."

Brian nodded and stepped away from a still-tremulous Barry, just as the six-foot rabbit and the gingerbread man arrived on the scene, followed by Raine, wielding the brass poker, and Maggie clutching Maeve's sword. Rob bent down to rip the double-faced mask from the prone body.

"I thought we were rid of him," Haggerty said, lifting the rabbit head from his shock of white hair.

Stooping beside the body and feeling for a pulse, Dugan, minus his gingerbread mask, retorted, "'Tis sar-tain we are ... *now.*"

***

"You'll never need to fret over that divil again." Rob tied up yet another bag of garbage. The household– Rob, Barry, Nora, Frank, Brian, and the Sleuth Sisters– were all pitching in for the remainder of the after-ball clean-up.

Barry paused in her dusting, pushing aside a lock of hair with the back of her hand. "I don't know about that, Rob. He has often bragged about his so-called influential friends. He was so unbalanced, he may have hired someone to finish the job, in the event he failed."

"Since the ruddy sod's dead, they'd keep the money and do nothing," Brian volunteered. He glanced over at Rob, who nodded his agreement.

"Right."

Barry, too, looked to Rob, "Maybe they don't know he's dead."

"He *is* dead, and your worries are behind you now," Rob pronounced with firmness.

"Th' man died a just death," Frank concluded, "as ofttimes happens." He firmly placed the lid on one of several barrels scattered about the Great Hall.

"Lucky I got there when I did," Brian interjected. "I caught Raine's cry, 'the gardens!' so I aimed m'self in that direction, as though th' Fiend of Hell was on my heels! And that's when I heard Barry's scream." He yanked down a garland of fall flora and tossed it into one of the barrels, where they were putting the decorations.

"I'm truly grateful, Brian," Rob repeated. He moved one of the decoration drums out of the way and climbed a ladder to take down a spray of colorful fall leaves.

"Here're the last of the costumes," Raine said, entering the room with the two gowns she and Maggie had worn.

"The accessories are here too," Maggie added, extending her arms to indicate the tissue-wrapped items she held. "We'll be happy to take them back up to the attic for you, Nora."

The housekeeper turned from her task of polishing a buffet table. "I would be thankful for that. Those steps seem steeper and more numerous with each year that goes by."

"And while we're up there, we'll put everything to rights," Raine volunteered, tossing a quick look to Maggie.

"'Twould be a blessin'," Nora replied. "The other fancy dress things are over there, on that table. They all go back upstairs."

"All except Barry's," Rob countered. "Hers goes back to Sullivan's Fantasia in Ennis. I'll take it back later."

The Sleuth Sisters began gathering the fancy dress items Nora had pointed out.

"That costume is supposed to be back today, but Frank's goin' to need help with those barrels that go back to the attic," Rob said. "Brian, can you stay and lend a hand?"

"'Tis sar-tain I can," he answered. He glanced at his watch. "I have to meet someone later on, but it won't take us much longer here."

"Good, then we can finish before Frank's card cronies arrive over at the carriage house. Barry and I can take the costume back tomorrow. One day late won't matter much."

"I'll take it back." Barry wiped her hands on her jeans. "You stay and help Frank. I need to practice my driving, and I could take this opportunity to solo. It would be good for me." *Very good. I have got to be alone to think.*

"Will you be all right?" Rob descended the ladder and kissed her on the cheek.

"Of course," she answered, picking up her boxed costume. "See you later." She swept out of the room before Rob could protest.

"As soon as we finish here, I'm going over to th' carriage house to prepare Frank's mates some sustenance for their night of cards, then I plan on a nice, quiet lie-down," Nora announced.

"My plan as well," Rob concurred. "I could use a bit of ease."

"There! That's all the costumes!" Raine closed the carton she had just filled, and the Sisters, carrying the lightweight boxes, left the Great Hall, headed for the attic.

En route, they nearly collided with Barry, who was just exiting her room to leave for Ennis.

"I hope now you can forgive," Maggie said, a gentle hand on Barry's arm.

"It's going to take me awhile to forgive Bill," she answered.

"It wasn't Bill I was referring to, darlin'. It was *you*. Old sins cast long shadows, but perhaps now you can forgive yourself for ever having thought you loved him, even momentarily. You were just lonely, and he happened into your life at a vulnerable time." After kissing Barry's cheek, she added, "Don't navigate life looking through your rear-view mirror."

Old fears and layers of guilt were cleansed away, as the fire of Truth blazed through her like a powerful absolution. It was an exhilarating feeling, and for the first time in her life, Barry felt completely at peace with who she was. She hugged Maggie, then skipped down the stairs, where Rob was on a ladder, taking down a fall wreath. Having caught a bit of their dialogue, he exclaimed, his eyes shooting a golden passion of his own, "Forgive th' swine! Bah! That's God's business! Ours was to arrange a meetin' between th'm! You drive carefully, luv!" he shouted a moment later, as the sound of the closing door told of Barry's departure.

Raine set the last item in the trunk and sat back on her haunches. "I think that about does it. I just heard Rob's door close, so the coast is clear now."

Kneeling beside her, Maggie wiped her hands on her pants. "Well, what are we waiting for!"

The Sleuth Sisters rose and went immediately to the trunk containing the century-old clothing they had discovered the day before the fancy dress ball.

The time had come to put their long-awaited plan into action.

Unable to contain her mounting excitement, Raine raised the domed lid and drew out the Edwardian ensemble she had mentally reserved for herself. Holding it up, she admired, for a satisfying moment, the sweeping skirt and the long, trim-looking jacket with yards of black frogging accenting her shade of forest-green velvet. She dug deeper into the trunk. "The ladies of the 1890s called these 'traveling suits.' Here's one for you, Maggie!" She handed over a rich velvet costume in a luscious shade of rosy peach.

Laying their modern slacks and sweaters aside, they quickly stripped down to their underwear and slipped into the antique clothing, helping one another with the endless buttons and hooks. Then standing before the tall pier glass, they each, in turn, admired the results of their efforts. The garments fit the attractive pair almost perfectly.

Next, they did their hair, aiding one another with the pins they had brought along. Maggie's deep-red, shoulder-length hair was no problem for an old-fashioned, up-swept coiffure, but Raine's shorter do was more difficult. Finally, the black chignon, inadvertently brought to Ireland in a compartment of her suitcase, was blended into her own glossy raven locks.

"Since, as you like to say, I dress either serious-black gothic or à la Stevie Nicks, the shoes for me are no problem. I'm wearing a pair now that look almost exactly like those authentic high-button shoes. Anyway, the too-small shoes in that trunk over there aren't the sole problem," Raine added, "pun intended. I don't think we'll be able to eat a thing while we're gone. I don't know about you, but the waist on my outfit is snug. Just a bit," she amended with a grin.

"We could really use waist cinches." Maggie turned to the side, smoothing the long skirt over her hips and admiring herself from a new angle. "You have to admit, though, we look pretty good." She raised her skirt a couple of inches. "These ankle-high paddock boots look passable, don't you think?"

Raine glanced down at Maggie's feet. "Oh, yeah, they look good. Only the toes of our shoes show anyway."

"Now," Maggie's eyes traveled around the attic room, "we will each need a nice warm shawl and a reticule."

"What'd you say?" Raine was tugging at the waist of her skirt.

"A drawstring purse, worn over the wrist. It was all the rage in Victorian times, and it won't be so easy to lose."

"I know what a reticule is, Mags. I thought you said something before that."

"Probably just the wind," Maggie answered. "I hope the rain holds off till *we're* off!"

After searching out the shawls and reticules, the Sleuth Sisters made a few last-minute repairs to their hair and faces, using only a gossamer touch of cosmetics. At last, they looked with critical eyes into the attic's ornate pier glass.

The women who gazed back at them were charming, genteel and, unquestionably– from a century past.

Outside the old manor, a wayward October wind seemed to whisper "Time-Key" and "Destiny" in a recurring, rhythmic chant, as it rattled the attic's diamond-paned windows.

***

From the windshield of the rental car, the 4500-year-old standing stones of Poulnabrone looked rather lonely. There, amidst the wild beauty of County Clare's Burren, the ancient portal stood waiting, the thin stone slabs silhouetted against the ink-blue night sky, like a primitive flying machine ready and waiting for take-off.

"Aisling is all prepared," Maggie stated, as she turned off the Blackberry and stashed the smart phone into their rental car's glovebox. "We've synchronized our watches."

"Right," Raine answered. What more was there to say?

At that, the Sisters stepped out into the cool evening, dressed in the century-old clothing from Barry Hall's accommodating attic. They stood for a suspended moment, taking in the majesty of the mysterious monument that loomed before them. Threatened by a cloud of regret, they started walking slowly across the frosty terrain toward their destiny.

From under the bodice of her costume, Raine paused to extract the talisman, suspended from its silver chain around her neck, then to brush a finger across its gem-studded surface. As she did, moonlight, reflected off the encrusted jewels, flickered like a dance of stars, a beacon to light their path, grant them emotional support on their journey, and favor from their angel and spirit guides. It always gave her a comforting feeling to touch the antique piece, and never more than now. She grasped it, sensing its powers, and its strong energies expanded, settling over her like a protective cloak.

Tonight, Aisling's amulet rested in the hollow of Maggie's full bosom, together with the redhead's own powerful talisman.

In another moment, Raine began striding toward the standing stones. Abruptly, she paused again. "Look at that sky! Doesn't it seem to you that there are millions more stars tonight?"

"It's the absence of city lights. That makes more stars visible to us." Maggie looked up at the great dome of velvet sky gemmed with a myriad of glittering stars and glowing moon. The stars seemed inviting now, in a warm, welcoming sort of way. Then she started walking purposefully forward, toward the soaring Poulnabrone.

Raine, however, remained where she stood, staring at the intimidating stones. "Great balls of fire, Mags, you don't think there's *really* a chance we could be zapped into two different places, do you?" She gripped her talisman even tighter.

Maggie turned, extending a hand to her cousin, her Sister of the Craft, and her lifelong best friend. Her voice was soft when she answered, "We'll make certain we aren't."

Shivering, Raine nodded, but remained rooted to the spot, continuing to stare fixedly at Poulnabrone. "Come fly with me!" it seemed to cry out to her.

"C'mon; we mustn't dally." Maggie grasped the other's cold hand. "You're not losing the legendary McDonough courage at this inopportune hour, are you?"

"Of course not!" Raine lied, knotting her fringed shawl over her chest. She gave an abrupt nod, thinking, *I am the courage and strength of all my McDonough ancestors!* "You're right," she said aloud. "We'd better make haste. We don't want to be out of sync with Aisling. Thank God and Goddess she has always been wizard at astral projecting."

Without further hesitation then, the Sleuth Sisters walked to the waiting megalith and entered the arcane Doorway of Time.

Positioning themselves directly under the horizontal stone lintel, Maggie secured her shawl as Raine had done, then extracted from her reticule a tiny key-chain flashlight and a small, red leather notebook. This was the item the Sisters called their portable *Book of Shadows*.

Checking her label watch, Maggie stated, "Aisling will be beginning ... *just about now*. Let us do likewise."

Raine reached into her bag for the sea salt, matches, and the bundle of white sage. She drew their circle of protection with the salt, then struck a match, cradling it against the wind. In an instant, the air filled with the pungent aroma of smoking sage. It was a familiar, comforting scent.

As one, the pair began to chant, "Wind spirit! Fire in all its brightness! The sea in all its deepness! Earth, rocks, in all their firmness! All these elements we now place, by God-Goddess' almighty strength and grace, between ourselves and the powers of darkness! So mote it be! Blessed be!"

The Sisters opened the small *Book of Shadows* to the ribboned page. With careful expression then, they intoned aloud the ancient Gaelic words, the arcane phrases in Old Irish, they had, over the long years, so diligently ferreted out, the secret words of the sacred Time-Key bestowed upon them in the old tongue by Dana, the golden-haired Goddess of the *Tuatha De Danann.*

Their unified voices rising with each line in crescendo, they concluded, "To honor the Olde Ones in deed and name, let Love and Light be our guides again. These eight words the Witches' Rede fulfill: 'And harm ye none; do what ye will.' Now we say this spell is cast, bestow upon us the Secret at last! So mote it be! Blessed be!"

They stood perfectly still, waiting. Not a sound reached them.

The night was hushed– *as though something momentous were about to unfold.*

"We *need* the power of three, *especially* the first time we do this. Let's recite the secret passage over," Maggie said, rechecking her lapel watch. "And this time– focus and *believe.* Feel, with all your essence, love and gratitude to the God-Goddess for the success of our mission. Cast Fear from you, Sister! As will I. *This* is what is holding us back."

Again, the Sisters chanted the long, ancient passage, eyes closed, hands raised in calling forth. Satisfied, Maggie quickly secured the small leather notebook containing the precious Time-Key inside the velvet reticule attached to her wrist.

Presently, little sparks of light zigged and zagged above and around them– hundreds of them, like shooting stars in the most dazzling meteor shower the pair had ever witnessed.

Of a sudden, an ethereal vision of Aisling appeared before them, her long blonde hair billowing out behind her. A terrific wind was rising, and carried on it was a strange, flute-like music, otherworldly in its timbre.

Out of the literal blue, a multitude of ghostly faces, skeletal figures, and vaporish human forms appeared in the rising swirling mists, some with their gaunt arms extended beseechingly. In an instant, claw-like hands wrapped tightly around the Sisters' ankles and, with supernatural strength, drew Raine and Maggie into the mouth of a pitch-black tunnel– a twister of helical wind that threatened to pull them deep inside with the force of a gigantic vacuum!

A flash of lightning– and the mystic wind howled and whirled with accelerated ferocity; so strong was it now that, beneath the table of the great standing stones, Raine and Maggie, trembling, held fast to one another.

Just outside Poulnabrone's Doorway of Time, the eldest Sleuth Sister stood her ground, her long, ash-blonde locks blowing violently about her upturned face, her arms raised skyward, her black robes billowing out from her tall, slender body.

Aisling's courage infused pluck and purpose into Maggie and Raine, and holding hands, they raised their arms, repeating the final line of the arcane passage yet again.

Thicker fog and mists rose from the depths of the earth, and a dreadful feeling of being suffocated by the very air around them threatened to overwhelm the trio.

Speechless perhaps for the first time in her life, Raine squeezed Maggie's hand hard, as another bright bolt of lightning speared the earth before them, a tremendous clap of thunder knocking the pair to the ground. They looked up just in time to see Aisling disappear in a brilliant burst of white light, the sound of her voice echoing after her, **"Bles—sed Beeeeeeeeeeeeeeeeeeeeeeeeeeeeeeeeeeeeee!"**

The powerful wind continued to whirl round and round the standing stones, the ever-rising mists clouding Raine and Maggie from view– as, at last, it wholly engulfed the still-chanting, clinging-together pair.

The oppressive sensation of being crushed by the surrounding atmosphere soon gave way to an acute feeling of being violently pulled deeper and deeper into the long, black tunnel.

"Hold tight!" Maggie's voice reverberated above the blustering din to a resolute Raine. **"Wherever we're going– we're goin' together!!"**

Chapter Fifteen

Raine and Maggie opened their eyes as they lay on the cold, damp ground under Poulnabrone's horizontal slab. For several moments, they could not move. Their bodies felt numb, as though they were intoxicated. The numbness, however, was caused by something electrical, something so powerful that even their minds, for a timeless time, felt deprived of any and all awareness.

Raine endeavored to sit up and, taking a deep gulp of the chill night air, felt it burn all the way to the bottom of her lungs. Still feeling woozy, she looked down at the antique clothing she was wearing, took a second deep breath, then let it out slowly. Another, and that seemed to clear her head, then she looked to what appeared to be a very pale Maggie, who was, by this point, also attempting to sit up. "Maggie, do you think it worked? The landscape," she glanced around, "looks the same. Are we *there?*"

"I don't know. I can't tell." Maggie shook her head as though to clear her brain.

"Breathe deeply, Mags. It helps." Again, Raine sucked in the crisp air. "I have a feeling we made it. *Breathe;* you'll see what I mean. The air seems ... cleaner, fresher than I have ever experienced in my life."

Maggie took a deep breath, filling her lungs and savoring the air. "I don't know. Ireland *is* clean and fresh. We said that–" She stopped abruptly, looking at Raine. Immediately she burst out laughing.

"What's so damn funny?"

"You look as if you stuck your finger in a light socket!" Maggie pulled a brush and some pins from her reticule, and the two began to make repairs.

After giving her deep-red hair a final pat, Maggie gazed out into the night. "Raine, I think you're right– *we made it.* Look," she pointed, "our rental car's *not there.*" She started to get up, but the barren landscape and the magnificent, dark-blue dome of night sky, with its myriad of glittering stars, began to spin sickeningly around her. "Ooooh," Maggie leaned back on her hands. "I'm so dizzy. We'd better take it slowly."

"I'm ... a bit queasy myself," Raine said hoarsely, as she sat back down, waiting for the woozy feeling to pass. "For a second there, I suffered the ultimate dread that I was ... *going back.* Let's get up as *slowly* as we can." She smoothed a stray wisp of ebony hair from her eye.

"I don't think I have a choice." Maggie gradually got to her feet. She stood waiting for her equilibrium to right itself, then extended a shaking hand to her cousin.

Raine clasped the hand and stood. "I feel a little better now." She took another deep pull of the clean, crisp air, her eyes scanning the area about her. Everything was beginning to assume a natural perspective.

Fighting off sweeping spells of vertigo, the Sleuth Sisters brushed themselves off, adjusted their shawls, replaced, to their wrists, their drawstring purses, then ventured a few tentative steps away from Poulnabrone, their legs ready to buckle, their progress slow and listing like two light crafts in a spinning sea that threatened at any moment to engulf them.

"The more we walk, the better we'll feel," Maggie said, hoping to the great Goddess that it would prove true. "We'd better perfect our plan for getting into Barry Hall. What will Robert de Barry, aristocrat and gentleman, think of two strange women arriving at his door, unchaperoned, in the dark of night?"

Always thrilled to use her skills as a raconteur, Raine picked up her skirts, to prevent their dragging on the damp ground, and began bending the tale. "We're two wealthy American women, whose husbands are involved in importing-exporting. We're friends of the bride's family, but not close friends. The bride's home was overflowing with guests, hence we decided to see if we could stay at Barry Hall, since we had determined to attend the wedding at the very last minute, and the bride's family wasn't expecting us."

"Let's say too," Maggie added, "that our husbands were to accompany us, but pressing business forbade their departure the very morning the ship was sailing."

"Good, good! And we had our hearts set on seeing Ireland, so we persuaded them to allow us to travel unescorted. We're Americans, after all. Our proprieties are more relaxed even then ... now. Gracious! I'm getting my chronologies all mixed up! Speaking of which, I do hope this *is* the night before the wedding," Raine said, sounding a bit anxious.

"Well, we were very specific in our invocation. Very clear in our intent. We've cast enough spells in our time to know that *intent* is everything." Maggie paused. "Hold on!" she shouted. The color had returned to her face, and she no longer felt dizzy. "I want to make sure we're walking in the right direction for Barry Hall. Let's see," she pursed her lips, "it was a twenty-minute drive in the car to Poulnabrone, so I figure we have about a two-hour tramp, moving at a good clip that is."

Raine groaned. "We'll still need to explain why we were on the roads after dark, two ladies alone."

Maggie kept walking, her gorgeous face, in the moon's silvery light, reflecting her deep thought. "Hmmm, that's a tough one."

"I've got it!" Raine exclaimed, picking up her pace a bit and talking in the rapid, excited way she sometimes did. "Our ship docked at Galway a couple of days ago. We wired the bride's family, and they, as you said, replied that the house was overflowing with guests, but to come ahead. However, we learned that Barry Hall was closer, and probably not as crowded, so we decided to take our chances there. We rented a horse and buggy near the hotel– which, should anyone ask its name, we completely forgot, so nondescript was the place– then we decided to see the standing stones, since there's absolutely nothing like that in America. While we were visiting Poulnabrone, the horse wandered off, consequently we were forced to walk to Barry Hall, and that's why we're arriving after dark and afoot with no luggage. Our valises were in that runaway buggy!"

Maggie smiled, patting her cousin on the back as the pair continued walking. "Sounds plausible. We'll stick to that then. You missed your calling, Raine. I always said you should have been a writer. You can concoct a story in a blink."

Raine grinned, her husky voice returned to its usual low pitch now. "Are you calling me a damn good liar?"

An hour later, the Sleuth Sisters were still walking, when they came upon the quiet waters of the Shannon. "If we follow the river south, it'll take us right to Ennis," Raine said. She stopped and stood on the dirt path, listening intently.

Maggie stopped too, turning around and looking back at Raine. "What's wrong?"

"Nothing. I was trying to feel the MacNamaras and the O'Briens, who once vied for control of this area. For many long years, bloody battles raged between the clans, right here, right on this very spot."

"That was *long* before where we are now," Maggie replied, cocking her head and listening for whatever it was her cousin seemed to sense. "C'mon, we must keep moving."

It was not long afterward, however, that they noticed some lights up ahead. "Ennis," Maggie said with a sigh. "Let's rest for a few minutes. Thank the good Goddess we had sense enough not to squeeze our feet into those tiny Edwardian shoes!"

"I seemed to have gotten my second wind. Let's not break our stride, if we want to reach Barry Hall any time tonight." Some minutes later, however, Raine made a vexed face. "I wish we could have whisked a horse and buggy through Time with us. That's something we should work on."

"Darlin', not even the most docile of mules would have stood for what we just went through!" Maggie started off again, toward the lights of the country town up ahead. "Waist cinches and hair nets next trip for sure though. Remember that!"

"We might try bicycles sometime, depending on when and where we're going," Raine considered, saucily giving her reticule a twirl.

A tiring Maggie turned her emerald gaze on her cousin, made a derisive noise and kept walking.

The narrow streets of Ennis had a medieval feel to them— not so very different from the Ennis they had seen prior to their more extraordinary "journey."

"Let's move quickly through the town," Maggie said in a low tone. "I don't want us picked up for ladies of the night or some damn thing. Raine, quit twirling that purse, or we *will* be picked up!"

"That could be interesting, don't you think?" Raine giggled, her curiosity prompting her to peer into a window, where she saw a family gathered round the supper table. The fare was plain, but the pair had walked so far in the cold that the steaming bowls of stew looked exceedingly appetizing.

A deep rumble interrupted the silence. "What was that?" Raine asked, turning abruptly.

"My tummy," Maggie laughed. "I hope the lord of the manor will feel obliged to set his table for us."

Their gaiety came to a screeching halt when a deep male voice behind them asked, "Aire you little things lost?"

Raine gulped, her mind working fast, as she came face to chest with a hulk of a man looking down on them with what she translated as a definite leer. "No, sir, we are not. You see, we're on a pilgrimage for the good ..." she gulped, "sisters."

"A pilgrimage? Two ladies alone– in the dark of night?" His eyes swept over the pair.

"Aye," Raine answered, affecting a slight brogue. "'Tis a ver-ry special quest altogether. You see, at the end of our journey, we'll be takin' th' vows ourselves, we will. Our families and friends address us even now with th' venerable utterance, 'Sisters.' I entreat you pray f'r our success, f'r we have a long way t' go yet, and we must be permitted to do it all ourselves with help from no man at all, at all."

The leer instantly vanished from his face, and the man quickly removed his tweed cap, placing it over his heart. "Ye have me prayers, Sisters. On that ye can count. Godspeed t' y' both."

Maggie gave a solemn nod, as did Raine, adding, "God bless you, sir."

"And the wee wheels in those wily wits of yours," Maggie breathed to her storytelling cousin. "A true *seanchaí* ye aire at weavin' a tale, jus' like Grand-*da* McDonough himself!" she concluded with a fine brogue.

The cover of night prevented any further encounters, and within minutes the pair left the town and its lights behind them.

"This dirt road is the N 18 we've traveled by car so many times." Maggie looked to Raine. "I hope, however, we'll recognize, in the dark, the turn-off to Quin when we come to it."

"Once we pass the old abbey, it will be that far again to the turn-off," Raine answered. "I'm glad these traveling suits are as warm as they are. Even with the shawls and all this walking, it's brisk ... and damp."

"Be happy it's not raining. That's another thing we didn't think of."

"Yes, umbrellas in certain climates, such as this one, would come in handy against the rain ... and the sun. They'd be good for protection all round. And money. We must go to a coin shop and purchase suitable money before our next trip. Of course, that won't always be feasible, but it would be nice to have coin. I've been thinking," Raine rambled, "that it's most convenient that we're long-time members of our community theatre. Perfect when we'll need period clothing beyond our own vintage wardrobes, and–" her hand shot up to tap her forehead with the sudden thought, "you know what else? Fort Haleigh! They have scores of things we can use for our 'special travels'!"

Presently, the duo arrived at the high-arched, fifteenth-century Franciscan friary standing solitary in an open field. They could hear, flowing next to it, the quiet waters of the abbey's lazy stream.

Stopping to take in the sight, the Sisters were struck by its moonlit grace.

"Why, it looks the same," Raine noted. "The place possesses the same unruffled tranquility in our time as it does then. I mean 'now'," she quickly amended. "Spell me! This timebinding is tricky."

"If we hadn't just passed through an 1890 Ennis– and even it didn't look that different–" Maggie assented, "I'd never believe we succeeded in our mission, by the look of the abbey here."

No sooner had the Sisters pushed on, when they heard creaking sounds behind them. Turning, they saw a horse and wagon coming toward them, the farmer atop looking more than a little surprised at seeing two well-dressed ladies walking unescorted down this lonely, dark road. He pulled up his horse just ahead of them, and Raine, ever the more talkative, approached the side of the wagon.

"Good sir, could you see your way to driving us to Barry Hall? We're in a bit of a crux, we are."

"Aye, I could that." The farmer continued to gape at them. Then he scrambled down from his seat and helped the women into the back of the wagon.

"Thank you!" the pair chorused.

"… And the silly beast wandered off. It's lucky for us you came along. I don't know if my poor little feet could have carried me a step farther," Raine finished, a hand to her chest, so nearly breathless was she from her storytelling.

"Ye'er th' first Americans I've met." The farmer, middle-aged, looked at them in the thin moonlight. "'Tis a long way t' come f'r a weddin', a long way."

"It was much farther than you think," Raine murmured, stifling a laugh. Maggie nudged her, and she quickly covered her mouth, feigning a yawn.

"... There's nae goin' t' be a Home Rule in my lifetime so long as the House of Lords remains in England, and it has the right of veto. Mebbe nothin' will iver change," the farmer concluded sadly.

"It **will**," Raine McDonough blurted in her husky voice, the words unbidden, her blood instantly rising. Ireland **will**–" For the second time, Maggie poked her into an abrupt silence.

The wagon creaked to a halt. "Here's the lane to Barry Hall," the farmer announced. "I'll carry y' right to th' door."

"No, there's no point in troubling yourself, turning off your road to home. You're most likely late for your supper as it is," Maggie answered. "We'll get out here and walk up to the manor. It's quite all right. Really it is." The farmer, however, was not convinced. "I assure you, kind sir, we will be fine now. And we thank you. I only wish I could pay you, but, as we said, the horse wandered off with our things."

The man tipped his beaked wool cap. "An act of goodwill needs no payment. I'll leave ye then. I've a wife t' home whose voice kin split rocks whin I'm late. *Slan.*"

"*Slan leat.*" The pair waved as the kind farmer gently slapped the reins to the horse and continued down the murky road.

"I wonder if everyone is friendlier in this epoch," Raine mused, looking after him. "We're bound to meet more of what has nearly become, in our time, a dying, vanishing breed– *gentlemen*." When Raine uttered the word "gentleman," she always gave it its full Victorian flavor– an echo from an era well before her own, of course, but nonetheless, the listener was conscious at once of dashing, full-blooded (and probably whiskered) males, sometimes a tad wicked, but always gallant. "What say you, Sister?"

"Well now, that's going to be hard to tell in a country with the slogan '*Céad míle fáilte*,' 'a hundred thousand welcomes.' What I mean is that I think the Irish have lived up to their motto in every century." Maggie pulled on Raine's sleeve. "Come on."

As they approached Barry Hall, the Sisters could not, in the misty moonglow, tell much difference in the place. One thing they did immediately notice was the fancy landau parked in front of the manor house, a regal family crest on its side, a plumed tall pair of matching bays hitched to it.

"I'll bet those beauties belong to Carlotta. Even *they* look Spanish," Raine remarked.

"They look blooded, at any rate." Maggie laid a hand on Raine's arm. "Perhaps she's here now."

"Why would she be? Isn't it bad luck for the groom to see the bride–"

"In her wedding dress."

Raine's tip-tilted green eyes danced, and the dimple in her cheek deepened. "I'll wager he wanted to present her with the Love Gardens tonight!" Raine glanced nervously about, whispering loudly, "Where's the coachman, do you suppose?"

Maggie placed a cautioning finger to her lips, entreating her overzealous cousin to lower her voice. "The custom would be for him to go round to the manse's backdoor for refreshment. Let's get to work. Perhaps we'll learn something of the relationship between Carlotta and Robert."

Except for the fact that the shrubs were smaller, and ivy did not fully cover the walls, the Love Gardens, too, looked virtually no different as the Sisters crept silently along the outer fringe of yews, keeping to the shadows and making themselves as invisible as they could. It wasn't long before voices reached them, a man's and a woman's, his with a passionate Irish lilt, hers with the fire and the music of Spain.

"I heard about that *rogue* of a cousin of yours from a mutual friend of your father's." Robert de Barry sounded more than a little annoyed.

"He's only come for our wedding, Robert. I can't think why you are so jealous of him, of someone you've never even been properly introduced to, of someone with whom you've never so much as exchanged a single word!" Anger carried on Carlotta's voice as well, and under the flickering torchlights, her dark eyes shot fire, as Raine and Maggie caught a glimpse of the strolling pair.

"I did not say I was jealous. I simply said th' man is a rogue!"

Secreted in the yews, but a few feet distant, the Sisters pressed closer, so as not to miss a word of the heated exchange.

"I shouldn't have to remind you that Amador is a *marqués*, and that our family is of a very old lineage. And a very proud one! You insult me, Robert! And you insult my family! My cousin is *not* a rogue!" she glowered. "He merely bears– unwarranted, I might add– the unfortunate reputation of one."

"And his *reputation* most brashly precedes him!" After a quiet moment, De Barry paused on the torch-lit path, and picking up

Carlotta's hand in its fingerless, black lace glove, pressed it to his lips. Still holding her slender fingers in his, he said, his voice contrite, "I would never insult the woman I love … *adore*. Forgive me. Perhaps, you are right. Ah, I suppose 'tis truth in your words. I am jealous of a man much younger and far more exciting than myself. How could I not be? I love you to distraction! Worship you, th' very ground upon which you walk. You must forgive me, *a chuisle*. It is simply that I find myself in a black mood this night."

Carlotta looked stunned. "A black mood! The night before we are to be wed? Again you insult me!"

"Oh, my darlin' girl! I assure you, it has naught to do with you. The jeweler's courier was here earlier, and," he paused, regretting acutely what he had to say, "there was an error– a very **stupid** error!– in what I commissioned the daft firm to do. I am afraid I will have to send the ring back after the wedding to be re-engraved."

Carlotta paused on the path, and toying with her betrothed's silk cravat, she purred, "Robert … why don't you give me the jewels tonight? All except the wedding band, *claro*. Why make me wait until after the wedding? I want to wear them to be wed tomorrow. *Por favor*." Rising on tiptoes, she placed her small, gloved hands on his broad chest and kissed his cheek. "*Por favor, Robert, mi amor.*"

De Barry thought for a few moments before answering, as if weighing his words to this volatile woman he so loved. When he spoke, his voice was gentle but resolute. "No, darlin', I want to give them to you on our wedding day. Isn't it enough that this evening I presented to you the Love Gardens? You haven't uttered a solitary word about them. Don't they please you?"

"They are pleasing, to the estate. But if you *really* wanted to please *me*, you would do what I am entreating you to do now. I want to wear the jewels on my wedding day!"

He kissed her cheek and, taking her arm and looping it through his, patted her gloved hand. "And so you shall wear them … on the morrow." Hoping to divert her attention, he remarked, "Ah, I have just noted that tonight you are wearing my very first gift to you. Do you remember the verse I sent with them?" Not waiting for her response, Robert quoted, "'If that from glove you take the "G," then glove is love and that I send to thee.' The hand, Carlotta, depicts, in my … *our* country, unwavering trust and loyalty, as symbolized in the claddagh." Again, he pressed her lace-adorned hand to his lips. "Do I have your loyalty, my love? Tell me that I do."

In response, Carlotta snatched her hand from his, stamped her foot, and if looks could kill, Robert would have dropped down on the spot. She stood, glaring at him in grim silence, while her beautiful eyes, in the flickering light from the torch lamps, flashed in temper. "I want the jewels tonight, Robert, **tonight!** If you do not concede to my wishes, I will make you sorry … and you know I can!"

From their hiding place behind the shadowy yews, the Sleuth Sisters had a fine view of the lovers' quarrel. "She wants the jewels now, because she knows she's going to elope with her cousin … that *marqués!*" Raine whispered to Maggie. "Look at her! It's crystal clear!"

Maggie clamped a quick, firm hand over a big-eyed Raine's open mouth, pointing to the path through the yews before them. A heavy-set woman, draped from head to toe in black, lumbered along some yards behind Carlotta and Robert. Once she had safely passed, Maggie removed her hand.

"The *duenna*, the chaperone!" Raine breathed. "Carlotta would *never* be alone with Robert until after the wedding. We were nearly discovered! Thanks, Mags."

Maggie peered through the hedges to see the couple, the duenna in their wake, heading for the manor. "C'mon, let's brush off our clothing, try to make ourselves look our parts, then approach the house from the front door. It looks as though Carlotta is just about to leave."

"… Thus you are truly a knightly gentleman to rescue us from our dilemma like this." Maggie dabbed daintily at the corner of her mouth, where a crumb of soda bread was about to escape.

The Sisters were seated at table in the familiar dining room of Barry Hall, where a uniformed maid removed their emptied plates.

"Friends of my fiancée's family are always welcome here." *Their manners are genteel enough, but they devour food like a couple of poor souls newly released from the workhouse.* "How did you say you knew my Carlotta's family?"

Raine nearly choked on a large hothouse grape, and hastily reached for her wine goblet. After taking a sip of the ruby liquid, she came to Maggie's aid. "Actually we have never met the family. It was our husbands who met them in Kinsale on a business venture, two, perhaps three years past."

"I see." Robert brought his large hands together as if in prayer. "Now that you've had refreshment, you no doubt wish to retire. You must be greatly fatigued from your unaccustomed exertions. I'll have Fíona show you up to your room. She will see to your needs. Should there be anything further you wish, please, do not hesitate to ask." He stood. "I'll bid you good-evening then. Sleep well." He effected a slight bow before turning to leave.

"He puts me in mind of Rob, but seems to lack his sense of humor … or any humor whatsoever. Do you think he bought our story?" Raine asked in an anxious whisper, behind the closed door of their bedchamber. She began to remove the numerous pins and the chignon from her short, glossy black hair.

"I think he did. It's more believable than the truth I daresay. We're fortunate that Barry shared with us as much as she did about the contents of his diary." Maggie, who had already removed the pins from her dark-red chignon, gave her shoulder-length hair a toss and began undressing. "Let's get out of these clothes and give them to Fíona to brush and steam for tomorrow. We don't want to look like a couple of down-and-outs. I was able to read fragments of De Barry's thoughts, and, I am sorry to say, that was one bit I caught."

A tap came at the door. Hastily wrapping a towel around her head, Raine handed the traveling suits and their shawls to Fíona, who provided them with two nightdresses smelling strongly of camphor. "These were Mr. de Barry's mother's. I found them at the back of the linen closet, m'am."

"Thank you." The Sisters tried to look appreciative despite the smell. Once the door was again closed, Maggie tossed the reeking night garments aside and sank down into a chair in her shift. "How I wish I could take a long, hot shower!"

"I know. I'm not going to feel really clean, bathing, like a cat, out of that bowl and pitcher." With a sigh, Raine began the unwelcome task.

Within a half-hour, the pair were abed. Though they had been thinking they would be too excited to sleep, they drifted off the moment their heads hit the heather-scented feather pillows.

The morning of the wedding dawned clear. Fíona knocked at their door at sun-up, bringing strong breakfast tea and warm, flaky scones with butter and a delicious black-currant jam.

No sooner were Maggie and Raine dressed, when, from the downstairs foyer, rose the bellowing sound of Robert's angry voice.

"*Och!* The jade and the carpet knight, quite a pair, that! A fine meld f'r a halfpenny novel! May the pair of them meet th' Divil at every turn! And **you**! What kind of a father are you to let your daughter run off with a man everyone knows to be a philandering, unprincipled blackguard! A rogue with a reputation as black as Satan's himself!"

Maggie and Raine scurried to the landing at the top of the stairs, hiding themselves behind the ornate railing and a trio of colossal potted plants to witness the escalating confrontation.

The distinguished-looking Señor Montoya reddened, but kept a tight rein on his Latin temper. His words were measured, his accent heavier than his daughter's. "Indeed her behavior was unpardonable; however, what's done is done. Now we must, all of us, learn to live with it."

"***You*** live with it, Montoya! You and that sly little minx! As far as I am concerned, all dealings– *business* and otherwise– between me and your … *farcical* family are severed." He flung open the front door. "Starting **NOW**!!!"

Señor Montoya drew himself up to his fullest height. "Perhaps," he stated, his voice ice, "my daughter *did* make the better choice!" He turned and strode pridefully from the entrance hall, De Barry violently slamming the heavy door after him.

"A pox on th' lot of you!"

Fíona suddenly appeared in the foyer, wiping soapy hands on her apron, her face registering concern.

Turning toward his housekeeper, Robert yelled, "The wedding is off! Inform the guests!"

"Whew! Spanish aristocrats are as proud as Lucifer! I know that from my mother's side of the family," Raine murmured in a low tone. "And Robert's temper deserves the legendary status his descendants have given it. But I thought he was left standing at the altar."

"Figuratively," Maggie returned in a whisper, a finger to her lips to silence her chatty cohort, "he was."

A dejected Robert de Barry was bent over his massive desk, penning the last lines of his lament to his lost love, when Raine and Maggie came to the partially open door of his study. Since Robert was talking aloud and seemed to be deeply submerged in his keening, they hesitated to disturb him, though they stood, silent, behind the door, immobilized by the pain carried on his words.

"Thus to cleanse my soul. Your heart is as cold as stone!" He continued putting pen to paper. "Reveal to me a broken heart … there the hidden beauty."

For a long moment he sat back in his chair, seemingly in thought, then he took up his pen once again, dipped it into the inkwell and rapidly wrote out several more lines. After reading through what he had just drafted, Robert, in explosive anger and swift motion, ripped the page from the journal, crushed it into a ball and hurled it to the floor. "If my heirs– should I ever produce any– have any wits about them, they can bloody well figure it out for themselves!"

Raine and Maggie looked to one another, then to the crumpled paper lying on the floor across the room. With tilt of head, Maggie motioned to the doorway, the fear of discovery prompting them to rap lightly. "Excuse us, Mr. de Barry, but we are ready to take our leave now," she said softly.

"We hesitated disturbing you, but we so wanted," Raine continued, "to thank you again for your chivalrous hospitality, and to bid you *adieu*."

Robert turned his wet-eyed gaze on them, then stood, pushing the high-backed, maroon velvet chair away from the desk. "Yes, yes, come in." He motioned to a pair of padded, tapestry-print chairs before the fire. "Please, sit down and warm yourselves. I must see to your carriage. Excuse me. I'll be but a moment." He walked briskly to the door and called, his voice once again stentorian, "Thomas! Thomas!! Where is that infernal lad? I entreat you; make yourselves comfortable, ladies. Would you care for something warming to drink?"

The Sisters shook their heads, answering together, "No, thank you."

Robert left the study, grumbling on about his absent servant, whilst Raine shot nimbly out of her seat to snatch up the crumpled page from De Barry's diary. She quickly stuffed it into her reticule.

"And if he notices it missing?" Maggie whispered with a quick glance toward the door.

Raine shrugged, "I'll tell him I threw it into the fire, thinking it scrap."

Maggie's silent response was to raise a hand with thumb and index finger forming the circle that symbolized the avant-garde "Way to go!"

Grim-faced, Robert stood at the side of the buggy, helping first Raine, then Maggie onto the seat. "Are you sar-tain you can manage? 'Tisn't seemly, sendin' you off without a driver or chaperone. I wish you'd change your minds and allow me to send young Thomas to drive the buggy and accompany you."

"We will be fine, sir," Maggie assured him. "Please, rest easy on that account."

"We would feel very naughty, indeed, taking your coachman," Raine teased à la Scarlett O'Hara, "when all we want to do is meander along, sightseeing as much as we can en route to the docks at Shannon. American ladies," she dimpled prettily, "as you most likely divined, are much more independent than women elsewhere."

Robert made a vain attempt at a smile. *Aye, I have noticed that.* "'Tisn't far," he said aloud. Then he handed them a heavy, cream-colored envelope with his seal on the back. "Once you get there, give this missive to the gentleman I told you about, a Mr. Liam Flynn. He will see to the tickets for your return passage. Leave the horse and trap with him, and I will have my man collect them in a day or so. Forgive me for not showing you about the area myself, but I am afraid I would be exceedingly poor company at this," he lowered his head, for a moment pausing, afraid perchance that his voice would break, "*regrettable* time."

Raine laid her small gloved hand on his. "We quite understand. You've been most kind. Perhaps, one day, we will meet again." Then, as an afterthought, she added, "Time, Mr. de Barry, has an ingenious way of setting matters straight. I have a good feeling that will happen in your case."

Maggie smiled. "We sincerely appreciate your rescue of us. Godspeed, Mr. de Barry." She gently flapped the reins over the horse's broad back.

"Godspeed," Robert returned, his baritone voice a bit shaky. He stood watching as the Sisters drove down Barry Hall's long, tree-lined lane and out onto the road. Then he turned and walked slowly back to the empty manor house, head down, shoulders slumped.

As soon as they were out of earshot, Raine said, "Let's secure the horse in those trees over there, so we can read the discarded page. I simply cannot wait a moment longer!"

The trees cast long shadows across the road. Maggie pulled in the reins, securing them on the brake. Raine already had the sheet in her hand, smoothing it out over her skirt-covered knees. She held the page so that they could both read it.

"I knew it!" Raine nearly gasped. "It's what he intends doing with the jewels!"

"We'd better stick to our plan and sneak back and *see* what he does with them, before we return to our own century. In his state, he's capable of just about anything," Maggie reasoned.

"I agree, and I don't think we'll have long to wait. I think he'll cache the jewels away tonight– his foiled wedding night." Raine rolled the smoothed page and slipped it back into her green velvet reticule.

"I have a keen witchy feeling that you're right," Maggie replied, "but we shall see, as the saying goes."

It was the magickal hour of twilight when the Sleuth Sisters, hiding in the bushes near the entrance to the Love Gardens, saw Robert come out the back door of the manor, carrying a box, a lantern, and what appeared to be a couple of tools. The Sisters waited until he entered the gardens, then they stealthily followed, keeping to the deep shadows.

"That last was a surprise," Raine whispered to Maggie not long afterward, as the pair watched Robert de Barry, finished with his rueful task, walk, like the broken man he now was, from the torch-lit gardens back toward the manor.

"Mission accomplished," Maggie breathed with a long, satisfied sigh. "We may as well start back."

At Poulnabrone, Raine and Maggie unhitched the horse and removed all his trappings. Whacking him with her hand smartly across his sleek brown rump, Maggie exclaimed, "Skedaddle, you balky beast!" With an answering whinny, a toss of his head, and a backward kick toward the Sisters, the horse shot off at a gallop south, in the direction of Barry Hall.

"I hope he finds his way back," Raine said, looking after him and shaking her head.

Maggie scoffed, "The way we had to grapple with him at every turn! He'll be back at Barry Hall within the hour. I *am* sorry Robert's out a trap, but," she concluded, cocking her fiery red head and locking eyes with her cousin, "unfortunately, there is nothing we can do about that."

"There is!" Raine exclaimed. "Why don't I compose a note and leave it with the buggy? These farmers around here are honest folk. Someone will return Robert's trap to him."

Maggie nodded, patting Raine on the shoulder. "Good idea." She glanced up at the moon. "And the Goddess is providing the needed light."

Opening their small *Book of Shadows*, Raine dashed off the brief missive, ripped out the notebook page, and secured it with a rock on the buggy seat, then she turned, looking with angst at the looming, nighttime Poulnabrone. "It's calling to us, Mags. We'd best get going. I've been gearing myself up all evening." She let out a huge sigh. "And this time, we're on our own."

"Yes, but now it'll be a breeze," Maggie joked with a weak smile. "A *breeze*," she repeated, nudging Raine, "get it?"

Raine essayed a smile of her own. "Oh, I get it all right!" *Buck up, McDonough!* she told herself sharply. *The Old Ones are watching and waiting!*

Maggie reached for the small, red leather notebook and opened to the ribboned page. "No time like the present, huh?"

The Sleuth Sisters clasped hands tightly and, for the second time in their soon-to-be illustrious career, began the ancient Gaelic invocation– *the magickal Key that unlocked the door of Time.*

The manor was dark and silent when the exhausted Sisters entered the front door and started quietly up the stairs. "We must tell Rob before we do anything else," Raine said, stifling a yawn. "Excuse me, but I'm …" she started to yawn again, "beat. But, Mags, we did it! We really did it!" She reached over and hugged her Sister of the Moon.

With depth of feeling, Maggie returned the embrace, and for a long, private moment, the pair stood thus, silently channeling their deep bonds of love and respect, each to the other.

At Rob's bedroom door they paused. Raine was just about to knock, when Maggie stopped her, grasping her cousin's hand the second before it struck the thick oaken panel. "We don't want to undo our welcome here," she whispered.

Raine made a baffled face.

"We're still in these outfits," Maggie explained, holding her voice to a whisper, "I'll remind you, borrowed *unsanctioned* from the attic. *And* ..." she cocked her head toward the closed bedroom door with a lift of one arched brow. "Hmmm?"

Realization struck her, and Raine dropped her hand, an impish expression passing over her face. Following Maggie's lead, she silently crept a safe distance down the hall, dark except for the flickering flame-like bulbs in the intermittent wall sconces. "You're right; Barry's probably in there with him." She yawned again, this time not even bothering to cover it. "It'll keep till morning." She slipped out of her shoes, picked them up, and yawned even bigger. "Anyway, the tale I invented for how we found the telling page from the diary isn't worthy of my storytelling ... isn't convincing ... whatever. And I'm too sleepy to craft a better one right now."

Maggie caught the still-yawning Raine by the seat of her long velvet skirt. "This is an easy fix. Give me his ancestor's note, and I'll just slide the page under Rob's door– and we say nothing."

"We know nothing," Raine mumbled, as she handed Robert de Barry's missive to Maggie and padded off to bed.

"The real secret is believing in yourself."
~ All the great avatars

Chapter Sixteen

Driving through the darkening Irish countryside, Barry soon discovered, was tricky business. Sweeping grey mists and a sudden, heavy rain shower did not help matters. The roads were narrow and winding, and there was virtually no illumination at all, except for the occasional lights from another vehicle. Before dusk, she stopped several times to allow sheep to cross. Once, a kindly old man atop a horse-drawn wagon waved encouragingly to her.

In Ennis, she had returned her costume to Sullivan's Fantasia. Afterward, she strolled Ennis' main streets, window shopping along the colorful and inventive store fronts. She had even taken a leisurely, light meal in the quaint dining room of one of the town's most historic hotels– all the while doing some serious thinking.

She drove slowly as she continued to reflect on the events of the past few days. *I must return to Pittsburgh to collect my belongings, sell some of my things and give up the apartment. I am afraid, though, that I may never get a commitment from Rob. He's sort of fractured the faerie tale. That thing he said the other day about not being able to oblige Maeve with a commitment ... did it mean he was incapable of one to her, or to any woman? I really don't know that. And when he said he could not understand how his great-grandfather could put a love interest above everything else ... I think, though, to be fair to Rob, I did rush to judgment with that one. He didn't actually say **he** couldn't put a love interest before everything else. He said he couldn't understand how his great-grandfather could. Rob was talking about **him**. Or at least I hope he was.*

Barry pulled the car off the road and turned off the ignition. *I think, to be honest, I was still smarting over 'Little-Miss-Hunt-Club.' And at the ball, when Tim Callahan grabbed Maeve, and Rob interceded ... . But it was only right that he should protect a lady, and especially one who was a guest in his own home. He did seem to be enjoying her company last night. Then again, she's not the kind of woman a man would run from. Any man!*

She looked around for a road sign. There was none. *I don't know where I am. My problem is I'm afraid of losing Rob– in more ways than one. Even with Bill no longer a threat, I feel the presence of danger– a very great danger– and I **know** I'm not imagining it. I won't leave Rob's side until I know for sure this ... lurking evil has* *passed. To be perfectly honest, I'm still scared to death— about everything!*

She leaned forward, resting her forehead on the cold steering wheel, her thoughts suddenly returning to the reading she had done the night Rob left to return to Ireland. *All of my dreams are held in the blankness of Destiny.* She closed her eyes, trying to remember the most important facets of the reading.

Receiving the Destiny rune is a clarion call for courage. The whole reading was veiled in mystery, danger, and intrigue. But I must remember to stop acting out of Fear. There is nothing that cannot be changed, warded off. We always have choices.

Barry turned the overhead light on and checked her watch. *It's late, and I am most definitely lost.* She opened the glovebox and unfolded the map, perusing it several moments. *I need to find N 18, then R 469.*

She reached for the ignition key, but paused before actually starting the car. A feeling of determination was gradually settling over her. *I'll find my way back. I've made my choices. I'm going to tell Rob that if he was serious about giving me a job, working for him, then I want to take him up on it. After all, as Raine said, thoughts are magick wands– powerful enough to make anything happen, anything we choose.*

I've been wondering how it's going to affect me when I actually make the official move from Pittsburgh to Ireland. She gazed out the car window. It was nearly dark now, but streams of light shone where the sun had set behind some green-black trees in the distance. The rain had stopped as suddenly as it had come. The darkening landscape seemed to shimmer, and a spectacular rainbow arched from one side of the quiet valley to the other. *Another omen. This changeable Irish weather… it throws one backdrop after another across its ever-changing canvas of sky.*

Her eyes skimmed the countryside. *Ireland. Moss and fern draping grey stones with emerald velvet ... grey-green fingers of sea plus roaring ocean foaming white against sheer, dark cliffs ... purple ridges of mountain– all coming together in mystical solitude. The salt-tanged sea wind ... the sheep dotting the rolling, green hills ... the white-washed, thatched-roof cottages tucked into quiet folds of the land ... the charming country roads ... the tranquil blue loughs ... the high-spirited, deep-feeling people.*

Ireland has drawn me in. I have fallen in love with this passionate land nearly as much as I have with Rob.

She started the engine, putting the car into gear, finding it hard to believe that places like this still existed in the world today. Feeling better at once, she executed a U-turn and headed back in the direction she had come, gazing anew in wonder at the unfolding, twilight beauty of the misty Irish countryside.

***

In the fireplace, the flames flickered and snapped, making ghostly, dancing shadows on the walls of Phillip's bedchamber. Kneeling before the brass-bound trunk, Rob rummaged through the contents, checking to see if anything was missing. Though everything seemed to be there, he continued searching. At the very bottom was the ornate box. He lifted it out, took the tiny baroque key from the top bureau drawer, and opened it, raising the lid.

The box's dark recesses unexpectantly released a mystical green light. He sat back on his heels, hardly daring to believe he was actually in possession of the magnificent emerald jewelry. *Could it be? There must be magick infused in the De Barry jewelry!*

One by one, he ran his fingers over the large, sparkling emerald and diamond ring, the stunning earbobs, and the matchless beauty of the magnificent necklace. Then he lifted out the ring, gazing long into its cool green depths. He could not tear his eyes from that shimmering center stone. In fact, he could not put the jewel down, so drawn was he into its undersurface.

Enchanted, he seemed to have no will of his own, as he traveled deeper and deeper into the emerald's mysterious crystal cavern.

Beset now with dreams of Venus, Rob tossed on the bed, mumbling incoherently.

Clothed in a green velvet drape, the Goddess of Love beckoned to him, a sardonic smile on her parted lips. When he reached out to her, she gleefully slipped away from his reach, disappearing into the engulfing, eddying mists.

Rob moved farther into the mystical green depths, only to find, not Venus, but his great-grandfather, Robert de Barry, dressed in 1890s attire and seated in candleglow at his massive desk, composing his lament to his lost Carlotta.

"List' to me … my tristful heart shall tell, how, in my sorrow, my love's delight concealed–" A mocking laugh interrupted him, and Robert looked up to see Venus, ever beautiful, fluttering in and out of the encircling mists that hung like a pale green shroud around the surreal scene.

Heedless, Robert continued to compose his poem. "Oh, show me, my angel, the way to gain the flood of tears … thus to cleanse my soul. Oh, Goddess of Love … ." He looked up, at that instant, entreating the capricious Venus to hear him. Mocking his pleas, she laughed merrily, her laugh falling on him like broken shards of green glass, as she continued to beckon. Yet every time Rob approached her, she deftly eluded him, cradling the ornate box to her bosom.

His great-grandfather returned once again to his lament. "Nay! Your heart is as cold as stone! Lift away your robes of emerald green … reveal to me a broken heart … there, the hidden beauty."

Staying just out of reach, Venus opened the box, drawing out the exquisite necklace. Holding the glittering *rivière* in her hands, the emeralds and diamonds dripping from her slim fingers, she continued to taunt Rob. The jewels tinkled like wind chimes. He moved toward her, reaching for the jewels, but as before, she evaded him. Again she laughed, and this time the timbre of her voice sounded like a carillon– or perhaps it was the tinkling sound of the jewels as she returned them to the shiny, metal casket she yet clasped to her heart. Spellbound by the goddess's antics, Rob watched as Venus' face transformed into the haughty aristocratic visage of Carlotta.

The older Robert, too, saw the Carlotta-persona of Venus, his face wretched as he completed his exorcising lament. "Nay! Your heart is as cold as stone! If the walls of Barry Hall could tell of my sorrow, my chagrin, they would, in a word, whisper *C-a-r-l-o-t-t-a.*"

When Rob made a last, rigorous attempt to snatch away the jewels, Venus gave a *banshee* wail, disappearing into the swirling mists with her cradled treasure.

The incredible thing was that before she vanished, Carlotta's face, losing its hauteur, softened into Barry's equally stunning features. It was Barry who ultimately eluded him, disappearing into the swirling emerald mists.

Venus' *banshee* wailing, however, continued, as Rob tossed on the bed, the white lace curtains billowing into the shadowy bedchamber. A strong autumnal wind rattled the panes, its runic keening and cold, icy fingers wakening him from his misty dreams with a sudden flooding of the senses– a wild rushing of thought and brightly colored images. For a few moments, the furor of the dream, or perhaps just its unearthly qualities, remained, scarcely ebbing in the ghostly light. He sat up, engulfed in magick.

Something about the dream left him with a sad feeling of loss and a painful lump in his throat. "Barry."

Disoriented, Rob sat on the bed like one drugged, trying to remember. When his half-open eyes began to focus, his gaze came to rest on the small lighted lamp on the dresser across the room. Glancing at his watch, he ran his fingers through his hair, then his eyes traveled to the open window with its flapping white curtain and the chill and damp of night beyond. *I must have dozed off.*

Wearing only his shorts, he got up and moved to the window. After lowering the sash, he stood there, looking out. *The banshee wail portends a death. Surely there's not to be another.* As if in response to his thought, the wind, with its keening cry, wailed forlornly.

Below, a torch lamp near the pointing Cupid romantically illuminated the entrance to the labyrinthine gardens. Rob remained at the window, gazing down at the angle of the arm, the shoulder aligning perfectly with the fountain and its statue of Venus that peered out of the misty darkness like a ghostly sentinel.

Only from this position, at this particular window in the master bedroom where he now stood, above the maze of yew hedges, was this alignment visible, accentuated by the nighttime lighting.

"Wiz-zard, fanciful planning, that," Rob said softly. "I never really noticed it before." Standing there, looking out on the Love Gardens, he began quoting from the lament.

"'Oh, show me, my angel, the way to gain the flood of tears … .'"

Ruminative, he turned from the window, switched on the bedside lamp, picked up the old diary from the nightstand, and located the translation of the Gaelic poem. He unfolded the sheet, reading aloud and skimming down the page. "'Goddess of Love … your heart is as cold as stone. Lift away your robes of emerald green … reveal to me a broken heart …'"

Rob's expression changed as realization crashed over him like a tsunami wave. He repeated the last words in a whisper, *"'there … the hidden beauty.'"*

Hurriedly, he pulled on jeans and a sweater, his gaze falling on the smoothed-out sheet of paper lying on the floor, his ancestor's missive slipped under the door earlier courtesy of the Sleuth Sisters.

Picking it up, he moved to the light to read it, his eyes skimming the antiquated script. "The hidden beauty!" he repeated, nearly shouting the words. "But where th' bloody hell did this come from? Could it have fallen out of the diary th' first night we searched through the trunk, fluttered under somethin' and– *This says it all!*" With a shrug, he laid the page on the dresser and set the diary over it. The translation he slid into his pocket.

At Barry's room he paused with the intention of knocking. No light showed from the crack under the closed door, and when he put his ear to the door, no sound came to him. *It's late. She's probably asleep. What a surprise this will be for her in th' morning!*

Without further delay, he dashed down the stairs and out into the night. From the public room of the ancient manor house's ground floor, the Gothic grandfather clock was dutifully chiming midnight.

Rob swiftly made his way to the gardener's shed. Finding the door unlocked, he entered the pitch-black interior. Pulling a book of matches from his jeans pocket, he struck one, his eyes scanning the area in the feeble light. He had to strike several matches before he located what he needed– a lantern, a pick, and a pry bar. Then, carrying the tools, he exited the shed and walked briskly through the garden maze to the Venus.

The light from the bullseye lantern cast a yellow glow across the sheet of paper in his hand. "Bollocks! The damn thing is so clear. Now I wonder how I didn't see it immediately." He read, "'… how in my sorrow, my love's delight concealed.' The 'love's delight' is the jewelry." He skimmed down, while the *banshee* wind tugged with ghostly fingers at the parchment in his hand. "'Show me, my angel, the way' is the pointing Cupid, indicating the fountain. 'The Goddess of Love,' of course, is the Venus. 'Robes of emerald-green,' the ivy. Therefore …"

Rob set the lighted lantern on the fountain's edge, knelt, and began tearing away the thick and tangled veil of ivy, the bullseye casting a circle of golden light over him. There, at the base of the wall, on one of the bricks, was a crudely chiseled heart, a slash through its center.

"'Reveal to me a broken heart … there, the hidden beauty.'" Rob shoved the translation back into his pocket. The tools were on the ground beside him. He took up the pick, glanced at the brickwork, then hurriedly cast it aside. Digging into his jeans for his pocketknife, he crouched down and started chipping away at the dry, powdery mortar. Using the pry bar, he pulled out the single loose brick. When he reached inside, his fingers touched cold metal, and a grin spread across his face. Expectantly, he withdrew a metal casket. Lifting the lid, he found a second box, ornate and intricately carved. It was locked. "Th' key in the trunk!"

Eager to get back to his room, he started to rise and felt a sharp, fiery pain shoot from his shoulders to the tip of his fingers, as his assailant– eerily silhouetted in the flickering light from the lantern– struck him a heavy blow with a shovel.

Swiftly then, the shadow-man replaced the brick, wove the torn strands of ivy over the exposed portion of the wall, and extinguished the lantern. Lastly, he dragged Rob's body down the yew-lined path and out of the shadowy, serpentine gardens.

The *banshee* wind, with its dire and ghostly warning of death, wailed even louder.

"Women are like tea bags.
We don't know how strong we are until we're in hot water."
~ Eleanor Roosevelt

Chapter Seventeen

In their spacious double room at Barry Hall, the Sleuth Sisters, both in pajamas, were back to work on their doctoral, excitedly discussing their recent experience. Books were spread across the chamber's floral chintz-covered couch, over the twin beds, and on the carpeted floor between them. Leaning against the mahogany headboard, using her knees as a desk, Maggie was busy taking down copious commentary, exposition and analysis in a thick notebook. Beside her, an outsized book on Ireland was open to a page illustrating Poulnabrone. "Eventually," she mumbled to herself, "everything connects– people, things, thoughts. The quality of the connections is the Key … ."

Raine stood at the quaint diamond-leaded window, brushing her teeth. "Didn't it feel good to shower! Ah, the delights of the modern age!" she sang out.

"My shower gave me a second wind too." Maggie paused in her writing, glancing over at Raine. "We've *got* to get this all down while it's fresh in our minds. Now," she emphasized with her pen, "Einstein said that nothing is ever lost or destroyed. Every light image, every sound wave that ever was still exits. Time, as we think of it, does *not* exist. Past, present, future– it's all *simultaneous*, like a great ball of yarn we lay out in a straight line to organize our lives into hours, days, weeks, months and years."

"I think I understand," Raine remarked, not even bothering to take the toothbrush from her mouth, "after what we've been through, why Einstein's hair always looked the way it did. You know … as if he combed it with firecrackers."

"When we checked our watches upon our return to our own time, not a second had passed from the moment we left! Isn't that amazing?! Truly amazing?!" Maggie tilted her head, pensive. "Do you realize what this means?" she exclaimed, holding up her notebook. "We can go back in time to solve any mystery that History has kept secret from our world. It's *Brilliant!*"

Raine yanked the toothbrush from her mouth, affecting a foamy reply. "Like Napoleon said, 'Impossible is a word found only in the dictionary of fools!'" She turned back to the window, gazing out at the twinkling stars and the moon, still high in a cobalt sky, glowing white and partially obscured by ragged, silver-edged clouds. "Einstein also said that 'The intuitive mind is a sacred gift, the rational mind a faithful servant. We've created a society that honors the servant and has forgotten the gift.' Think, Mags, of all the possibilities now. Every year, every event is *there*," she gestured toward the star-sprinkled nightsky with the toothbrush, her voice taking on a dramatic tone, "out there … *somewhere*. Just waiting to be visited– and explored."

"And now that we have the Time-Key, and won't have to research the logistics of our travel, we can prepare more thoroughly for each trip. Your thought about borrowing costumes from our theatre group is excellent, but forget about the fort. The folks at Fort Haleigh are not going to loan us anything from their collection; I can tell you that right now. And rightly so," she added in the fort's defense. "We'd do better ferreting out our needs from our area's exceptional costume-rental shops. Then there're the flea markets and antique shops, and we've plenty of those in the Pittsburgh area," Maggie mused, adjusting her back against the bed's headboard.

"We've a good start on the lot already!" Raine laughed, thinking about their home with its myriad of treasures, attic to cellar, of their combined wardrobes of vintage clothing and antique jewelry. Raine reached for her night cream, dabbing it round the delicate skin of her fabulous feline eyes, then massaging it upward into her flawless complexion.

A delicate apricot stained Maggie's milky cheeks, and her emerald eyes glittered. "This is *exhilarating*! We can meticulously research the period we're going to visit– clothing, speech patterns, customs, the works." Her expression was pensive for a moment. "Period money presents more of a challenge. I noted what you said, that we could visit a coin shop before a trip, but antique money is often quite costly."

"Oh, I realize that," Raine replied, giving her ebony hair a few brisk strokes with her brush. "It won't always be feasible, but as I mentioned, it would be nice to have coin, as the saying goes."

"I know!" Maggie's face again lit up. "We could take something with us to sell, a small item or two, in sync and of value to where we're going."

Raine grimaced. "'He who would travel happily must travel light.' Antoine de Saint-Exupéry," she recited, remembering how Maggie had smirked at her bicycle idea.

"Light, of course. I said something small … and easy to transport. Then we'd have emergency funds, and it wouldn't cost us an arm and a leg each trip."

"That's *wizard*, Mags!"

"You've been using that old expression a lot lately. Where'd you hit on it? It's linked almost exclusively to preppie schoolboys nowadays."

"I heard Rob say it the other day, and I've adopted it."

Maggie smiled at her gamin cousin. "Getting back to our discussion of period money, if all else fails, we can revert back to our old standby– 'Our things were stolen.' By the way, did you experience, both times, a high-pitched sound as we sped through the long, black tunnel?"

"Uh-huh," Raine answered, absently staring out the window, her hairbrush still in her hand. Their room overlooked the carriage house flat where Nora and Frank resided. "Frank's card game must not be over. The 'Forty-Fivers'' cars are still in the lot."

Maggie nodded, leafing through a pictorial on Stonehenge, while she rambled to herself, "Mind over matter. Noetic science– the human mind and its untapped potential– *it's the last great frontier.* Did you hear me, Raine? The last great frontier is not space, as so many think and say, but *the mind!* Oh, Raine, what a door we have opened!" Maggie went into instant reverie, her Mona Lisa smile lending mystery to her beautiful face.

"What th'–" Raine quickly ducked behind the drape, and brush in hand, began gesturing frantically to Maggie, who was at the moment oblivious to her cousin's wild antics. Quickly then, she voiced in a ragged whisper, "Pssst! Maggie! McHendrie and somebody else are wrestling what looks to be a body wrapped in," still hidden behind the curtain, she leaned closer to the window, peering out, "a tarp, I think, into the trunk of Frank's Ford!"

"What!" Maggie swept the books aside and, leaping off the bed, ran to the window. From a nearby chair, she snatched up the jeans and sweater Raine had worn earlier that day and, shoving them at her, exclaimed, "Hurry and dress! Try not to let them out of your sight. And for Heaven's sake, don't let them see you. I'll run downstairs and phone the Gards!" After yanking on a pair of slacks and a sweater over her pajamas, she rushed down the stairs and into the shadowy foyer.

Raine had begun pulling on her clothes as rapidly as she could behind the draperies, where she could still see McHendrie and his accomplice.

A few seconds later, a trio of events occurred nearly simultaneously. Barry, who had finally found her way back to the manor– and driving the rental car in the middle of the roadway– turned into the carpark at the precise moment McHendrie and his passenger were speeding away, without lights, in Frank's Ford, the passenger ducking down to hide himself.

Hell's Fire! Where'd that car come from! Barry jerked the wheel sharply to the left. Both vehicles swerved to avoid crashing head-on but sideswiped at the entrance, the harsh, drawn-out shriek of scraping metal setting her teeth on edge. *Damn it! Who **was** that maniac?*

The game of "Forty-Five" was just breaking up, when Frank went to the window to air the smoky room. Hearing the collision and screeching tires, he threw up the sash and leaned out over the sill. "What th' hell's goin' on down there?"

Below, Barry stepped, a bit shaky, from the rental and, looking up at the opened window, yelled, "Frank! Someone just tore outta here in your car!"

Frank hung as far as he could out the window, looking toward the carpark entrance.

"I couldn't see who it was," Barry shouted. "They were runnin' without lights 'n layin' rubber. They sideswiped me!"

"Jaysus!" Frank yelled. "Someone stole me car!" Dashing across the room to the door, Frank grabbed, en route, a fowling piece and a handful of shells, his excited cronies close behind him. Nearly tripping over one another, the four men, including Sheriff Brennan, burst from the carriage house into the dimly lighted carpark, leaving in their wake a flustered, irate Nora, in nightdress, at the top of the stairs. "Francis Dillon, where d'ya think you're goin' at this time-a night! **Francis!!!**"

"Into my car!" Brennan gestured. "We'll catch th' bloody bastid!" There was a mad rush to get into the car. Barry pushed her way into the front seat, next to the sheriff. "This is police wur-rk, lass. You stay here!" Frank, O'Shaughnessy and Garrity piled into the back.

"I've got a press card; I'm used to this sort of thing. Go!" Barry pointed in the direction of Frank's stolen vehicle. *I don't know why.*

I just know I've got to go along! And it's not a good feeling that I'm feelin'!

"**Go!**" Frank resounded. "What 'r we sittin' here for!"

Brennan floored it, and with a screeching of tires, the chase was on.

"Ye'er sar-tain it wasn't Rob?" Frank asked as they sped down the dark road.

"I don't know who it was, but it wasn't Rob," Barry answered. "He buzzed off so fast– hey! Taillights up ahead!"

"I think that's me car!" Frank yelled. "Looks like he's makin' f'r Ennis!"

"He could be goin' to the airport," the sheriff grunted, leaning forward in the seat. "We'll shadow him and find out. Damn! Fog's startin' t' roll in."

"Does the radio work?" Barry asked, glancing over at Brennan.

"Use ye'er wireless 'n have th' Gards set up a roadblock, Pat!" O'Shaughnessy shouted from the backseat.

"I can't call th' Gards on this set. All I can do is call Ennis and have them telephone to th' Garda," the sheriff answered.

"Well, what 'n hell are ye waitin' for?" Frank roared, reaching for the controls.

Brennan snatched the speaker from Frank's anxious grip. "Quiet whilst I talk! Frank, give me ye'er license tag number."

"08-CE-481311." Frank leaned forward now too. "That's my car all right," he ground out between his teeth.

"This is Sheriff Brennan, County Clare. I'm reportin' a car theft. The description of th' vehicle is as follows: two-thousand-eight, two-door Ford Focus, dark blue. License tag number: 08-CE-481311. I am in pursuit. Please advise Garda for roadblock immediately. We are headin' toward Ennis, on the Quin-Ennis Road." The sheriff was about to replace the speaker, when he stopped, his hand in mid-air. "Hold on now! Th' suspect … suspects– looks like *two* in the vehicle– have just turned into the Old Ground Hotel. Send Gardai straightaway. I'll hold 'em till you arrive. Make haste!" He disconnected, mumbling to himself, "This fog's goin' t' be a hindrance."

Brennan turned into the guest carpark of the Old Ground, pulling into a space within sight of Frank's Ford– from which the driver was just emerging.

From the backseat of the sheriff's car, Frank gasped, "Bloody Hell! Sure 'tis McHendrie, our new gardener!"

Garrity smirked, slapping Dillon on the back. "Ye'll have t' revise ye'er hirin' practices, Frankie."

Frank responded with a muttered oath, when Sheriff Brennan, with a dissuading hand, waved them to silence. "Quiet now, lads! The other one's gettin' out too. Lass, you keep out of th' way. Let me have that fowlin' piece."

Frank handed the shotgun and shells over the seat. "Here, Pat, an' take some extra cartridges. Have a care now. Both barrels 'r loaded."

The sheriff nodded. "Appears like they're lookin' t' steal another vehicle."

McHendrie and his passenger, a tall strapping man wearing a hat pulled down over his eyes and carrying a valise, were, indeed, casing a new, dark Mercedes near Frank's car.

"Everybody out!" Brennan ordered softly. "And remember; I'm in charge. Now, here's what we're goin' t' do."

In the dimly lit carpark, the Forty-Fivers moved to their assigned positions, Barry close behind the sheriff, who kept his weapon hidden under the coat draped over his arm. McHendrie was conversing, in low tones, with his accomplice.

At the moment the brawny pair were about to enter the Mercedes, the sheriff stepped forward, holding the gun on them. "Stop where ye are! Ye'er under arrest!"

The bigger man, with the valise, whose hat was masking his features, stepped back.

"You too!" Brennan commanded, with tone and gun.

Spying Frank close by, McHendrie assumed an air of innocence. "Mr. Dillon, would y' be listenin' to me, please? I should've asked you f'r th' use of ye'er car, 'tis true, but this was an emergency. Allow me, please sir, to explain. I was faced with an unforeseen dilemma," the gardener twisted his hands in anguish, "with no other remedy at all. None at all."

Frank's face and attitude conveyed that he did not buy it, but he said gruffly, "I'm listenin'."

"It's like this. Me wife's sister arrived, unexpected, t'night from New York, and–"

A loud thump from the boot of Frank's Ford interrupted the dialogue. Looking toward his vehicle, Frank mumbled, "What th' bloody hell?" He crossed the short distance to the rear of his car, fished the keys from a ring in his trouser pocket, then unlocked and raised the trunk lid. Inside, a man groaned and, struggling free of the heavy confining canvas, sat up. By this time, Garrity and Barry had moved to join Frank at the rear of his car. Both Barry and Frank cried out, "Rob!"

"I *knew* I had to get in that car with the sheriff!" Barry said, rushing forth to the object of her affection, as he stepped gingerly out of the trunk, his face and shirt bloody. "Are you okay?" She began to search for his head injury. "How bad is it?" She turned to Frank. "Call an ambulance!"

A bit off-balance, Rob sat on the rear bumper and gingerly touched the back of his head, wincing. Barry took out a handkerchief and gently began dabbing his wound. "Oh, Rob, it's like my nightmare– the blood, the two people, the fog."

"I'm all right. Never mind that ambulance." He stood, flexing his shoulders, then rubbed the small of his back.

While Barry continued to fret over Rob, Brennan was still holding the loaded shotgun on the two men. Rob stood, kissed Barry on the forehead, then closed the trunk to the Ford. Slowly, the man with the valise started to back away. "Don't do it!" The burly sheriff advised. "I'd hate t' have to summon a priest t'night. My aim's never been too keen."

At that, Rob looked closely at the man, though the slouch hat covered most of the thief's face. "Brian. Why am I not surprised?"

Frank's face took on an expression of profound disappointment. "Saint Michael 'n Saint George!"

While attention was on Brian, McHendrie, with his forearm, walloped the loaded shotgun out of the sheriff's grasp, the blow forceful enough to knock the surprised Brennan to the pavement. The sheriff hit the back of his skull and was instantly out cold.

In a flash, Brian dashed for the Mercedes, but Rob smoothly tackled him. With the valise then, Brian struck Rob a terrific blow to the head, a look of intense hatred demonizing him. "I'm going to **kill** you!"

"Trust to Time to set matters straight."
~ Old Irish adage

Chapter Eighteen

Beside Sheriff Brennan's body, Barry knelt frozen in fear, as the brothers battled it out in an *explosive* fight, the two bouncing off the parked vehicles and rolling over car hoods, exchanging all the while relentless, savage punches, body slams, shoves, kicks and gouges.

Simultaneous with the fistfight between Rob and Brian, McHendrie, after having knocked Brennan down, rushed for Frank's Ford, the pilfered set of keys still in the ignition. With surprising speed, Frank and O'Shaughnessy brought down the erstwhile gardener, while Garrity grabbed for and recovered the shotgun. Holding the loaded weapon, Garrity moved with the action, reluctant to fire.

McHendrie and O'Shaughnessy were yet on the ground, as Frank jumped to his feet and began bobbing and weaving, keeping his bout-clenched hands in front of his face. "Step aside, O'Shaughnessy, 'n leave th' blackguard t' me!" Blue eyes twinkling, Frank spat on his readied fists. "Lightweight champion, County Clare."

McHendrie got up, amazing metamorphoses coming over him. He no longer smiled his cherubic smile, and his brogue completely vanished, morphed by curt, clipped English. "When was that, old man? When Victoria was still queen?" McHendrie, the heavier of the two, though not as fast as Frank, took the first swing, which Dillon easily dodged.

"Janey Mac!" The Irish expression of surprise registered in Frank's eyes, but in a moment, a mischievous grin played on his face, as he continued to bob and weave, his left fist poking, provoking his former employee into throwing the next punch. Lightening fast, Frank delivered a left jab, followed swiftly by a mean right, catching the stunned McHendrie solidly on the left jaw and sharply turning his broad face.

Now there were two fistfights in progress, with Garrity still following the action with the loaded shotgun. The sheriff was just beginning to regain consciousness. Opening his eyes and taking in the scene, he struggled to sit up to join the fray, but fell immediately back, narrowly missing hitting his head again as Barry caught him.

Frank was so wiry, it took several exchanged blows before the brawnier, streetwise McHendrie could snare him in a head lock. Finally succeeding in getting a firm hold on him, McHendrie expertly flicked open a wicked-looking switchblade and, pressing it to Frank's neck, shouted, looking to Garrity, his eyes reflecting his manic frenzy, "You! Drop th' gun and get back, or I'll slice 'is throat!"

Garrity promptly let the gun fall to the pavement, but Frank, ever the faster, raised his shoulder, twisted his body deftly to the side and, at the same time, stomped as hard as he could with the heel of his boot on the instep of McHendrie's foot. The gardener yelled in pain, "I'll get you, you mickey sonivabitch!"

"Blubbery *eejet*! Let's see ya try!" Frank took the knife slash across the shoulder, blood rapidly soaking through his shirt.

His face still showing pain, McHendrie, with furious force, shoved Frank forward. In a split second, the gardener snatched the valise Brian had dropped, dived into Frank's car, started it and floored it, sending the Ford careening wildly across the lot, scattering witnesses in all directions.

By this time, Garrity had once again recovered the loaded shotgun, and taking careful aim, he let go with both barrels, blowing out the Focus' rear window as it sped from the carpark and out onto the main road, tires screeching.

The commotion had drawn several people from the hotel, though it was well past midnight.

Barry thought the fistfight between Rob and Brian was beginning to slow; both were showing wear. Their blows looked less forceful, and each appeared unsteady.

Suddenly, with a squealing of tires, a Garda Ford whipped into the carpark, whereupon Frank, holding a handkerchief to his injured shoulder to staunch the bleeding, rushed to their vehicle, yelling at the top of his voice, "Th' filthy beggar stole m' car again! After him!" Peering into the car, Frank gave a surprised start. **"You two!"**

Ignoring Frank's exclamation, the Sleuth Sisters, taking in the situation at a glance, replied in unison to the officer at the wheel, "You heard th' man– **after him!**"

"That way!" Raine shouted, pointing in the direction Frank was excitedly indicating. As the Gards sped off, tires screaming in hot pursuit, the blue light rotating atop their marked vehicle, the Sisters, from the backseat, sent Frank a brisk simultaneous thumbs-up.

The assembly of hotel personnel and guests, gathered round the brothers' fisticuffs, watched as Rob delivered a rapid left-right to his brother's face, quickly followed by two quick slams to the gut, finishing him off with a hard blow to the jaw that knocked his head back forcibly, pummeling him to the ground. Still conscious, Brian tried once again to rise, but at last he was beaten, his battered countenance, as he looked up, contorting into an ugly snarl.

The coals of his rage yet hot, Rob, with disgust clearly visible on his face, turned away, casting his brother from his life with a final, dispelling gesture of his arm.

Bursting into tears, Barry flew to Rob, who was exhibiting battle scars of his own. His lower lip was cut and bleeding, and there was a contusion above his left eye that was already beginning to swell. He held the sobbing Barry. "I'd kiss you, but it would hurt too much."

She stroked his bruised face and dabbed the blood from his mouth with a tissue. "I'm sorry, Rob, I want you to know I was wrong the other day. I love you. *I love you so.*"

He grinned. "I think it would hurt too much *not* to kiss you." He pulled her to him, and their lips met softly. Rob turned to Frank. "That's a nasty slice. We'd better get you to hospital."

Barry gave a nervous laugh. "We'd better get you there too, not to mention the sheriff."

Before anyone could respond, she caught a movement out of her peripheral vision– Brian was pulling from his boot a small automatic pistol and aiming for Rob's back. Horrified, she felt as though paralyzed in a fog-engulfed nightmare in which Time had suddenly slowed, for in that brief moment, Barry *knew* she could not live without him. As if sprung from a trap, she lunged at Brian, her heart in her mouth, "Noooooooooo!" Kicking the gun from his grip, she bounded for it.

"Bitch!" Brian reached for her and his weapon, but Frank's thick-soled brogan came savagely down on the cursing man's clutching hand.

"Enough!" Frank growled. "It ends here– **now!**"

Rob yanked his brother roughly to his feet, while Sheriff Brennan cuffed him. For the second time that evening, Barry and Rob came together, clinging to one another. "You saved my life," he whispered, holding her close.

"When, Mr. Carroll," she asked, pushing away and gazing deeply into his eyes, her hands on his broad shoulders, "are you ever going to start watching your back? I see now that I'm going to have to start accompanying you on your expeditions!"

Rob smiled then. "I'm countin' on it." Presently, his gaze came to rest again on Brian.

His anger rekindled, Rob advanced on his brother, grabbed him by the lapels of his torn jacket, and fiercely shook him. "What did you do with th' jewels?" He looked quickly around. "Damn your eyes! Where's that suitcase you had?"

Barry suddenly remembered. "Rob! McHendrie tore outta here with it in Frank's car!"

It was then Rob caught the eye of a slight man dressed in loud plaid slacks and matching sports cap, who had witnessed most of the donnybrook. In a flash, he tossed Rob a set of keys. "Take my Jag! She'll catch th' ver-ry Divil himself!" He indicated a sleek, green godsend of a car a few feet distant.

Barry and Rob rushed for the Jaguar, jumped in, and within seconds, *roared* out of the carpark, with Frank pointing and yelling, **"Th' Cliff Road!!!"**

While Brennan was holding Frank's double-barreled shotgun on the cuffed Brian, Frank dashed for the sheriff's car, gesturing, "You drive, Garrity!"

Garrity hurriedly got behind the wheel, Frank at once sliding into the passenger's side, his hand instantly reaching for the controls, as O'Shaughnessy leapt into the backseat.

"Come back here!" Brennan yelled, "I'm the only one permitted t' drive that vehicle!"

But the Forty-Fivers were off, speeding after the Jaguar, with blue light rotating and siren blaring.

"Rob," Barry said softly, looking over at him from the passenger side of the Jaguar, "my heart goes out to you over your brother. I know this must be hard for you, very hard."

Rob did not take his eyes from the road. In the semi-darkness, his profile was intense, the taut muscles of his jaw indicative of the profound and stressful feelings he had been harboring. "Barry, I will never forget our father telling us that the most valuable gift he would ever give us was his name." He clenched his teeth, and a determined look was stamped on his features. "'I give this name, a grand old name, a *proud* name, to you both, untarnished. Carry it well, for if either of you disgrace it, you'll not regain it. Something of pride and honor will be lost to you, to your ancestors, and to your children, forever.'" After a moment he added, "My parents died sick at heart over him, Barry. Brian never cared a whit about them, either of them."

Barry reached over, placed a hand on his arm, and felt the powerful muscles rigid with tension. The dark of night could not keep her from seeing every detail of that beloved face she now knew better than her own. Though Rob kept his eyes to his front, Barry thought she detected, in the moonlight off the dash, a tear glistening on his bearded cheek.

Patches of thick, swirling fog and mist made driving on the steep, twisting coastal road even more hazardous. Up ahead, McHendrie rounded a bend, narrowly missing a shadowy figure who was crossing the dark road, the man instantly opting for the cliff edge rather than being mowed down. Driving like a demon, his facial cast desperate, a laughing McHendrie checked his rear-view mirror to see the pedestrian waving a fist, while the Gardai were steadily gaining on him.

Behind them, in the Jaguar, Barry was holding on with clenched fingers. "Are you sure this is the road? Are you sure we're *on* the road? Sometimes I can't see a thing. And the ocean sounds … *awfully close.*"

Rob kissed his finger and, without taking his eyes from the road, reached over and touched it to her lips. "Shh, I know this road. Learned to drive on it. Sing somethin', luv. It'll help you relax."

Barry sent him a weak smile, then in a slightly trembling voice, she began an off-key rendition of an old Girl Scout tune, "Over hill, over dale …"

The Gardai were hot on McHendrie's tail, their rotating blue light and high beams flashing in warning for him to pull over, the dazzle bouncing off his rear-view mirror and onto his jowly face. "No bloody way, Mate!"

Sergeant Dugan, who was doing the driving, exclaimed, incredulous, "He's goin' t' make a run f'r it!"

Detective-Inspector Haggerty, in the passenger seat, shook his head. "Stupid *amadan!*"

Leaning anxiously forward, her hands gripping the seat in front of her, Raine urged, "You can't let him get away!"

Dugan threw a glance at the inspector. "Let's take 'im!"

"Not with th' ladies in the car," Haggerty gestured toward the pair with his white head.

Maggie, too, leaned forward. "Never you mind about us. He's likely killed three people … that we know of!"

The sergeant threw another fleeting look at the inspector. "I'm a capable driver, Dennis, and quite used to this road. We can take him."

"*We* put you on to the SOB," Maggie pressed, "and *we sure as hell* don't want to be the reason you lose him!"

The men looked to one another, the Sleuth Sisters prompting, **"Go!"**

The inspector gave a nod, the sergeant put the pedal to the floor, and the car shot forward, with siren blasting, blue light flashing. "I have t' give you ladies credit. I'd have thought you'd be as nervous back there as two Orangemen in a Falls Road pub on Saint Paddy's Day."

Raine smirked. "Apparently, sir, you've never taught school. I taught high school for a couple of years before I moved on to my professorship, and I can tell you–"

"Can't you go any faster!" Maggie spurred, her sharp nails digging into the driver's shoulder. **"He's getting away!"**

Constantly checking his rear-view mirror, McHendrie again laughed aloud. "Not this time, Bahstads! Cheer-r-r-i–o!"

A thick patch of fog enveloped them, and in that instant, McHendrie's rear lights disappeared. In frustration, Sergeant Dugan slammed his hand down hard on the steering wheel.

"I can't see a bloody thing!" Haggerty groaned. "Excuse me, ladies."

"D'you *want* him to get away!" Raine incited.

"I was goin' like billy-o back there!" the sergeant shrieked in his defense.

"Do y' realize, Dugan," the inspector began, his speech measured, "how much paper work is involved, if y' crash a Garda vehicle?"

The sergeant shot him a look of annoyance. Suddenly, his seeking gaze caught a set of fast-approaching headlights in the rear-view mirror. "Hel-lo! Looks like we've got company."

The Sisters and the inspector turned to see the Jaguar about to pass them. "What sort of *eejet* would overtake the Gards on this road in these conditions! Let's try 'n get the tag num–" Dugan yelled, cut off by Raine's fervent shout, as she rapidly lowered the back-seat window —

"It's Rob! He's going after him!"

As the curve-hugging XKE came alongside, she and Maggie, with excited, pointing gestures, yelled above the din of engine and siren, the sharp wind whipping their hair wildly about their animated faces, **"Head 'em off at the pass! We'll box 'em in!"** With an exhilarating laugh, Raine gripped a breathless Maggie's shoulders, "I always wanted to say that!"

A second before, without the least bit of hesitation, Dugan had shouted, **"Right!"** And in the passing Jag, Rob echoed the prompt reply, his handsome profile resolute.

Her fears suddenly vanishing, Barry let go a rousing victory cry, gesturing with uplifted arm, **"Alllll—RIGHT!"**

"Dreams are held in the blankness of Destiny."
~ Ancient Runes

Chapter Nineteen

Driving like one possessed, McHendrie shot out of the fog pocket, laughing and checking his rear-view mirror. Seeing the Jaguar on his tail, his laugh froze on his face. "What's this?" Looking to his front, he saw, through the gap in the swirling fog and mist, a clear straightaway. Switching off his lights, he slammed the Ford's pedal again to the floor, his mad laughter and the engine acceleration noise filling the cold, drafty car with its shot-out rear window.

Rapidly, from out of the thick fog and headed right for him, came the blurred headlamps of an approaching vehicle, its horn blaring. Jolted into action, he jerked the wheel, barely avoiding a head-on crash. The horn of the advancing car reverberated for what seemed to the crazed McHendrie an extraordinarily long time, as it continued past the three chase vehicles behind him.

In the Jaguar, Rob and Barry, also emerging from the fog pocket and veering to avoid the oncoming, horn-blaring vehicle, looked ahead into the pitch-black void– there was no sign of McHendric! Frank's Ford had completely vanished into the foggy, black night.

"Sonivabitch!" Rob gunned the Jag, and the powerful car shot forward on the steep cliff road. To combat her queasiness, Barry had her window down a bit, and she could hear the roar of the Atlantic seven hundred feet below them. "Oh my God!"

"Th' Ford's gone off th' cliff!" Haggerty, in the Garda vehicle, exclaimed to the sergeant, who was leaning over the steering wheel attempting unsuccessfully to peer through the murky soup. The men exchanged quick glances, both making the Sign of the Cross. "Must've swerved too far 'n gone over!"

"We don't know that!" Maggie stated fiercely, giving Dugan's shoulder a hard whack. "Let's keep going!"

"He's crafty; could be that's what he wants us to think!" Raine blurted, excitedly clutching the sergeant's already-smarting shoulder.

Up ahead, in Frank's filched Ford– the only illumination the thin, silvery moonlight reflecting off the dash– the elusive McHendrie made an eerie figure, his shaggy hair whipping about in the cold, windy car, his face that of a madman. Suddenly, he glimpsed a secondary road off to the right. Oblivious to the fact that he had three pursuit vehicles hot on his tail, he slammed on the brakes, turning the wheel hard to starboard. In a dreadful screeching of tires, the Ford spun a hundred eighty degrees, hitting a steep embankment and propelling him forward. He violently struck his head against the steering wheel, and blood began flowing into his stinging eyes.

In the Jaguar, Rob and Barry were still searching the road for the missing Ford. "Rob, why did you slow down back there? I'm afraid we've lost him."

"I know this road. Barry, if we would've met that car comin' in the opposite direction round that last curve, there could've been a head-on smashup in this gumbo. As much as I want to collar McHendrie and recover the jewels, I don't want to jeopardize your life. You mean too much to me!"

Barry was just about to respond, when she pointed abruptly, **"Ho!** I think I saw a side road back there!"

Rob jammed on the breaks, threw the XKE in reverse, popped it into gear and, tires screaming, roared down the narrow byway.

Meanwhile, Sergeant Dugan, Inspector Haggerty, and the Sleuth Sisters were searching the black night for signs of either car, four pairs of eyes straining.

"No taillights at all, at all," the inspector repeated for the third time.

"I told you to speed up!" Raine nearly shouted. **"Damn it!"** And that she did shout.

"Let's hope they–" Maggie stopped unexpectedly, pointing to the right. "There! A side road!"

"What-d'ya think?" the sergeant queried.

"Right!" came the unanimous, resounding responses of his passengers.

Smoke billowed out of the Ford, as McHendrie staggered out into the gusty night, the swirling fog, and the sea mists. Dazed, he fell, face forward, onto the cold, damp ground. Struggling to his knees, he wiped blood from his eyes with the sleeve of his dark jacket. He blinked and swiped his sleeve across his face again. He could hardly see. It was as though he were under water. A vehicle was coming, the headlights shining above him. He attempted to stand, shielding his eyes from the dazzle. Finding it easier to crawl, he began moving forward as quickly as he could.

On the steep, slippery downhill route, the truck driver, seeing something– someone– just ahead, leaned on the horn. "Get out of th' way, man! **Get outta th' way!"**

McHendrie pulled himself to his feet, swaying in the middle of the road, as he madly attempted to wave down the oncoming vehicle.

Concurrently, the Jaguar arrived on the scene, Barry and Rob witnessing the dazed McHendrie in the path of the huge lorry that was rapidly bearing down on him. "What's he doing!" Barry screamed. **"Dear God!"**

There was a horrific protesting of truck and trailer brakes followed by the sickening sound of impact as McHendrie was hurled, like a rag doll, high into the air.

Barry braced herself as the Jaguar fishtailed and screeched to a stop near the truck on the narrow cliff road. The lorry's headlights flooded McHendrie's broken body where it lay on the ground, and from the back of the long vehicle came the sounds of frightened, screaming horses. The driver jumped from the cab and ran to McHendrie's motionless body, Rob and Barry swiftly joining him.

Rob knelt, feeling for a pulse. "He's still alive. We'd better not move him though." He removed his own jacket and laid it over the injured criminal.

The truck driver, his face pale and anxious, wrung his hands. "Thank God! I didn't see him till th' last second. I *couldn't* avoid him." He turned and hurried to the rear of the trailer to check on the horses that were kicking frantically at the inside walls of the van and neighing shrilly. "I couldn't stop," the truck driver repeated. *"I couldn't stop."*

When Barry's gaze followed him, her eyes came to rest on the side of the long trailer, there the words portended by her Pittsburgh rune reading– CAUTION HORSES. Below, in smaller print, was the name of the firm, *O'Hanlon & Sons Livestock Transport Ltd., Quin, Co. Clare*.

Rob moved to Frank's wrecked Ford, reached inside and lifted the suitcase from the floor, depositing it into the Jaguar. Then he joined the truck driver at the rear of the van, where the opened door revealed that the horses were wearing protective gear– helmets, blankets, and leg wraps. Nostrils flared, their large eyes showing white, the panicked animals continued to kick, toss their heads and scream. Both the driver and Rob began attempting to soothe and calm them.

"Ho now, big fella. Easy … *easy*." Rob's mellow voice reached Barry, who had stayed at McHendrie's side. She drew in a large draught of tangy sea air, releasing it slowly. Somehow, despite the pandemonium, she knew that for the rest of her life that deep, resonant voice would be calming and soothing *to her*.

Muffled through the wind, the shrill wail of a siren was getting closer, and in a few moments, a rotating blue light bounced off the cliffside above her.

"We'd best not move him," the inspector said. "I've radioed for an ambulance." On either side of the delirious McHendrie, Haggerty and Dugan knelt, trying to make sense of the injured man's babbling. "Can you tell me ye'er name?" Haggerty asked, trying to determine if the criminal was coherent.

McHendrie grasped the detective's arm. "Is that you, Brian? I took care of the gardener … couple of drops in his Guinness … spilled the stuff in the shed … made it look … accident."

"What's that about the gardener? What gardener? Who?" Dugan pressed, trying to gain as much information as he could.

"Mannion … Mannion." McHendrie again grasped Haggerty's arm. "Did you fence the jewels? You promised … bonus."

"Ask him about Máire Nolan," Raine pushed. "And Phillip Barry! Don't coddle the man!" She moved in closer, between the Gardai, kneeling beside the babbling suspect and fixing him with her witchy stare. "McHendrie! Ever hear the old saying, 'Better late than never'? Well, I hear the late bell ringin' now. If you believe in a hereafter, you better start talkin'! What!" Raine retorted in response to the Gardai's surprised looks. "This might be the only chance we have to get the truth outta him! Great Goddess!"

The siren was ear-splitting as Frank, Garrity, and O'Shaughnessy arrived on the scene in the pirated sheriff's car.

McHendrie groaned as Raine continued to stare down at him. "Brian," he pulled on the inspector's arm, "my cut … my share of the take–" McHendrie's voice faded away, and his grip on Haggerty's arm loosened, his hand falling to the ground beside his twisted body.

"Blast it; he's out." The detective checked for a pulse. "That's a bit of a hitch!"

Raine's hands flew up to cover her ears, and Sergeant Dugan looked up in exasperation, shouting over the din, "Jaysus, Frank, turn that bleedin' siren off!"

Inside the sheriff's clamorous vehicle, Frank was fumbling at the controls from the passenger's side of the front seat. He stuck his head out of the open door, his expression that of a naughty little boy, "I can't turn th' blasted thing off!"

With that, a muttering Dugan jumped to his feet and ran to switch off the screaming alarm. Maggie joined Raine beside McHendrie's body. "He's not dead, is he?" she asked, her tone and face apprehensive.

"No," the inspector answered, "but he's lost a lot of blood." He looked to the Sisters. "He did *some* talkin'."

"Let's hope he lives to do some more." Raine stood and began moving her arms to generate heat. "Damn, it's cold!" she swore, as the salt-tinged wind, whipping off the sea, slammed against her.

No sooner had the sergeant extinguished the one siren, when another could be heard approaching in the distance. "Sounds like the ambulance coming now. Someone get down to the end of the road," Haggerty shouted, "so they know where we are."

"There's a little witch in every woman."
~ Wise women throughout the ages

Chapter Twenty

[A few days later …]

A cheery fire burned in Barry Hall's public room. Nora and Frank, his arm in a sling, were behind the bar, Frank supervising, Nora pouring and serving the champagne they had opened for the occasion. Also present were the Forty-Fivers– Sheriff Brennan, with bandaged head, Garrity, and O'Shaughnessy. "I wouldn't trade m' usual jar of stout for this French fizz," Garrity murmured to the sheriff, who nodded his agreement.

Barry was seated on the divan next to Rob, a patch on the back of his head, his face still showing wear from the bout with his brother. "I've always loved your face, but now it seems to have taken on," she leaned back, as if judging a work of art, searching for the proper word, "I don't know … *color!*"

Rob laughed. "Oh, I'm a *rainbow* of colors, black, blue, green, purple."

Sergeant Dugan, in civvies, was standing before the fireplace, an elbow on the mantel. Raine and Maggie were each seated in Morris chairs, across from one another before the fireplace.

Today, since Nora had told them that the gathering would be a celebration of sorts, Raine was wearing a long-sleeved, black, gothic-style Edwardian blouse with a stand-up collar that framed her face to perfection. Her diamond magick-wand brooch sparkled against the soft, ebony fabric. The forest-green riding skirt she sported was also Edwardian, the black belt coming to a point over the gentle curve of her abdomen. In contrast, Maggie's sexy figure did justice to a vibrant turquoise flapper-style dress with matching, jeweled turban from which a few, carefully arranged, fiery curls had been permitted to escape.

Everyone was sipping champagne except Frank, who nursed a mug of his favorite stout. "Well, we're all waitin' t' hear. What did y' learn about that thievin' reprobate?" he asked, his bright blue gaze on Dugan.

"Aye, the final *dénouement*," the hefty, ruddy-faced sergeant teased. "McHendrie's right name is Jack Miller. He's a former English actor turned from petty crook to gouger." For the benefit of the Americans, he translated, "Big-time thief."

"A 'gow' till my brother talked him into murder," Rob corrected, echoing the Garda slang.

"Some actor!" Frank's voice dripped with scorn. "I suspected from th' start he wasn't Irish. 'Top o' th' mornin',' indaid! I never had th' phrase spoke at me in m' life till McHendrie!"

"I didn't take it as a clue," Rob cut in. "I took it as a bit of humor. The man did appear to be a jovial sort."

"Him and that perpetual smile of his!" Frank blurted with fire.

"Some people wear a smile like a disguise," Raine interjected. "A useful tidbit from a good friend of ours, stateside."

"During the interrogation, McHen– Miller– used many such theatrical phrases. Must be th' effect of actin' in so many second-rate plays," Dugan chortled, shaking his head. "For my part, I think th' man's become a tad unhinged."

"I feel like I'm in the emergency ward at hospital!" Nora handed a tray of hors d'oeuvres to the bandaged Rob.

Barry looked thoughtful. "Rob, if your brother was excluded from your great-uncle's will, how did he find out about … anything?"

"Several days ago, I talked on the phone with th' manager of my agency in London," Rob answered. "He informed me Brian had called there, asking for me. Naturally, he saw no harm in tellin' my brother that our great-uncle was dying. How was *he* to know that Brian was an international criminal? I sar-tainly had never discussed him."

"And, as you've said, the jewels are legendary," Barry added.

"Yes. When Brian learned that our uncle was near death, he and his crony began workin' out a plan," Rob continued. "Brian was familiar with the estate, so it was *he* who killed Uncle Phillip."

"Quite right, Mr. Carroll," Sergeant Dugan confirmed, moving away from the mantel to take a seat in one of the room's comfortable chairs. "Inspector Haggerty and I *both* apologize to you for our initial misgivin's. He'd tell ya himself, and he tanks ya f'r the invitation to join the festivity of th' settlin' of th' estate, but he was called back to Dublin early this mornin' on another case. As I was sayin', you were correct all along in your feeling that your uncle's death was not a suicide … nor was it an accident. Your brother finally confessed to 'hurryin' him toward his heavenly reward,' as he put it. On the fatal night, he entered the house through a rear window, quietly stole up to your uncle's bedchamber, and, in the dimly lit room, pretended to be *you*, sent up on orders from Nora to administer the nighttime medication, a killin' dose, as it turned out. In his twilight state, th' poor old gentleman did not realize that it was *not* you, and that Nora had *already* given him his medicine."

Nora paused in her bar-polishing to make the Sign of the Cross, Frank and the Forty-Fivers adding softly, "God rest him."

"God rest him," chanted the others.

"Raine and Maggie– and may I say, you two ladies are the 'goods'– " Dugan continued, "had us check on whether or no Brian was even in the merchant fleet. Turns out he was for a time, until he was arrested for orchestrating a ring of thieves, stealin' and sellin' freight they were carrying– Waterford crystal, Irish spirits, and other high-ticket items."

Maggie smiled to herself. *He told me his pirate costume reflected his alter ego.*

"'Twas in prison he met McHendrie," Dugan went on about Brian. "Thinkin' he was dyin', McHendrie– I meant t' say Miller– confessed to killin' Tom Mannion so he could get himself hired as gardener here." Dugan pursed his lips. "That business in the shed with th' spilt herbicide– too pat ... too pat. Tom, a gardener f'r over tar-rty years, would niver have been so careless. Miller did th' durty deed in Kelley's pub."

"Poor old Tom ..." Sheriff Brennan shook his head sadly, "poisoned by th' jar of stout he always took after wur-rk. God rest him as well."

Again, the others took up the blessing.

"Thanks to you ladies," Sergeant Dugan gestured across the room to the Sleuth Sisters, "and those fingerprints you provided when you gave us that teacup, we found a list of prior convictions. *Och!* His name– I should say *names*– appears on the books more times than th' Church has holy days. Miller's a *career criminal*, known in crime circles as the 'Handyman' due to the variety of roles he's played."

Maggie gave a short laugh, glancing over at Raine and mimicking the halfpenny actor's fractured Irish parlance, "Faith 'n begorrah! Sure 'n didn't he tell us he was a '*humble* handyman' who niver sought a *fanciful* career. An' him so modest! Why, he's the standout lead in th' cast iv characters!"

Nora belatedly lit up. "Soooo that's where the missin' teacup 'n napkin went off t'!"

"As we told you, Sergeant, we caught the man in a couple of lies at lunch," Maggie remarked, "the day Raine and I nipped the teacup. He tried making us believe he was Dublin-born. Our first clue was his accent. Dubliners– especially those born and reared in the working-class North Side–have a very *distinct* accent. And from where he said he lived, it's not a long tramp at all to Trinity. In fact, it's a very short one from all areas of the North Side."

"And … as Frank so succinctly pointed out, his stage-Irish was all too apparent," Raine added.

Rob nodded to the Sleuth Sisters and smiled. "Brian wasn't lying to Frank when he said he was in Ennis all day. He was with a–" Rob cleared his throat, continuing, "woman. He slept most of the day, so he could prowl round here nights. That was probably *his* shadow we saw under the door that time we were reading the old diary." He looked to Barry, who gave a little shiver. "It was Brian's hand that pushed over that urn, nearly killing me, and it was Brian who went through my things th' night we were at the castle."

"Aye. Poor little Máire must have surprised him takin' th' photographs of th' diary we found on him. We know *he* killed her because of th' skin under her nails and the deep scratches on his forearms. God rest her." The sergeant slipped his champagne, and the assembly was silent for some moments, the blessing seeming to softly echo round the cozy, hearth-lit room.

"Th' filthy divil!" Nora blurted with abrupt intensity. "Takin' th' life of our sweet Máire!"

"Brian said he regretted takin' her life. 'Hated t' waste so lovely a woman' was the way he put it," Dugan related disgustedly. "Máire's was the murder th' rotters hadn't planned on. And they did their best t' make it look as if there was no connection. That's another thing we owe to your resident sleuths."

"Seeds planted in our heads from friends," Maggie interjected modestly, "and family."

Again Dugan indicated Raine and Maggie. "We owe them a debt of gratitude for the discovery of Máire's body and for rendering, the night of the chase, Brian's alibi at Bunratty null and void … most helpful in obtaining his confession. That flooz–" the sergeant caught himself, continuing, "the *friendly* little blonde's partner at the castle that night was a redhead, not Brian, as he so wanted all of you to believe."

"We knew how verbal 'Little Miss Hot-to-Trot' was, so we followed her into the Ladies' and overheard her relate the details of her latest conquest to her friend," Raine recounted. "She said she could not decide between Brian and another man, but that she chose the other because of his, and I quote, 'gorgeous red hair.' Seems she was partial to redheads."

"Why do you suppose Brian gave money to that priest in Ennis?" Barry asked.

Crossing her booted legs, Raine began in her husky voice, "I'm no psychologist, but I've had to take plenty of courses in the subject to obtain a permanent teaching certificate. I think it was to create a good image for himself around the area, good PR I suppose we could say."

"After all, he imagined he was going to become lord of the manor," Maggie concurred.

"I think you're both right about that," Barry responded. "Thanks to your shouts for help, he did save me from Bill the night of the fancy dress ball. He did his level best to *impress* us with that ... and, earlier, with his other accomplishments, at dinner the night the Conroys were here. He certainly had them fooled."

"As for Conroy," Rob said, "he is no longer the solicitor of *this* estate. I've always retained my own solicitors, and I never felt comfortable around him or Margaret. Ah, well, I'm finally to get the estate money. It was always there, but that blasted bloody barrister kept stallin' me. Frank," he gestured to his affable manager, "we can start plannin' a fine restoration of th' place now."

"By th' bye, I stumbled into Margaret this mornin' when I was out and about," Frank remarked, indicating for Nora to refill his mug. "I felt kinda sorry for her. The old gurl looked down in th' mouth over sellin' her stable of horses– all except her favorite hunter. She confessed to me she's been after her husband to purchase Barry Hall. 'Take th' burden of th' place off Rob's shoulders' is how she put it, 'so he can resume his Gypsy life.' She always had it in mind to become mistress here."

Barry rolled her eyes.

"Ah," Frank began anew, "Once-st you get t' know her, she's not half as bad as she seems, she's–"

"Much worse," Nora finished, glancing up from her bar tasks.

Everyone laughed, including Nora, the rusty laugh pulling loose from her lips and rippling softly about the room, warming it. "That

Margaret! I kin just see th' selfish wheels iv manipulation turnin'.'"
A brief silence followed, as everyone, including Frank, stared at the
still-smiling housekeeper.

"With all th' killin's goin' on round here, I didn't fancy bein'
alone nights in the carriage house," Nora admitted. "Of course,
Frank had volunteered for that church committee long before any of
this began. However, I am not ashamed to say that I slept with a
loaded gun next to th' bed. Bein' that it was a fowlin' piece, I
figured I'd hit *somethin'*!"

"*Shotgun*," Raine mouthed, unnecessarily, to Barry.

"What **I** want to know," Frank queried, "is how *McHendrie* got a
key to m' car?"

"Did you have an extra set lyin' about?" Dugan asked.

"Be right back." Frank hurried from the room.

Barry reached up and touched Rob's bruised face. He caught her
hand and pressed it to his lips. In a moment Frank returned to the
public room via his usual rushing walk. "It's gone." He crossed to
his position behind the bar. "I always kept the extra key on th' peg
in the kitchen." He shrugged. "'Tis lucky I had insurance; th' car's
totally destroyed."

"Lucky for me Raine snw McHendrie ... Miller stuffing me into
Frank's Ford," Rob said with a grin. And thanks to you," he kissed
Barry's cheek, "the Sleuth Sisters were here in the first place. Oh,
and remind me never to doubt your presentiments again, luv."

Barry responded with a smiling nod, "I'll do that."

"What's all this about presentiments? I stepped out for a
moment," O'Shaughnessy asked from the doorway.

"I knew that there were two people plotting to murder Rob. I saw
the blood on Rob's face ... even the horses! Suffice it to say I *knew*
Rob was in grave danger. It's why I followed him to Ireland in the
first place!" Barry squeezed his hand.

"If it weren't for th' lot of you, I'd be at th' bottom of the ocean
right now. Before Miller even arrived at hospital, he confessed that
their plan was to stage an accident." Rob paused, the weight of what
he just said causing him to reflect a moment. "Excuse me; I'll be
right back." He stood and left the room, Barry looking after him, an
expression of concern on her face.

"That's bloody well what they intended– to put Rob behind the
wheel of Frank's Ford, then to push th' car off th' cliff and into the
ocean," Dugan reported.

"His own brother," Barry breathed.

"Brian was always jealous of Rob," Frank recalled. "Blamed him f'r his own miserable failin's. Ah! He was a bad lot, even as a wee lad."

"Always tormentin' one of th' dogs 'r cats," Nora added. "Aye, he had a black heart altogether. I told his father an' mother, God rest 'm, that he'd come to a bad end. Tsk, tsk, a Carroll in prison. Life with hard labor."

"Is that what McHendrie will get too?" Frank queried. "If so, they'd do well t' have someone behind 'im with a blinkin' cattle prod."

Sergeant Dugan nodded. "Aye, once he's out of hospital, it's life, no parole." He shifted his attention to Barry. "I heard a bit o' gossip couple of days ago, which might be of interest. Maeve O'Brien and Tim Callahan eloped the night of the ball. Like I said, 'Life, no parole.'"

Maggie sent Raine one of her mysterious smiles, the 'life no parole' remark bringing a hearty laugh from the gathering, including Rob, who had reentered the public room, carrying the large, ornate jewel box. He took his place again on the divan, next to Barry. Lifting the lid and removing the sheepskin wrap, he took out each magnificent piece, arranging them on the coffee table before him. Everyone gathered round to see the legendary De Barry jewels.

"Oh, Rob, they're exquisite! How old are they?"

"They've been cached away for over a century." Rob took a dainty hand-painted portrait from the elaborately carved box, "as was this miniature of Carlotta."

The Sleuth Sisters rose and, moving to the couch, leaned over Barry's shoulder to see Carlotta's sultry likeness. "Why, she could be your twin!" Maggie exclaimed with feigned surprise.

"Great-grandfather buried 'her' along with the jewels." He handed the porcelain to Barry. "If it hadn't been for Barry kicking the gun out of Brian's hand– at *huge* risk to her own life– **I'd** be buried! I'm a lucky man. And a grateful one. Lucky and grateful, indaid." He smiled, and the love he felt for the woman at his side was apparent in his expression. "You know, Barry, it was your talk of the poem– the Venus and the Cupid– that triggered my dream from which I awoke, wandered over to the window and, within minutes, uncovered the jewels. *You* planted that very important seed in my head."

Rob's face took on a look of bemusement. "There remains yet one enigma– that page from great-grandfather's diary, disclosing what he intended to do with the jewels. It just *appeared* in my room– out of nowhere! *Strange yoke that!* I hadn't noticed before that a page had been torn out, so deep was the tear into the binding. Upon close inspection– dead close– I saw where it had been ripped from the journal. The leaf matches perfectly *to* the tear, but the odd thing is– it doesn't appear as *old* as the other pages in the diary. And if it had, at some point in time, been returned to the journal, why hadn't Grandfather and Uncle Phillip ever made use of it? They both searched for the jewels, painstakingly, over the years." Rob shook his head. "I suppose it will forever remain a mystery."

A secret glance flew between the Sleuth Sisters, as each smiled in her own mysterious way, Raine dropping her gaze almost instantly to fiddle with one of the enchanted rings on her hands. When Maggie turned her head, she became aware that Barry was staring at them, though the latter remained silent.

"I'm of the mind, Rob, that your ancestor *wanted* a descendant to find it, but he decided to leave it to Destiny to orchestrate," Raine interjected.

"Why, I think Raine has got it in one! It's the old Irish saying, 'Trust to Time to set matters straight,' come to pass," Maggie added, her voice full of innocence."

Noting Barry's stare, Raine remarked, reverting back to the subject of the miniature, "You and Carlotta really do resemble one another."

"I suppose I can see a resemblance," Barry said, glancing, from the small portrait, to herself in the bar mirror.

"I can understand why my great-gran*da* was bewitched. Carlotta was," Rob picked up the emerald earbobs, the glittering stones like cool green drops of water, and held them to Barry's ears, "*so beautiful.*" In a moment, he slipped the French hooks through Barry's pierced ears. "They were made for you, darlin'," he pronounced softly.

Barry studied the haughty woman in the portrait, with her flashing dark eyes, night-black hair parted in the center, and her aristocratic face. *I wonder if she found love with her marqués? For all her fiery looks, her eyes tell me she was not capable of real love.*

Rob took up the necklace and fastened it around Baranya's slender throat. She was wearing her dark auburn hair up, and loose tendrils fell softly about her lovely face. The jewels were perfect with the heart-shaped neckline of the crushed velvet dress she wore– a dress so dark a green, it was nearly black, like dewy Irish moss in veiled moonlight.

"Craftsmanship like this is a thing of a bygone era. Look at the intricate scrollwork and beading. What a lovely gift for a bride," Rob voiced softly. "You show off the jewels impeccably, my love."

Barry blushed becomingly, and tears glistened in her almond-shaped eyes. "Oh, Rob." She caught another glimpse of herself in the wall mirror, the emeralds and diamonds flashing. *He's asking me to marry him! At least I **think** he is.*

"Sure 'n Rob has found a treasure!" Frank intoned. "Lad, I never meant to keep you from findin' your legacy, but I never thought th' jewels existed. I still can't believe a frugal man like ye'er great-grandfather would've kept somethin' he never intended to do anythin' with. Why?"

"Probably for the same reason he left the Love Gardens intact … as a constant reminder of what he considered his supreme folly," Rob concluded.

"I think you are absolutely correct in your assumption," Maggie smiled her enigmatic smile, and again she and Raine traded knowing glances.

Rob picked up the ten-carat emerald surrounded by glittering European-cut diamonds. "The engraver had been instructed to inscribe the initials *C.B.* for *Carlotta Barry* on the inner surface of this ring and the traditional claddagh wedding band. He erred, *reversing* the initials." He turned the ring slowly, reading the inscription aloud, "*B.C. ~ To Destiny.*" Moving closer to Baranya, Rob took her left hand and slipped the fabulous ring onto her third finger. It fit perfectly. "As Fate would have it, the engraver did not err. *B.C.*– Baranya, or more *à propos*– *Barry Carroll*."

He knelt, and her hand still in his, he asked in his knee-weakening brogue, his voice replete with emotion, "Barry, will you be my wife and my partner in every way, for the rest of our lives?"

"Oh, yes," she breathed. "Yes!"

"Let's seal that with a kiss." He embraced her then, and his kiss was full of promise. Pulling her even closer, he whispered something in her ear. She blushed, a low laugh escaping her, and the Forty-Fivers, Sergeant Dugan, and the Sleuth Sisters all cheered.

Radiant with joy, a tear falling onto her cheek, Barry smiled brightly. "For me, coming to Ireland has been a journey to," she touched Rob's bruised face delicately, "the rainbow's end."

Everyone cheered again, and Nora dabbed at her eyes with her apron.

"With all this talk about rainbows and presentiments, I feel as though I'm marrying a witch." Rob patted Barry's hand, sending her a wink.

O'Shaughnessy said aside to Garrity, "Sure an' did I, but I pronounce th' wur-rd a tad different."

Raine laughed her sexy laugh. "There's a little witch in every woman."

Frank nodded vigorously, raising his glass of stout, "Hear–" He stopped sharply, his glass in mid-air, his jovial visage frozen by what he often referred to as 'one of Nora's glacial glares.' "Here now," he rapidly shifted gears, "everyone, more champagne! This calls for a special cheerin' cup!"

Nora poured champagne all round, then hoisting his own glass of stout, Frank began anew, "A Toast … to Robbie and Barry! And to their rendezvous with Destiny or Time, or whatever its name, fur finally settin' matters straight!"

"Wiz-zard!" Raine purred to Maggie.

"Hear! Hear!" the assembly chorused with raised glasses.

"Hear! Hear!" Nora echoed quietly, smiling widely at Barry who, raising her glass, added a toast of her own.

"And to Raine and Maggie, the Sleuth Sisters, for adding their energies to sorting out every last mystery of Barry Hall!" Barry sent the Sisters a warm and meaningful smile.

"To the Sleuth Sisters!" the group intoned in happy refrain, as Raine and Maggie looked at once pleased and blushing. *Where there's a witch– there's a way*, the pair reflected as one.

At that express moment, the white lace curtains billowed into the room, carried by a mystical wind, a wind breathing whispers of ancient, treasured secrets.

Out in the Love Gardens, surrounded by a whirlwind of multicolored autumn-leaf confetti, it looked as if Mother Nature, Destiny, Cupid and the Goddess of Love herself were all celebrating. It was– if only for an instant– a delightful reminder that a bright, wordless magick still existed in the world.

~Epilogue~

The Sleuth Sisters settled into their places and fastened their seat belts. The huge *Aer Lingus* jet, with the big shamrock on its tail, slowly began to taxi down the runway.

Raine, who had the window seat, gazed at the passing green landscape. "We'll have to come back soon." She dabbed at her tip-tilted cat eyes, careful not to smear her mascara.

"To me, Ireland is as much my home as our Pennsylvania Tara," Maggie replied, trying unsuccessfully not to cry, as her own green eyes welled with tears. She reached into a pocket of the tailored, sixties-era Chanel suit she was wearing for a tissue. Always one for color, the jade-green outfit was adorned with a designer shawl in a splash of jewel tones.

Raine nodded, absently straightening the antique Chantilly flounce that overlapped the black, Goth frock coat she was sporting, what Maggie christened her "Raine gear." The garment was lightweight for travel, with matching, close-fitting, black pants beneath.

"Beau and I have said that if we marry– and Goddess knows he's likely the only man who'll be able to live with my hail, thunder and lightning, my storm surges, as he calls them– we'll go to Ireland on our honeymoon. Some day." Her emerald eyes danced. "Who knows? We might even stay at Barry Hall." She adjusted herself to a more comfortable position in the seat, slipping her feet out of the witchy pair of high heels she was wearing. "How did it go with your ex? Did you have a pleasant visit? I was too sleepy to talk last night when you got back. I think I must have fallen asleep as soon as my head hit the pillow."

"Rory McLaughlin will never change," Maggie replied. "He's still got more charm than the law should allow. Still an incurable womanizer, but a 'good ole boy' nonetheless. I enjoyed our dinner together immensely. He reminded me that we are always welcome to stay at his family's castle whenever we wish, just to be sure to check with them ahead of time."

Raine looked over at her cousin. "How you manage to stay such good friends with an ex-husband and a bevy of ex-boyfriends is beyond me, but you do. And you do it so creatively. Did he try– "

"Of course."

"And?"

Maggie responded with her effervescent laugh. "Some things should remain a mystery." The sexy redhead closed her eyes for a long moment, and her signature enigmatic smile fleetingly passed over her features. She glowed like a gorgeous rare jewel, a second later opening those magnificent emerald orbs to see Raine staring at her. "You're looking at me as though I just suggested you vote the straight Republican ticket, darlin'."

"You are *incorrigible!*" Raine gave a mischievous smile, curving her lips just enough to reveal the dimple that lurked in her left cheek.

"I hope so!" Maggie answered. After a moment, she sighed, "I so love to travel, but I especially miss the cats when we're away. And how wonderful it will be to sit down for a long visit over tea with Aisling! We've so much to tell her. And to thank her for." She rested a hand over the twin talismans suspended from her neck, hidden from sight under her clothing; then she opened her outsized leather purse to extract two photographs cached between the pages of a guidebook. "Take a look at these." She handed the photos to Raine. "Notice anything about that one of Barry and Rob I took in the Love Gardens?"

Raine studied the photographs for several seconds. "Orbs. Definitely orbs of what might be two separate entities floating above and around Barry, Rob, and the Venus. I'd venture an educated guess—"

"Robert de Barry and Phillip Barry," Maggie finished. "Of that, I have no doubt."

"And in high spirits, both!" Raine joked.

"Most happy, I'd say, about how it all turned out," Maggie laughed. "Look at the other photo, of Poulnabrone. I caught the setting sun just as it flashed, star-like and centered, beneath the horizontal slab of the great standing stones."

"Oooh! It's a *magickal* image!"

"I'm going to paint it, one for us, and one for Aisling." Maggie carefully returned the photographs to the guidebook in her purse.

"Aisling's Celtic music enchants, and I'm the family *seanchaí*. Storytelling's my talent. I guess it's because I've a heady addiction to the texture and color of words, like your creativity reveals itself in your brilliant paintings. Aisling will be *thrilled*, Mags, and so will I. The painting will be a beautiful souvenir of the most significant journey we ever made." Raine returned her attention to the window.

The gigantic Irish airliner lifted gracefully off the runway and banked, giving the Sleuth Sisters a grand view of the isle they so loved, with its forty shades of green in a patchwork quilt of Divine arrangement. Raine dabbed again at her glistening eyes. "That brilliant green jewel called 'Eire.' You know, Mags, our constant reassurance that magick does exist, that there's so much *more* to life than what we see, never fails to delight me." She brushed away another tear.

Leaning over her cousin and glancing out the window for a parting look, Maggie patted Raine's arm. "Your sense of wonder and your passion are what make you such a good historian ... and a good person. C'mon now, we'll come back again soon." She readjusted herself in the seat. After she was again comfortable, she said, "Tell me what Beau and Hugh had to say about things at *our* Tara."

"We owe a huge 'Thank you' to Beau and Hugh as well." Raine smiled, deepening her dimple. "Beau ran into a couple of our fellow theatre members in town yesterday. The Whispering Shades committee has voted on next year's plays. They want us to revive our 'three weird sisters' role for *Macbeth* next fall. And there was something else. Something weird for sure. His exact words were, 'the Shades desperately need you and want to know when you're coming home.' It seems we may be going home to yet another mystery. And it *appears,* pun intended, that the situation at home in our theatre, whatever it is, has upset our resident ghost. According to Beau, Élise has really been out-of-sorts lately. I didn't get the details. Could just be Hallowe'en pranks. Oh, and that reminds me. He said over Hallowe'en, a couple of our students– I think we have some pretty good ideas who– nailed up a sign reading 'Witch-Way' over the Tara plaque at the entrance to our lane."

Maggie shook her head. "It's one fraternity or another. They never miss a Hallowe'en for the Witch-Way sign. Do we care?" she asked, not really fancying an answer, then adding, "We should keep it ... I rather like it. Did you tell me that Beau did get your MG tuned up?" She offered Raine a hard candy.

"Yes indeed." She accepted the sweet and began unwrapping it. "Mmm, cinnamon. He said the men at the garage were teasing him about the car. They asked him if he were Peter Pan."

"Surprising that, considering Beau's size. Rob really put me in mind of Beau, don't you think?"

Raine tilted her head. "He did. I thought that several times. Anyway, Beau got the detailing done that I wanted on my little Tinker Bell. Ever since I was a little girl and read Nancy Drew, you know I *just had to have* a vintage roadster of my own one day. When I saw that little '53 MG TD, I *knew* she was the car for me," she rhymed, her fabulous eyes sparkling. What could be more purrrrrr-fect? The red and black interior and grill are our high school and college colors, and the cream body the perfect canvas for the wee magick wand I had painted on the driver's door, with my initials on the wand." She gave a little flourish as though waving the instrument of magick. "It suits her."

"And you," Maggie quipped. "You always were what Granny used to call a 'corker.'"

"Ooooh, the magick wand is my cachet," Raine replied in her throaty voice, touching her diamond brooch and sending Maggie a little cat smile. "And we've both seen the proof of what I've always advocated: 'Thoughts are magick wands, powerful enough to make anything happen … *anything we choose!*'"

"Soo," Maggie mused, arching her back and stretching, "the Shades desperately need us at our 'little theatre in the woods'?"

"It followed us to Ireland, and it's following us home," Raine sighed.

"Now, honey, what would any woman, and especially any witchy-woman be without mystery? What would *life* be without a little mystery?" Maggie effervesced with her delightful laugh.

"I doubt we'll ever find out," Raine replied. "We're mystery magnets."

"That only stands to reason," Maggie quipped, leaning toward her cousin and whispering, "After all, we always were and always will be– *the Sleuth Sisters!*"

"And now," Raine whispered, "that we've the magickal Time-Key, we'll be able, as we said, to unlock the door that will whisk us through yesteryear … and who knows what skeletons and dangers dangle in all the closets our Key will open?"

"Of one thing we can be certain," Maggie concluded softly, "at the creak of every opening door– magick, adventure, and surprise await us!"

~About the Author~

Author with Athena Award

Ceane O'Hanlon-Lincoln is a native of southwestern Pennsylvania, where she taught high school French until 1985. Already engaged in commercial writing, she immediately began pursuing a career writing both fiction and history.

In the tradition of a great Irish *seanchaí* (storyteller), O'Hanlon-Lincoln has been called by many a "state-of-the-heart writer."

In 1987, at Robert Redford's Sundance Institute, two of her screenplays made the "top twenty-five," chosen from thousands of nationwide entries. In 1994, she optioned one of those scripts to Kevin Costner; the other screenplay she reworked and adapted, in 2014, to the first of her Sleuth Sisters Mysteries, *The Witches' Time-Key*, conceived years ago when Ceane first visited Ireland. As she stood on the sacred Hill of Tara, the wind whispered ancient voices– ancient secrets. O'Hanlon-Lincoln never forgot that very mystical experience.

Fire Burn and Cauldron Bubble is the second of the Sleuth Sisters Mysteries, *The Witch's Silent Scream* the third in the bewitching series. Watch for the fourth exciting Sleuth Sisters adventure– *Which Witch is Which?*– coming soon.

Ceane has also had a poem published in *Great Poems of Our Time*. Winner of the Editor's Choice Award, "The Man Who Holds the Reins" appears in the fore of her *Autumn Song* anthology.

William Colvin, a retired Pennsylvania theatre and English teacher said of her *Autumn Song*: "The tales rank with those of Rod Serling and the great O. Henry. O'Hanlon-Lincoln is a *master* storyteller."

Robert Matzen, writer/producer of Paladin Films said of *Autumn Song*: "I like the flow of the words, almost like song lyrics. *Very evocative*."

In February 2004, O'Hanlon-Lincoln won the prestigious Athena, an award presented to professional "women of spirit" on local, national and international levels. The marble, bronze and crystal Athena sculpture symbolizes "career excellence and the light that emanates from the recipient."

Soon after the debut of the premier volume of her Pennsylvania history series, the talented author won for her *County Chronicles* a Citation/Special Recognition Award from the Pennsylvania House of Representatives, followed by a Special Recognition Award from the Senate of Pennsylvania. She has since won both awards a second time for *County Chronicles*– the series.

Ceane shares Tara, her century-old Victorian home, with her beloved husband Phillip and their champion Bombay cats, Black Jade and Black Jack O'Lantern.

Her hobbies include travel, nature walks, theatre, film, antiques, and reading "… everything I can on Pennsylvania, American, and Celtic history, legend and lore."

~~~

~ A message to her readers from
Mistress of Magick–
Ceane O'Hanlon-Lincoln ~

"I write because writing is, to me, empowering. Writing is creation. When I take up a pen or sit at my computer, I am a goddess, a deity wielding that pen like a faerie godmother waves a wand.

Via will, clever word-choice and placement, I can arrange symbols and characters to invoke a whole circuitous route of emotions, images, ideas, arm-chair travel– and, yes indeed, even time-travel. A writer can create– *magick.*

"I am often asked where I get my inspiration. The answer is 'From everything and everyone around me.' I love to travel, discover new places, and meet new people. And I have never been shy about talking to people I don't know. I love to talk, so over the years, I've had to train myself to be a good listener. One cannot learn anything new, talking.

"People also ask me if there is any truth to my stories about the Sleuth Sisters. To me, they are very real, though each is my own creation, and since I have always drawn from life when I write, I would have to say that there is a measure of truth in each of their essences– and in each of their adventures."

How much, though, like the author herself– *shall remain a mystery.*

Love and Light ...

. . . and all that is Bright!

Printed in Great Britain
by Amazon